Love's Promise

Love's Promise

PENNY ZELLER

Maplebrook

ALSO BY PENNY ZELLER

Maplebrook Publishing

Standalone Books
Love in the Headlines
Freedom's Flight
Levi's Vow
Heart of Courage

Wyoming Sunrise Series
Love's New Beginnings
Forgotten Memories
Dreams of the Heart
When Love Comes
Love's Promise

Horizon Series
Over the Horizon
Dreams on the Horizon
Beyond the Horizon

Hollow Creek Series
Love in Disguise
Love in Store

Love Letters from Ellis Creek Series
Love from Afar
Love Unforeseen
Love Most Certain

Love in Chokecherry Heights Series
Henry and Evaline (Prequel)
Love Under Construction

Whitaker House Publishing

Montana Skies Series
McKenzie
Kaydie
Hailee

Barbour Publishing
Love from Afar
(The Secret Admirer Romance
Collection)

Freedom's Flight
(The Underground Railroad Brides
Collection)

Beacon Hill Press (Nonfiction)
77 Ways Your Family Can Make a
Difference

Dedicated to those who have temporarily lost their way, but later find Truth in the Savior.

That if thou shalt confess with thy mouth the
Lord Jesus, and shalt believe in thine heart that
God hath raised him from the dead, thou shalt be saved.

Romans 10:9

CHAPTER ONE

POPLAR SPRINGS, WYOMING, 1897

"GOOD MORNING, GRANDMAMA. HOW is Mr. Alvarado today?" Silas asked as he set a variety of items on the counter at the mercantile.

Grandmama peered at something in the distance before answering. "As well as can be expected, I suppose. I'll be glad when Amaya arrives in Poplar Springs. She and her grandfather are close, and I wouldn't want him to pass before she can say goodbye."

"I'm sorry to hear he's not doing well, ma'am. Has Doc given any indication that Mr. Alvarado will recover?"

"He's just not sure—but we keep praying. The Lord is faithful." Grandmama closed her eyes, perhaps to pray once again for her ailing husband.

Silas prayed as well. He had come to know the couple reasonably well during his short time in Poplar Springs and had grown fond of them. He recalled recently when Mrs. Alvarado asked him to refer to her as "Grandmama". Silas had tamped down the emotion that threatened on that day. He'd had to remind himself that referring to her as "Grandmama" as she requested did not take away from precious Oma and what she'd meant to him. Between her expectant gaze and the empty void

1

she'd filled in his life, he'd agreed to Mrs. Alvarado's appeal.

Grandmama's eyes flung open. "I almost forgot to ask. Would you...could you..."

"Yes?"

"I know this is a lot to ask and you are busy with spring chores on your ranch and helping the sheriff when necessary, but..." Twin lines formed on Grandmama's forehead. "Might you be willing to ride halfway toward Bowman and make sure Amaya's stagecoach arrives safely? Deputy Eliason said there's been an increase in stagecoach robberies."

"Say no more, Grandmama. I will be happy to oblige. When are you expecting the stage to arrive?"

"It leaves Bowman tomorrow morning at nine a.m." She reached over the counter and pinched Silas's cheek. "You're a sweet boy, Silas McFadden."

The endearment reminded him so much of Oma. Silas swallowed the lump in his throat and focused on the present. "Thank you." Grandmama needn't know he'd not always been the "sweet boy" she surmised him to be.

Grandmama raised her chin. "Now, I insist you allow me to pay you for your time, or at the very least apply a credit to your account."

"And I insist, Grandmama..."

"Ah, no." She shook her head.

Silas chuckled at the woman's stubbornness. She was all of five feet tall, but a lot of spunk was wrapped in that small package. He briefly wondered if her husband had ever won a disagreement. "The payment I *would* like is some of your delicious gâteau Basque."

The woman firmed her hands on her hips. "How could I forget how much you love those homemade blackberry-filled tarts? All right, then, Silas, it is a deal. Your parents raised a stubborn young man, but alas, who am I to argue with someone who's doing me a much-needed favor?"

If only Grandmama knew that his parents had nothing to do with his upbringing.

"Thank you for agreeing to see that the stagecoach arrives in Poplar Springs safely. We do not want anything to happen to Amaya and she's been through so much with having lost Russell. Have you met her?"

Silas shook his head. He'd regrettably been out of town on the day of Russell's funeral. "No, ma'am, I haven't."

Silas loaded his pack and gave instructions to his hired hand. Assured his growing ranch was in good hands, he mounted his horse. A ride through the beauty of God's Creation that stretched all the way from Bowman to Willow Falls on the other side and Prune Creek over the mountain was something he never tired of.

After about an hour of riding, Silas eyed the horizon.

Shouldn't he have met up with the stagecoach by now?

The hot Wyoming sun beat upon him, and sweat trickled down his back. He stopped his horse, removed his hat, and wiped the moisture from his forehead.

Silas had long ago learned to listen to the sounds around him and to have complete awareness of the on-goings nearby. Two crows bickered from a nearby tree,

3

their obnoxious calls disturbing the otherwise quiet surroundings. Silas dismounted and placed an ear to the ground.

Nothing.

He scanned the area around him. Too many stagecoaches had fallen prey to nefarious outlaws. And while travel by rail replaced much of the need for the stagecoach line, places such as Poplar Springs still waited for spurs to be completed, rendering stagecoach travel a necessity.

Prairie grasses waved in the breeze, and to his right, timbered hills melded into majestic mountains, their tips still covered with snow. Snow that would likely remain throughout the year while the valley below experienced a toss between pleasant and hot summer temperatures.

Silas raked his fingers through his hair. Perhaps the stage had been delayed from its departure in Bowman. If so, concern wouldn't yet be warranted. Or maybe Grandmama mistook the time of its arrival to Poplar Springs. Or maybe Silas harbored a cynical outlook when it came to opportunities for crime. After all, he knew what it was like to live on both sides of the law.

He raised his canteen to his lips and guzzled a fair amount of water. Never could the Wyoming heat compare to the Texas heat with its high humidity. Nonetheless, the spring day was uncharacteristically warm.

Silas mounted his horse, returned his hat atop his head, and continued on his way.

Before he'd become a praying man, Silas depended fully on himself and the men who pledged their loyalty to him. After surrendering to Christ, that all changed. Now his every breath was dependent on the One who'd given him his first breath.

Antelope on a nearby hill briefly drew his attention from the road. In the sky, several birds circled an area just ahead near where the Poplar River wound through a grove of willows. He squinted, thoughts pummeling his mind. Could be a dead animal. Could be nothing.

Or it could be something he needed to investigate.

Riding with the Poplar Springs sheriff's posse and being deputized when assisting in the search for criminals gave Silas an even keener sense of awareness. Briefly resting his fingers on his revolver, he did one more sweep of the area before beckoning his horse and riding at an efficient clip toward the willow grove. Adrenaline coursed through his veins, reminding him that the life he'd chosen as a rancher was much more preferable.

At the crest of the hill, Silas again stopped his horse and inspected the area as far as he could see. On the second perusal to the right, he glimpsed something that caused him another, more lingering glance.

A stagecoach overturned in the middle of the Poplar River, its red wheels still spinning. Silas's heart lurched, an uneasy feeling settling in the pit of his stomach.

"Giddyap!" Silas pushed his horse as fast as safely possible. Minutes later, he dismounted, and half-sliding, half-running, he headed down the embankment toward the river, the tall weeds attempting to impede his travel. He nearly tripped when he stumbled on a hole in the ground, likely the home of a prairie dog. The sound of the rushing river, a child's whimpering, and an obnoxious cawing from a well-fed crow flying overhead filled the air.

He wasn't prepared for the site before him, nor the greeting he would receive.

Water rushed through the stagecoach's windows. A man lay prostrate near the river's edge. To the right, a woman huddled near a wounded man, a young child in her arms.

"What happened?" he muttered, attempting to piece together the scenario that caused the accident.

"Hold it right there, mister."

A woman appeared, holding a Winchester on him. Her long dark brown hair hung in clumps around her face, and twigs and leaves clung to her blue skirt.

Silas raised his hands and took a step back. "I mean no harm, ma'am." He'd had a lot of guns held on him over the years, but this was the first time it was a woman pointing a shotgun at him.

CHAPTER TWO

THREE HOURS EARLIER

AMAYA ALVARADO ATE ANOTHER of the crackers Ma had packed for her. Anything to quell the nausea that arose from riding in the swaying stagecoach. Her stomach lurched as the stage hit a bump, then righted itself.

"Do you think we're almost there?" Cecily, a fretful woman with a high-pitched voice, perfectly-styled coiffure, prominent blue eyes, a slender stature, and one of the other three stagecoach passengers asked her husband, Herman.

"I don't rightly know, my dear." Herman peered about the stagecoach with almond-shaped, hooded brown eyes as if looking for an answer.

Cecily snuggled their chubby baby and planted a kiss on his bald head. "Herman Jr. will begin fussing soon."

Herman Jr., or H.J. as Cecily periodically referred to him, was the opposite of his nervous parents. He babbled and drooled, his pudgy arms batting at the air. He released a giggle, his baby laugh causing Amaya to smile.

"Is this your first time on a stagecoach?" Amaya asked, attempting to ignore the queasiness.

Cecily's fraught expression and audibly shallow breathing answered Amaya's question more than the woman's words could. "Yes, it is. We hail from Massachusetts. Herman has accepted a position in Thornsby. We're accustomed to trains." Cecily peered out the window. "I was so worried the stagecoach would tip over when we first boarded."

Herman placed a skinny arm around his wife. "Please try not to fret, my dear. The man at the Bowman station said it was only a few hours aboard this mode of transport. Soon, we'll be in Poplar Springs and on a train to Thornsby."

Amaya did not want to be the bearer of disappointing news, but the spur in Poplar Springs was not yet complete, and Cecily and Herman would be boarding another stagecoach instead of a train when they traveled south to Thornsby.

The stagecoach stopped then, and Amaya straightened in her seat. The stretch between Bowman and Poplar Springs could be a dangerous one with the possibility of nefarious individuals seeking to take advantage of unsuspecting travelers.

"Is something wrong?" Cecily's eyes widened and she gripped Herman's arm.

The shotgun messenger opened the door. "We're only stopping for a break. There's no station between Bowman and Poplar Springs, so we decided to allow you a minute to stretch your legs and whatnot."

Amaya released the breath she'd been holding. While she might not appear as frantic as Cecily, concern had briefly overwhelmed her. She deboarded, tin of crackers in hand.

The bright sunny day was warm for this time of year, but then, spring in Wyoming was known for being unpredictable. Today could be pleasant with no wind, while tomorrow could usher in rain, or even snow. She cast a glance toward the white-tipped mountains and the plush green meadows below. A black-capped chickadee, her favorite bird, chirped from the tree, its persistent and easily-identifiable warble a welcome sound. She wandered ahead a bit, relishing the chance to move about before again boarding for the final stretch to Poplar Springs.

The stagecoach driver and the shotgun messenger stood just ahead of her in deep conversation. She inclined her ear to hear, not wishing to be nosy, but figuring it was imperative she stay abreast of any occurrences given the occasional dangers of traveling in an area where bandits often lurked.

"I'm just fine. Quit worrying yerself," snapped the driver.

But even from her standpoint, the driver did *not* seem "just fine". In fact, a considerable swath of perspiration covered his entire back, soaking his tan shirt.

"You were saying your shoulder was giving you fits just a few minutes ago," the shotgun messenger countered.

"Yeah, and it still is. What of it? I have a bad case of indigestion too. Shouldn't have had that meal in Bowman before we left. Sausage never sits well with me."

"Let me drive and you can rest. We're almost to Poplar Springs."

The driver shook his head. "No can do. You were hired to be the shotgun messenger, and what with the gold, we need to keep you in that position." He paused for a minute and rubbed his shoulder.

Gold? They were transporting gold?

Amaya should have realized that with the shotgun messenger accompanying them. She scanned her surroundings. Peaceful. Calm. Two house wrens landed in the poplar tree above and trilled in conversation. A downy woodpecker drummed on the pine just to the right of Amaya, a gentle breeze blew, and H.J. babbled.

Nothing to be concerned about.

Right?

The stagecoach arrived this far without any sign of outlaws or those wishing to plunder what didn't belong to them.

While there was nothing to be concerned about regarding the journey, the driver's apparent ailment notwithstanding, there were other items on Amaya's list of distresses. Paramount was that Grandmama needed her assistance with Grandfather. His apoplexy rendered him reliant on Grandmama, who also attempted to operate the mercantile. Thankfully, Ma had Amaya's younger sister to assist with caring for the ranch in light of Pa's recent injury.

Her conversation with Ma before leaving Bowman crossed her mind. *"While Grandmama needs you, your pa and I are hesitant to allow you to travel the distance by your lonesome. There are outlaws bent on nefarious actions. You could be hurt or worse."*

"Ma, I promise to take the utmost of caution. I don't think it's prudent to wait until someone can accompany me. Not when Grandmama needs me."

Ma framed Amaya's face with her hands, the worry etched in her sweet face. Amaya rarely argued with Ma, but for several reasons, namely to assist Grandmama and Grandfather, and secondarily to visit Russell's grave, Amaya determined to maintain her position.

"Grandmama knows the time of my expected arrival, and I promise to send a telegram the instant I reach Poplar Springs. Ma, you always remind me not to borrow worry."

Pa called from the bedroom, his voice weak. If Zurina wasn't there to assist Ma with Pa's care after his accident, Amaya would never have entertained the idea of traveling to Poplar Springs.

Ma relented and allowed Amaya's travel plans after a hushed discussion with Pa.

And now here Amaya was. Closer to Poplar Springs than to Bowman. God had protected her and would continue to do so.

Amaya took a deep breath. They were perhaps less than an hour away with the stagecoach's rapid speed.

The driver and shotgun messenger turned then. "Can we help you, miss?" the driver asked, interrupting her thoughts.

Perspiration beaded the man's forehead and his formerly reddish face had taken on a pale hue. From her years of caregiving for those hurt and injured, Amaya easily recognized the man was not well.

"No, sir. Just wondering if you are all right."

"Why does everyone keep asking that?" The driver scowled and motioned to the shotgun messenger. "Round up the passengers. Let's be on our way."

Moments later, the stagecoach sped along at an efficient speed. Amaya prayed for the driver, prayed that no bandits would meet them along this stretch, and prayed for her family and the many needs currently facing them.

Her stomach churned as the stage bounced along, her crackers threatening to make a reappearance. Cecily clutched Herman's hand and held the baby close.

Why were they going so fast?

And why did it feel like the stage was erratic? As if no driver controlled it?

They weaved along the road, never staying in anything resembling a straight line. Vociferous words, although she couldn't make them out, sounded from the front of the stage where the driver and shotgun messenger sat.

Lord, please keep us safe.

The stagecoach hit an enormous rut in the road, causing Amaya's head to collide with the back wall and snap forward again. She reached up and attempted to massage her neck. H.J. began to cry, and Cecily closed her eyes. Herman said nothing, but attempted to brace himself and his wife as the stagecoach jostled to and fro. A noise akin to cracking wood erupted, and Amaya gasped when she saw the horses going in a different direction without them. Still going a high rate of speed, the stagecoach bounded off the road and into the weeds, hitting bumps and rocks. Her heart pounded in her chest, and she squeezed her eyes shut for a brief moment before reopening them. She begged the Lord for His Providence.

Cecily shrieked. "Are we going to die?"

Herman leaned out the window.

"No, keep your body inside the stagecoach," Amaya pleaded.

"I think the shotgun messenger just threw the strong-box off the stage."

Amaya was about to again remind Herman to keep his head and limbs within the stagecoach when he settled back against the seat. He reached for Cecily's hand and squeezed it.

Just then, they hit another bump, causing the stage-coach to wobble out of control down an embankment. Amaya dug her fingernails into her palms, and she once again prayed—no pleaded—with the Lord to protect them.

The stage veered to the right with a deafening thump. She watched in horror as the driver was ejected from his seat, his body hitting the ground. Tears flooded her eyes and panic settled in her heart. *Lord, please have mercy on us.*

The stagecoach came to an abrupt stop before teeter-ing on what felt like the edge of a cliff. Then, without warning, it slowly tipped onto its side and rolled into the river, tossing the passengers about as it did so.

CHAPTER THREE

AMAYA HAD ALWAYS BEEN afraid of the water. It stemmed from an incident when she was a little girl. Her hands shook as she clutched the window frame and stood to an upright position. Water filled the stagecoach, but thankfully only came to her waist. She poked her head through the window and peered about.

They were directly in the river, the stagecoach resting on its side as the water swirled around it. "Is everyone all right?" she asked, realizing that it was by God's grace alone that they managed to survive the accident.

"I don't think I am." Cecily's tremulous tone matched her wobbly balance, and she steadied herself against the wooden seat and held tightly to H.J.

"And the baby?"

Cecily kissed him on the top of his head, a brief moment of calm in the midst of her excessive distress. "He's fine."

Herman shifted and attempted to stand. "I think my leg is broken," he moaned.

Amaya's first three attempts to hoist herself through the door were for naught. The water had drenched her skirt, making it all the more difficult to lift her body weight. Finally, on the fourth time, she was able to elevate herself enough to sit on the side of the stagecoach, swing her legs over, and hop into the water.

She spied a man on the bank near the edge of the river, his crumpled body motionless. Amaya gasped and covered her mouth with her hand as tears formed.

The shotgun messenger.

Blinking, she attempted to mentally list the types of aid everyone required. "Herman," she said, slushing through the water, "I must go help the shotgun messenger. I'll be back to assist you and Cecily to the riverbank."

"No, don't leave us," wailed Cecily.

Herman placed a hand on his wife's arm. "She'll be right back, and we're safe in here at present." He grimaced and his face grew paler.

Amaya allowed her gaze to travel briefly to Herman's fractured leg. She needed to get him to the river's edge. But first, she must see if there was anything she could do for the shotgun messenger.

The matted grass lining the flat riverbank crunched beneath her feet as she made her way toward him. She thought she detected slight movement.

Lord, please let him still be alive.

Her sodden dress made movement at a steady pace impossible, and she lifted her skirt, the water dripping from it as she continued toward the man.

The shotgun messenger lay sprawled prostrate, his head turned to the left side. The shallow rise and fall of his rib cage gave her hope.

Thank You, Lord!

Amaya fell to her knees beside him. "Sir, can you hear me?"

Thankfully, he was a slim man, as one much larger would be impossible to budge. She placed her hands beneath his upper body and endeavored to roll him over. He released an agonized moan, and she rocked back on her heels. "I'm so sorry," she whispered. "But I have to roll you over so I can check your injuries."

Something about him reminded her of Pa, and she swiped a tear. "I'm going to try again."

She took a deep breath and, with all the strength she could muster, she rolled him to his back.

Blood oozed from a sizable gash on his forehead that extended down the left side of his face. She covered her mouth with her hand and attempted to remind herself she'd seen injuries—some worse—when she and Ma had assisted those in need of medical care in Bowman before a doctor moved to town.

Amaya pulled on the bottom of her skirt, hoping to rip a portion of it to dab at the wound, but because her clothes were still wet, the attempt was futile. Instead, she rose onto her knees and dabbed at the wound with the hem of her skirt.

His pulse was weak and his breathing shallow. "I'm going to help you."

"Nothing to be done," he rasped.

"But..."

The shotgun messenger reached toward her. "Listen to me. You need to get the key from my pocket. The key for the..." He took a labored breath.

"Please, don't attempt to talk." Amaya gazed around her. Nothing but birds, an antelope in the near distance, and Cecily peering above the stagecoach in her direction.

Nothing else.

And no one else.

How would she help this man on her own? If only Herman hadn't been injured. She checked the shotgun messenger for other visible injuries and broken bones, noting he likely suffered a concussion. He'd lost a lot of blood from his head wound, which required stitches.

"The key for the strongbox—it's—" The shotgun messenger paused, each of his words laborious.

"Don't try to talk."

His hand gripped hers with likely all the energy he could muster. "No. You have to—the key is my shirt pocket. Get—get it."

Amaya retrieved the gold-plated key and fingered its rounded corner. "I have it."

Urgency lined his weary features and he heaved a strangled breath. "Open the strongbox. Remove the gold and cash and hide it somewhere in case the bandits come."

He closed his eyes for a moment, and Amaya thought she'd lost him. "Sir?"

"Hide the money and tell Winslow or Eliason about it. They'll know—they'll know what to do."

"All right."

"Promise me."

She leaned closer to better hear his words, which emerged as gasps. "Promise me you'll hide the money and tell the sheriff and deputy when you get to Poplar Springs."

"I promise."

The shotgun messenger opened his eyes "The driver. He didn't make it."

Amaya gasped. "What happened?"

"Likely a heart attack, but I ain't no doctor."

Somewhere, amongst the trees and weeds lay the driver. What if he did survive? Amaya would need to aid him as well.

She placed a hand on the man's arm. "We're going to get you some help." But even as she said it, doubt gripped her. Amaya stared in the direction of Poplar Springs. It wouldn't be prudent for her to embark on the lengthy walk to town on her own and leave the injured behind.

"Nothing to be done, ma'am." He peered up at her, his breathing swift and shallow. His lips were dry and cracked, and a pile of blood had formed beneath his head.

But Amaya wasn't willing to give up so easily.

"Ma'am, I'm thirsty," he rasped.

Amaya jumped to her feet and scooped some water into her hands. The shotgun messenger couldn't lift his head on his own, and she needed both hands to retain some of the water, so she moistened his lips, hoping to satiate some of his thirst. His vacant gaze peered somewhere past her.

Had she lost him?

But a few seconds later, the man again cried out in pain. She rested a hand on his arm, noting it was cold to the touch, and averted her attention towards the stagecoach. Perhaps there was a piece of clothing she could hang to dry that could later be used in lieu of a blanket.

"Ma'am, like I said—I—I ain't gonna make it." His voice grew weaker and his words nearly incoherent.

"Yes, you are. You'll be all right. I just have to get help." Her words came in a slew of babbling. She could no more get help than drag the stagecoach from the river.

Lord, please let him survive.

"Don't worry yourself none, I know Jesus, and I know where I'm going."

Relief overcame her. "If I could just tend to your wounds. I have some nursing experience."

"Tell my employer I did all I could."

He was giving up. Tears formed in Amaya's eyes. "Do you have a family?"

"No family."

The man would die alone. Except for her.

"Promise me about the strongbox."

"I promise."

Amaya held his hand as he breathed his last. Then the uncontrollable sobs wracked her body, her wails emitting through the otherwise peaceful day.

Once she arrived in Poplar Springs, she would send someone to retrieve the driver's and shotgun messenger's bodies for proper burials. The shotgun messenger mentioned there was no one, but what about friends? Did the driver have a wife waiting at home for him?

No one should have to lose the man they loved.

Only with the Lord's help did Amaya compose herself several minutes later. She trudged to the stagecoach, her heart heavy. While the shotgun messenger was now in the presence of Jesus, she grieved for the loss of life.

Amaya stopped at the river's edge and splashed her face with water. She would do as she promised with the strongbox once she assisted Herman and Cecily. She'd left the key beside the shotgun messenger so as not to lose it while wading through the water.

"Is the man all right?" Cecily asked when Amaya approached the overturned stagecoach.

For the briefest moment, Amaya was tempted to lie to protect Cecily's sensitive nature. But sooner or later, the woman would discover the truth. "No, he has gone Home to be with the Lord."

The tears cascaded down Cecily's face. "Oh, dear," she breathed.

Worried she too might begin to blubber again, Amaya cleared her throat and focused her attention to the task before her. "Herman, you'll go first. I'll hand H.J. to you once you're to shore. Then I'll be back for Cecily." Her voice shook in her own ears. Could she do this? Could she assist a man with a broken leg from the overturned stagecoach?

Could she gather her thoughts well enough after what happened with the shotgun messenger?

She recalled the verse from Philippians 4:13 that she'd memorized as a child. *I can do all things through Christ which strengtheneth me.*

Fortunately, Herman was a thin, fine-boned man, half the width of Amaya's slender figure.

When he was safe with H.J. resting in his arms, Amaya went back for Cecily. "I can't do it," the woman whined. "I just can't."

"You can, and you must."

Cecily's distraught appearance—with her tousled auburn hair once so perfectly set, now in disarray, her rapidly blinking eyes, ashen face, and the way she'd bent her fingers into her mouth caused Amaya more than momentary concern. Cecily would have to cooperate if Amaya was to get her to the riverbank.

"Give me your hand."

Cecily shook her head. "No, I can't do it."

"Once we are able to remove you from the stagecoach, it isn't far to the side, and the water isn't deep."

"No, I can't."

"Cecily, God will help us. We were able to rescue Herman and the baby. Now it's your turn."

"But I can't. I'm too scared."

Amaya prayed for the words that would settle Cecily's apprehension. "It's not that far," she repeated. "But I do need you to hoist yourself up as I did. As Herman did. He was able to do so with a broken leg. Then once you are able to do that, I can take you to the riverbank."

Cecily again shook her head, her entire body trembling.

Amaya knew what it was like to face fear. Had done so on several occasions. She also knew what it was like to feel hopeless. Her fiancé, Russell's, face flashed through her mind.

"What if I slip and fall?" Tremors in Cecily's tone made it difficult to understand her jumbled words.

"Now just put her hands on either side of the door and push yourself up."

"No."

"Do you want to stay in the stagecoach?" Amaya chastised herself for being harsher than she ought, but if they were to seek some sort of shelter before nightfall, Cecily would have to cooperate. That, and they needed time to dry in the sun before the chilly night set in, provided no one came for them.

What if no one came for them?

No. Amaya wouldn't think that way. Grandmama knew she was coming. The station in Poplar Springs would wonder if something was amiss when the stage didn't arrive.

And she needed to keep her promise about the strongbox should any outlaws discover their whereabouts.

Amaya took a deep breath, inhaling a mixture of pine and blooming willows. "I will help you, Cecily, but we must get you to the side."

Cecily bit her lip and nodded. She pushed herself up and onto the top of the door's frame.

"I'll help you down into the water, and then we'll walk to the riverbank."

Cecily's foot slipped and she fell on Amaya, her weight causing Amaya to submerge beneath the water. Pain seared through her as Amaya struck her knee on a rock beneath the surface. Opening her eyes, she saw the bottom of the river, tiny pebbles, a trout swimming in the opposite direction, and the weeds swaying with the water's current.

Confusion reigned for a moment.

She closed her eyes again, the real possibility of drowning engulfing her thoughts.

Panic set in. Reminders of that day so long ago.

The day when the deep water swept her along, farther and farther away from the shore. Her head bobbing as she pleaded her lungs to take in air.

No one realized her foot had slipped, plunging her into the river.

It wasn't so different now as water whirled around her, the cold rush of it shocking and unexpected as it covered her head and her face and threatened to drown her.

She couldn't hold her breath much longer.

Lord, please help me.

Amaya moved her arms in the motion she'd seen Ma, Pa, and her younger sister, Zurina, do when they swam in the nearby pond. But she remained in one spot, crouched beneath the water.

She wasn't ready to die yet. Wasn't ready to see Russell and her maternal grandparents in Heaven. Not yet. She needed to be there for Grandmama and Grandfather. To return home to her parents. To assist her mother and sister with Pa after his accident.

Lord, I can't swim. I'm so afraid. It will be by Your grace alone...

Long seconds ticked by when suddenly realization settled in. She could stand. The water wasn't deep.

Amaya shot upright and gasped for breath. *Thank You, Jesus.*

Dizziness overcame her as the world around her spun, the twirling threatening to unsteady her and pull her beneath the water again.

A hand clutched her arm. "Amaya? I think I'm going to drown."

Amaya blinked, her vision clearing as the spinning ceased. Cecily. Standing there in front of her, teetering, her eyes bulging and her mouth chattering.

"Please, Amaya, can you help me? It's so cold in here."

Amaya forced her feet to move, and together she and Cecily plodded towards the riverbank.

Moments later, Amaya and the other passengers clustered beneath a tree not far from the river's edge. She tended to Herman's leg, reassured Cecily that all would be well, prayed with them, held H.J. for a few minutes while Cecily rested, then realized something important.

She needed to find and hide the strongbox.

Convincing Cecily that Amaya would return for her was not an easy feat. The woman lived in a state of anxiety and disquietude.

The last thing she would do would be to tell either Herman or Cecily about the strongbox. If outlaws did arrive, the less they knew, the better. "I'll be back in a moment. Perhaps I can find us some wild berries or something to eat."

"That would be delightful. I'm famished." Cecily fed H.J. while Herman rested on the ground, his broken leg elevated. She'd dressed his wound, dabbed at his forehead with a cool wet piece of cloth Cecily had torn from her own skirt, and was satisfied it was all she could do until help arrived.

If help arrived.

No, she wouldn't allow discouragement to cloud her thoughts. The Lord had brought them this far. He was faithful and would see them to safety.

Now to fulfill her promise. Where was the strongbox? Herman mentioned he'd seen the shotgun messenger toss it from the stagecoach as they headed down the embankment. She followed the path the stage had made, its wheels temporarily matting the vegetation in its wake.

The zig zag impressions made it clear that it hadn't been her imagination that the stagecoach was out of control. Amaya followed the tracks a short distance before discovering the shotgun messenger's double-barrel shotgun. She lifted and carried it as she continued her perusal toward the strongbox.

She glanced to the right, then to the left. Where could it be? Amaya climbed to the top of the bank and peered down the road. Nothing but pines, aspens, willows, and meadows as far as the eye could see. At the crest of the hill, looking down she noticed something concerning.

The stagecoach wheels spun in the breeze. Wheels anyone paying a minute amount of attention would notice while traveling on the road.

Her heart lurched. They were targets. Amaya veered to the right and could see Herman, Cecily, and the baby from her vantage point. A sweep of the area included a perfect view of the shotgun messenger.

If only the driver hadn't suffered a fatal illness. If only the shotgun messenger hadn't been thrown from the stage. If only the horses had stayed attached to the stagecoach. If only none of it happened in the first place.

But dwelling on "if-onlies" would do no good.

She planted herself on a smooth gray rock and lifted her skirt to reveal an angry red abrasion on her right knee, streaked with blood and meshed with some purple discoloration. She winced. If only she hadn't fallen while attempting to reach the shore.

Desperation consumed her. How could Amaya care for Herman, Cecily, and the baby if she herself was injured? How could she keep her promise to the shotgun messenger if she couldn't find the strongbox? How long would it be before someone came to look for them?

Ma's words rang in her ears. *"Your worries are getting the best of you, Amaya Alvardo. The best remedy to worry is to call upon the Lord."*

Indeed.

She bowed her head in prayer, and after several minutes passed, felt the Lord's peace overcome her.

Amaya peered around at the tall green grasses waving in the mild breeze. The rushing water, H.J.'s babbling, and birds chirping overhead echoed around her. She stood and started back down the embankment, shotgun in hand.

An uprooted tree lay on the ground a short distance away, its roots exposed and a massive crater left where the tree once stood. Amaya continued forward when she noticed something rectangular-shaped.

The strongbox.

She limped toward it, the key gripped tightly in her hand.

The wooden strongbox with metal reinforcements, green paint with the words WELLS FARGO & CO. printed on the front, lay nestled against a pile of dried leaves.

Amaya crouched down and inserted the key into the lock. Inside, a bag of gold and a stack of currency greeted her. She inhaled a sharp breath. There was no way she could move the heavy strongbox. She'd have to remove the contents. But if outlaws arrived, wouldn't they know the box was empty given how light it was?

Think, Amaya, think.

She searched around her and noticed numerous granite rocks littering the immediate area. What if she gathered several of those and replaced the gold and currency with rocks? If so, when the outlaws attempted to lift it, they could reasonably be assured there was still gold in it.

If bandits came. Which, she hoped they wouldn't.

Amaya gazed into the sky. Afternoon was setting in, and she still needed to find some sort of shelter for the four of them until help arrived.

Chapter Four

AMAYA POSITIONED THE BAGS of money and gold in the hole created by the downed tree. She scooped dirt, rocks, grass, pine cones and pine needles over the bag in an attempt to hide it. Standing, she dusted off her skirt and hobbled back to the strongbox. Collecting multiple rocks, she placed them inside the strongbox, closed the lid, locked it, and tucked the key inside her blouse.

Before returning to Herman and Cecily, she hid the shotgun in the brush several paces behind them. No sense in Cecily seeing the gun until necessary.

Herman was not doing well. Pale, lethargic, and in obvious intense pain, he had few words to say when she returned. Amaya gathered wood for a fire should help be delayed, then dampened the piece of cloth in the river and dabbed Herman's forehead. They were close enough to the river that she was also able to cup her hands and bring small amounts of water for Herman to drink.

Cecily asked a million and five questions, her brows perpetually lowered and pinched and her movements frantic as she cared for H.J.

And Amaya continued to pray and keep her eyes on the road above them.

Herman stirred, in and out of consciousness, and Amaya held H.J. while Cecily tended to Herman's wounds. The woman whimpered as she did so. "Oh, Herman, why did we ever agree to come West?" She placed her head on Herman's chest. "We never should have left the city's confines."

H.J. gurgled and grinned at Amaya, his features a perfect blend of his parents. She pulled him closer and planted a kiss on his bald head. He giggled and batted at her face with chubby hands.

If only Russell had lived, they might have had a little one of their own.

A happily ever after with a husband she loved and the blessing of a child.

Amaya choked on the emotion stirring within her. Right now she musn't give thought to anything but seeking safety for the four of them.

Cecily stood and retrieved H.J., and Amaya collected some wild huckleberries. If they remained stranded at nightfall, she'd build a fire and use the shotgun to find them some supper from the plentiful rabbit and pheasant supply.

A short time later, three riders came into view. Grandmama must have sent them! Amaya waved her arms to garner their attention and heaved a sigh of relief as they drew closer.

Three men dismounted at the top of the embankment, tethered their horses, and stalked toward them. A peculiar niggling formed in her stomach, but Amaya ignored it. "Thank goodness you're here. There's been an accident." She motioned toward the stagecoach.

"Yes, thank goodness we're here." The tallest man's mocking tone set alarms down her spine. He rested one hand on his revolver and with the other, stroked his bristly reddish beard.

And her heartbeat quickened as realization dawned. These men were *not* here to help.

"Ain't never known a time when people were happy to see *us*," snorted one of the other men, one with long brown hair and cold, dark eyes that were spaced far too close together.

The third one removed his hat and scratched his head. "Me neither now that you mention it." He chortled too, his already-oversized nostrils flaring even wider. His ebony head was skinnier at the top and wider at the bottom, and his yellow teeth gleamed with his amusement.

Suddenly, without warning, the first man with the reddish beard, drew his revolver from its holster and held it on Amaya. "Where's the strongbox?"

Cecily screamed, causing H.J. to wail.

"Shut the baby up or I will," said the first man.

For a minute, Amaya forgot to breathe. The whooshing sound of her heartbeat pounded in her ears, and her legs wobbled. The barrel of the gun, just feet away and aimed at her, caused bile to rise in her throat. Her body went cold while sweat chilled her forehead.

The man took a step toward her. "Well?"

From his close proximity, she could see the whites of his eyes, and the gap between his top teeth.

"I..." her breaths came out in gasps. "The stagecoach."

"It's in the stagecoach? Fertig, go check," the man directed to the one with the misshapen head.

"Why is it my job? You go do it, Spitler."

Spitler, the man with the dark eyes shrugged. "I don't mind goin' for a swim. It's a hot day anyways."

"Check the boot too. We might find some of the passengers' loot." The first man kept his attention on Amaya as he directed orders to Spitler. "Maybe the strongbox is bolted to the floor inside the stage."

Fertig shook his head. "Ain't seen nothing like that up here in the northern part of the state. This ain't the Cheyenne to Deadwood route."

"Well, aren't you just the smartest of us all? You have to go north from Cheyenne to get to Deadwood, you idiot." The first man nodded toward Amaya. "You four all that's left?"

Amaya thought of the shotgun messenger and the driver. The loss of life already on this trip was two lives too many. Her stomach clenched as fear choked her. Tell the truth and allow the men to know they were alone and vulnerable? Lie, but have them find out anyway?

"Since you've lost your ability to speak," sneered the man, "we've already seen the one man over there dead. Where's the other one?"

"I'm not sure."

"That don't sound reassuring," said Fertig.

"Shut up, Fertig. You worry too much. If the other driver is alive, we'd have seen him by now."

"Hey, Boggs!" Spitler exclaimed from his place in the stage. "Found some things." He threw Amaya's worn trunk onto the shore, along with two other pieces of luggage.

Boggs briefly averted his attention from Amaya and peered toward Spitler. "Check the stage for the strongbox."

Spitler waded through the water and peered inside the stage. "Don't see it."

Boggs stepped forward and pressed the gun against Amaya's shoulder. "I'm gonna say this one more time. Where is the strongbox?"

Herman raised himself up on his arms. "Sir, with all respect, can we handle this peacefully? The woman doesn't know where the strongbox is, nor do I. It likely fell from the stage when we drove down the embankment."

In a brisk motion, Boggs turned and bridged the space between him and Herman. "Settle this peacefully?"

"Yes, you know, discuss it man-to-man. We don't want to see anyone hurt."

Boggs and Fertig both chortled, their chorus of hateful amusement echoing in the formerly quiet surroundings. In a fleeting moment, Boggs's eyes enlarged, his face contorted into a harsh scowl, and he leaned over and whacked Herman in the side of the head with his gun. "Didn't anyone ever teach you that you can't negotiate with those bent on killing you?"

Cecily screeched again and rushed toward Herman, H.J. whimpering in her arms. "Please can you leave us alone?" she pleaded.

"Did you see what I did to that man?" Boggs asked.

Cecily nodded, her face pale.

"I ain't above hurting you or the baby. So keep yerself quiet."

Amaya lifted her tenth prayer to the Lord for protection. If she'd kept the shotgun close by...but no, she would have had no chance against three men, and they likely were all experienced quick draws.

Spitler emerged from the water and began to unpack the three trunks, strewing clothes, possessions, and unmentionables. He found Amaya's coin purse and some dollars folded in one of the other trunks and pocketed them.

"Quit taking all the spoils for yerself," snarled Fertig.

Boggs again held the gun on Amaya, and she struggled not to panic as the fear pulsed through her. "I'm going to give you one more chance to tell me where the strongbox is."

"I—I think it fell from the stage when we came down the embankment. It could be over there." She pointed toward the direction of the strongbox.

Boggs regarded her. "Fertig, go see if you can find it."

The other man started in the area she pointed, and minutes later, announced he'd found the box.

"Come on, Spitler." To Amaya, he shoved the barrel into her shoulder, nearly knocking her off his feet. "Don't do nothing foolish, and we might allow the four of you to live." He backed away, still holding the revolver on her and never taking his eyes from her.

Even if Amaya wanted to, there was no way she could efficiently reach the hidden shotgun and fire it toward Boggs or the other men. Not when her hands shook so violently. Not with the threat of immediate retaliation.

"It's a heavy one," said Fertig. "'Course, we heard it was gonna be filled with gold." He hoisted it onto his shoulder, and the three men rushed to their horses.

Amaya released the breath she'd been holding as the men rode away. Would they return once they discovered the weight wasn't caused by gold?

Chapter Five

Amaya and Cecily had scarcely finished the meager ration of huckleberries when Amaya spied a man with a black Stetson on horseback in the distance. He tethered his horse on a tree just slightly down the embankment and walked toward them, his large presence demanding attention.

Her heart constricted. Had the men from earlier sent him for revenge?

No, that didn't make sense. They all would have returned.

Was he another outlaw? Looking for the spoils from an overturned stagecoach? Did he mean them harm?

Cecily sniveled and clutched a sleeping H.J. tighter while sliding down beside Herman. The stone in Amaya's throat thickened, and her heart raced in her chest. With shaking arms, she raised the shotgun and aimed it at the man.

Was he alone or were others waiting at the top of the hill?

"Hold it right there, mister." Amaya gripped the shotgun tighter.

The man held his hands in front of him, palms facing her, but she'd noticed the revolver on his hip.

"I mean no harm, ma'am." He took a step back. His tone, with a drawl that indicated he might be from elsewhere, was opposite of the outlaws who'd retreated earlier, and was instead polite, calm, and respectful. The man didn't look like them, but appearances could be deceiving. She surmised him to be slightly older than her, tall, broad-shouldered, and muscular with tan trousers and a blue plaid shirt. Were there others?

His open body stance seemed friendly enough, but he could easily access his revolver. Amaya inwardly cringed when she recalled the gun pointed at her by the outlaws. Pressed into her flesh. Threatening to take her life with a simple pull of a trigger.

Cecily shrieked. "Please don't hurt us!"

"Ma'am…"

"Stay where you are." Amaya's voice squeaked, and she regretted it sounded more mousy than authoritative.

"Don't take another step closer." The woman blinked rapidly, her rifle still trained on him. She displayed confidence, but Silas didn't miss the shaking of her arms as she struggled to hold the gun steady. In truth, he was a quick draw so the woman was no threat.

"I assure you, I just saw the overturned stagecoach and thought I could offer some assistance."

"Yes, you and the last men who happened by."

Other men had stopped by? But hadn't rendered aid? "I know nothing of the last men, ma'am."

Several heartbeats passed before the woman spoke again. "You're sure you're not with them?"

What had they done? An unsettled feeling gnawed at him. The two women, injured man, and young child were vulnerable to anyone with ill intent. Silas turned to again focus on the man to the left. Was he even still alive?

"Ma'am, I assure you I am not with those other men. I was asked to ensure the stagecoach arrived safely from Bowman to Poplar Springs."

She quirked an eyebrow. "Asked by whom?"

"By Mrs. Alvarado at the mercantile."

"Grandmama?"

"Yes. Are you Amaya?"

Her posture slumped, and she lowered the gun. "Praise the Lord." She released a deep breath. "Yes, I'm Amaya. We need help."

Silas silently thanked God for keeping her safe until he could arrive. "Can you tell me what happened here?"

The relief in her countenance apparent, the woman set the shotgun against a tree. "Our stagecoach went out of control and down the embankment into the river. Herman has a broken leg as well as a likely concussion caused by the bandits."

Silas clenched his hands at his sides. So, the outlaws had caused trouble. It was God's Providence alone they hadn't attacked the women, or worse. "Are you and the other woman and child all right?"

"Yes."

"The man over there—has he passed on?"

"The shotgun messenger. Yes, he has." Her voice wavered.

"Was there a driver?" Or perhaps the driver had been part of the plan? Silas heard of that on more than one occasion.

"There was. The shotgun messenger said the driver had a heart attack. I believe he passed before the stagecoach crashed." She pointed to an area several paces away. "He's over there."

Silas followed her gesture. He'd need to come back and retrieve the men for a proper burial. A man suffering a heart attack—another dead likely from the impact—a man injured from the accident and at the hands of bandits... Silas shook his head. The evil in the world got to him at times like these. He returned his attention to the man nearby. "Is he conscious?"

"Right now he is."

"He needs a doctor. I can help. Name's Silas McFadden. I was asked to ride along the road from Poplar Springs to Bowman to ensure the stage arrived safely, although I can see I may be too late. You were robbed?"

"Yes, but after the driver lost control of the stagecoach."

Silas strode toward Herman. The woman holding the child backed away slightly, relief in her otherwise weary features. "Will my husband survive?"

"I'm no doctor, ma'am, but he is still breathing, and whenever there's breath, there's hope."

She covered her mouth with her free hand. "Thank you."

"This is Cecily, her husband, Herman, and their son, H.J."

Silas nodded. "Wish we could have met under different circumstances, ma'am, but I assure you I will do whatever is necessary to get help for your husband."

"The outlaws wanted the strongbox. They rode off with it, but..." Amaya's words trailed, and Silas stood and faced her. She motioned for him to step away from Cecily, then whispered, "There wasn't gold in the box."

Recognition dawned. "Something else, perhaps?"

"Rocks."

He removed his hat and scratched his head. "That was some quick thinking on your part. I'm sure Sheriff Winslow and Deputy Eliason will want a full description of the men. Were you able to get a good look at them?"

She shivered and wrung her hands. "Yes. He...one of them...held a gun on me."

Anger coursed through him. "I'm sorry. Did he—did they hurt you in any other way?"

"No."

He released the breath he'd been holding. He'd ridden with the Poplar Springs posse long enough to know many outlaws didn't stop at theft.

Amaya wrapped her arms around herself. "Do you know Deputy Eliason well?"

"I do. He's a good friend of mine."

It was her turn to release a breath. "I'm so grateful you arrived. I know John Mark and his wife, Hannah. John Mark was one of my fiancé, Russell's, best friends."

"I'm sorry about Russell. I met him briefly. We lost a good man that day."

"Yes, we did." She paused. "We don't have any horses. They were separated from the stagecoach."

39

"I have my horse, and we'll need to make a stretcher for Herman. But we will need to hurry so we can make some headway before nightfall."

An hour later, the unlikely group was on their way toward Poplar Springs. Mr. McFadden—Silas—worked efficiently to gather two long, durable branches before attaching shirts from Herman's trunk of clothing between the branches. He then lashed it to his horse's saddle and carefully placed Herman on it.

While Cecily and H.J. rode Silas's horse—which Silas led—Amaya walked alongside him on the way to Poplar Springs.

The trudging up the rolling hills proved somewhat difficult with her knee, but Amaya refused to complain. God had blessed them richly in sending someone to rescue them, and so far, there was no sign of the bandits.

"I've heard of those outlaws," Silas said after Amaya described them. "Winslow hung a wanted poster about a month or so ago about the Spitler Gang wanted for robbery, assault, murder, and horse theft. When we get to town, the sheriff will form a posse and hopefully find them."

Amaya shivered despite the heat. Things could have progressed so much differently with the outlaws. She and the other passengers could have easily been their victims. She studied the man beside her. Strong, brawny, broad-shouldered, and confident, Silas would be a deterrent should the bandits return. He could have been anyone—another lawless man or even part of the gang bent on stealing the strongbox.

"I'm sorry I pointed the shotgun at you."

A corner of his mouth quirked up. "Reckon I had a bit of a time convincing you I was on the side of justice."

"One can never know. My ma almost didn't allow me to travel to Poplar Springs because this stretch of Wyoming is known for its stagecoach robberies."

"Most towns now have the railroad. With the spur expected to be completed soon, we'll no longer have to worry about stagecoach robberies, but highwaymen will find ways to board trains and pillage them as well. Although agents will deter that somewhat." He paused. "How did you convince your ma to allow you to proceed with your plan? I've never had a daughter, but I imagine I might be protective of her, especially with so many bent on doing innocent people harm."

"My father was injured in a ranching accident, and Ma and my younger sister, Zurina, have been caring for him. When we received the telegram from Grandmama about Grandfather, we knew someone had to assist Grandmama not only with his care, but also with the mercantile. It's their livelihood, and while they could hire help, Grandmama was of the mind to favor family over a stranger." Amaya recalled the worry lines etched in Ma's face. "Pa is usually the more cautious one, but he actually convinced Ma to allow me to go. My entire family was concerned we might lose Grandfather, and truth be told, I'm worried I might not be able to tell him goodbye before he succumbs to his illness."

"He's been doing better. Doc says it's a lengthy process, and he may not fully regain use of his arms and legs."

The sooner they arrived in Poplar Springs, the sooner she would be reassured about Grandfather's condition. She surveyed the distance ahead. Prairies with an abundance of wildflowers, aspens, and pines scattered throughout, and the mountains arcing in a half circle to the right, loomed in her vision. Miles and miles awaited them, especially at the slow pace from walking and pulling the stretcher.

Amaya averted her attention to Silas's comment. "I'm grateful to hear he's doing better. I've been so worried about both him and Grandmama." She ignored the pain that shot through her knee. "Were you there on the day it happened?"

"I was. It happened at church. We just finished singing the final hymn before Reverend Fleming's sermon. Grandmama nudged me, and I noticed immediately something was awry with Grandfather. His mouth was droopy on one side. I asked him if he was all right and was unable to understand his response."

How frightening that must have been for Grandmama!

Silas continued. "Thankfully, Doc was only a few rows behind us. With his knowledge and experience, he was able to save Grandfather. John Mark and I carried him to Doc's office, which has an infirmary attached to it. Doc performed surgery with his wife, Florence's, help. The rest of us held a vigil outside the building, praying for Grandfather. We thought we were going to lose him."

What if they had lost her precious grandfather? "Poor Grandmama."

"Yes, she was..." Silas's voice trailed. "She was beside herself, understandably so. Folks came alongside her and provided comfort. Grandfather survived the surgery, but he's not been the same since."

Amaya briefly squeezed her eyes shut as the tears threatened. "I'm so thankful for the Lord's Providence."

She found herself comfortable in Silas's presence as if they'd known each other for years instead of hours. Soon they were discussing a myriad of topics from Silas's arrival in Poplar Springs, his ranch, and his time riding with the posse, and Amaya's life in Bowman, her parents' desire to move to Poplar Springs, and her love of birds.

And on that day, Amaya found a friend in Silas Mc-Fadden.

CHAPTER SIX

SILAS FOUND AMAYA EASY to converse with, almost as though they'd met years ago. They continued in conversation as they trudged along at a slower pace than he would have liked due to the stretcher. It was then that he noticed Amaya's gait.

"How much farther to Poplar Springs?" Cecily asked.

"Still a ways yet." Silas squinted at the bright sun. Sweat dripped down his back. Hopefully they would make it to town before nightfall. "Are you limping, Amaya?"

"My knee is a bit stiff is all. When we were attempting to make it to the riverbank from the stagecoach, I hit it on a rock."

Silas stopped the horse and placed a gentle hand on her arm. "You shouldn't be walking on it."

"I—Silas—I'm fine."

"There's room on the horse."

If she remained walking on it, it could cause more damage. "I'll help you." Without waiting for her response, Silas took her elbow and assisted her on top of the horse behind Cecily. He then checked on Herman, who had fallen asleep on the stretcher.

Two men on horseback just over the rise caught Silas's attention. He rested his hand on his revolver, but as they neared, he realized they had nothing to fear. "It appears help has arrived."

John Mark and Nowell approached minutes later. "It is good to see you," Silas said, clapping John Mark on the back.

"When the stationmaster realized the stage was late, he notified us. What happened?"

After Silas and Amaya relayed the story to John Mark and Nowell, it was decided John Mark would ride back to town to alert Doc about Herman and to secure a wagon to retrieve the driver and shotgun messenger. Nowell rode to a nearby ranch to borrow another wagon to more easily transport Herman. "We'll form a posse tomorrow to locate the outlaws and deliver them to Poplar Springs," said John Mark.

Grandmama embraced him in a hug. "Thank you for rescuing my Amaya," she said as tears spilled from her eyes.

"It was my pleasure, ma'am."

Grandmama took a step back and pinched his cheek. "You are such a sweet boy, Silas McFadden. I do believe this occasion merits supper every night for two weeks."

"You don't have to do that, what with Grandfather and all." The poor woman had enough to think about without preparing an additional plate.

"You wouldn't deny an old woman something that matters to her, would you?" She peered up at him with twinkling brown eyes.

Ornery. Just like Oma.

"If you insist, I'd be much obliged."

"Now, you stop by here each evening, and I promise you I'll fix the best Basque suppers you've ever tasted."

Silas wouldn't complain about Grandmama's invitation. Eating a home-cooked meal prepared by a gifted cook appealed to him much more than relying on his own paltry cooking skills.

He approached the mercantile the following evening and noted the wooden *closed* sign. He rapped on the door twice, and Amaya offered him a smile as she opened it.

The first thing Silas noticed was her hair. Tendrils framed her face.

Her face. That was the second thing he noticed. Her brown eyes shone and a rosy hue colored her cheeks.

Yes, she was beautiful when he'd first met her yesterday after the stagecoach accident. But now?

With effort, he tore his gaze away from her and focused on a ladybug attempting to climb the mercantile's outer wall.

"Hello, Silas. Please come in. Grandmama is expecting you."

"Thank you." He wiped his sweaty palms on his trousers and followed her inside the mercantile and up the stairs to the living quarters. Before he reached the first step, the aroma of peppers and ham greeted him. Silas closed his eyes and inhaled, his stomach growling in response.

When he opened his eyes, Amaya stood two steps above him. "Wait until you taste it. I've not yet met someone with Grandmama's cooking skills."

A mixture of onions and tomatoes meshed with the peppers and ham lingered in the air when Silas meandered through the door to the humble apartment.

To the right stood a cookstove, sink, two shelves with dishes, and a weathered table with four place settings. On the opposite wall, a potbelly stove and trunk doubled as a second table, which displayed a Bible and two picture frames. A doorway led into the bedroom where Grandfather rested in bed.

The Alvardos were known in Poplar Springs for their generosity, but from the appearance of their living quarters, had few possessions.

"Welcome. You're just in time. We were about to sit and eat." Grandmama bustled about, placing a pitcher and three cups on the table. Amaya stirred a concoction in the skillet on the stove.

"Can I help?"

"No, you just take a seat. Or..." Grandmama's brow furrowed. "Would you mind checking on Grandfather?"

Silas strode the short distance to the bedroom. Grandfather's pallor, fragile body, and thin arms covered in purplish veins reminded Silas the man he'd grown to think of as a grandpa had declined rapidly in the days since his apoplexy. Silas stood above the bed, quietly so as not to awaken Grandfather, and prayed for the Lord's healing. And for Grandmama and Amaya as they cared for him.

He returned to the table a few minutes later and took a seat at an empty chair between Grandmama and Amaya.

Upon Grandmama's request, he led the prayer before doing his best not to eat the appetizing meal all in a matter of three bites.

"Do I understand correctly that you are fond of piperade?" Grandmama asked.

Silas swallowed the bite of food before responding. "Oh, yes. Very much so."

"Sometimes we serve it with eggs. Other times, we add ham to the sauce." Grandmama sat up straighter in her chair, adding a few inches to her petite stature.

"It's delicious."

Amaya dabbed at her mouth with a napkin. "This is a family recipe passed down to us from our ancestors in Spain."

"Indeed," said Grandmama. "My own dear grandmother developed just the right proportions of each ingredient. I daresay we Alvarados could eat this every evening."

Amaya laughed, her soft giggle reminding him of bubbling water in the creek on a summer's day. "Pa for sure wouldn't argue with you about that. He's been known to pester Ma on more than one occasion, especially when we have fresh peppers from the garden."

"Amaya's parents and sister, Zurina, plan to move here soon. Were it not for her father's untimely accident, they would perhaps be here now." Grandmama set her spoon near her plate. "How good it will be to have the family all in one place."

"Honestly, Grandmama, they cannot wait to move here. Pa talks of nothing else but how he plans to manage a ranch and hopefully someday build Ma her own home."

Grandmama's eyes crinkled at the corners. "Ah, yes, but until then, we shall see just how many Alvarados we can squeeze into the mercantile living quarters."

"What meals that Oma made were your favorite?" Amaya asked.

Silas pondered her question. How many times when he was a young'un were they unable to eat much more than a thin broth with a few sparse vegetables? "Well, we're German, so when I was older, she made a lot of Kartoffel Kloesse, which are dumplings made from potatoes. We also ate plenty of cabbage. But mostly, we ate rabbit, beef, and deer."

"Do you have any of her recipes?" Grandmama asked.

"Only for her famous carrot cake." A flood of emotion filled his chest. What he wouldn't give to have Oma sitting here with them right now. She'd take quickly to Grandmama. Amaya too.

Silas, Grandmama, and Amaya, talked late into the night before Grandmama walked him to the door. "See you tomorrow evening. And remember. Our home is your home."

And so it was. Each evening for the next two weeks, Silas planned to ride into town and share a meal with the Alvarados. While he was there, he vowed to complete any chores Grandmama needed, check on Grandfather, and further his friendship with a beautiful woman named Amaya Alvarado.

With trepidation, Amaya hobbled to the sheriff's office to identify the men apprehended by the posse last night. The morning had been an eventful one assisting customers at the mercantile, checking on Cecily, Herman, and H.J., and now preparing for a task she dreaded.

Silas met her just outside the sheriff's office. "How is the knee?"

"Doc said it's badly bruised, but will heal in time. He suggested I stay off it, but with the mercantile and..." her voice trailed. No sense in complaining. Grandmama and the others needed her help. "Although I am a bit anxious about seeing the outlaws again."

"Don't worry. Winslow, John Mark, and I will not allow anything to happen to you. But we do need you to properly identify these men. If they aren't the ones who threatened you and the others, assaulted Herman, and stole the strongbox, you need to let Winslow know."

She inhaled a stuttering breath and nodded. "I will do my best."

"That's all the law asks of you."

His encouragement and the warmth in his eyes emboldened her. Silas opened the door, and she limped through. He hurried ahead of her and joined John Mark, and the two of them stood on either side of her in front of the two cells where the three men were held.

Winslow remained at his desk, shuffling through a stack of wanted posters, and stood when Amaya entered. "Thank you for coming, ma'am. We apprehended these three last night and need you to let us know if they are the men who paid you a visit after the stagecoach accident."

One man gripped the cell bars and attempted to shake them. "We did nothin' wrong," he growled.

The man with the reddish beard, whom Amaya recognized as Boggs, leered at her, his eyes resting just below her neck. Fear paralyzed her, and Amaya worried her legs might fail to adequately bear her weight. "Well, well," he snarled.

Sweat trickled down the back of her neck and her belly cramped. Her voice trembled as she spoke. "Sheriff?"

"Yes?"

"These are the men."

"We ain't the men!" Fertig stomped his foot and pressed his face against the bars. "We ain't the men yer lookin' for!"

Spitler narrowed his eyes at Amaya. "She don't know what she's talkin' about. If we're the ones, then what did we do?"

John Mark peered from her to the men behind the bars. "You don't have to answer that, Amaya. All we need to know is if you recognize these men as the ones who paid you and the others a visit that day."

"They are the ones."

Boggs, the one who'd held the gun to her, took a step forward and attempted to reach Amaya through the bars, his fingers swatting at her. She stood frozen to the floor, unable to move. His upper lip curled and he gritted his teeth. "I should have killed you when I had the chance."

In an instant that took Amaya aback, Silas reached forward and covered Boggs's flailing fingers with his own and squeezed. His massive presence caused Boggs, who was nearly as tall, but half his muscular girth, shrunk back, attempting to take his hand with him.

A vein throbbed in Silas's jaw, and he pressed his face toward the man. "Whatever justice you receive won't be enough."

John Mark stepped up behind Silas and cupped his shoulder. Heeding John Mark's unspoken warning, he released Boggs's fingers.

"I think we have what we need," said Winslow. "Thank you, ma'am. McFadden, I'd be much obliged if you'd escort her from the jail."

Silas heeded Winslow's directive and led Amaya out the door and onto the boardwalk. Her body felt numb from the experience and the continual thoughts of what could have been were it not for the Lord's protection.

"Are you all right?"

"I will be. Thank you."

Silas regarded her. "Let's return you to the mercantile."

Were it not for his supportive hand on her elbow, Amaya wasn't sure her buckling legs would carry her back to safety.

CHAPTER SEVEN

AMAYA GREETED REVEREND FLEMING and flipped the *open* sign to *closed*. "Thank you for agreeing to sit with Iker while we attend the festivities," said Grandmama.

"Happy to do so." The reverend removed his hat and hung it on the hook just inside the entrance.

Grandmama patted her gray bun and smoothed the wrinkles in her colorful skirt. "Are you ready, Amaya?"

She linked her arm through Grandmama's. "I can't wait to see Ina's face when Pritchard makes his announcement."

"If no one has accidentally divulged the secret."

"True. While I have only lived here a couple of weeks, I imagine such a secret might prove difficult to keep in a town this size."

Grandmama laughed. "Indeed, although it wouldn't be charitable of me to name just who might tattle." She clutched a leather zippered pouch. "I hope we get enough entries for the horse races to provide a befitting prize."

Amaya tightened her grip on her own coin purse, her money thankfully recovered when the Spitler Gang was arrested. She hadn't yet revealed that she planned to join one of the races. Perhaps she ought to share that tidbit with Grandmama *before* she presented her with the entry fee.

They continued down the boardwalk and towards the steps of city hall where the event would take place. Twice, Amaya began to open her mouth, only to think better of it. What would Grandmama say? She was what some termed, "old-fashioned".

Her grandmother stopped and peered up at Amaya, her forehead puckered. "What is on your mind, my dear granddaughter? For the past several minutes, it would seem you have something to share, but yet, you haven't shared it."

Ma was correct when she mentioned the difficulty of keeping something from Grandmama. "I—"

"Yes?"

"Well, I—"

"If you don't tell me post haste, we may miss the event entirely, and that will never do as I am the one to collect the entry fees. Besides, if we hasten, we'll procure a spot in front of the crowd and be able to see Ina's face."

"I plan to join the horse race." There. She'd said it.

Grandmama's mouth rounded. "I beg your pardon?"

"I think I have just as good a chance as any."

"You could be injured or worse, and your ma and pa would have my hide and then some."

Amaya shook her head. "Don't worry about that, Grandmama. It's a short distance, and Zurina and I have entered many of these races, all with Pa's permission."

"Well, I suppose I can't stop you, but you do know it's a team of two that will be doing the riding?"

"Yes, and I'm sure other women will join."

Grandmama pursed her lips. "If your parents allow it, who am I to argue? But do be careful."

The anticipation of joining the race was nearly too much to bear. Especially with the thought of potentially winning and being able to assist her parents with purchasing the supplies to build a home when they moved to Poplar Springs later this year.

She and Grandmama joined Silas near the right-side edge of the crowd moments later. She looked up just in time to see Ambrose Eliason hurtle toward them. "Guess what, Uncle Silas and Mrs. Alvarado? I'm going to enter the pony race!"

Silas ruffled his blond hair. "I reckon you'll do a fine job at that."

"I been practicing at home every day." He turned toward Amaya. "Where are my manners?" He bowed. "In case you don't remember me, my name is Sheriff Ambrose Miller Eliason."

She extended a hand to him. "It's a pleasure to meet you, Sheriff. I'm Amaya Alvarado. Thank you for keeping the folks of Poplar Springs safe."

He shook her hand with exaggeration. "My pleasure, ma'am. Well, I best go. There are things to be done before the big race."

Mayor Pritchard planted himself on the steps of city hall, and the crowd hushed. "Thank you for coming today for this special celebration. As most of you know, we aren't here merely for some horse races, but to commemorate the love of my life." He held out his hand. "Ina, would you join me here?"

Ina threaded her through the throngs of people and took her place beside her husband.

"Happy birthday to my lovely bride."

Those in attendance cheered. A blush mottled Ina's face. "Thank you," she squeaked.

"In celebration, there will be cake and lemonade for everyone, courtesy of my in-laws at Pearson's Restaurant, the finest eatery in Wyoming. If you join them for the noonday meal today, you'll receive your meal with a five-cent discount. We'll also have horse and pony races and a foot race. The horse race will commence at one-thirty p.m. sharp and will include teams of two for two heats of four-hundred yards each. One person will ride the first heat, while the second person will ride the second heat. Entry fee is five dollars per person. If you haven't already signed up, submit your fee to Mrs. Alvarado and join us at one p.m. near the livery. The purse is fifty dollars to be split between the two winners. For the children's pony race, the entry fee is fifty cents, and the purse is ten dollars. All proceeds go to repairing the church's roof."

Twenty minutes later, Amaya stood in line to hand Grandmama the five dollars then met at the livery. She inhaled a sharp breath. Five dollars was a lot to lose, but she and Zurina won the last competition with two riders at last year's Bowman Founder's Day Celebration. While she didn't have her own horse this time, she did have the one Silas loaned her. But she'd only ridden it once, and that was earlier today. Several folks wished her well, and she thought of how she'd regret it if she didn't try. If only Zurina were here to join her.

Besides, winning would put her parents that much closer to having the funds to build a home in Poplar Springs. The first home they would ever own.

That alone was worth any consternation she may have.

When Amaya first told him she planned to enter the race, Silas hadn't believed her. Not that he didn't think she was capable, because she was. But with having only practiced once on the horse he lent her, such a feat might not be as easy as she anticipated.

"Please choose your partner," said Mr. Valdez, the livery owner and the one in charge of the race.

Burtlow, a man who'd been in and out of jail primarily for drunkenness and petty theft, sidled up alongside him and wiggled a finger at Silas. "Hey, McFadden, you and me."

Silas was about to refuse when he noticed Kekich, a scrawny man with skinny limbs and a round stomach, a foul reputation, and a permanent stench that was a mixture of body odor and manure, slink up next to Amaya. "How come I haven't noticed you before?" He leaned too close to her, and she backed away. "How about you and me be partners?"

"How about not?" Silas snapped.

"No one asked you, McFadden."

"Doesn't matter if anyone asked me or not. Amaya, would you care to be my partner?"

Amaya nodded. "Yes."

"Hey, what about me?" Burtlow asked. "You were supposed to be my partner. You're a fool." He jabbed his thumb toward Amaya. "You'd have a far better chance of winning the purse with me than her."

Silas ignored him and instead focused on Amaya. "Do you want the first heat or the second?"

"I'll take the first."

Valdez stepped to the starting line. "Lady and gentlemen, may I remind you that cheating disqualifies you. Will those who are taking the second heat ride slowly to their destination before we begin?"

"See you at the finish line," Silas told Amaya before riding four hundred yards ahead. A minuscule moment of uncertainty about Amaya's riding abilities entered his mind before he brushed it aside. Whether they won or whether they lost, choosing her as a partner was his best bet.

Burtlow leaned forward in his saddle "You'll regret choosing that woman over me."

"Doubt it."

Burtlow's lips drew back in a snarl. "We'll see about that."

"You and Kekich are a better team anyhow."

The jarring sound of Valdez's revolver rang through the air, and Silas's pulse pounded in his ears. He loved such competitions. Craning his neck, he watched for the moment Amaya arrived and crossed the line so he could take his turn.

She rounded the corner. Her dark brown hair had loosened from its bun and now flowed behind her, captivating his attention. Her determination, dedication, and fortitude impressed him. Her beauty enthralled him. And her friendship meant everything to him. For a moment, he almost forgot what it was he was supposed to do.

As Amaya neared, common sense returned to him just in time and he hastened his horse down the road and toward victory.

Valdez handed Silas and Amaya each twenty-five dollars. Amaya held the amount to her heart before stuffing it into her coin purse. Wouldn't Pa be proud when he heard she'd raised some funds to go towards his and Ma's new home? Ma would fret a bit that Amaya had actually entered the race, and Amaya was confident Grandmama had fretted the entire time she rode those four hundred yards.

"Congratulations, partner." Silas offered her a lopsided grin.

"We made a good team, didn't we?"

"That we did."

As they walked back towards town to tether their horses and watch the pony race, Amaya thanked the Lord for the friendship she'd found with Silas and for the win that would assist in enabling Ma and Pa's dream to come true.

CHAPTER EIGHT

AMAYA LEFT THE NEW hotel where Cecily, Herman, and H.J. were staying while Herman continued to recover from his injuries. She greeted passersby as she hurried back to the mercantile to assist Grandmama with customers. It had been busy as of late, not that she was complaining. She knew her grandparents struggled at times since most of their customers put items on account.

When she entered the mercantile, Grandmama was nowhere to be seen. Nor did any customers peruse the wares. A clattering noise caused her to jump, and she started toward the stairs.

Grandmama staggered down the steps, her right hand clenching the railing. Tears streamed down her face.

Amaya rushed towards her. "Grandmama?"

"Oh, Amaya."

"Is it Grandfather?"

Grandmama nodded.

"Is he all right?"

"He's all right, it's just that..." Grandmama lowered her head, and Amaya wrapped her arms around her.

"Please tell me what's wrong. What was that noise?" Amaya's heart lurched, and the threat of tears stung her own eyes at Grandmama's distress.

Grandmama took a step back from Amaya's embrace, peered about them—likely to check to see if anyone else was in the mercantile—then a shaky breath. "I don't know what to do."

Amaya took Grandmama's hands in her own and prayed the Lord would keep customers from entering during this time.

"Iker has not been eating like he should. I'm so worried for him. He's become so frail in so short of time. I—I have been feeding him in the days since he first had his apoplexy. At first, he had no strength at all, but now, just as Doc mentioned, he's improved, especially his leg. So today, I attempted to convince him to hold the spoon since one arm has not suffered as much as the other."

Amaya rubbed Grandmama's arm and urged her to continue.

"He became angry and dropped the spoon. He kept pointing at me, and in his garbled words, telling me I should be the one to feed him. But I want him to heal. I want him to be better." Her sobs wracked her petite frame, and Amaya again folded her arms around her, this time, tears falling freely from her own eyes.

"I'll fetch Doc. Perhaps he'll know what to do."

Grandmama's body shook with stuttered breaths. "Yes, please do."

Amaya released her and frantically dashed toward the door. Just as she exited, she collided with Silas.

"Oh!"

"Amaya?"

"Begging your pardon, Silas, but I must fetch Doc. Grandfather isn't well." Without awaiting a response she darted down the boardwalk, tears misting her vision.

She returned with Doc minutes later and found Silas in the mercantile with Grandmama. "Oh, Doc. Thank you for coming. Iker is not himself."

Amaya was torn with the decision of whether to remain downstairs to oversee the mercantile or join Grandmama and Doc.

As if to read her mind, Silas said, "I'll manage the mercantile. You go upstairs."

"Are you sure? You've never..."

Grandmama rested a hand on Amaya's arm. "We've already discussed it."

"Besides, how difficult can managing a mercantile be? I manage cows every day." His statement, along with his lopsided grin, offered a brief reprieve from the strain of the past few minutes.

"If you're sure."

"I'm sure."

The kindness and sincerity in his gaze made her again appreciate their friendship.

Silas wasn't concerned in the least about temporarily overseeing the mercantile. He'd herded cattle, delivered calves, branded, mended fences, tracked predators, and more. Oftentimes in frigid or stifling weather. He was, however, concerned about Grandfather and those who loved him.

He straightened the canned goods and swept while he waited for customers. While being a clerk wasn't on his list of ambitions, it proved a pleasant reprieve from the at-times grueling labor on the ranch. Not that he would trade ranching for anything, because he fully believed it was what he was meant to do.

Silas took his place behind the counter and watched the passersby on the boardwalk. He regretted not asking Grandmama if she had some freight for him to unload. A small round face pressed against the window drew his attention a moment later. Ambrose's nose and lips, squished against the window, caused him to chuckle.

Ambrose saw him and entered the mercantile with Hannah and Little Russell. "Guess what, Uncle Silas!" Ambrose ran towards him, then halted. "Wait. Why are you behind the counter?"

"I'm helping Mrs. Alvarado and Amaya today."

Ambrose shrugged. "All right. Say, did you hear I won second place in the pony race?"

Silas ambled from behind the counter. "I saw you cross the finish line. Congratulations!"

Ambrose puffed his chest out and removed his over-sized cowboy hat. "Thank you, sir. It's what we sheriffs do. Practicing in races helps us become faster so when the outlaws try to outride us, they don't stand a chance."

"I an outwah," said Little Russell pointing to himself.

Hannah bent to his height. "No, sweetie, you're one of the good men." To Silas, she added, "We rode to town today to retrieve a few provisions and share a noonday meal with John Mark."

Ambrose jumped up and down. "And..."

"And so Ambrose can choose something with his winnings."

"I've been having my eye on that battleship over there." Ambrose bolted toward the shelf that showcased a variety of toys. He lifted the wooden ship, complete with an American flag and two soldiers on board. "It's a pull toy, Uncle Silas." He tugged on the string, and the boat rolled along the floor. "Pa told me a man divides his funds three ways. Tithe, save, and spend on the necessities. Reckon this battleship is a necessity."

Little Russell reached for it, and Ambrose swatted his hand away. "This is only for big kids. Maybe when you're older, you can play with it." Ambrose plucked fifty cents from his trouser pocket and put it on the counter before eyeballing the candy jars. "Reckon I best take a few of those peanut taffies too. How much are they?"

Silas found the price on the back of the jar. "Ten cents a pound."

"I'll take a whole pound." Ambrose reached into his pocket for a dime. "And some stick candy too."

Silas added a pound of stick candy at seven-and-a-half cents to Ambrose's order.

"Is everything all right with Amaya and Mrs. Alvarado?" Hannah asked.

"It's Mr. Alvarado. Doc is up there now." Silas wasn't sure how much to say since it wasn't his place, but he knew Amaya and Hannah shared a close friendship.

Hannah added a few items to the purchase of the battleship, and Silas completed the transaction before they went on their way.

The next customer purchased farm implements and bullets. An easy task since Silas had knowledge of both.

Mrs. Fleming bought some sugar, flour, and a few canned goods.

Silas grinned. So far the transactions proved easy, and if there ever had been a doubt in his mind that he couldn't oversee the mercantile, those qualms quickly disappeared.

Until...

Mrs. Shawdale, a woman he knew only from having briefly met her and her husband at the surprise birthday party for Ina, entered next. "Dear me. I had no idea you worked here," she pursed her lips. "Perhaps I can shop another day."

"No need to worry, ma'am. I'm only here temporarily."

"Well that's a relief." She scrutinized him, her gaze resting on his dirty shirt. She wrinkled her nose. "If you were here permanently, it's doubtful the Alvarados would allow you to arrive in soiled clothing."

"I was working on the ranch and had to come to town for some barbed wire and lumber."

"Far be it from me to concern myself over your comings and goings." Mrs. Shawdale meandered toward the section with the notions. "I'll be needing some fabric and thread . But first, do you have any of Dr. Price's Special Flavoring Extracts?"

"Never heard of that, ma'am."

Her eyes shot sparks at him. "No, I'm sure you haven't. For your ease of understanding, do you have any of Dr. Price's vanilla extract?"

Silas rummaged through the different shelves searching for vanilla extract. How difficult could it be in a store as small as the Alvarados' mercantile? "I don't see any of Dr. Price's vanilla extract; however, Doc does keep some elixirs available. You might check there."

Mrs. Shawdale's nostrils flared, and she crossed her arms across her chest. "Mr. Alvarado..."

"Mr. McFadden."

"Mr. McFadden, I do not appreciate—as a matter of fact—I abhor your attempts at being comical. Doc would not carry cooking supplies."

How was he to know Dr. Price's vanilla extract wasn't a tonic? Silas now realized why he esteemed cattle over people at times. He bit his tongue, knowing that how he conducted himself would directly influence the mercantile's reputation. "Did you mention something about needing fabric and thread?"

A glower breached her mouth. "Yes. I did." She marched closer to the fabric shelf and pointed at some purple cloth. "I need two yards of the calico, please."

That, he could do. "That'll be four cents a yard." He grabbed the bolt of fabric and unrolled it over his arm like he'd seen a shop owner do one time when shopping with Oma as a child. Then he carried it to the counter and smoothed the unrolled material to measure it.

There was just one problem. When he smoothed it, he failed to remember that his hands were blackened and smudged from handling the lumber and barbed wire.

Streaks of dirt covered the light purple fabric. Would Mrs. Shawdale notice?

Fortunately, her attention remained on a tea set a few paces away. Maybe if he cut it and placed it in brown paper before she returned to the counter, she wouldn't be the wiser.

His conscience niggled at him. Honesty was important.

In that case, Silas would just attempt to remove the grime, and if that failed, he'd cut her another piece and pay for this section himself.

He withdrew his trusty pocket knife from his trouser pocket, flipped it open, and wiped the blade on his pants to clean it. Then he measured out two yards, pressed the material once again to remove any creases, and prepared to cut through it.

"Mr. McFadden!"

He nearly ripped the fabric at Mrs. Shawdale's exclamation. Was something wrong? Had someone been injured? He scanned the mercantile, but it was still just the two of them. "Yes, ma'am?"

Through gritted teeth, she seethed, "How dare you prepare to incise the cloth with your filthy pocket knife."

"I'm not sure I understand the problem."

"No, of course you wouldn't. Nevermind. I don't wish to purchase the calico. I will return when there is a more capable clerk. You, Mr. McFadden, are an uncouth cad who belongs toiling outdoors in the soil rather than employed as a salesman." She turned on her heel and stomped toward the door. "Good day."

To say he was relieved was an understatement. Silas rolled the fabric back onto the bolt as best he could and would keep it at the counter so he could pay for the soiled portion.

Silas heard footsteps and saw Amaya descend from the stairs. "How is Grandfather?" Weariness tugged at her shoulders, and he wished he could fix all that worried her.

"He'll be all right. Doc said the good news is that Grandfather's chin is dry, which means he's able to swallow. If he wasn't able to..." Amaya's voice trailed and she briefly looked away before continuing. "Doc has given Grandmama some advice and has also discussed a few matters with Grandfather." She paused. "How was your first day working as a mercantile clerk?"

"I reckon Mrs. Shawdale doesn't care much for me." He explained about the fabric and insisted on paying for it. Perhaps he could donate it to Mrs. Fleming for one of her charitable items.

"Mrs. Shawdale is a challenging sort. Silas, thank you so much for being here for us and for overseeing the store in our absence."

"My pleasure."

The gratitude in her expression warmed places deep inside of him.

And he knew he would do anything for her.

CHAPTER NINE

SILAS STIRRED THE BEAN soup in his bowl but had no appetite, not even for the delicious meal he'd purchased from Pearson's Restaurant earlier in the day. Last night was the final night to eat at Grandmama's, and tonight he was on his own.

He already missed the company.

It didn't help that today was Oma's birthday. Had she lived, she would have been seventy-four. As he always did when this day arrived, Silas struggled with the guilt piling up and weighing heavily on his shoulders. But today wasn't the only day he wrestled with wishing he could have changed things. Oftentimes discouraging thoughts about the past entered his mind without much warning.

He rose and walked to his bedroom. A tintype of Oma held a prominent place next to his Bible on the bureau. While no one smiled in photographs, he could still see the joy in her eyes. A joy she possessed because of her love for the Lord.

Certainly not because she was proud of the way Silas had lived his life.

Silas clutched it to his chest and hung his head. If only he had been the grandson Oma deserved.

He'd arrived home late after dawdling with the group of young men Oma did not approve of. Once again they'd slipped into the saloon and joined the men for some drinks. He reached his hand into his pocket and produced the two leftover coins after his whiskey expenditures. Oma was expecting enough to purchase some necessaries at the mercantile. Silas rolled the nickels through his fingertips. The remainder of his wages wouldn't be enough to purchase much.

He slid through the door as quietly as he could. Hopefully Oma was already in bed. But as soon as he entered, he heard her voice. English, combined with intermittent German from her motherland, spoken softly and rapidly.

She was praying.

Again.

Silas tiptoed quietly toward the ladder that led to the tiny loft where he slept. But Oma's words drew him in. He paused, setting his jaw in a straight line.

Surely she wasn't praying for him *again.*

"Precious Lord, I beseech You to save mein süßer junge—to save my sweet boy."

Silas gritted his teeth. He may have been a sweet boy years ago, but the life he'd chosen and the other rebellious young men he kept company with had tainted him.

"You say in Your Word to *'train up a child in the way he should go: and when he is old, he will not depart from it'.* I have trained Him in the way I know best. But I must have done something wrong. Something very wrong." Oma choked on the words.

The thought of hurting her caused a deep pain in his chest. She blamed herself for the choices he made. But what could he do? What was done was done.

"I have trained Him in Your ways, Lord. I have taken him to church, read the Bible with him, instructed him about what is right and what is wrong. But it's all for naught."

Oma was fond of saying things were all for naught, and now he was included in the things she found hopeless.

Although he knew she would never consider him hopeless. To Oma, no one was without hope.

"Please bring him to You, Lord. Convict him of his errors. Give him a heart for Jesus. I beseech thee, Lord."

Silas swallowed the lump that had formed in his throat. He'd disappointed the one he loved most in this world, and day after day she prayed for him.

But he was beyond prayer.

Thank goodness she didn't know about the stealing. The drinking and gambling was enough.

Silas bemoaned his calloused heart. When had he not cared what Oma thought? What the Lord thought? When had having fun and causing trouble become paramount to him?

He'd changed in the last two years. And not for the better.

Silas could see Oma kneeling beside her bed, her wrinkled hands folded and her shoulders quaking.

He'd caused that pain.

"Lord, soften his heart and..." Oma lapsed into German again. "Bring back my Silas. Mein süßer junge. The one who used to bring me flowers from the field. Who used to go on walks and we would talk about everything. The boy who opened his Bible with such eagerness and who did all he could to help others. A helpful sort, that's what my Silas once was."

Silas had become accustomed to Oma's prayers for him and not once had he allowed his grandmother to know he eavesdropped.

Tonight, listening to his beloved Oma cry out to the Lord did something all those other times hadn't.

It shook him.

But how could he change? How could he be the sweet boy Oma wanted him to be?

The following day, Oma fell ill. She'd collapsed in the kitchen while preparing supper and Silas hadn't been there. He'd been with his friends seeing how many items they could steal from neighboring barns and not get caught then prepare to sell them in a neighboring Texas county.

When he arrived home that evening, he carried Oma to her bed before mounting his horse and riding faster than he ever had to fetch the doctor. All the while, he did his own crying out to the Lord. Begging Him to save his grandmother. To heal her.

Cancer. The word stuck deep in his throat, the pain of the diagnosis that she had a tumor caused a grief he'd never known.

Silas made deals with God that if He would restore her to good health, Silas would change his ways and seek the Lord's guidance.

Oma survived for a short time, but was never the same. Weak, fragile, constantly fatigued, and with belly pain and vomiting, the doctor said she had little time left. In truth, it wasn't the cancer that stole her life, but the pneumonia that winter.

Silas cherished the last days of Oma's life. He stayed by her bedside most of the day when not doing chores, working at his job, or fixing meals for his grandmother. He prayed the Lord would restore her.

"I'm so sorry for the way I've behaved. Will you forgive me?"

Oma's blue eyes, so like his own, crinkled at the corners and a smile lifted her lips. "Oh, mein süßer junge, of course I forgive you. You have been such a treasure to me all these years."

Silas knew he hadn't been a treasure for the past two years at least, and his heart constricted at the thought. Why had he not been wiser and owned up to his ways long before today? It had always been just he and Oma. She raised him when his parents decided they had no room in their life for a child. A woman who became pregnant without being married sullied not only her own name, but also her mother's and her son's. His pa never wanted him in the first place.

"I gave my life to Christ last night."

Tears slid down her soft and wrinkled cheeks.

"Don't cry, Oma."

"It's happy tears, mein süßer junge happy tears." But her voice faltered.

"I love you, Silas," Oma said.

"I love you, Oma."

Two things happened that day. Silas secured his future for eternity. And he lost Oma.

A knock on the door interrupted Silas's recollection of that day. Who would be visiting at this time of the evening? Exhaustion wearied him. First early morning chores, then the stint at the mercantile, then home for more chores.

He flung the door open to see a portly man slightly older than him with a too-tight silk-faced frock coat, a faded fawn-colored felt hat, and trousers with a button that threatened to pop in response to his rotund stomach.

"Can I help you?"

"Yes, you can. I'm Palmerston Liptack. Might I interest you in some of the wares on my peddler's wagon?"

"How did you find my place?" It wasn't easy to access his house from the main road leading to Poplar Springs, something Silas appreciated.

The man shrugged. "Why don't you come and see what you can't live without?"

Silas hadn't the patience to deal with a swindler, but he followed Mr. Liptack to a mustard-yellow wagon. In the waning sunlight, Silas could barely see the pots, pans, washboards, lanterns, and other goods stacked haphazardly on the top, corralled by thin red railing.

A wheelchair, strapped to the wagon, its one smaller wheel spinning in the evening breeze, caught his eye. He'd seen such a contraption once while in Colorado.

Such a device would be perfect for Grandfather.

"How much for the wheelchair?"

"Ah, I see you've discovered my most important product. Constructed in a manufactory in New York, this fine wood chair with three wheels, two at the sides, and a much smaller one in the back is the epitome of durability. There are foot rests and a high back for the invalid's ultimate comfort."

"How much are you asking for it?"

Mr. Liptack stroked his clean-shaven chin. "Well, I didn't cheaply acquire such an appliance." The man stated a price Silas found ridiculously high.

"I best get back to my supper before it gets cold." There was no way Silas would pay that amount, even if he did have it, for a dilapidated old wheelchair he'd have to fix.

"Wait! Since you are such a charming gent, allow me to offer you my best price." He offered a price a few dollars less than his original price.

Silas shook his head. "I'll give you three dollars."

"Three dollars? But this is a superior wheelchair."

"One I will have to fix, not to mention the rusted wheels."

Mr. Liptack rested his hands on his ample stomach. "Three dollars and ten cents."

Silas waited a moment before agreeing to the sum.

An hour later, he'd cleaned and fixed any broken parts on the chair. And tomorrow, he'd present it to Grandfather.

Maybe, just maybe for the first time since his apoplexy, both he and Grandmama could attend church together.

Sunday morning arrived quicker than usual, and Amaya rolled up her bedroll and assisted Grandmama with breakfast. "Please, let me stay with Grandfather today," she whispered.

"No, you go to church. I'll stay with him."

It pained her to see Grandmama's pain and Grandfather's ailing condition. Grandmama put on a brave front, but Amaya heard her muffled cries in the night and her fervent prayers for God's healing.

Amaya had only told one other person of the sadness in Grandmama's eyes at not being able to attend church with Grandfather, and that was Silas. While she couldn't do anything about her grandparents frequenting Pastor Fleming's church together, she *could* ensure that Grandmama could attend. She was about to argue again when she heard a knock on the mercantile door.

Who could be visiting on a Sunday morning? She tiptoed past Grandmama and Grandfather's room and down the stairs. A hasty peek through the window revealed it was Silas. She pressed the wrinkles from her skirt and opened the door. "Silas?"

"Good morning, Amaya."

She'd always thought him a handsome man, but today, he was especially so with his red plaid shirt stretched across his wide shoulders and tucked into his trousers to reveal his trim waist.

Amaya pushed the notion aside and chastised herself for noticing his appearance. "What brings you to the mercantile on a Sunday morning?" And what was that contraption with wheels beside him?

"I've come to help Grandfather attend church."

"Oh, Silas, he's not well enough."

"Can he sit up?"

"Yes, when propped against the pillows in case he were to fall over, but he can't stand."

Silas pointed to the chair beside him. "I purchased this from a peddler yesterday. Apparently he was making his way through Poplar Springs as I saw him parked near the blacksmith shop this morning. Anyhow, this is a wheelchair, and I figured we'd wheel Grandfather to the church. We can bring pillows, and we can even somehow strap him in so he doesn't fall out."

Amaya remained skeptical as the questions and concerns loomed in her mind. "What if Grandfather—"

"Amaya? Who's at the door?" Grandmama interrupted their conversation.

"It's Silas."

Grandmama padded down the stairs, and her distressed expression from moments ago softened when her entire face lit up. Amaya often thought that if Grandmama could choose a grandson, she'd choose Silas.

He explained about the wheelchair, and Grandmama clapped her hands together. "Goodness, but it would be delightful if we were once again able to worship together. I've so missed Reverend Fleming's insightful sermons."

"Well, now you can. I'll carry Grandfather to the chair, we'll make sure he's comfortable, and I'll push him to the church. It isn't that far."

Grandmama pressed a hand against the disheveled hair she'd not yet had the chance to braid. "It will take a moment for me to continue making myself presentable, and Grandfather isn't properly dressed and hasn't eaten yet." Her shoulders slumped. "While I appreciate the thought, we may have to postpone it until next Sunday."

"You go upstairs and make yourself presentable. Amaya can feed Grandfather, and I'll ready the chair for him."

Uncertainty lined Grandmama's features and her brows drew close together. "If you're sure we can make it on time."

Silas's gaze caught Amaya's. "Not if we dawdle."

Grandmama didn't need any further prodding. Amaya hadn't ever seen her move as swiftly as she did when she flew back up the stairs to ready herself.

Fifteen minutes later, Silas carried Grandfather down the stairs and set him in the chair. He gave a half-smile as Grandmama tucked him between the pillows and draped a crocheted blanket over his lap. Finally, she placed the Bible on top of the blanket.

Joy transformed her face as they made their way to church. Silas went ahead of them through the door and arranged for Grandfather to sit at the edge of the pew in their customary row.

"That Silas is such a sweet boy. Kind, thoughtful, and handsome too." Grandmama whispered to Amaya. "You might ought to consider him."

Silas *was* kind, thoughtful, and handsome, and Amaya appreciated their close friendship. But she would never see him as more than a friend because her heart would never belong to anyone but Russell.

CHAPTER TEN

THE FOLLOWING WEEK, SILAS pulled out the oak chair and took a seat at the round table across from Nowell at Pearson's Restaurant. It was the same table where they always sat, near the pot-bellied stove on one side and the window to Nowell's back. The aroma of potatoes, chicken, and cornbread muffins lingered in the air. Silas perused the menu noting that tomorrow's special would be ham and veal loaf, cabbage salad, brown bread, and applesauce for twenty-five cents. Perhaps he'd be eating here tomorrow as well.

"Hello, Silas and Nowell. May I take your order?" Mrs. Pearson, a plump woman with a constant smile and gray-blonde hair, stood with her pencil in hand. "The special today is mashed potatoes, baked chicken with dressing, celery sticks, and cream pie."

Silas and Nowell both ordered the special along with some coffee, and Mrs. Pearson promised to return soon with their meals. Nowell leaned across the table and lowered his voice. "Ever since John Mark married Hannah, I've really had it on my mind to find a woman and settle down."

"Yes. We speak of this nearly every time we eat a meal here."

Nowell feigned surprise. "We do?"

"Yes, for at least the past couple of years."

Nowell's reddish-brown mustache twitched. "It's been that long?"

"It has."

"The ranch can be a bit lonely at times. It would be nice to have a wife."

It was the same thing Nowell always said when he brought up the topic. "You might have noticed that there aren't a lot of choices here in Poplar Springs."

Mrs. Pearson deposited two cups of coffee at their place settings, and Silas added a liberal amount of sugar.

Nowell tilted back on two of the legs of the chair and clasped his hands behind his head. "I think I might have a solution."

"A solution to what?" While Nowell had been and was a good friend, his "solutions" weren't always the brightest.

"To my dilemma of not having a wife."

"That's a dilemma?"

"To me it is."

Silas took a drink of his coffee. "And what's your solution?"

"A matchmaking service."

Coffee spewed everywhere before Silas regained control of his shock.

"Just listen a minute." Nowell inclined forward again, a glint in his brown eyes. "I heard from Hank and Frank..."

"Now you sound like a chattering hen."

"They have some worthwhile stuff to say sometimes."

"Not sometimes. More like rarely."

Nowell nodded. "This was worthwhile. You know how Hank has fancied Widow Holmes?"

"Unlike you, I haven't kept abreast of the elderly townsfolks' romantic notions."

"Everyone knows about Hank's fondness for Widow Holmes. Everyone. Even someone who doesn't stay abreast of the elderly townsfolks' romantic notions."

Silas steepled his fingers. "All right. What about them?"

"Gertrude's Matrimonial Agency arranged to help them begin courting."

"Gertrude's Matrimonial Agency?"

"Here are your meals, gentleman. Please let me know if you'll be needing anything else." Mrs. Pearson set down the two steaming plates and hurried away to her next customer.

Silas and Nowell prayed for the meal before Silas took a bite of his chicken. Nowell continued prattling on with his crazy notion about matchmaking services.

"Hear me out, Silas." Nowell shook his knee beneath the table like he always did when excited. "Gertrude Duckworth, the woman who recently purchased the old barbershop across from the livery, has opened a new business. Two, in fact."

"Is she the one from back East?" Silas recalled the reverend introducing a woman who'd recently moved to Wyoming.

"I think she's from Iowa. She has a mending service on one side of the building and her matchmaking service on the other. The businesses are both connected." Nowell paused long enough to stuff a bite of mashed potatoes into his mouth before continuing. "Let's you and me go in there and hire her to help us find wives."

"What?"

"If she finds us someone we don't cotton to, we don't have to accept. You go in there with me, hire Miss Duckworth, and I'll pay for today's noonday meal. Both of your helpings."

While Silas would like to find a good Christian woman with whom to share his life, he wasn't about to hire a matrimonial service. "You can go in there, but I'm not interested."

"You never know. She might find you the perfect wife."

"Here in Poplar Springs?"

Nowell chewed and swallowed his food so fast his Adam's apple bobbed double-time and Silas thought he might choke. "Her advertisements say if she can't find you someone to court here in Poplar Springs, she'll handle the correspondence for a mail-order bride. Reckon that sounds like a worthwhile guarantee to me."

"I'll go with you, but I'm not hiring her."

"Good enough for me." Nowell's satisfied smile gave Silas pause for concern.

An hour later, Silas and Nowell strolled down the boardwalk to Gertrude Duckworth's business. "I hope this doesn't take long. I've got to get back to the ranch." Silas considered everything he had to do. Visiting with the owner of a matrimonial agency was not among them.

"Here it is." Nowell opened the door to the former barbershop, and they both stepped inside. However, Silas was not prepared for what he saw.

The room took Silas aback. It no longer resembled a barbershop. Light pink wallpaper covered the walls and an ornate desk stood to one side. A lacy curtain hung on the front window, and two fancy chairs were placed on the right-hand side of the room in front of the desk. On the left-hand side was another chair, a table with needles and thread, and a basket full of clothing items. A few pictures hung on the wall, and in the middle of the floor was a yellow and brown rug.

It was quite opposite from the barbershop Silas once knew. The masculine furnishings had been replaced with feminine frippery.

He turned to leave when Nowell grabbed his arm. "Remember the noonday meal?" he hissed.

Oh, Silas remembered all right. He reached for some coins in his trouser pocket. The amount wouldn't set him back much as he'd already planned on paying for his own meal.

Nowell narrowed his eyes, a warning glance. Silas wasn't concerned. While Nowell matched him in height, Silas was easily two of him in muscle, girth, and strength. But a promise was a promise, and Silas valued the friendship he'd found in Nowell. For that, he could suffer a few minutes in the froufrou business.

A woman about Silas's age, tall, thin, and awkward with wire-rimmed spectacles and a mass of curly brown hair approached them. She held a calico cat in her arms and offered a broad smile. "Welcome to Gertrude's Mending and Gertrude's Matrimonial Agency. For which business might I assist you today?"

"Hello, Gertrude."

Silas noticed Nowell had pasted on his best smile. The one he used when charming the ladies. Except it hadn't been effective or Nowell wouldn't be a patron at Gertrude's Matrimonial Agency.

"Hello, Nowell."

"We're here to enlist your matrimonial services."

Was it Silas's imagination or had Nowell puffed up his puny chest?

Gertrude's eyes lit. "Delightful! Have a seat in the Matrimonial Agency, and I'll just retrieve a piece of stationery and be right with you."

Nowell, of course, took the larger chair, his lanky body barely filling half of it. Silas had no option but to sit in the high-backed chair with fluffy pink cushions and gold plating around the edges. "How about we trade?" he asked Nowell. The chair's lack of width forced him to partially sit on one of the excessively-curled ornate arm rests."

"Sir," said Gertrude, setting the cat on the floor and settling herself behind her desk, "did you know that chair is a Rococo chair? It's quite elaborate, especially for the Wild West."

Silas didn't care if it was elaborate or not. The narrow back filled the center of his back, and the rest of his torso extended far beyond the measly chair. He crammed himself between the armrests as discomfort settled in.

"Now, gentlemen. Who would like to go first?"

"Oh, I'm not..."

But Gertrude wasn't paying him any mind. Instead, she stared intently at Nowell.

"I'll go first, ma'am," Nowell offered another of his charming smiles.

Gertrude tapped her pencil on the desk. "Excellent! Now, from our previous discussion, I already have your name since we met heretofore at church."

Nowell nodded as if he'd won a prize. "Yes, ma'am."

"I'll just need your age."

"Thirty."

Gertrude scrutinized him. "Physical description..." her pencil scratched the paper as she wrote. "Tall, slim, in good condition, brownish-red hair, mustache, brown eyes." She paused. "Your occupation?"

"Rancher, and I do assist the posse with hunting outlaws from time to time," he beamed.

Gertrude clapped. "Splendid! A law-abiding man." Her brow wrinkled. "You've never been in jail, have you?"

At her inquiry, Silas was grateful he couldn't squirm in the miniature chair. If she asked him that question, would he be able to tell the truth?

"No, ma'am, I have not."

"And you are a God-fearing man?"

"Yes."

Gertrude offered him a vivacious smile. "Now tell me, Nowell, what is it you are hoping to find in your future wife as it pertains to characteristics and traits?"

Nowell sat up straighter in his comfortable and spacious chair. "She must be a God-fearing woman. About my age, maybe a few years younger or older. Easy on the eyes, smart, and have a sense of humor."

"Is that of utmost importance to you?"

"The God-fearing, age or appearance part?"

"The appearance part."

Nowell seemed to ponder her question. "My ma always said character is most important, so I suppose not, but she needs to have all her teeth and be somewhat attractive."

Gertrude nodded. "I completely understand. Anything else?"

"Yes. She has to want to live on a ranch. If she's a city woman, it won't work for us. I live two miles from town."

"So she must also like animals?"

Nowell shrugged. "She has to at least like some of them. No sense in living on a ranch if you don't like God's creatures."

"I have your application completed, Nowell. If you'll kindly pay the fee, we can begin. If I cannot find you a wife here in Poplar Springs, which might be a challenge..."

"A challenge?"

Gertrude placed a hand to her heart. "Oh, dear me. Allow me to rephrase that. If I cannot find you a wife here in Poplar Springs due to the shortage, not due to your, appearance and ahem, qualifications, then I shall look elsewhere. Are you amenable to a mail-order bride?"

"If she's honest and forthright. I've heard of some who aren't."

"Indeed. If the time comes for us to travel that path, I'll assist you in writing the advertisement, placing it, and responding—for an additional fee, of course."

Nowell sat back and extended his legs to the front of him, crossing them at the ankles. "Reckon that sounds good to me."

"After you both meet here two times with me as your chaperone, you will then partake in a meal at Pearson's Restaurant. At that point, you should be able to ascertain whether or not you would like to continue spending time with the woman, begin courting her, or decide friendship is the best course. If the latter, then we'll start over in the process. And if you and the woman I've chosen to be your bride do decide to proceed to marriage, I am happy to arrange it all for you, from securing the reverend, to inviting the guests—for an additional fee, of course."

Nowell chuckled. "If you can succeed at this, I'm happy to pay the additional fee."

"Oh, I will succeed. Of that I am sure." Gertrude stood, lifted her cat, and walked around the desk towards him. "This is Lady Austen, named after my favorite author. Are you a reader, Nowell?"

"Sure. I read the Bible, the newspaper, and population signs when I come to other towns."

The woman held Lady Austen toward him. "Would you care to hold her for a moment while I gather your friend's information?"

"All right." Nowell reached for the cat, and it settled into his arms, snuggling against him.

"Ma'am..." began Silas, "I'm not here for an interview or to apply. I was just along to help Nowell."

Gertrude waved her hand at him. "Poppycock! Now tell me your name, please."

"Silas McFadden."

She scribbled it down. "Now, Silas, may I call you Silas?"

"Yes.

"Let's see...physical description." Gertrude squinted her eyes as if to see him better. "Oversized, tall, and in good condition, dark blond hair, blue eyes, clean-shaven. And what is your occupation?"

"I'm a rancher as well, ma'am."

Nowell decided to interject at that moment. "He's also ridden with the Poplar Springs posse."

"My, but that will sound appealing for the women who peruse your files."

"We have files?" asked Nowell.

Gertrude nodded. "Most certainly. Everyone who is a patron of Gertrude's Matrimonial Agency does. I keep them stored safely in a drawer." She patted the top of her desk. "Here at the Agency, we aim only to do our utmost best in finding the one you'll want to spend the rest of your life with."

Silas wanted—no yearned—to find a woman to spend the rest of his life with, but he was fairly sure Gertrude wouldn't be the one to help him with that aspiration.

"Now, tell me, Silas, what is it you are hoping to find in your future wife as in characteristics and traits?"

"Well, all of the things Nowell said and she must love children. I'd like to have a large family."

He just realized he'd poured out a part of his heart to the mousy woman behind the desk and she wasn't even listening to him. Instead, Gertrude focused on Nowell. "Oh, look, Nowell, Lady Austen adores you!"

Silas peered at his friend. The cat purred and curled into Nowell's lap as if she belonged there.

Gertrude again held a hand to her heart. "You know what they say about animals and babies."

"No," said Nowell. "What do they say?"

"They say that if an animal or a baby likes or is drawn to someone, that person is of good character. I purposely wanted to know of your character to..." Gertrude rifled through a stack of papers on the top of her desk. "To make a note on your application to share with your potential beloved."

As if Nowell needed any more confidence. The man was already arrogant. "Well, I am of good character. Wouldn't you say, Silas?"

"Sure."

"Oh, Silas, yes, now where were we?" Gertrude cleared her throat. "I wrote down your description, and you were about to answer my question about what it is you are hoping to find in your future wife, such as characteristics and traits."

Apparently Gertrude had been too immersed in her thoughts about the cat and thinking Nowell was of good character to have listened to Silas's prior statement, so he repeated it.

"A large family." The woman wrote the words on the paper, then held her pencil in midair. "Now, then, have you ever been in jail?"

The question that Silas dreaded had just been asked. He pondered his options. He could lie and say 'no'. But even at his worst, he knew from God's Word and Oma's teaching that lying was wrong. He could say 'yes', and explain. Or he could say 'yes' and end this ridiculous questioning once and for all.

But before he could speak, Nowell did the honors. "Remember when you were in jail?"

Silas's heart raced. Would Nowell share what he knew about Silas's past? No, he wouldn't do that. Nowell was a loyal friend. "Uh..."

"That time with Sheriff Ambrose and Deputy Grumbles?"

The air whooshed from Silas's lungs. "Oh, yes. I do remember that time."

"Sheriff Ambrose and Deputy Grumbles?" Gertrude tilted her head to one side. "They must have been lawmen before I arrived in Poplar Springs."

"No, ma'am." Nowell chortled. "They aren't lawmen at all."

Silas laughed at the thought of the young Ambrose and his pet pig.

"Is that a humorous inquiry?"

For the first time since they'd arrived, Gertrude appeared perturbed with Nowell.

Silas shifted in the too-small chair. "Ambrose is a little boy who wants to be a sheriff. He already thinks he is one, and his pet pig is his deputy."

"Oh." Gertrude emitted a nervous laugh. "Well, good then."

"It was Ambrose's birthday last year, and he asked me if he could pretend like I was the outlaw and he was the sheriff. He's like a nephew to me, so I allowed him to take me to the jail, put me in the cell, and lock the door. With his pa, who is a real deputy's, permission of course." Silas thought of Ambrose and the broad grin on his face when Silas acquiesced to his request. John Mark hadn't been so sure about it, and Hannah attempted to dissuade Ambrose. But Silas had agreed. If it created a fond memory for Ambrose, it was worth it.

"Goodness, but I'm glad it wasn't that you really were arrested." Gertrude tapped her pencil on the desk once again. "I believe that is all I need from you at the moment. Both of you do stop by next week to see the progress."

"You'll know by next week?" Silas wasn't sure where Gertrude would find two eligible women to his and Nowell's liking in Poplar Springs, especially so quickly.

"I'll know whether or not it's possible to help you. Oh, and Nowell as well, although I doubt it will be a problem." She tossed a generous smile Nowell's way, and Nowell, of course, returned it.

Silas would be content if Gertrude lost his application. When he did find the woman God had planned for him, he aimed to do it on his own, not with the help of some crazy lady who thought she was a matchmaker.

CHAPTER ELEVEN

A WEEK LATER, SILAS again joined Nowell at Pearson's Restaurant. The topic of finding a wife once more dominated the conversation.

Silas much preferred discussing cattle prices, outlaws who'd recently been captured, or even the weather.

Nowell swiveled in his chair and stared out the window, his attention obviously on the woman who traversed the boardwalk as if she owned it.

"Gertrude told me she thinks Jolene and I should court."

Silas watched Jolene talk to another woman. She would be considered comely by some with her light brown hair, large round eyes, and slender figure accentuated by extravagant clothing.

"Reckon I want to be sure you're fine with that."

Nowell's comment brought Silas's attention back to his friend. "Reckon that's fine with me, but why Jolene?"

Nowell shrugged. "I'm thirty years old. It's time I found someone to share my life with. I'm lonely out there at the ranch."

Hence the reason why Nowell was *rarely* at the ranch and instead hired two hands to assist him. Still, his comment failed to surprise Silas. For as long as he'd known him, Nowell needed to be around people. All the time.

"I know Jolene set her cap for you."

Silas groaned. That had been last year when she'd fluttered her lashes at him on numerous occasions, told her sister, who told a mutual friend, who told Silas that Jolene was interested in him. Quite forward in Silas's opinion, but he supposed it was almost the 1900s. He'd considered her interest and spoke with her on more than one occasion at church and at the Christmas celebration.

"She attends church, is a handsome woman, and comes from a respected family."

"If you think she's the one God has planned for you, then take Gertrude's advice."

Nowell shrugged. "Not sure she's the one God has planned for me."

Jolene hadn't been the one for Silas, and for that he was grateful. Shortly after expressing interest in Silas, she began to express interest in the smithy. As such, Silas and Jolene never courted or got past the cordial state, and he had no regrets. From what he'd heard, Jolene didn't stay interested in the smithy for long before she expressed interest in the new hotel owner's son. "Does no harm to talk with her and get to know her."

"That's what Gertrude said. Apparently Jolene paid a visit to Gertrude's Matrimonial Agency. Are you sure you don't still cotton to her?"

"Never did. But are you willing to marry just anyone?"

Nowell didn't answer immediately. Instead, he pushed his food around on his plate, buttered a piece of bread, took a drink of his coffee, re-tucked his napkin into his shirt, and pushed his food around on his plate once more. Finally, he cleared his throat and took a deep breath. "I don't know if considering courtship with Jolene will eventually lead to marriage. Her pa does own a ranch, so she knows about the occupation. She is comely."

"So you've mentioned."

"Don't you ever wish you were married?"

Why did Amaya's face fleetingly enter his mind?

all the time. "Yes, but I prefer to marry someone because we love each other, not because it's convenient."

Nowell forked his pile of broiled potatoes. "Look at Hannah and John Mark. They didn't know each other well at all before they married. They weren't in love, but they did grow to love each other."

"Maybe their marriage was an exception."

"Not everyone can know they love someone right away like Pritchard did with Ina."

Silas couldn't argue with him on that point. Pritchard had fancied Ina from the moment he met her, and from what he'd overheard Ina telling Mrs. Fleming, the fondness was mutual. "Still, he may have thought he liked her—and he did—but he couldn't possibly love her that quickly. They courted for a time before their marriage."

"All I'm saying is that maybe Jolene is the one God has planned for me, and if so, I could grow to love her in time, and she could grow to love me."

Silas regarded Nowell and the desperation in his expression. "If you want to take Gertrude's advice and spend time with Jolene to see if maybe you should court her, by all means, do so. But I'd pray about it before marrying her or any other woman. It's a lifetime commitment once you make those vows."

"You're starting to sound like John Mark's pa with your advice."

"Reckon that's a compliment." Silas smirked. "I'm surprised Gertrude isn't placing an advertisement for you for a mail-order bride."

"That's next if Jolene isn't the one for me and I'm not the one for her."

Silas doubted they were right for each other, but who was he to know about such ridiculous romantic notions? Perhaps they *could* fall in love like John Mark and Hannah had, even if it happened after their marriage. "All I know is that I'm not going to rush marrying someone until I know she's the right one for me. If that takes some time, it takes some time. If I have to wait for a woman to move to Poplar Springs from elsewhere, so be it." But while Silas attempted to sound confident in his statement, his voice sounded dubious even in his own ears. "There's not a rush when it's something as important as marriage."

"In the meantime, Silas McFadden celebrates his ninety-eighth birthday next month."

Silas chuckled at his friend's teasing, but he truly hoped he wouldn't be ninety-eight before finding a woman to marry.

Amaya placed the items for Mrs. Fleming into the crate and bid her farewell before she noticed Gertrude perusing the bolts of fabric. "Hello, Gertrude. Can I help you find something?"

"Amaya! Just the person I wanted to see. Would you like to join me for coffee sometime at my place of business?"

Gertrude's hopeful expression—with her spectacles inching down her nose and her enlarged eyes—made it difficult to refuse her request. Even if Amaya surmised Gertrude's reason for wanting to meet with her. "I would love to meet with you, but I may have to wait until a better time as I'm helping Grandmama with the store."

Grandmama stepped beside Amaya. "You go ahead, dear. I'll be fine. Grandfather is taking his nap, and there are no customers at present. Go enjoy yourself." She gave Amaya a push toward the door.

"If you're sure..."

"I'm sure."

And Grandmama, never one to allow argument once her mind was settled on something, went about organizing spools of thread on the shelf.

Amaya removed her apron, hung it on the hook, and followed Gertrude to her businesses. The woman ushered her inside and bustled about, returning to the two chairs on the matrimonial side with a pot of coffee and two cups.

"I'm so glad you decided to come for a visit." Gertrude rested the pot on a nearby table. "I've been meaning to ask you a question."

Amaya surmised she knew what that question was. Gertrude had started earning a reputation for "meeting" with folks so she could sign them up for her matchmaking services. "Yes?"

"You moved here recently from Bowman, correct?"

"I did. But I'm not sure how long I'll be here as I'm temporarily assisting Grandmama with the care of my grandfather who suffered an apoplexy. My parents and sister do intend to move here later this year, but I may be returning to Bowman before then."

Gertrude nodded a somewhat exaggerated nod that caused her spectacles to again slip down the bridge of her nose. "Yes, I remember you mentioning that when we first met at church. Your grandmother is blessed to have you. Please accept my condolences for your grandfather's ill health."

"Thank you. We've been praying for the Lord's healing, and I truly believe Grandfather will recover, although I'm not sure he will ever return to his former condition." She thought of Grandfather and the paralysis and weakness he suffered on one side of his body, his struggle with speaking, and his melancholy. At least they'd been able to go to church last week, thanks to Silas and his idea for the wheelchair.

They sat in silence for a few moments before Gertrude spoke again. "If you don't mind me asking, do you have a beau?"

So Amaya had been correct in her presumption. Gertrude aimed to arrange a courtship for her. "I do not."

"Oh!" The woman clapped her hands together, stood and rushed to her desk to retrieve a stack of papers and a pencil, then returned to her chair. "Would you like to become one of my clients? I'm offering an extraordinary discount this month for first-time applicants." Gertrude took a half a second to catch her breath before continuing her spiel. "I am adept and come highly recommended for assisting matrimonially-minded folks with finding their one true love. You could be next."

Amaya inhaled a sharp breath. How could she explain to Gertrude that her one true love was with the Lord and that for her there was no other? "Gertrude..."

"I know what you're thinking. Truly, I do. You're thinking, 'Gertrude, how could you ever manage to find my one true love in Poplar Springs? After all, I've seen the pickings, and they are anything but impressive. But let me reassure you, Amaya, there is someone out there for you."

But Gertrude's friendly animation could do nothing to resolve the real fact that Amaya would never fall in love again. Russell's image flashed in her mind. The way he smiled, his kind heart, and his giving nature. His love for the Lord and for her.

She'd only met the woman before her a few weeks ago at church, and while she liked Gertrude, she wasn't close enough to her to share the private matters of losing Russell. Still, Amaya knew she needed to explain why she would need to refuse Gertrude's generous offer.

Amaya took another sip of her coffee, intertwined her fingers, and prayed for the words to speak. "Gertrude, I appreciate your offer. I have heard of your reputation for matching people together in matrimony. However, I will have to respectfully decline. You see, I loved a man once. His name was Russell." Amaya swallowed hard and forced herself to continue. "He was killed, and suffice it to say, there is no other for me."

Gertrude held a hand to her mouth. "Oh, Amaya. I am so sorry. I had no idea."

"You couldn't have known."

"I just kept thinking you would be a wonderful candidate, and I've had some fine men apply as of late. But, yes, I understand fully. Please do forgive me for asking."

Amaya blinked back the tears that threatened. "There is nothing to forgive."

"Thank you, Amaya."

"I did hear you were successful in encouraging the courtship of Widow Holmes and Hank."

Gertrude's smile returned. "Yes, those two are such a delight. I've been trying in earnest to find someone for Hank's brother, Frank. Nothing yet, but I've never been one to give up easily."

"I'm sure you'll succeed." Amaya paused, a conversation she'd had with Hannah recently re-entering her mind. "I see you are a talented mender. How would you like to join several of us at next week's sewing circle?"

Gertrude's mouth dropped open and her eyes darted about. "Me?" She pointed a thumb at her chest.

"We'd love to have you. Hannah Eliason, Ina Pritchard, and I were discussing this just the other day. A group of us meet, most often at Hannah's or Ina's houses for a time of camaraderie, delicious desserts, and sometimes we actually get some sewing done as well."

"I just...you'd invite me?"

"Of course."

Gertrude peered down at her hands. "I, well, it's just that some see me as eccentric for being the proprietress of a matchmaking business, and I can be a bit, shall we say, whimsical."

"I don't think you're whimsical at all. It really is a grand time. Please do consider. It will be on Tuesday at two in the afternoon at Hannah's house. That time has worked well for us since it's after naptime for Hannah's and Ina's younger children."

"I will most certainly be there. Thank..." but Gertrude's attention had wandered from Amaya to something or someone outside on the boardwalk.

Amaya turned just in time to see Nowell's face pressed against the window.

"It's Nowell," said Gertrude. She waved at him and stood. "Please excuse me a moment."

Nowell must have meandered down the street because Gertrude moved quite swiftly toward the door, flinging it open, and stretching her neck outside. "Nowell!" she called before rushing to meet him.

Amaya walked to the window in time to see Gertrude and Nowell conversing on the boardwalk, Gertrude's arms flailing about and Nowell with a broad smile on his face as he nodded.

Minutes later, Gertrude returned. "Do excuse me for that interruption. I'd forgotten I needed to speak with Nowell. He'll be back momentarily."

Was that a blush covering Gertrude's face?

"I do need to get back to the mercantile. I'll see you at church and then Tuesday at the sewing circle."

But Gertrude's mind must have been elsewhere, for she scarcely noticed Amaya's departure.

⁂

Silas exited the church with Amaya that Sunday as he always did when they attended service. Amaya's grandparents were slightly in front of them, Grandmama slowly pushing Grandfather in his wheelchair.

"Grandmama invited you for the noonday meal," said Amaya. "She's making piperade."

Silas couldn't refuse any of Grandmama's meals, especially not the piperade, but if he continued to be her guest, he'd need a larger pair of trousers. "Sounds delicious."

"Of course, Grandmama will likely have made enough to feed Wyoming's entire population."

Silas chuckled and offered his arm. Amaya placed her hand through his elbow. He attempted to convince himself he was unaffected by the warmth of her hand on his arm. That they were only friends, and from what John Mark and Nowell mentioned, she'd never love anyone else besides Russell.

After Silas carried Grandfather upstairs, settled him in his wheelchair at the table, and the family had eaten, Amaya joined him on the boardwalk before he headed for home.

"I heard Gertrude was unable to arrange a courtship between Nowell and Jolene," Amaya said.

"Apparently Jolene set her cap for someone else. She's known for being a flighty and fickle woman."

Amaya shook her head. "Poor Nowell."

Silas chuckled. "He'll be fine, but I suspect he's disappointed. Gertrude is meeting with him next week to write his first advertisement for a mail-order bride."

"I do applaud Gertrude's manner of finding one's true love if conventional matters aren't successful."

"I just hope it goes well. Mr. Guldager here in Poplar Springs advertised for a bride, but when she arrived, she instead fell in love with his cousin. They married not long after."

"Oh, dear. We had an interesting occurrence in Bowman as well. Mr. Denby placed an advertisement where he listed in length all of the qualifications for a wife. Mr. Denby was apparently far too particular because not one woman in Wyoming or elsewhere answered his advertisement. It did lend some assistance to a Mr. Richmond in the southern part of the state who had been searching for Mr. Denby's whereabouts for some time in regards to a sizable amount of money owed to him. From our dear friend who was witness to the incident, Mr. Denby procured the long-overdue amount in less than a minute. Mr. Richmond shared his information of locating Mr. Denby with the sheriff, and Mr. Denby's shenanigans quickly came to a halt. So perhaps, even if Gertrude isn't able to secure a bride for Nowell, some other good might come from it."

"I hope for Nowell's sake Gertrude is able to find him a wife. He's talked of nothing else for the past several months."

"You're a likable fellow, Nowell." Amaya raised the pitch in her voice, just as Gertrude would do. "And therefore, it's only a matter of time until you find your one true love."

"You sound just like her." Just another trait of Amaya's he'd grown fond of. Her sense of humor.

"She's animated and perfect for the job."

Nowell was animated too. Silas smirked as a thought occurred and turned to Amaya. "What about..." they both said at the same time.

Silas deferred to her, but figured she thought the same thing he did.

"Nowell and Gertrude."

"Exactly!"

"Why not? I think they secretly are fond of each other. I've seen the way Gertrude looks at him, and when I last visited her his name came up in conversation several times. She even rushed after him when I was meeting with her at the Matrimonial Agency."

"And Nowell talks about her all the time." Silas paused. "Did you know he took Lady Austen a gift?"

"He did?"

"Yes, a yarn ball."

Amaya's eyes widened. "I wondered why he purchased pink yarn during his last visit to the mercantile."

"That would be why." Silas slapped a hand on his thigh. "Why didn't we think of this before? It would have saved Nowell the pain of Jolene spurning him."

"A few days ago, I was speaking with Gertrude at her business, and Nowell peeked in the window. You should have seen it, Silas. His nose all pressed flat against the window as he gaped. Gertrude noticed immediately, and she could hardly finish our conversation quickly enough.

I've never seen her move so fast as she did when she hurried through the door to speak with him."

Silas recalled Nowell mentioning Amaya was at Gertrude's Matrimonial Agency. He wanted to ask if she was there arranging for her own match, and a niggle of disappointment rose in him. But how could that be if she still mourned Russell? "Nowell did mention he saw you there."

"Yes, but when Gertrude saw Nowell, she prattled on only about him until I took my leave." Amaya grabbed his arm. "What if we become matchmakers? Wouldn't that be an ironic turn of events?"

"It would be. We should try it." Disappointed he hadn't discovered the reason for Amaya's visit to Gertrude's, Silas instead concentrated on Amaya's suggestion. It made perfect sense. "How do you suggest we start?"

"It's imperative we determine a way to bring them together so they realize they're perfect for each other. Of course, Gertrude may already have secretly set her cap for Nowell, but how can a matchmaker succeed in her business if she allows herself to be the one who is matched?"

Silas raked a hand through his hair. "But they already see each other often. Nowell has appointments for matchmaking services just about every week. I've also noticed that he suddenly has need to have every pair of his socks mended. Last Wednesday, a button popped off his trousers, and he, of course, visited Gertrude's. The Nowell I've always known isn't handy with a needle and thread, but he *does* know how to sew on a button. Plus, they see each other at church every Sunday."

"Indeed. And not only do they see each other at church every Sunday, but they also sit by each other in the same pew."

They both stood silently pondering a scheme. He tore his eyes away from Amaya's hand still gripping his arm. Had she forgotten? From his side-eye while pretending to think about Nowell and Gertrude, he instead noticed Amaya's long slim fingers and slender hand. He caught a glimpse at her profile, the way she pressed her lips together when deep in thought. Her thick eyelashes, and her dainty nose. The way tendrils of dark hair framed her face.

If Gertrude were here, she'd likely tell him he was besotted with Amaya.

Which was true. But for now, he'd appreciate their friendship.

She turned then, her eyes meeting his. A gentleman would avert his attention, but standing this close to her, taking in her beauty, and wondering what could be if she allowed him into her life, such a feat didn't come easily. Her loveliness, especially at this close proximity, stole his breath as though he'd run for miles upon miles without once stopping.

Amaya removed her clutch on his arm. "Oh!" she exclaimed, a deep crimson covering her lovely face.

Silas hadn't minded one bit that she'd held his arm, but he could see she was clearly embarrassed. So he cleared his throat and redirected his attention to a pebble on the boardwalk.

A few seconds ticked by. "I—well—what would you propose then?"

It was a challenge to return his attention to Nowell and Gertrude. "How about having them meet for a noonday meal at Pearson's?"

"How would we go about arranging that? After all, that's usually where she suggests couples meet for step three after they've met at the Matrimonial Agency with her as a chaperone."

Silas wanted to ask how Amaya knew about "step three", but with effort, he kept his curiosity to himself. His mind conjured up the dismal images of available men in Poplar Springs. Was Amaya set on having Gertrude arrange a courtship for her? Did she have her cap set for someone? He shook his head. No. She still mourned Russell. He was sure of it. Unless...

"Silas?"

"I—sorry. Just thinking."

"I just thought of it!" Amaya's eyes lit. "I'll see if Gertrude would like to meet me at Pearson's for a noonday meal."

"Of course, she would do that." And when they met for the noonday meal, would Gertrude provide advice to Amaya regarding finding her a suitable match?

"And you could see if Nowell wants to meet you there at the same time. But in actuality, you and I won't be there."

"We won't? I mean, right. Sure. Reckon that'd be a fine plan."

Amaya's wide smile lit up her entire countenance and was so contagious, he himself offered his own smile. "They'll sit across from each other and perhaps realize just how enjoyable time spent together is. And if that isn't successful, we can plan a second 'meeting' for them. Perhaps skipping step three and going directly to step four."

"Are you sure you're not a matchmaker yourself? Perhaps Gertrude's assistant?"

She laughed, the tone of her amusement drawing him in. "Perhaps I could ask her if she needs help some time." Amaya peered up towards the sky, then back at him. "Yes, having them meet at Pearson's is an extraordinary idea."

"As long as they realize they're each other's one true love just by sharing a noonday meal," he teased.

Amaya tapped her chin. "I do believe, Silas McFadden, that we should become professional matchmakers ourselves." She pretended to write in the air. "Silas and Amaya's Matrimonial Agency. I like the sound of it."

And he liked the way she combined their names together.

CHAPTER TWELVE

AMAYA SETTLED INTO THE high-backed chair with pink cushions in Gertrude's Matrimonial Agency while Gertrude took her usual customary seat behind her desk. Today Lady Austen wore a pink crocheted scarf around her neck. Someone, presumably Gertrude, had sewn a tan button on the end of the scarf near a white fringe.

"Doesn't Lady Austen look extraordinary? I dare say she'll be perfectly prepared for winter in Wyoming." Gertrude patted the cat and set her on the floor. "There now, Lady Austen. Don't wander too far."

Lady Austen meowed as if in response and batted at her toy mouse made from a pinecone.

"She does look charming."

"Indeed. One of my clients purchased some yarn for her scarf. I'd say she looks rather exquisite."

Gertrude perhaps forgot that there was only one place to purchase yarn in Poplar Springs, and there were only two clerks at Alvarado's Mercantile, one of which was Amaya.

She prattled on with nary a breath in between sentences. "It's always most gracious when a client brings a present to Lady Austen." A rosy glow covered the woman's face, and they shared pleasant conversation before Gertrude asked, "Pray tell, what brings you to the Matrimonial Agency?"

"I was hoping you'd join me for the noonday meal at Pearson's Restaurant tomorrow."

Gertrude clapped. "Most definitely. What time shall we meet?"

"How about noon?"

"Delightful."

"Let's plan to meet at table four."

"Table four it is. And thank you, Amaya, for befriending me. I had no idea how lonely it could be moving to a new town."

Amaya knew from the moment she met Gertrude that the woman loved people and hadn't a shy bone in her body. Something she and Nowell had in common, according to Silas. "You are welcome."

"Ooh! Did I tell you?" Gertrude rose, her arms flailing about. "I just had another successful match."

"Oh?"

"Yes. You'll recall the new deputy, Mr. Hilliard? He ambled in here one day to secure both matchmaking and mending services. Of course, I gave him a discount."

Gertrude's words spilled from her mouth so rapidly Amaya had to lean forward and concentrate to catch them all. "Yes?"

"He was in search of a wife. Now, he's no longer a young man at age forty, but I told him I'd do my utmost best to find him his one true love. Suffice it to say, if there's one thing about Gertrude N. Duckworth, it's that she has never met a challenge she didn't wholeheartedly embrace. So Mr. Hilliard completed the application, and

I set about doing what I do best—besides mending, of course. I searched high and low and thought I might have to find someone from another town with whom Mr. Hilliard could correspond. But just as I was about to give up hope, I met Widow Sumner while visiting the millinery. She is new to the area, recently having moved here to be closer to her son and his wife." Gertrude paused ever so slightly, drew in two deep breaths, then continued. "And then, with my keen ability to sense those who would make impeccable couples, I invited her to complete an application."

Amaya managed to slip in six words— "I'm so happy for you, Gertrude."

"Happy for me? Oh, yes, thank you. I'm happy too. I always wondered what my gifting and talents may be. My older sister was a pianist. My younger sister was adept at baking. Me, I am not accomplished at either of those disciplines. Now, mind you, I do mend well, but I knew there was another talent I possessed. I dithered a bit before I made the decision to open the Matrimonial Agency here, and believe me when I say there were numerous prayers for guidance and direction. But alas, here I am, ensuring that the fine folks of Poplar Springs find the one God intended for them."

"Are Mr. Hilliard and Widow Sumner courting?"

"They are as of two o'clock yesterday afternoon."

The words slipped out before Amaya had the wherewithal to stop them. "Do you ever contemplate finding *your* one true love?"

"Me? Well, yes, I have contemplated it, but save for one man, there just haven't been any that have garnered a second thought from me."

Could that one man be Nowell? Amaya usually wasn't given in to profound curiosity, but she did want to know.

Speaking of Nowell...the tall, lanky man walked through the door. "Hello, Gertrude." As if a second thought, he added, "And Amaya."

"Nowell," Gertrude gushed. "How are you?"

"Good. Just keeping my appointment to work on the advertisement." He took all of two steps and dropped into the chair beside Amaya. "I'm not sure this will be an easy task."

"You'll do splendidly, I'm sure."

Amaya watched the interaction between the two. She couldn't wait to tell Silas. While proper etiquette dictated she leave the two to their advertisement writing shenanigans, she couldn't help but stay firmly planted in her seat.

Gertrude removed her gaze from Nowell for the briefest of moments to retrieve a sheet of paper. "Now, then, Nowell, let's begin with describing you. I have your application, which we can acquire some information from, but first, do tell me some of your most pleasant traits."

Nowell puffed up, and a smirk tugged at the corner of his lips. "Well, I'm a Christian gentleman with good manners."

"Indeed, you are."

"I'm witty and somewhat smart."

Gertrude scribbled the words on her sheet of paper. "All right, now tell me again what you are looking for in a wife."

Nowell's and Gertrude's gazes rested on each other for the next several seconds, and Amaya wondered if they'd forgotten her presence.

"Of course, she has to be easy on the eyes," said Nowell.

"Naturally."

"She can't be lazy. I don't like lazy."

"Goodness, but no. You do not want to marry a slothful woman. Anything else?"

Nowell smoothed his mustache. "She has to want to live on a ranch and know how to cook. If she's not the best cook, that's all right, but I don't aim to starve, and eating at Pearson's everyday could get mighty expensive."

"No, we wouldn't want you to starve."

Lady Austen jumped into Nowell's lap. "Is this scarf made from the yarn I bought?"

Gertrude's face rivaled the color of the scarf. "Indeed, it is. She looks elegant, and I have you to thank."

Nowell grinned. "You are most welcome, milady."

"Oh!" Gertrude tittered, then settled herself. "Now, where were we? Do tell me some other attributes you wish for your future bride to possess."

"She has to be smart and not shy. It would make me crazier than crazy to be married to someone who doesn't speak much. 'Course, I don't want a chattering hen either because then I would never have the chance to speak, and I do have stuff to say on occasion."

From what Amaya knew of Nowell—and from what Silas insinuated—Nowell had a whole lot to say and on many occasions.

"Approximate age?"

"Between the ages of twenty-five and thirty-two."

Gertrude nodded. "Anything else?"

"Can't think of anything."

"Give me five minutes," said Gertrude.

Even from her location, Amaya could see Gertrude's oversized loopy writing taking up half a sheet of paper.

Nowell twiddled his thumbs and shook his right leg. Clearly, the man was nervous. And why not? This was a momentous occasion in his life. Of course, if he fell in love with Gertrude like Amaya and Silas hoped, he'd have no need of an advertisement.

"Finished!" Gertrude announced. She waved the paper in front of her before returning it to her desk. "I'll read it aloud, and you can tell me what you think. If all is well, you can pay the fee, and I'll place the advertisement tomorrow morning."

Gertrude stood. "Attention!" she said as if a teacher. "How does this sound?

"Handsome Wyoming rancher in good condition, a Christian gentleman with faultless manners and a witty sense of humor, intelligent, tall with all his teeth and a full head of brownish-red hair, brown velvety eyes, mustache, aged thirty-years-old, seeks stylish and attractive lady between the ages of twenty-five and thirty-two for correspondence. A brunette with hazel eyes preferred. Spectacles are fine. Must be jolly and entertaining, not slothful, must love animals, especially

cats, cook a decent meal, and be an adept seamstress. Matrimonially inclined. Will answer all letters."

Amaya didn't reveal the fact that Gertrude described herself.

"Reckon you're a mighty fine advertisement writer, Gertrude," said Nowell.

Gertrude held a hand to her heart. "To hear you say that means the world to me, Nowell. Thank you."

As if suddenly remembering Amaya was in the room, Gertrude directed her next question to her. "What did you think?"

"I thought it was quite thorough."

"Delightful!"

Amaya rose. "I should return to the mercantile. I'll see you tomorrow, Gertrude."

But Gertrude scarcely heard her as she and Nowell had again commenced conversing. Maybe she and Nowell didn't need Amaya's and Silas's help after all.

CHAPTER THIRTEEN

SILAS MET AMAYA AT the mercantile where they discussed their conversations with Nowell and Gertrude the day before.

"That Gertrude is an amusing sort. Most of the characteristics she listed for Nowell's future bride described her. I'm not so sure Nowell is partial to brunettes with hazel eyes."

"She wrote that in the advertisement?"

Sweet laughter bubbled from Amaya's lips. "She did. Of course, Nowell agreed to every word. Gertrude could have written that he hoped to find a homely woman who preferred the city over a ranch, detested animals, and couldn't boil water, and it's likely Nowell would have agreed as his attention was fixated on her, rather than her words."

"I'm glad Nowell has found someone he cottons to. He's been a good and loyal friend, and I know how much he'd like to be married. He has eight siblings, so I think as a young'un, he became accustomed to people. On his ranch, there's just him, the cattle, chickens, a dog, and sometimes his hired hands. He's lonely."

"I did not realize he came from such a large family. I think Gertrude is lonely too. She talks nonstop to everyone and was so grateful when I invited her to the sewing circle."

Grandmama appeared around the corner carrying a plate with several thin wedges of gâteau Basque. Silas's mouth watered. He could almost taste the delicious buttery pastry dough filled with preserves.

"If you two want to proceed with your special mission, you best hurry. It's already five past the hour." Grandmama placed the plate on the counter for customers.

Silas was a customer. A devoted one who purchased all his provisions at the lone supplier of goods in Poplar Springs. He'd even been an employee once.

"I see you eyeing that gâteau Basque, Silas." Grandmama placed her hands on her hips. "Those are for the customers."

Would it do any good to argue with Grandmama? "But..." He reached for the dessert.

Grandmama swatted his hand. "Off with you now. Amaya told me in confidence your plan for Nowell and Gertrude. If you want to witness how it all unfolds, you best skedaddle."

"But..."

Grandmama shooed him away. "Off with you, Silas McFadden."

Amaya giggled. "Grandmama is correct. If we don't hasten our steps, we'll miss spying on Nowell and Gertrude. And from the way they prattled on yesterday, I imagine it will only be a matter of minutes before they continue their conversation at table four in Pearson's Restaurant."

Silas reluctantly agreed to allow Amaya to tug on his arm and remove him from the temptation of eating every single one of those gâteau Basque slices. Hadn't Grandmama seen his disappointment? His distress?

"Don't worry about the gâteau Basque, Silas. Grandmama knows you are fond of it."

How could he not worry? He'd postponed his own noonday meal so he would arrive on time to the mercantile.

Oma always quoted the saying that patience was a virtue. When it came to gâteau Basque, Silas had *no* patience. He took a deep breath and offered his arm to Amaya. She slipped her hand through it as though it was the most natural thing to do. He briefly placed his hand over hers and wondered what it would be like to walk with her like this every day.

And in a matter of seconds, Silas forgot about Grandmama's famous dessert, and thoughts of first Amaya, then the plan for Nowell and Gertrude filled his mind. "I've been thinking that if this scheme isn't successful, I could somehow encourage Nowell to ask Gertrude to accompany him to the barn dance on Saturday."

Amaya peered up at him as they walked, and for a moment, Silas contemplated asking *her* to accompany *him* to the barn dance. Would she say "yes"? He knew she considered him a good friend, and they had grown that friendship even more so in recent days. But as he spent more time with her, he hoped for something more. However, for a woman still grieving her fiancé, patience would be a virtue, and one he needed to heed if he hoped to someday win Amaya's heart.

Because for her, he'd wait forever.

"I've heard there will be quite a crowd at the barn dance. I think your idea has merit. It's humorous how neither of them realizes the other is fond of them."

Did Amaya realize *he* was fond of her? That he'd fallen in love with her strong faith, compassionate nature, kindness, and beauty? That he respected how she tenderly cared for both of her grandparents and her dedicated loyalty to her family? That he admired the way she protected the other passengers the first day he'd met her? That he was impressed by the way she'd ridden the horse that day that helped them win the race?

"Silas?"

He reluctantly tore his eyes from her lest he collide with a passerby on the boardwalk. "I'm sorry. What were you saying?"

"Do you have a plan for how we can eavesdrop without being seen?"

"I do. On the way to the kitchen, there's a partial wall we can hide behind. We'd have to tell Mrs. Pearson and Ina's sisters ahead of time so they don't wonder why we're lurking there, but I think we could hear a good lot of the conversation from that location."

"And how do we sneak in without them seeing us? The last thing we'd want is to have to join them at the table."

Silas had already thought of that. "We'll enter through the back door. Pritchard should be waiting for us."

"Pritchard?"

"He has a key, and I figured it would be better than disturbing the Pearsons when it's during their busiest time of day. Besides, Pritchard can get away with doing things that would make anyone else look suspicious."

Sure enough, when they arrived at the back entrance, Pritchard was leaning against the door, hands in his pockets.

Pritchard was a godly man, a husband and father, and the mayor of Poplar Springs, but if someone came upon him lounging in the back next to the alleyway, they might deem him an outlaw waiting to rob the restaurant. Not that he appeared dubious, because he didn't, but Pritchard was Pritchard, and typically no one dawdled near the back of a restaurant. Even if he could get away with things most people couldn't.

"Thanks for agreeing to let us in," said Silas. He clapped the scrawny man on the shoulder.

"You know how it is, Si. Anytime I can aid someone in a worthwhile endeavor, I'm happy to do so."

Pritchard was the only one who called him "Si", just like he was the only one who called John Mark "J.M." Pritchard inserted the key into the back door and ushered Silas and Amaya into the building. The aroma of steak and potatoes drowned Silas's lungs with a heavenly scent that rivaled Grandmama's gâteau Basque. His stomach rumbled, and Pritchard chuckled.

"If you're going to be doing surveillance, you might want to restrain your stomach from making noises that can be heard all the way to Nelsonville."

"Funny, Pritchard."

Silas and Amaya paused by Mr. and Mrs. Pearson and explained their scheme. Pritchard helped himself to samples of the food, and the Pearson children bustled about retrieving plates to serve to the customers. Grandmother Pearson shuffled in, a bright red apron around her waist. "Hello, Pritchard. How are my great-grandbabies?"

"They're well, Grandmother Pearson. Growing like weeds, as the saying goes."

Grandmother Pearson stood taller, but it did little to assist her short frame. "Well, that's good to hear. When are you going to bring them by again?"

Pritchard laughed and slung an arm around the older woman's shoulders. "We were just here yesterday, but you're right, we do need to bring them by again. How about tomorrow? I know Ina mentioned something about showing you the new quilting square she's working on."

Grandmother Pearson, twice the width of Pritchard and a whole head shorter, beamed. "That will do just fine." She paused and focused on Silas and Amaya. "And what are you two doing here? You resemble questionable characters."

Amaya smiled. "We're here to do some secret work."

The elderly woman moved away from Pritchard and toward Amaya. "Do tell."

"We are attempting to be matchmakers. Do you know Nowell and Gertrude?"

Grandmother Pearson bunched her mouth into a lopsided pucker and furrowed her brow. "Don't believe I do."

"You'd recognize them if you saw them," said Silas. "We need to be covert while watching them. We're hoping to eavesdrop on their conversation and see if we were successful in arranging a noonday meal for them together."

The woman jabbed a finger toward the stairway that led to the upper level. "I have a hearing horn upstairs." She lowered her voice. "Shall I retrieve it?"

Amaya shook her head. "You don't have to do that, Grandmother Pearson."

"Oh, but I want to. It's a special ear trumpet I received in 1851 as a gift from my late husband. Seems he wanted to make it easier on me to listen in on the ongoings." She offered a grin that enhanced her abundance of wrinkles.

Silas's gaze met Amaya's and she nodded. "In that case, we'd be much obliged."

"Wait right here." She hobbled toward the staircase. "I'll be right back."

Amaya had come to treasure the folks in Poplar Springs. Having grown up in Bowman, she and her family were blessed with many friends. However, in her short time in the new town, she'd grown accustomed to the variety of people and their kindness. Grandmother Pearson was no exception. Nor were Mr. and Mrs. Pearson and Pritchard.

Silas leaned toward her. "We should go see if they've found a way to sit together yet."

"Oh, they've found a way to sit together," said Mrs. Pearson. "I was just out there taking another order and there they were, blathering on at table four."

A glint touched Silas's eyes. "We best go see if we're to start our own matchmaking agency." To Mrs. Pearson, he added, "Thank you, ma'am, for your help."

Mrs. Pearson beamed. "Oh, you're welcome. I'm always thrilled to participate in a ploy to assist someone, or two someones, in finding true love."

Amaya and Silas peered around the corner, and sure enough, Nowell and Gertrude sat at table four in deep conversation.

Nowell looked in their direction, and Amaya slunk back behind the wall, nearly stepping on Silas's toes in the process. "We can't let them see us," she whispered.

The clanging of utensils, the chatter among the patrons, and the hum of noise from the kitchen all competed with Nowell's and Gertrude's voices. Amaya inclined forward again, and Silas did the same, his head above hers. They faced the couple once again, carefully allowing only the top portion of their faces to lean out from the wall. "I wonder if they even miss us."

"Likely not," Silas whispered, his warm breath tickling her cheek. A peculiar warming shiver ran through her and she shoved it aside.

Amaya flinched when Grandmother Pearson tapped on Silas's shoulder and he jolted her. "Here's the hearing horn," whispered the woman, although not too quietly. "You stick the porcelain ear tip into your ear like so." She removed the lanyard from around her neck and placed it around Amaya's neck.

Amaya stuck the porcelain tip into her ear.

"Now you turn toward the noise," directed Grand-mother Pearson. "You'll find it works wonders for the hard-of-hearing."

Amaya wasn't hard of hearing, but she certainly did want to snoop on the conversation between hers and Silas's first customers.

Pritchard swaggered past them and toward Nowell and Gertrude. He stopped and chatted with them before returning to Amaya and Silas.

"Well?" asked Silas.

"Sounds like you may have succeeded in your endeavor." Pritchard flipped his suspenders.

"Much obliged for your help." Silas gripped his shoulder, nearly toppling the skinny man off his feet.

"Always a pleasure helping an old friend. By the way, I could see the hearing horn all by its lonesome protruding out from behind the wall."

CHAPTER FOURTEEN

SILAS AND AMAYA RETURNED to the mercantile several minutes later. When they entered, Silas proceeded directly to the counter. Perhaps there were still a few remaining pieces of gâteau Basque. But the plate's contents consisted of a meager crumb.

"Erdutza?" Grandfather's weakened tone drew Silas's attention from the dismal trace of food to the stairway that led to the building's upper portion.

Amaya placed a hand on Grandmama's arm. "I'll go," she said, and not leaving Grandmama the opportunity to argue, progressed up the stairs.

"Thank you, Amaya." Grandmama hung a piece of paper on a nail on the board near the sewing notions. "How did your mission go?"

"We're confident Nowell and Gertrude will soon be courting." Had he ever imagined he'd be a matchmaker? He stood next to Grandmama and noticed unshed tears in her eyes. She pressed the paper against the board with gnarled fingers and took a step back.

"Is something wrong with Grandfather?"

"He had an arduous morning." Grandmama's attention lingered on the paper she'd hung, and Silas followed her gaze.

Barn dance and potluck
This Saturday at the Swofford Ranch.
Fun for the entire family.
Bring a plate of food to share.

"Grandmama?"

Seconds ticked by before Grandmama turned her attention to him. "I'm sorry, Silas. I was just thinking of all the many dances Iker and I had been to in our younger years." A tear slid down her cheek. "And now my sweet Iker cannot stand for any length of time, let alone dance."

Silas recalled Oma's discussions of the times with Grandpa and how she missed them. *"We didn't have nearly long enough together before the Lord took him home,"* she'd always say.

While Amaya's grandfather hadn't passed, Silas suspected there was a degree of mourning on Grandmama's part all the same—to know her husband could no longer do the things they formerly enjoyed together.

He slung his arm around her shoulder, just as he had Oma when sadness engulfed her.

Grandmama leaned into him. "I miss those days. I miss them for me, and I miss them for him. He wants so badly to feel well, but every day is a struggle, and now with the melancholy setting in..." Grandmama retrieved a handkerchief from her apron pocket and patted at her eyes. "I'm sorry. I don't mean to share all of this. He's done significantly better in recent days, especially with being able to attend church and join family meals, thanks to you and the wheelchair."

Instead of responding, Silas pulled her closer and allowed her to grieve. Doc mentioned the road ahead would be lengthy for Grandfather and that he might never fully recover. But there had to be something that could be done. For Grandfather and for Grandmama.

Finally, Grandmama reached up and pinched Silas's cheek, just as Oma always had. "You're such a sweet boy," she said just as she'd done numerous times before. And once again, realization hit Silas in the gut that if Grandmama knew his past, she'd not think of him as a "sweet boy". Mr. Meacham's face flashed in his mind and the disappointment of finding out that Silas was partly responsible for his cattle leaving his ranch.

After all Mr. Meacham had done to help Silas, that was how he repaid him.

Silas cleared his throat, begging the Lord to remove painful memories—memories he himself caused. "If there's any way I can help..."

"You've already done so much." Grandmama tilted her head back and looked at him.

Could she see the shame? The guilt? The regret? The pain that continually remained at the thought of how he'd disappointed Oma? Would Grandmama allow him to spend time with Amaya if she knew of his past?

The thought smothered him. God might have forgiven him, but he'd never forgive himself.

"I have a surprise for you behind the counter. But first," Grandmama tucked the handkerchief back into her apron pocket. "Would you accompany Amaya to the barn dance? I'll ask her if she'll accompany you. She needs a reprieve from helping me with Grandfather and the mercantile."

Would Amaya agree to accompany him? The expectant expression in Grandmama's eyes prompted his answer. "Sure."

"Thank you." Grandmama walked toward the counter. "As you and Amaya left the restaurant, your bewilderment was a site to behold. All along I was keeping this for you." She withdrew a plate of gâteau Basque, eyes twinkling. "A grandmother knows when something is her grandson's favorite."

Her grandson? Grandmama would never know how much her referring to him as someone so important as her grandson meant to him.

The following day proved a busy one. Numerous customers entered the mercantile, Grandfather again refused to eat, and sat in his wheelchair staring out the window and ignoring Grandmama and Amaya.

Grandfather had for certain slipped into a state of melancholy. His previously jolly self had been preplaced with despondency to the point his appetite waned even more so than when the apoplexy first occurred.

Doc visited several times, assuring Amaya and Grandmama they were doing an admirable job of caring for Grandfather and that being able to attend church made a significant difference. Grandfather had also regained much use in his arms and legs, although he still could not walk.

Even so, Amaya witnessed the trepidation in Doc's eyes. A downcast mind could preclude one from healing as well as they should. And Amaya had seen firsthand the woebegone and low-spirited countenance Grandfather had succumbed to.

She could understand. He could no longer do mundane things that most people took for granted. He still needed help getting dressed, he couldn't wait on customers, haul the freight on delivery day, or even walk. A robust man had been replaced with a fragile one.

Amaya perched in a chair at the table after checking on Grandfather and folded her hands. Many times each day, she lifted her gratitude and petitions to the Lord. *Father, I thank You for the healing work You've done in Grandfather. I remember receiving the news that we may lose him. Thank You for Grandmama's dedication in caring for him and for Silas's grand idea for the wheelchair. Lord, I ask that You please help Grandfather overcome his melancholy, become stronger, and to heal according to Your will. Please help Grandmama and I know how to best aid him.*

"Amaya?"

Grandmama's voice shook her from her prayer. Amaya turned to see her grandmother standing in the doorway, a brightly-colored dress draped over her arm. "I'd like you to attend the barn dance. Silas has already agreed to accompany you."

"I couldn't. You need me here."

"Nothing I can't handle. I'm already planning to read the Book of John to Grandfather again since that's his favorite Book in the Bible. Besides, you need to spend time with your friends and become better acquainted with folks in Poplar Springs."

"I spend a lot of time with friends," countered Amaya. "I attend church, the sewing circle, Silas and I just arranged a successful matchmaking endeavor, and I've also spent time with Hannah, Ina, Mrs. Fleming, and Gertrude. I see customers everyday except Sunday and enjoy conversing with most of them, Mrs. Shawdale being the exception."

Grandmama's eyes crinkled at the corners. "Yes, well, Mrs. Shawdale is a challenge. As far as those other things you mentioned, Silas is a dear friend, and those other activities are wonderful, but not enough. You're young. You've been working hard without much rest. Some time at a festivity will do you good. I hear most of the town will be there."

Grandmama didn't know there was another, more profound, reason for not wanting to attend the dance.

"Besides," Grandmama continued, "I dug this out from the trunk. It was mine when Grandfather and I attended dances years ago." She held up the red skirt with its purple bodice and multi-colored jacket. "Hard to believe I was once slender."

"Grandmama..."

Her grandmother laughed. "I've never been tall, but once upon a time, I was half the woman I am now. This ought to fit well, and I'll sew a lace trim since the skirt will be too short."

Amaya loved and cherished her Basque heritage and was honored to wear Grandmama's dress, but leaving her here alone when Grandfather was struggling caused her great apprehension. She took the garment from Grandmama's outstretched arms.

"There now, Silas will be here within the hour. Will you consider allowing him to accompany you?"

"An hour?"

Grandmama patted her arm. "I didn't want to give you much of a chance to argue. Now then, that boy is always hungry, so I'll prepare an early supper with plenty of leftovers to take to the dance."

The woman was persistent, but Amaya wouldn't deny Grandmama's request. "All right, I'll go."

When Grandmama offered a beaming smile in response, Amaya knew she'd made the right decision.

CHAPTER FIFTEEN

SILAS HADN'T EVER GIVEN much thought to his appearance. He bathed, shaved, visited the barber regularly, scrubbed behind his ears as Oma always demanded, and kept himself clean with good hygiene when not working in the fields. But today, he wanted to look his best.

For Amaya.

Not that she would ever think of him as more than a friend. Besides, he'd never be able to compete for a heart that belonged to another man.

He buttoned his favorite blue plaid shirt and tucked it into his trousers then rolled up the sleeves and combed his hair.

The first thing he noticed when he strode through the mercantile's door was Amaya's dress. Not her customary skirt and waistcoat, but a brightly-colored skirt, shirt, and fitted jacket. She was always beautiful to him, but something about the vivid clothing especially heightened the deep brown of her eyes and her raven-colored hair.

He drew in a sharp breath and did his best not to stare. "Hello, I'm here."

Of course you're here, McFadden. What a dolt!

He drummed his fingers against his trousers and tried again. "Hello, Amaya."

She smiled at him with full lips, and with effort, he directed his attention to Grandmama who rushed towards him, a plate in hand. "I'm not sure what kind of food there will be at the barn dance, but I prepared supper if you'd care to eat before you go."

Silas didn't need any further convincing. He perched near the counter, prayed, and took a bite of the meal Grandmama had prepared.

Several minutes later, he and Amaya rode in silence to the Swofford Ranch, Amaya folded her hands in her lap and worried her lip, a trait he noticed she did when something was bothering her. "Amaya?"

She glanced his way, and he saw the emotion in her distant stare.

Silas waited patiently for her to speak. Surely with as close as they had grown in the past weeks, she would feel comfortable sharing with him whatever it was that caused her consternation.

"I'm afraid I won't be good company this evening." Her downturned expression remained.

"Is it Grandfather?"

A slight smile emerged. "No, but thank you for asking about him. Although I am concerned because his melancholy has increased. It's difficult for him and Grandmama to communicate due to his warbled words. This is, understandably, frustrating to Grandmama as well."

Silas spent time in prayer last night seeking God's wisdom in how he could further help Grandfather—Grandmama and Amaya too—with the care of a man who meant so much to them.

He was about to mention such when Amaya continued.

"When Russell was alive, we attended a dance in Bowman. He did it for me as dances were never something to his liking."

Silas swerved around a pothole in the road. "I'm sorry about the memories. We don't have to attend the festivities tonight. I can take you back to the mercantile."

"Grandmama insisted I go. She's concerned that I've been working too hard helping care for Grandfather and assisting with the mercantile." Amaya sighed. "It just makes me think of Russell. That was our last time spent together before..."

"I can turn around and take you back. Grandmama will understand."

"No, it's all right."

They continued down the road, and Silas figured he needed to say something to remove her mind from the topic that grieved her. "I spoke to Nowell. Seems he and Gertrude enjoyed their time together at the noonday meal."

"That's delightful to hear. Did you mention the barn dance?"

"I did. Nowell was already planning to ask her to accompany him. Reckon you and I should open that matchmaking agency."

Amaya's face brightened.

And the heaviness in his heart temporarily eased.

Amaya hadn't planned on sharing her angst about the barn dance with Silas. But in the short time they'd known each other, she'd come to appreciate and value their friendship. She also respected his opinion. More than anyone else, with the exception of her parents and Zurina, Silas knew about the complexities of her grandparents' situation.

Speaking about Russell was an entirely different matter.

She cast a glance at Silas's profile. He'd shaved, making his strong, square jaw more pronounced. She'd not noticed before the slight upturned tilt of his nose. Calloused hands, indicating the hard work he undertook each day, guided the reins. His blue plaid shirt stretched between his sturdy shoulders and outlined the muscles in his upper arms.

Silas McFadden was a dapper man.

Not that this was the first time she'd noticed.

Silas faced her then and smiled. Amaya focused her gaze straight ahead as the guilt washed over her. Russell had been her one true love. Russell, so different in appearance than Silas, with his slim and smaller stature. Built more like Grandfather, only a few inches taller. But both Russell and Silas shared similar traits of godliness, kindness, and inner strength.

She worried her lip and pondered whether to ask Silas to turn the wagon around and take her back to the mercantile. But as they drew closer, she heard a banjo's faint strains. Perhaps Grandmama was correct about time spent with friends.

Wagons and buggies filled the area surrounding the Swofford barn. Children ran and played in the meadow area near the house. Several chickens foraged just beyond the coop, and a brown dog with long droopy ears lounged at the fence beside the corral, as if overseeing activities.

Silas assisted her from the wagon, his hand holding hers for a brief moment longer than usual. "Are you sure you want to attend the dance?" he asked.

"I—yes."

"Because I'm willing to take you back at any time."

"Thank you, Silas."

He smiled again at her, and a fluttering took up residency in her belly. Amaya's gaze drifted to his hand holding hers, and he quickly pulled his hand away and instead offered his elbow to escort her into the barn.

When they entered, Silas set the plate of food Grandmama prepared on the long, narrow table with numerous other offerings. The music stopped, and Mayor Pritchard stood at the front of the barn on a makeshift wooden platform.

"Ladies and gentlemen, the first lady and I would like to welcome you to the barn dance." Mayor Pritchard held out his hand to Ina. She took his hand and juggled their baby daughter in her other arm.

The crowd clapped. Pritchard and Ina took slight bows before Pritchard continued.

"A huge thank you to Mr. and Mrs. Swofford for the generosity of their barn. Also, a thank you to Mr. Epps who brought his fiddle along, and Mr. Newby who will play his banjo."

The men held up their instruments, then both also took a bow.

"Some excellent news before we proceed." Pritchard waited until the crowd quieted. "The Driessen-Evers Railway Company informed us that the spur from Poplar Springs to Nelsonville will be completed and ready for passengers on Monday."

Those in attendance clapped and cheered. "Good news also is that there will be an agent on board to assist in preventing robberies. Without further ado, let the festivities begin!" Pritchard and Ina stepped down from the makeshift platform, and Mr. Epps and Mr. Newby began playing their instruments.

Folks greeted Amaya and Silas, and Amaya reveled in the fact that although she'd been in Poplar Springs such a short time, the town welcomed her.

Hannah and John Mark stood beside her and Silas. "I'm so thrilled about the spur," said Hannah. "That means our family from Willow Falls will be visiting more often."

Amaya thought of her parents and Zurina. If for some reason they weren't able to move to Poplar Springs this fall, perhaps they, too, could visit by rail once the spur from Poplar Springs to Bowman was completed.

"How about you and John Mark go dance? I'll take care of Little Russell for you," Silas said.

A relaxed smile crossed Hannah's face. "Are you sure?"

"Absolutely." Silas crouched to Little Russell's height. "What say you and me go get something to eat while your parents dance?"

Little Russell nodded and reached for Silas's hand. "Okay, Uncle Siwus."

"Enjoy yourselves," said Silas to John Mark and Hannah. "We'll be in the food line eating far too much supper."

John Mark clapped him on the shoulder. "Thank you. It's been a while since I've danced with my wife."

"Little Russell, you be a good boy for Uncle Silas." To Silas, Hannah added, "He's particularly rambunctious today."

Silas leaned toward Amaya. "I wonder if Oma ever said the same about me." His eyes crinkled at the corners.

"I didn't know you as a little boy, but far be it from me to say that it's quite likely Oma would have said that."

Silas held her gaze as several seconds ticked by. Finally, she turned her attention to Little Russell and was about to ask if she could join them in the food line when Ambrose approached them in his Sunday best. "Howdy, ma'am," he said. "Would you care for a dance?"

Amaya laughed. "I think that would be lovely, Sheriff Ambrose."

Ambrose puffed up, the buttons on his black vest threatening to pop.

Silas watched as Amaya joined Ambrose on the cleared space that had become a dance floor. Perhaps later he'd ask her to dance.

He led Little Russell, who was full of nonstop babbling, to the food table. Silas noticed immediately a plate of sugar cookies. While he'd eaten plenty of food at the mercantile, there was always room for dessert. "How about a cookie, Little Russell?"

"Me like cookies."

Little Russell, who, with the exception of his mother's eyes, was a miniature John Mark, tugged on Silas's arm and attempted to weave through the crowd in front of those standing in line.

Silas reached down and swooped him up. "What say we see how many desserts we'd like to eat?"

The little boy didn't need to be asked twice. He pointed a chubby finger toward the numerous apple pies, cookies, cakes, and pastries. "Wittle Wussell wikes all of them and all of those." He pointed to his stomach. "Wittle Wussell's tummy is hungry."

Silas doubted the boy, who was set to be taller and with more girth than his older brother, Ambrose, was hungry. "Did you eat supper?"

Little Russell nodded, then pointed in the direction behind Silas. "Uncle No."

Silas turned in the direction of his point, and sure enough Nowell and Gertrude stood in line. "Surprised you two aren't dancing."

Nowell ruffled Little Russell's hair. "Gertrude and I both discovered we love peach cobbler, and we heard a rumor Mrs. Pearson sent some of her famous cobbler with Pritchard."

"If it was sent with Pritchard, it didn't make it here."

"Where does he hide all the food he eats?" Nowell patted his stomach. "If that was me, I'd be plump."

Silas harrumphed. "You, my friend, would never be plump. You're a taller version of Pritchard. Me, on the other hand, if I keep eating Grandmama's food, you'll be able to roll me down the street."

"That'd be a sight to see. But it's never gonna happen. Never seen a man with as much muscle as you. Getting some practice at being a pa here with Little Russell?"

"His parents are dancing, so I offered to get us something to eat."

"You'll make a great pa someday."

Silas hoped so, even though he had no example to follow.

Nowell offered his arm to Gertrude. "You might as well be the first to know. Gertrude and I are courting."

"You both decided that rather quickly." But why was Silas not surprised? He glanced behind him at those dancing and searched for Amaya. Wait until he told her. "Congratulations."

Gertrude's smile spanned her entire face. "Thank you. We discovered our fondness for each other at the restaurant. How could we not have known sooner? And do not distress yourself about it being a rather quick happening. Nowell and I plan to court for a lengthy time."

If Silas knew Nowell, he wouldn't want to court for "a lengthy time". He quirked an eyebrow at his friend, and Nowell shrugged. "With Gertrude's success rate at matching couples in Poplar Springs, we may not be able to secure Reverend Fleming's services for some time."

"And speaking of my success at matching couples through the matrimonial agency, this is yet another victory to add to the list of those I have aided in finding their one true love."

Silas wouldn't share that he and Amaya assisted in this most recent victory. Had Nowell and Gertrude even realized he and Amaya weren't there for their noonday meal get-together?

Little Russell tapped on his arm. "Uncle Siwus?"

"Yes?"

"Wittle Wussell hungry."

CHAPTER SIXTEEN

AMAYA CLUTCHED THE LETTER from Ma to her heart. Yes, she enjoyed her time in Poplar Springs, but she missed her parents and sister and couldn't wait to see them again.

She broke the seal and unfolded the letter that displayed Ma's perfect handwriting.

Dearest Amaya,

I hope this letter finds you well and adjusting to life in Poplar Springs. I daresay it won't be long until we join you there. Pa, especially, can barely wait. He's somewhat restless as he continues to heal, but is doing remarkably well. We are grateful his boss has allowed us to stay in this home rent free until the fall even though Pa cannot engage in his ranch hand duties. We are ever grateful for the Lord's Providence.

How are Grandmama and Grandfather faring?

Zurina says hello and that she misses her favorite sister. She's been busy assisting me with midwife duties and tending to the garden.

Love you and miss you.

Ma

Amaya tucked the letter back into the envelope. Fall couldn't arrive soon enough, and she hoped by then Pa would be completely healed and that a home for them would become available to rent or purchase.

She stopped to peer into the millinery's window. An elegant cobalt-blue dinner gown of striped silk satin with a lace bodice sewn over the blue fabric and a high-necked lace neckline hung in the window. While she would treasure such a possession, nothing would be quite as cherished as wearing Grandmama's dress to the barn dance.

Memories of the dance two nights ago and how she'd enjoyed herself far more than she imagined lingered in the forefront of her memory. While she'd not admit it to anyone else, dancing with Silas had been the highlight of the evening. They'd discussed much on the way home from the festivities, their easy camaraderie reminding her once again of how close they'd grown.

She continued down the boardwalk to the hotel to meet Cecily, Herman, and H.J. and tell them goodbye. Today they'd leave Poplar Springs.

H.J. reached for her when she entered the hotel, and Amaya scooped the precious baby into her arms.

"Thank you so much for everything. For helping us during..." Cecily shivered. "When the stagecoach crashed and those horrid men arrived. We shall never forget your kindness."

"You are welcome." Amaya held H.J. to her, and he gurgled, drool running down his chin as he batted at her cheeks and giggled.

Oh, but to have a little one like H.J. If only Russell...

"Thank you for visiting while I was healing and for the desserts your grandmother made," added Herman, interrupting her melancholic musings. He stood, leaning on a cane. "Doc says the leg should heal fully."

"I'm so glad to hear that. You three will be among the first to ride on the train."

Cecily released an exaggerated sigh. "For that we are most grateful. No more stagecoaches for us. Oh, Amaya, we shall miss you."

Amaya handed H.J. back to his mother and extended a hug to Cecily. "And I shall miss you. Do be sure to write once you reach Thornsby. I'm eager to hear all about the train ride."

She prattled on with her friends a while longer before leaving the hotel for her final errand of the day.

Her weekly visit to Russell's grave.

Silas retrieved Widow Kingston and delivered her to the cemetery, just as he did once a month every month.

"Take your time, ma'am."

While Widow Kingston visited her late husband, Silas gave her privacy and sat beneath the aspen trees, thinking of Oma. He no longer lived in Texas where he could visit her grave. But he knew she wasn't there anyway. Oma was in the arms of her Lord and Savior. And he would see her someday, of that he was certain.

Silas rolled his shoulders, attempting to release the guilt that so often and so easily found a way to settle there. He glanced up at the blue sky with nary a cloud.

An eagle spread its wings and soared peacefully on the breeze.

He missed Oma. Missed her more than he ever thought possible. She'd taken a rejected little boy and raised him to a man. Loved him unconditionally, even when he'd broken her heart.

"Oma," he whispered. "I wish you were still here. You'd like Wyoming."

Silas peered down at his dirty fingernails in need of a good scrubbing. He'd been busy as of late tending to the continual chores a ranch his size demanded. Being at the cemetery brought back memories of Oma.

Sitting by the fireplace at night while she read the Bible aloud. The first time they'd tried watermelon—and both loved it. They'd eaten an entire melon in one day causing stomach upset for both of them. But it had been worth it.

Or the time he'd surprised Oma with a carrot cake for her birthday. One he'd baked himself.

He'd worked several extra days after school at the Meacham Ranch. Usually, he only worked there on Saturdays, but he'd begged Mr. Meacham to allow him to earn some money for the ingredients for Oma's cake. Since he was a hard worker, big for his age, and stronger than many grown men, Mr. Meacham gladly agreed to Silas's request. The only problem was having to not be quite as forthright as he ought when giving Oma his earnings.

Then, the day of Oma's birthday, he'd asked the reverend's wife if she'd keep Oma at her house until evening so he would have time to bake her a cake. Silas purchased extra flour and sugar so as not to use their meager rations. Carrots came from the garden and butter from Oma's freshly-churned stock. The chickens were cooperating, so eggs were not a concern, but he'd almost not had enough money for the cinnamon and baking soda.

Finally, back at their humble cabin, he'd followed Oma's recipe. It was then he realized he didn't care much for baking or cooking or anything to do with being in the kitchen. Big clumsy hands weren't helpful when it came to cracking the eggs and scooping the batter into the pan. He'd opened the oven door at least twenty times in the course of the cake baking just to be sure he didn't burn it. For if he did, there were no more ingredients.

The icing was runny, but Oma hadn't minded. When she finally returned home, Silas had the cake waiting for her. She had cried, told him how much she loved him, and then they'd eaten the entire cake that evening.

When he was fourteen, he'd worked an additional job besides his one at the Meacham Ranch, and saved up enough money over the course of two months to purchase the brooch Oma had been eyeing at the mercantile. She'd worn it every day after receiving it. Before she died, Oma told him that she hoped he'd give the brooch to his wife someday when she was gone.

Silas had assured her she had at least thirty more years.

But she hadn't had that long. Not even close.

And that year when he was fourteen was the last year they celebrated her birthday in such a gregarious manner. Other, seemingly more important things took the place of Oma and her birthday. Silas recalled the pain in her eyes the first year he'd forgotten the day of her birth.

He'd disappointed her in a way that could never be forgiven, even after all she'd done for him.

Silas swallowed the lump that formed in his throat. "Just one more day with you, Oma. That's all I would ask for. Just one more day."

Just one more day to prove to her he was worthy of her love.

Silas closed his eyes, willing the image of her disappointment to fade away. Disappointment at the man he'd become.

He opened his eyes once again and reverted his attention to Mrs. Kingston. The woman still knelt at her husband's grave. She was at least ninety years old, hard of hearing, blind in one eye, and hunched over with back problems. As though a little bird who'd fallen from the nest, Mrs. Kingston needed someone to take her under their wing. Silas had been the one to do so, and now every month, without fail, he brought her to the cemetery. He also often took food to her and made sure she was getting enough to eat. Her frail frame reminded him so much of what Oma's had looked like in those last days. And while she didn't resemble Oma in any other way as far as appearance, she was a godly and gracious woman. Just like Oma had been.

A noise in the opposite direction commanded his attention, and Silas turned to see Amaya visiting Russell's grave. Her back to him, her shoulders slumped as though she carried a tremendous burden.

If only he could have prevented Russell's death. No one had the foresight to know he would lose his life that day to nefarious individuals who sought his land.

Silas stood and meandered toward her, the desire to comfort her tugging at him.

Amaya's voice carried on the breeze and he figured it wasn't right to listen in on such a private moment, yet his feet refused to move.

"I should be here with you starting our new life together, Russell." Amaya's shoulders shook. "It was just so unexpected that you were taken from me. I loved you so much and for me there will never be another."

In an unanticipated moment, Amaya turned and her eye met his.

"I'm sorry, I didn't mean to..."

She rose and dusted off her skirt. "It's fine." She paused and walked slowly toward him. "Since I've been in Poplar Springs, I've been visiting him regularly. Not him, as I know he's not here, but his grave."

Silas nodded toward the elderly woman at a nearby gravesite. "I bring Widow Kingston here once a month to visit Mr. Kingston's grave."

A half-smile lit Amaya's face. "You are such a compassionate sort when it comes to widows and those in need."

"I try to be. Oma taught me what the Bible says about orphans and widows and to always be chivalrous, so I try."

"She taught you well."

But he hadn't listened to all that Oma instructed him.

Amaya pressed the front of her skirt with her hands. "I know you never met Russell, but if you had, you two would have been friends."

"I have no doubt about that. John Mark spoke highly of his character."

"Ah, yes, John Mark. Russell talked almost non-stop about him and their other friend, Tobias, and all of their mischievous antics while they were youngsters."

Silas thought of some of his friends he'd had as a young'un. They'd had their share of harmless pranks before he'd deserted them and fell in with the wrong crowd. His thoughts returned to Russell, an upstanding man who died at the hands of evil far too soon. "I'm sorry about Russell." The day flashed through his mind. John Mark finding Russell. The fire. The exchange of bullets.

"Ma says I'll never fully recover from losing him, but that it will get easier. And it slowly has, but..." A single tear slid down Amaya's face.

He wanted to take her into his arms and comfort her. To remind her she'd see her betrothed again someday.

"I'm grateful to be here to assist Grandmama with the care of Grandpapa, but I imagined I would be here under different circumstances. Starting a new life with Russell."

Pain etched her lovely features and tears slid down her face. Silas never figured he'd live in Wyoming. Hadn't he declared Texas his forever home? "While I didn't lose someone I was about to marry, I do feel the pain of losing Oma. At one time, she was all I had." *Until I broke her heart.*

"I'm sorry about your loss. She was blessed to have you for a grandson."

Her words meant more to him than he could express, even if he hadn't always felt like a blessing to the woman who rescued him from being placed in an orphanage.

Emotions had overwhelmed her as they always did following time spent at Russell's grave. As she did during the visits, she placed a bouquet of wildflowers near the wooden cross and spent time telling Russell of the recent ongoings and how much she missed him.

Oh, she knew Russell was not in the grave. But having somewhere to "speak" with him gave her comfort.

She'd dusted off her dress and plodded toward the edge of the cemetery. It was then that she saw a familiar figure. When he'd walked toward her, his strong and confident demeanor gave her no doubt as to his identity.

Silas now stood inches away, his muscular physique dwarfing her. She'd shared with him about Russell, and he'd shared with her about missing Oma.

The Lord had blessed Amaya with several friends over the years, but none so close as Silas. He knew about Russell. Had been there after her fiancé was killed. Had watched as justice was meted out to those who survived the posse formed by Sheriff Winslow.

She knew of the pain he carried at losing his grandmother. She couldn't imagine losing her own grandparents, and although she didn't know the specifics, Amaya figured Silas carried regrets that pertained to the woman who raised him.

They stood facing each other discussing their losses, and then, in an instant, Silas's arms enveloped her. She rested against his broad chest, feeling the comfort and safety of his embrace. Amaya heard his heartbeat pounding in his chest as her tears wetted his shirt. She felt him kiss the top of her head and rub her back gently.

Just as a good friend did.

But in recent days, Silas McFadden had become more than a friend.

How could it be that she was growing fond of Silas when she still loved Russell? When she vowed to never care for anyone else the way she'd cared for her fiancé? Her dear and sweet Russell. How could she be such a betrayer?

The tears came freely then. Tears at losing Russell, especially in such a horrific way just months before their wedding. Tears at the unfairness of life of how someone so young and so vibrant could be snatched in an instant. Tears at the thought that she wasn't keeping her promise to herself to love Russell and only Russell all the days of her life.

But she'd not share that last bit with anyone.

Amaya stepped back from Silas. "Thank you."

"You're welcome," he said, reaching up with a calloused finger and tenderly wiping the tears that continued to fall.

She determined to ignore her growing feelings for the man who'd unexpectedly claimed her heart.

CHAPTER SEVENTEEN

SILAS CUT ACROSS THE short distance between his ranch and John Mark's. Hopefully his friend would be home so he could deliver the colt that would someday be Ambrose's.

Ambrose and his pet pig, Grumbles, greeted him the second he rode up the stretch to the Eliason home. "Hi, there, Uncle Silas. Me and Grumbles just arrested some outlaws that were fixin' to rob a train."

Silas dismounted and ruffled Ambrose's hair, warmed as he always was that Ambrose considered him an uncle. He took the title seriously. "Sounds like you've been busy today."

"Yes, sir. As Sheriff Winslow says, 'There's much to be done in these here parts of Wyoming'".

Silas chuckled at the boy's vivid imagination. "On behalf of the fine folks of Poplar Springs, we're thankful Sheriff Ambrose and Deputy Grumbles are keeping us safe." He scanned the area. "Is your pa home?"

"He's not home yet, but Ma is over there." Ambrose pointed to Hannah who was near the house hanging laundry on the line. "Little Russell is here too."

"All right, thank you." Silas put the colt in the corral, tethered his own horse, and strolled toward Hannah. He patted his shirt pocket. He had something he might as well ask her while he waited for John Mark's arrival.

"Hello, Silas," Hannah greeted. "John Mark should be here any minute."

"Hello, Hannah. I brought the new colt and put him in the corral."

Little Russell waved at him. "Hi, Uncle Siwus."

"How's Little Russell today?"

"I fine."

Silas chuckled and patted him on the head. "Looks like you have more toy horses."

"Gwampa made them for Wittle Wussell."

John Mark's parents doted on the boys. "Pretty soon you'll have an entire corral full of horses." He turned his attention to Hannah and reached into his pocket. "I've been needing to talk to you about the Founder's Day Celebration."

"Oh?"

Silas reached into his pocket. "Could I ask you a favor?"

"Certainly."

He removed a stack of narrow papers and fanned them, causing Little Russell to giggle and reach for them. "Would you be willing to write my name on some of these for me? I've written quite a few myself, but maybe having different handwriting would be beneficial."

Hannah took the stack of tickets from him. "I see that this is to win Amaya's quilt in the raffle."

Silas kicked at a pebble in the dirt. "Yes, ma'am. I've been needing a new quilt."

"They do have those at the mercantile. Or perhaps you could purchase one from Gertrude. I hear she has one or two for sale at her mending business."

"Yes, well..."

Hannah smiled. "I would be happy to put your name on them. But doesn't whoever you purchased these from know it was you who is attempting to win the quilt? I'm not sure how it will help for me to write your name."

Silas cleared his throat. "Fortunately, it was Pritchard's clerk at the mayor's office who sold them to me, and I'm not sure she knows who I am. I just asked for a stack of them."

It was Hannah's turn to fan the tickets. "Did you buy every possible one?"

"Someone unfortunately purchased a few before I could buy the remainder of them." The heat climbed up his face. Good thing he hadn't shaved in a few days. He turned his gaze toward the far field. "Thought I could help raise money for a good cause and win a pretty quilt all at once."

It hadn't mattered that each ticket cost him ten cents, and he'd had to do without a few necessities in order to afford the generous amount of tickets that would likely enable him to win.

"I'd be happy to help. Perhaps Ambrose can practice some of his penmanship as well."

"Thank you. Oh, and Hannah?"

"Yes?"

"Can we not tell Amaya about this?"

Hannah pretended to button her lip. "Your secret is safe with me."

Silas released the breath he'd been holding. "Thank you."

John Mark arrived around the bend, and Silas ambled his way toward the man he considered his best friend.

"Pa! Pa!" Ambrose dashed from the barn and wrapped his arms around John Mark. Hannah and Little Russell, doing his best to keep up with his stubby legs, rushed toward him. John Mark circled Hannah's waist and drew her to him.

Silas turned to avoid interrupting the special moment between the family. A yearning in his heart that always struck him whenever he was visiting the Eliason home needled its way deep within him. He'd never known his parents and, until he was an adult, had rarely seen an example of abiding love between a married couple.

There was something so forceful, so intense that filled him with a longing for a family of his own, especially in moments like this. Not just a family to have a family, but a family to love, to care for, and to provide for. A wife to hug and kiss after a long day such as John Mark had with Hannah. A wife to cherish, protect, love, and care for all the days of their married lives. A son to set an example for what it meant to be a godly man. A daughter to protect and show her how a man should treat his wife through how Silas treated her own mother. He swallowed the lump that nearly choked him and focused on the mountains to the south.

Sometimes the Lord didn't see fit to answer certain prayers. But he hoped and hankered for God's will to be the desires of Silas's heart when it came to a family.

Hannah ushered Ambrose into the house to "practice" his penmanship, and Little Russell toddled along behind his mother.

"Silas, good to see you." John Mark interrupted his thoughts. "Staying for supper?"

"Can't say as I've ever refused a home-cooked meal. I brought the colt and put him in the corral."

"Thank you. What do I owe you?"

"Nothing. We'll call it even."

John Mark began to argue about not wanting to accept charity when Silas interrupted. "I think he'll make a good horse for Ambrose. Let me give him to you."

John Mark finally relented, and they stood near the corral and talked of agricultural prices, ranches, crime in Poplar Springs, and Sheriff Winslow's success in hiring another new deputy.

"Pa and Uncle Silas, it's time to eat," called Ambrose, his high-pitched little boy voice resounding over the otherwise quiet evening.

Silas followed John Mark into the house. He'd been here often enough for meals that he knew the routine. Ambrose was setting the table and Hannah was at the stove. John Mark carried over the food, Hannah placed Little Russell in his high chair, and Silas poured milk from the pitcher into each cup. It was the sense of belonging to this family that made him want to outstay his welcome on many occasions. But he'd relented and left soon after assisting with the clearing of the table. Hannah always sent him home with extra food, which never made it to his front door.

After they prayed, pleasant conversation ensued.

All except on the part of Ambrose.

"Pa, it just ain't fair."

"Isn't fair."

Ambrose pouted. "Pa, it just isn't fair," he repeated.

"What's not fair, Son?"

A scowl crossed the young boy's face. "I don't see why I gots to do book learning so late in the day."

"It's never too late to learn new things," said John Mark, helping himself to a second piece of buttered bread.

"I try not to complain and all seeing as how I'm supposed to be grateful, but today I had to practice writing Uncle Silas's name a hundred and five times on these pieces of paper." Ambrose scowled, his brows furrowing. "Ain't, I mean isn't fair, not one bit. Besides, I already know how to write names."

John Mark and Hannah exchanged a knowing glance before John Mark continued his conversation with his son. "Why were you practicing writing Uncle Silas's name?"

Ambrose shrugged. "Not sure, Pa. All I know is I had to write his name on that big stack of papers over there." Ambrose pointed to the pile of tickets on a small round table with a lantern.

Silas knew he would be in for some serious teasing from John Mark once he knew what he'd asked of Hannah and Ambrose. He decided to divert the topic somewhat. "You want to be a sheriff, isn't that right, Ambrose?"

"Yes, sir."

"Did you know it's mighty important to have good penmanship as a sheriff?"

Ambrose tilted his head. "How so?"

"A sheriff is a busy man. He has to write letters and send telegrams whenever there are outlaws to be caught. He has to know how to be a proficient reader in order to read the wanted posters. And he has to know his arithmetic to figure reward money and know how many outlaws to put in one jail cell."

"How do you know so much about sheriffs, Uncle Silas?"

"Because I have been deputized and have ridden with the posse. I've worked with your pa many times to know a man has to have intelligence and a whole lot of book learning if he's to be a successful lawman."

Ambrose seemed to ponder Silas's words. "I know Pa is smart and Sheriff Winslow too."

"That's right. If your pa hadn't done his book learning, he wouldn't be as good of a deputy as he is."

"Uncle Silas is right, Son," said John Mark. "And just about any job you might want as a man will require you to have good penmanship skills. What if someone couldn't read your writing?"

Ambrose sighed. "Reckon you are right," he mumbled before scooping an oversized bite of mashed potatoes into his mouth.

"Interesting that he's practicing writing *your* name," John Mark said to Silas.

Silas chewed his meatloaf extra slowly to prolong having to expound on the reasons Ambrose was penning his name over and over again on little sheets of paper.

"Silas is entering a contest at the Founder's Day Celebration next week," offered Hannah.

John Mark tilted his head. "Really? What kind of contest?"

"I'm aiming to win a new quilt."

"You can buy those at the mercantile, and I heard from Nowell about six hundred times that Gertrude has a few at her business."

"Yes, but this is a special quilt."

"What makes it special? The pink calico flowers?"

At John Mark's statement, he and Hannah laughed.

"I have no idea what color it is or what pattern it has other than I've been needing a new quilt for the coming winter."

"Since it's July, I'd say you have some time, even if Wyoming winters arrive sooner than in some other parts of the country."

"I reckon it's a good way to help support the cause of replacing the roof on the church. We're closer than ever to having all the money raised for the materials."

John Mark looked skeptical. "Let me guess...did a certain woman make the quilt?"

"I'm sure a woman did. Can't see any man wanting to sew a quilt except maybe Pritchard, and that would likely be because Ina's working on a quilt and he'd want to be a helpful sort."

"You're an evasive man, Silas." John Mark chuckled. "But I'm sure Amaya would be honored to see that you've spent a year's worth of wages attempting to win her quilt."

Silas groaned. Whatever he'd spent on the tickets would be worth it.

Hannah cut up Little Russell's meatloaf and placed it before him. "Ambrose and I are helping him by writing his name on the tickets so it's as if someone else nominated him to win, not just himself, should someone inspect the papers."

"I see," said John Mark. "Well, with that investment, you're sure to win."

Silas nodded, knowing this would not be the last time he heard about this subject. "Never hurts to enter contests. You never know when you could be chosen as the winner."

The camaraderie continued throughout the meal, and while Silas knew John Mark would tease him about the quilt, he wouldn't have it any other way. He'd often wondered what it would have been like to have a brother or a sister and figured this was the closest he'd ever come to that.

When the meal was over and the dishes cleaned, Silas prepared to take his leave.

"I hear the new spur from Nelsonville to Poplar Springs is a popular one. My entire family intends to visit in a few weeks. When they do, we plan to invite several friends to the get-together, you, Amaya, Pritchard, Ina, Nowell, and Gertrude included."

"If anyone needs a place to stay while they're here, I've got some room at my place."

"Much obliged. We may need to accept your offer."

Silas shifted as they stood on the porch. "Could you not say anything to Amaya about the quilt?"

"I wouldn't say a word."

"Thank you for the supper."

"We always enjoy having you for a visit."

Silas turned to look through the window. Hannah was wiping Little Russell's messy face, much to his annoyance, and Ambrose was talking, likely telling another story. "You're a blessed man, John Mark."

"That I am. God has blessed me richly."

"Little Russell sure looks just like you."

John Mark laughed. "He's an Eliason for sure, but he has Hannah's sweet temperament. Thank you again for the colt and for helping Ambrose see the importance of book learning. He really looks up to you."

"He'll make a fine sheriff someday. Can you see him talking nonstop to the outlaws and telling them stories while they're stuck in the cell?"

"He has a creative imagination. He's antsy as all get out for Little Russell to grow up so they can play sheriff and outlaw without Little Russell just running around chasing him and laughing."

Several minutes later, leftovers in hand, Silas rode toward his house. He lifted his gaze to the sky to the Lord who knew every desire of his heart, especially the one with the hopes of someday having a family.

CHAPTER EIGHTEEN

SILAS HAD AN IDEA that might just work. While Amaya was with a customer and Grandmama was upstairs checking on Grandfather, he wandered to an area adjacent to the mercantile. Crates lined the walls with freight and provisions A musty and dank odor assaulted him, and the sound of a critter skittering across the floor alerted him to a narrow stream of light filtering in through the window. What if he could remodel the mercantile's storage area into living quarters for Grandmama and Grandfather? Since Grandfather couldn't navigate the stairs, he remained trapped in the upper quarters unless Silas carried him downstairs for church.

If Grandfather was on the lower level, perhaps he'd be able to go more places and his melancholy would lift. If nothing else, he could sit outside on the boardwalk in his wheelchair in the bright sunshine.

And it would certainly help Grandmama to more easily care for him. Folks, including Doc, could visit him more readily as well.

Silas blew a film of dust off a worn table in the corner. A window overlooked the boardwalk. A window not cleaned in years. Dirt crusted in the pane as well as a collection of dead flies and a few wasps.

A bed, bureau, and a potbelly stove would fit easily in the spacious new living area.

It would take work—a lot of it—but it was doable. Would Grandmama agree to his idea, and if so, where would they store the freight and extra provisions?

Unless...

What if he sectioned off another small area for the extra items and the remainder could be used only for a bedroom for Grandmama and Grandfather? The kitchen could remain upstairs for now. Silas could coat the walls with fresh paint and put a lock on the door. Amaya could still reside upstairs, and when her parents and sister arrived, they could stay up there as well until they moved to their new home.

It would be crowded, but at least Grandfather would more easily be able to engage in day-to-day activities.

"Silas?" Amaya found him a few moments later. She shivered, although the fetid-smelling room was far from cold.

Silas explained his plan to her and hoped she'd agree.

"It's a delightful idea, but I'm not sure we can afford it."

"With your permission, I'll talk to Reverend Fleming, John Mark, Pritchard, Nowell, and some others. Perhaps we can raise some funds. Mrs. Fleming is always looking for people to help."

A smile jotted across Amaya's lips. A beautiful smile he'd never tire of seeing.

Amaya arranged the quilt on the table situated in front of city hall. The block pattern, with its blue, red, and cream-colored squares hadn't been an easy endeavor, but with Grandmama's patient instruction, she finished the quilt just in time for the Founder's Day Celebration.

Ma would be proud if she was here to see it. The quilt's vibrant colors would make a stunning addition to any bed. She'd been humbled when Mayor Pritchard's clerk mentioned many tickets were sold to people hoping to win.

Other items lined the table, including two other quilts, a basket of preserves, a canister of coffee from the mercantile, a rake from the blacksmith shop, a paper with Mrs. Pearson's precise penmanship for a free supper at Pearson's Restaurant, a free haircut at the new barbershop, and a chance to win a free consultation courtesy of Gertrude Duckworth.

Amaya lifted the latter and read the words:

Looking for your one true love?
Look no further!
Miss Gertrude Duckworth at Gertrude's Matrimonial Agency on Main Street will assist you in finding that true love.
Purchase tickets for your chance to win a free consultation with Miss Duckworth.

Gertrude had caused quite a stir in Poplar Springs with her matchmaking services. Her success rate continued to rise, and she was even of the belief she'd arranged for the success of finding Nowell. She'd been so excited that neither Amaya nor Silas determined it necessary to be forthright with her about who the *real* matchmakers were.

Amaya positioned the paper on the table and pinned it beneath a rock to keep it from blowing away. She then strolled toward where Grandmama, Grandfather, and Silas stood awaiting the announcement of festivities from Mayor Pritchard.

As was the custom, the mayor took to the steps with Ina and presented all of the happenings for Founder's Day in celebration of Mr. Gunnarsen, who founded the town.

"Every year since we've started Founder's Day, we've sold tickets for valuable prizes. Thank you to everyone who provided prizes for this year's celebration. Each year we also determine a worthwhile charity for the proceeds of the funds raised. This year, we were set to donate the earnings to the church for the new roof. Due to the large number of tickets sold, we have an excess of funds. Mrs. Fleming, will you join us and share what other charity we'll be donating to this year?"

Mrs. Fleming, a stylish woman with expressive green eyes and long, dark blonde hair, took her place beside the mayor and Ina. "Thank you, Mayor Pritchard. As most of you know, I am the president of the Poplar Springs Church Ladies Ministry Society. We determine who in our town is in need of assistance. As the mayor indicated, we have an excess of funds this year, in part to a sizable number of tickets purchased to win Amaya Alvarado's quilt."

The crowd cheered, and the warmth of a blush suffused Amaya's cheeks. She would have thought the other fine products more worthy than her humble quilt.

"As such, after learning of a need, we've decided that with the substantial amount of donations from tickets this year, we can both completely fund the materials to fix the church roof *and* assist a well-respected family in this town—a family who has done so much for others and now needs our help. With the remaining money, we will aid Mr. and Mrs. Alvarado with the remodeling of their freight room into living quarters."

Amaya's jaw dropped and she looked up at Silas who stood beside her. Affection glowed in his eyes as he smiled at her, his grin causing her pulse to skitter. She brushed aside the peculiar happening and whispered, "Thank you."

"You're welcome."

Grandmama's lashes were wet with tears, and one of the men in the crowd had placed a hand on Grandfather's shoulder and told him he'd assist with the painting.

"Thank you, Mrs. Fleming. We will now announce the winners. Miss Duckworth, would you please draw the names?" Mayor Pritchard summoned Gertrude, who stood beside Nowell to the right of the audience.

The mayor listed each item separately along with the winner for that item. Mr. Janda from the livery won Gertrude's Matrimonial Agency prize, and one would have thought he'd acquired a brand-new horse and buggy.

"Our final winner will take home this lovely quilt sewn by Amaya Alvarado. I daresay in speaking with Mayor Pritchard's clerk that this item exceedingly sold the most tickets. The winner is Mr. Silas McFadden."

For the second time today, Amaya's jaw dropped. Silas's excitement made Mr. Janda's pale in comparison. He strutted to the city steps to retrieve his prize. "Thank you, Miss Duckworth."

The crowd dispersed to partake in the other festivities, and Ambrose dashed toward them. "I'm so glad you won, Uncle Silas! Reckon my hand was gonna fall off after writing your..."

"There now, Ambrose. It's good to see you. Are you and your parents going to join the other festivities?"

"Yes, sir, we are. As I was saying, my hand was tired of doing book learning all them hours. But I'm sure I'll be the best sheriff ever now that my penmanship has improved after writing all them tickets with your..."

Silas put his arm around the boy. "You'll be a fine sheriff someday, Ambrose."

Ambrose stared up at Silas, his forehead wrinkling.

Warmth filled her heart as she pondered her suspicions that not only had Silas been the one to share with Mrs. Fleming about her grandparents' need, but he'd also been the one to purchase enough tickets to ensure the extra donation.

CHAPTER NINETEEN

SILAS JOINED JOHN MARK and Caleb beneath a sizable oak tree on John Mark's ranch. Amaya stood on the porch with Hannah, Annie, and John Mark's parents. Pritchard and Ina would arrive soon as would Nowell and Gertrude and the remainder of John Mark's family. Children ran through the yard, laughing and playing.

And for a moment, Silas imagined he truly was a part of this large and loving family.

"Looks like Charlotte, Tobias, the aunts, and Quimby and Stanley have arrived," said Caleb.

"Whatever you do, not eat any of Aunt Myrtle's baking," warned John Mark.

Caleb nodded. "Braver men have partaken in some of her huckleberry desserts and barely survived." He and John Mark chuckled and Caleb shared a story about their pa before he married their ma and how he'd nearly succumbed to an early death after eating some of Aunt Myrtle's huckleberry pie.

"Wasn't Ma unimpressed by Pa in those days?" asked John Mark.

"They tell the story much better than we do, but Pa said something about it not being fit for human consumption and being grateful Ma inherited her baking skills from Aunt Fern." Caleb laughed. "I wish we could have seen the entire exchange that day. Ma didn't cotton much to Pa in those days."

John Mark joined his brother's revelry. "And look at them now. Married for at least a hundred years."

Silas glanced at Reverend Solomon and Mrs. Eliason. The reverend had his arm around his wife as she leaned into his chest. He could see they loved each other.

And that was the type of marriage he wanted someday. His gaze lingered on Amaya. Her face lit with amusement at something Annie said.

"Have you told her how you feel?"

John Mark's question interrupted Silas's thoughts. "No."

"You should."

"I can't compete with Russell."

"Russell was a good man," said Caleb. "Ornery as a young'un just like John Mark here, but..."

John Mark playfully jabbed his brother in the rib. "Hey, now. As far as Silas knows, I was a model youngster."

They laughed again, and this time Silas joined in their camaraderie. Caleb sobered again and added, "While what happened to Russell was unfortunate, he would want her to be happy. That happiness might be with you."

Silas appreciated Caleb's encouragement, but he wasn't convinced.

A wagon arrived then and John Mark and Caleb's sister, Charlotte, her husband, Tobias, and two little girls disembarked. A buggy carrying whom Silas presumed to be Aunt Myrtle and Aunt Fern and their husbands,

Quimby and Stanley, followed the wagon and parked near the barn.

Ambrose raced to meet Charlotte and Tobias's oldest daughter, and the four of them walked toward Silas, John Mark, and Caleb.

"I don't believe you've met our daughters, Lanie and Baby Rebecca," said Tobias.

"This is Uncle Silas," interjected Ambrose.

"Nice to meet you, Uncle Silas," Lanie beamed, exposing a missing front tooth.

Ambrose tugged on Lanie's arm. "Come on, Lanie, let's go play sheriff."

Lanie clapped her hands together. "I can't wait until tonight when we sleep under the stars and pretend we're on the Oregon trail."

"We're gonna make camp tonight outside our place, Uncle Silas." Ambrose puffed out his chest. "It'll be me, Lanie, and our other girl cousins except for Baby Rebecca and not Little Russell. They're not old enough. But I'll be the sheriff in charge of keeping the law during our time on the trail."

Silas chuckled. "Reckon everyone will feel safe having a sheriff at camp."

"I hear congratulations are in order," said Charlotte.

John Mark turned to Silas. "We found out just yesterday that I'm going to be a pa again."

Silas playfully elbowed his friend. "Congratulations."

"Thank you. We'll be happy with whatever the Lord blesses us with, but Hannah would really like a daughter."

Pritchard and Ina arrived and Ina, carrying their daughter, met the womenfolk on the porch while Pritchard strolled toward the men.

John Mark's aunts and their husbands followed as well, and he introduced everyone.

"Silas and Pritchard, these are our aunts, Myrtle and Fern, and their husbands, Quimby and Stanley."

Aunt Myrtle stepped forward with something wrapped in brown paper. "Are you the one who likes to eat?" she asked Silas.

"I reckon so."

"I was going to bring you one of my famous huckleberry pies, but such a delicacy doesn't transport well. So instead, I brought you some of my famous huckleberry muffins." She handed the wrapped parcel to Silas. "If you can't bear the thought of waiting to eat them, we'll understand."

Silas heard John Mark choke and saw Tobias blanch. Caleb chuckled, and Pritchard raised his eyebrows and leaned closer.

"Thank you, ma'am. Much obliged."

"Don't eat those," Aunt Fern warned. "You seem like a nice fellow and too young to meet your demise."

"I declare, Fern. This young man is one who likely appreciates fine cuisine."

Pritchard nodded toward Aunt Myrtle. "Pardon me, but aren't you the one who is known throughout Wyoming for her baking skills?"

Aunt Fern snorted. "Not known in the way you're thinking."

Aunt Myrtle ignored her sister. "Why, yes, I am. How is it that I can help you?" She paused and scrutinized Pritchard. "You're a scrawny fellow. Perhaps Silas can share the huckleberry muffins with you. My most sincere apologies that I failed to bring more of my delectable desserts."

Pritchard chuckled. "I appreciate that, ma'am. I was hoping to ask a favor."

"Yes?"

"As you may or may not know, I am not only the mayor of our town, but I also join the sheriff's posse on numerous occasions to assist in the apprehension of outlaws."

Silas tossed John Mark a knowing look at Pritchard's arrogance.

"Goodness, but what an impressive young man you are."

Pritchard straightened his shoulders, attempting to add some height to his short stature. "Thank you, ma'am."

"Oh, you must call me Aunt Myrtle. I insist."

"Aunt Myrtle." Pritchard paused and flipped his suspenders. "At this very moment, as unfortunate as it may be, we have two jail cells full of despicable criminals who've languished here for some time while they await transport to the prison. Seeing as how you are known for your baking skills, would you perhaps be interested in supplying some huckleberry desserts while you are in town? The ingredients would be provided, and the town would pay you for your trouble."

Aunt Myrtle held a hand to heart. "My, but what a splendid request! I'd be honored."

Quimby placed a gentle hand on Aunt Myrtle's arm. "It is an honor, my dear, but Mayor Pritchard, I must inquire as to why such abhorrent criminals would receive such delicious food."

"I have a question too," said Aunt Fern. "Did these men do something worthy of a death sentence?"

Everyone but Tobias soon joined the womenfolk, and Silas and the men spoke of cattle prices. They then discussed the new railroad spur that offered discount rates until next month, how Frederick and Millicent at the mercantile in Willow Falls ordered two new Waverly bicycles from the Indiana Bicycle Company, and how they sold within days at their reduced cost of sixty dollars. The discussion then turned to the new hardware store in Nelsonville, which sold agricultural implements and nails.

Lola ran up to Caleb and wrapped her arms around his legs. "What's wrong, Lola?" he asked.

The little girl in a pink dress and matching bonnet answered with a muffled, "Where's Ma?"

"She was on the porch with Grandma, Aunt Charlotte, and Aunt Hannah." Caleb folded in half and gently tugged on Lola's arms which clutched his legs. "Are you all right?"

"No, Pa, I am not."

Silas hid a smirk at Lola's dramatic declaration. If the Lord someday blessed him with a family, would he have all daughters like Caleb did? Or would he have sons like John Mark? Or one of each?

"Can you tell me what's wrong?"

Lola finally released her tight grip. "It's that boy."

A knowing glance passed between Caleb and John Mark.

"Ambrose?" Caleb asked.

"Uh-huh."

"What did he do?"

Lola pointed to Ambrose. "Ambrose called me an outlaw. I'm not an outlaw, Pa!"

Caleb reached down and with an efficient swoop, gathered his daughter into his arms. She nestled her face into his shoulder and emitted a high-pitched whine.

John Mark covered a chuckle with his hand before calling out, "Ambrose? Can you please come here for a minute?"

"Esther and Lena, you too," Caleb motioned with one hand to his other daughters.

Tobias beckoned his oldest daughter. "You too, Lanie."

Ambrose, his too-large black cowboy hat sliding over his eyes, reached them first. "Yes, Pa?"

John Mark knelt to Ambrose's height.

Silas watched with amazement. He never knew his own pa. Would he have crouched down eye-level to Silas and cared about Silas's concerns? Would he have been a doting father like Caleb and John Mark? Likely not given the fact he couldn't be bothered to care for the son he helped bring into this world.

If Silas ever was a pa, would he be a caring one? Exhibit concern when his young daughter shrieked about the injustice of being called an outlaw by her cousin?

"Ambrose, did you call Lola an outlaw?"

"Ah, Pa, it ain't such a bad thing. Little Russell doesn't mind being an outlaw. Besides, we were just playing."

"But I'm not an outlaw, Ambrose," Lola interjected, giving Ambrose two seconds of her time before burying her face again in Caleb's shoulder.

Esther and Lena, who matched their younger sister with their pink dresses and bonnets, ran toward Caleb. Esther, the older of the two, clutched a dolly. "Yes, Pa? Is Lola all right?"

"And you said I was an outlaw too, Esty." Lola's lip quivered. "And you too, Lena."

"Ambrose and girls, Lola doesn't understand when you call her an outlaw," said Caleb.

"No," sobbed Lola. "I don't understand." She wrapped her arms tighter around Caleb's neck.

John Mark spoke calmly. "Ambrose, can you tell us what happened?"

"We were just playin' like the stagecoach was robbed and Lola here was the robber. But we found out she isn't a very good bad guy."

"That is true," agreed Lanie.

Esther patted Lola on the arm. "We're sorry, Lola. We didn't mean anything by it, and we're sorry we chased you."

"And put you in jail." Ambrose puffed out his chest and fingered the pinned-on badge on his chest.

"I'm sorry too," added Lena.

Lanie bobbed her head. "As am I."

John Mark placed a hand on Ambrose's shoulder. "Ambrose, do you have something to say to your cousin for upsetting her?"

Ambrose kicked a pebble on the ground. "Sorry, Lola."

"Perhaps you can all think of something else to play or maybe someone else could be the outlaw," proposed Caleb.

"Well, I can't be the outlaw," said Ambrose. "I'm Sheriff Ambrose Miller Eliason at your service, and I have to round up all the bad guys. Little Russell is napping in the house so he can't be the bad guy."

Lena's eyes grew large. "And I can't be the outlaw. I'm the grandma. Grandmas aren't outlaws."

"What about you, Esther?" Caleb asked.

Esther held her hands palm up. "I'm the deputy and also the judge."

"Lanie, maybe you could be the outlaw," Tobias suggested.

"Sorry, Pa. I'm one of the deputies."

Caleb scanned the area. "Where's Evangeline?"

"She's with Ma."

"How about you play something else then?"

"I know! I know!" Esther jumped up and down. "We can play Mayflower!"

Lena clapped her hands. "Yes, let's play Mayflower."

Ambrose scowled. "What's Mayflower?"

"I wanna play!" Lola squirmed out of Caleb's grasp and stood next to her sisters. She reached for Esther's hand. "Can we play that, Esty?"

"Yes, we can. We will find somewhere that could be a ship."

Ambrose crossed his arms. "Can I be the sheriff?"

"Sure," said Esther. "What we do is pretend we are on the Mayflower and it's a big ship. We are coming all the way to America and there are waves crashing against the boat and it's dark at night and it's an adventure. We will need a sheriff to keep us safe."

"And I could be that sheriff," said Ambrose.

They were soon all chatting at once describing their plans to play Mayflower. And as Silas watched, something inside him jolted. If the Lord ever blessed him with the family he so badly desired, he hoped he'd be a patient and gracious pa just like the men standing beside him.

CHAPTER TWENTY

AMAYA HAD JUST FINISHED Mrs. Winslow's order when Silas entered the mercantile.

"Hello, Amaya. I have a surprise for you out at the ranch."

A surprise?

Grandmama looked up from her task of unpacking new freight and waved her hand at Amaya. "I'll see you when you return."

"But Grandfather?"

"He's napping right now, and as soon as he awakens, he plans to sit out front on the boardwalk in the sunshine."

Grandfather had taken to sitting outside often now, and with the new living quarters completed last week thanks to Silas and a considerable number of men from town, Grandmama was able to check on him during the day much more easily.

Amaya planted a kiss on Grandmama's soft, wrinkled cheek. "Thank you, Grandmama." Minutes later, she mounted Grandfather's horse, and together she and Silas rode toward his ranch, curiosity besting her.

"It's to the north down by the river." Silas led her past the house, barn, corrals, and chicken coop, past an extensive field with numerous cattle, and through a grove of trees. The sound of the rushing river greeted them, along with the glorious harmony of birds singing. She identified several robins scurrying on twiggy legs, a downy woodpecker tap-tapping on a tree trunk, and two American goldfinches, her second favorite bird, chirping in the aspens above them.

Silas dismounted, removing his hat and hanging it on the saddle horn. As he lifted her from her horse, his hands lingered on her waist. His eyes searched her face, and she saw the interest written in his gaze. Something within her jolted and her breath caught.

When had she begun to fall in love with him? When had she begun to see him as more than a friend of her family? It was so unexpected that she would grow to care for someone again after losing Russell.

Silas leaned toward her and raised a finger to tuck a hair behind her ear. Amaya's heart skittered. What would it be like for him to kiss her?

That thought competed with the ever-present guilt of betraying Russell, and she averted her attention from Silas to a chipmunk to her right.

No matter her growing feelings for Silas, she wouldn't—couldn't—break her promise to Russell.

Silas released her and took a step back. "I—uh—I thought you might enjoy this place. I've nicknamed it Bird Haven." Silas made a sweeping gesture with his arms. "So far I've seen woodpeckers, meadowlarks, red-winged blackbirds, and robins, and just before I came to town, a blue heron in the pond."

"Silas, it's lovely here."

He reached for her hand. "I want to show you something," he said.

Amaya's heart flipped in her stomach when his fingers wound around hers. Conflicting emotions again surged through her as he escorted her beneath the canopy of trees, their fingers intertwined. The brown shirt he wore stretched against his muscular shoulders and his dark blond hair was flattened with a crease at the base of his neck from his hat. Lest she be caught staring, Amaya instead focused on the clearing with a wooden slatted bench.

"I built this bench for us to watch and listen to the birds. Care to sit for a bit?"

She took a seat on the bench and he plopped beside her. Amaya closed her eyes and listened to the marvelous sounds all around her. She counted at least five different types of birds tweeting their happiness on the hot August day. A frog croaked somewhere in the direction of the pond, created by a tributary from the river. A bumblebee buzzed, and every so often the serene sound of aspen leaves whispered on the wind.

"Amaya?"

She fluttered her eyes open and peered in the direction Silas pointed to where a great blue heron was wading through the pond. The heron moved slowly, his long neck exhibiting perfect posture while seeking a meal.

"He was here earlier. I'm glad he returned. I think he has a nest somewhere in one of those trees."

"This is so peaceful. Thank you for taking time from the ranch to bring me here."

"I know how much you love birds."

A robin bustled through the blades of grass. "Have you seen a hawk yet?" Amaya asked.

"Twice and a few nuthatches and sparrows. Of course, there are always magpies and crows as well."

"Black-capped chickadees are my favorite with their sweet chirps. I never knew you were so well-versed in bird types," Amaya teased.

Silas chuckled. "I've been known to thumb through the bird book you keep on the mercantile shelf a time or two."

The fact that he brought her here when he knew it would mean so much endeared him to her.

They sat for some time, reveling in the intricacies of God's Creation. Finally, Silas reached for her hand. He brought it to his lips and gently kissed her fingers. "Amaya..."

Her heart pitter-pattered against her ribcage. "Yes?"

"Would you do me the honor of courting me?"

The words he spoke were unexpected, yet how could they be? Amaya surmised his feelings for her through his thoughtful gestures, the care he gave to her grandparents, and the obviousness of his wanting to spend time with her.

Russell's image flashed in her mind. Ambitious, funny, and handsome Russell with his strawberry-blond hair and his mischievous green eyes. His wiry, but strong physique, and his love for the Lord and especially horses. His hopes and dreams for a future that was never to be.

"Silas..."

"You don't have to answer right this minute. Take some time to think about it."

"Silas…I can't court you." She pulled her hand from his.

The pain in his expression was nearly her undoing and she almost changed her mind, but for Russell. Silas turned his face from hers and his normally broad shoulders slumped. "Is it because of Russell?"

"Yes."

Silas stood and offered his hand. "I best get you back to the mercantile before Grandmama worries. I've got some fences to mend yet today."

"Silas…"

"Thank you for coming out here with me. I'll let you know if I see any other types of birds." But instead of his formerly jubilant tone, Silas's voice fell flat. As if he lacked energy, he plodded toward the horses.

"So there is no hope for a future for us?"

"No. I'm sorry, Silas." Tears dampened her eyes.

He said nothing more, only assisted her onto Grandfather's horse. The ride back to town was void of any words, and when they reached the mercantile, Silas bid Grandmama farewell, tipped his hat, and left.

But Silas's heart wasn't the only one that broke that day. And Amaya felt powerless to do a thing about it.

Amaya willed the sleep to come, but as it had the past several nights, it once again evaded her. Thoughts of Silas and how she'd hurt him remained on her mind. She'd seen him only once since the day at the ranch, and that was during church yesterday. He'd kept his distance —not in a calloused or spiteful way, but he had avoided her with the exception of sitting next to her while Reverend Fleming preached. She missed him. Missed their friendship. Missed their camaraderie. Missed his husky laughter, and his witty personality.

She was about to fetch a glass of water from the pitcher when she heard a commotion downstairs. Grandmama or Grandfather perhaps? If so, what if Grandmama needed her help?

She pulled her wrap over her shoulders and dashed down the stairs. A can of food rolled to a stop at her feet. Other cans were spread sporadically across the floor and a butter churn rested on its side. Near the counter, a glass bottle of perfume lay shattered on the floor, its lavender scent filling the air.

Amaya's heart pounded. Had someone attempted to rob them? She reached for a pan off the shelf, holding it in a firm grasp in case she had to wield it at someone. A breeze blew some papers from the counter, and Amaya peered behind her to see the door ajar.

Someone had definitely been in the mercantile, and had left chaos in their wake.

Grandmama appeared in the door adjacent to the new living area. "Amaya? What's going on out here?"

"Grandmama, please grab the rifle."

Without hesitation, her grandmother turned on her heel and returned less than five seconds later with the rifle.

"Someone's been in here."

"Yes, and they made a horrible mess." Grandmama shuffled towards her. "Look at this. Canned food everywhere, and what is that smell?"

"A bottle of perfume."

"They knocked the quilts off the shelf, and it appears one is missing."

Amaya followed Grandmama's gaze to the quilt shelf. "I hope they're not still in here, hiding somewhere," she whispered, more to herself than to Grandmama. She clutched the frying pan tighter and noticed her grandmother taking a firm grip on the rifle.

"If you're still here, show your face!" Grandmama commanded, her normally subdued tone elevated.

There was no sound save the papers rustling on the counter. Amaya lit a lantern, and together, they perused the remainder of the humble store. Every nook was void of a person crouching in the darkness, but much of the mercantile's inventory had been knocked off shelves, or worse, stolen.

Grandmama squinted into the dimmed area. "Appears they're gone now."

"Erdutza?" Grandfather's warbled, yet frantic, voice cut through the silence, and Grandmama backed toward the door to their living quarters.

"Just a moment, Iker." Grandmama peered up at Amaya. "Dear, do shut and lock that door. We'll contact the sheriff at dawn. There's no one in here now."

Amaya did as she was told, but fear wouldn't relent its hold on her. Who had been in the mercantile—why had they been there? And would they be back?

As the saying went, there was no rest for the weary. Amaya tossed and turned in her bed, her ear tuned to the ongoings below. Thankfully, Grandfather was fine and had only been concerned as to why Grandmama had leapt from their bed in such a panic. As the protector of his wife and family for so many years, it was likely difficult for Grandfather in his weakened state to be unable to effectively shield those he loved from danger.

Amaya stood and peered out the window at the street below. A drunkard plodded down the middle of the street, bellowing an off-tune ditty. He stumbled, his bottle of whiskey teetering in his hand as he did so.

A dog wandered along the boardwalk, its nose to the ground. And further down the street, a man on a horse stalled, his attention on the buildings on either side of the street.

Who had robbed them?

Poplar Springs had long been known for its lawlessness. She was reminded of Russell and his horrific death. But even before that, crime was rampant in the Wyoming town. She'd been somewhat shielded from the corruption while living in Bowman—and residing outside of town on the ranch where her pa worked.

And her parents desired to move to Poplar Springs once Pa recovered from his accident?

Amaya shook her head. If one couldn't even feel safe in a mercantile, where could they feel safe?

Several hours later, the light of dawn peeked through the curtained window. The aroma of Basque potato and pepper tortilla waffled through the air. Amaya buttoned her shirtwaist and pulled her hair into a bun. She'd fetch the sheriff right after breakfast.

Sheriff Winslow was riding with two of the other four deputies in a search for a gang who was wanted in Wyoming and Nebraska, and who'd been seen in the area two days ago. Deputy John Mark Eliason, who'd stayed behind with one other deputy to keep watch on things in town, followed Amaya back to the mercantile.

"Do you know of anyone who would want to do this?" he asked as he perused the scene minutes later.

"No," said Grandmama. "We don't have any enemies that we know of."

Grandfather attempted to utter a string of words. Frustrated, he gritted his teeth and tried once more. "They—how get in?"

John Mark rested a hand on Grandfather's shoulder. "Apparently, they were able to gain access to the store through the door."

"Bu—but locked."

"Yes, I'm sure I locked the door," said Grandmama, her face contorted with concern.

Grandmama had one other time forgotten to lock the door when she closed up the mercantile for the evening. Amaya had discovered it, locked it, and didn't say a word to Grandmama. No sense in upsetting her with all she had on her mind as of late. Could she have perchance forgotten once again? Or believed she had done so but was mistaken?

CHAPTER TWENTY-ONE

SILAS WAS JUST ABOUT to sit down for supper and eat his steak when he heard a ruckus outside. A pounding on the door alerted him that this was either an emergency or an unwanted guest.

It would take less than five seconds to determine it was the latter.

When he flung open the door, he was not prepared for the sight before him. The air whooshed from his lungs, and he gripped the door frame.

Hurst, Engstrom, and Kylian looked just as he remembered them, with the exception of some extra padding around Hurst's middle.

Silas wanted to close the door and reopen it again just to be sure what he was seeing was real and not just a nightmare he'd awakened from. How had they found him?

"Ain't you gonna invite us in?" Kylian asked. He sneezed and wiped his narrow, beakish nose with the back of his hand.

Engstrom shoved Kylian aside. "Don't need no invite." He stomped into the house and crossed his arms across his chest. "You done well for yourself, McFadden."

"You three need to leave."

Hurst removed his hat, revealing mangy dark blond hair that had thinned in the front since Silas last saw him. He chortled loudly enough for the neighbors to hear. "Is that any way to treat your friends? It smells good in here. Don't mind at all if we join you for supper."

"Except you weren't invited."

Hurst narrowed his eyes, strode past Silas, and took a seat at the table. He jutted his chin and smoothed his walrus-like mustache and scraggly beard with a dirty hand. "Don't mind if I eat do you, McFadden?" Without awaiting an answer, he tucked the napkin into his collar, picked up a fork and knife, and sliced into the steak. "See you got some buttered bread here too. What did you do? Decide to become a cook?"

Engstrom expectorated onto the floor before taking a seat at the table next to Hurst. Fetid body odor emitted from his person, and he fixed a dark, penetrating stare on Silas. "He did tell us about that time he made a cake."

"Oh, yes, for his dear Oma. Who could forget Oma? It was all he talked about when we first allowed him into our gang." Kylian shook his head and folded his tall and wiry self into the chair across from Hurst. "Oma this and Oma that. Who knew he'd upset her so?" For added effect, Kylian held a hand to his chest and lowered the tone of his voice. "You ain't disappointed in me, is you, Oma?"

At the mention of his grandmother's name and their mocking, heat flushed through Silas. "You men need to leave," he repeated, regretting that his voice didn't sound as strong and self-assured as it normally did.

"Have a seat here, McFadden. Let's talk this over." Hurst pointed to the vacant chair. He took another bite of his food and failed to close his mouth while chewing, the sound of him smacking his food echoing in the room.

Silas reluctantly took a seat. He knew these men. Knew the havoc they were capable of causing. Knew he was outnumbered. "How did you find me?"

Kylian snatched one of the buttered pieces of bread from the plate Hurst ate from and took an ample bite. "Let's see, should I tell him?"

Engstrom slurped the milk from Silas's cup before answering. "Go ahead."

Kylian leaned back in the chair and clasped his hands behind his head. "McFadden Ranch, offering the best steaks in the West."

"If this is one of them steaks, it ain't the best I've ever had, but it'll do for a black angus." Hurst cut another piece and popped it into his mouth. "Wasn't hard to find you. What did you think? That you could hide forever after what you done?"

That had been Silas's hope when he'd left Texas that July day and rode north until he'd reached Poplar Springs. A town he'd never heard of, had never visited, and had no idea if it would welcome him. Nothing but the clothes on his back, Oma's bible, his horse, and his worn Stetson. He regarded the three men who made themselves welcome at his table. Being a part of the Farris Hill Gang had seemed like a lifetime ago.

"What? You suddenly speechless?" Engstrom poured himself a second helping of milk.

"I've got a new life here." Sweat trickled down his back even as Silas said the words. The men wouldn't take it well.

Hurst peered around the room. "You done well for yourself, but it don't mean you can't ride with us a while and return."

Truth was, Silas never wanted to ride with them again. Those days were in his past, and he preferred to leave them there.

"'Course maybe we ain't good enough for you anymore, is that it?"

"My life is here. As a rancher."

Hurst leaned forward on his elbows. "Can't say Wyoming is all bad. We've made some money while working here."

Kylian chortled. "Working here. Yeah, that's what it is."

"There's a nice abundance of brothels in Wyoming. I kinda like it," added Engstrom. "Can't wait to visit one in Poplar Springs. You do got brothels in town, ain't ya?"

"Ah, yes, the women. Pretty here as they are in Texas." Hurst, always the crassest of the gang, looked into the distance. "You been to any brothels lately, McFadden?"

The men engaged in a round of raucous laughter. "McFadden at a brothel?" Engstrom asked. "Let's see, I think his last words on that subject were, 'Women ought to be respected'."

"I have always and will always stand by those words. Women were created by God to be respected and treated in high regard."

"You missed out on a lot of good times having that stance," said Hurst. "But who really cares what God thinks anyhow? I for sure don't."

Kylian nodded. "Me neither. Or maybe it was because you always thought you was better than us. All haughty-like."

"He was only that way because of dear Oma. You were always so sure you'd never want to disappoint an old woman," Hurst mocked. "Although you worried about all the pain you caused her when you were living your life as an outlaw."

Silas clenched his fists at his sides and felt the heat rise in his face. He gritted his teeth. "Leave Oma out of this."

"Or what? Gonna lose your temper like you are so prone to do?" Kylian took the last piece of bread and shoved half of it into his mouth.

Silas offered a quick prayer heavenward asking the Lord to put a lock on his mouth. "Nope."

"Right. I see the anger in your eyes. Your jaw all tense-like. It's just a matter of time before you unleash some of that rage toward us for talkin' about your Oma that way." Engstrom paused. "Let's see here. Your parents never wanted you so they leave you with this worthless sermon-preachin' woman, always talkin' about Jesus, who thinks she can take a boy meant to ride with one of the best gangs in Texas and turn him around. Teach him about the things of God. A God who never cared for you neither. If He had, why would He have given you worthless parents and left you in poverty? You think your God can change you? That He cares about you one way or another? Remember when you begged Him to save

Oma's life? He didn't listen to you. And Oma? Well, she only took you in because if she didn't, how would that look to the church? She didn't love you. Only wanted you to work hard to support her in that pitiful cabin she called home."

Silas slammed a fist on the table, causing the cup to jump and milk to spill over the side. "That's enough!"

"All we ever had to do was talk about Oma in a derogatory way, and you'd release some of that anger you been holdin' onto." Kylian leaned toward him. "Whatcha gonna do to us? Shoot us?"

"Well, he is the best shot of all of us," said Hurst.

Engstrom shoved Silas hard on the shoulder, although it failed to move Silas an inch. "Temper prone Silas Mc-Fadden. 'Member that time you got all drunk and was put in jail for disorderly conduct? Got all bent because someone said something you didn't like. Punched him in the face for it."

The memories of that night clouded Silas's mind. The first and last time he'd ever imbibed. And the first and last time he'd ever partaken in a fight with another man. He'd used his fists to solve the problem, although the issue hadn't been solved, and Silas was hauled to jail. Remorse stuck with him for years—still did—at his foolish mistakes.

Hurst shoved aside the plate of what was left of the steak and leaned toward Silas. "You ain't a Christian. You is the same as you always was."

The punch to the gut at Hurst's words took whatever comeback Silas could have uttered from him. Maybe Hurst was right. Maybe he wasn't a Christian. For if he was, why would he still lose his temper? Why was the anger coursing through his veins so forcefully at the words the men said about Oma and God?

"But we're not here to talk about your sorry state of disillusionment," said Hurst. "We're here to tell you we want you back in the gang. You left us in the middle of the biggest heist of our careers. We talked many a day about killin' you for that." He paused, his lip curled in disgust. "But you can atone for it. We've been holding up some trains and have been rather successful at it. Banks too. You can join us and all will be forgiven."

"No thanks." The words flew from his mouth before he could give them a second thought.

Kylian thrummed his fingers on the table. "You always was the best shot of all of us. Accurate as you were fast. A quick draw like no one I ever seen. Plus, you're intimidatin' with your size and all. Help us out for a few heists, then you can return here to your nice little spread."

The men stood. "We'll give you a few days to think it over," said Engstrom. "We got some matters to tend to in the southern part of the state, but we'll be back. And when we are, we'll expect an answer."

Silas stood as well, and Hurst neared him, bumping his chest against Silas's. "And if you don't..." Silas peered down at the man who was at least a head shorter and lacking in half the muscle Silas possessed. "And if you don't," Hurst repeated, "we'll exact revenge on you. And no one, not your Oma and not your God will be able to protect you."

On the way out, Engstrom purposely bumped Silas with his shoulder. "You ain't seen the last of us, McFadden."

Silas rested his head against his pillow that night. His weary body begged for sleep, but his mind raced through the events of the evening with the Farris Hill Gang. Those thoughts collided with details from his past.

A past he'd attempted to forget.

Engstrom's rehashing of the time Silas was arrested for disorderly conduct re-emerged in his mind. He'd never entered a saloon before that evening when his comrades pressured him to join them for a few rounds of whiskey. They'd traveled to Westenberg—a town a few miles away—and a town where they'd spent a fair amount of time.

Finally, Silas relented and followed Hurst, Kylian, and Engstrom into the dank saloon. The odor of cigar smoke, unwashed bodies, and alcohol filled the room, the smell still lingering in Silas's memory to this day. He'd told his friends he had no use for alcohol, but they'd seen fit to encourage him to try just one drink. When Silas countered with the fact he had only a few coins to his name, they enlisted several of the other patrons in providing multiple rounds of the hardest liquor the bartender could provide.

At his size, Silas figured it would take a while for the alcohol to affect him. And it had. But the willingness of the gang to procure drink after drink, combined with

194

Silas's steady decline in awareness and slowed reflexes, soon caused peculiar changes within him. Changes he hadn't prepared for.

Silas didn't remember a whole lot about that evening after becoming drunk. He vaguely recalled a man looking for a fight, and Silas answering that call. The gang goaded Silas when the man spoke unkindly about Oma.

How had the man even known about his grandmother?

Now Silas realized that it was due to the gang's willingness to share with him details Silas had shared in confidence.

Confidence with men Silas assumed were like the brothers he never had.

Silas's pulse sped at the thought. Those men were no more like brothers than the men who threatened Amaya and the other passengers that day when the stagecoach crashed.

The man had hit him hard in the nose, and Silas faintly recalled the taunting and the deafening roar of voices as his fist connected with the man's face in retaliation. A man whose name he couldn't even remember.

The next thing he knew, Silas was sleeping on a thin smelly cot in jail. His head throbbed, he'd vomited twice, the room spun, and he was beyond irritable. He was later charged with disorderly conduct, assault, and drunkenness. Jail time and a fine were his punishments.

But the worst punishment of all? Disappointing Oma.

Her expression when he returned home would forever be his undoing. Tears shone in her eyes. She'd said nothing, but later that evening, he'd witnessed her kneeling beside her bed, crying out to God.

Unfortunately, that hadn't been Silas's last time spent in jail. Three other times, he was caught and punished for two petty theft charges and a trespassing allegation. Fortunately, all charges were all misdemeanors or minor felonies in the eyes of the law, and his time in jail was minimal. Especially given the fact there were worse criminals, and the space was needed for them.

Silas gagged at the reminder of the taste of the food provided while he was incarcerated. Bland with no variation, the meat and vegetables were sparse and the broth plentiful. Oma came to visit him faithfully, and she prayed each time she did.

Her small hands folded, her head bowed, and her pleading with the Lord would forever be etched in Silas's memory. Prayers that went unanswered for a lengthy period of time.

Still, Oma never gave up on him.

After that day and for the remaining two weeks Silas lived at the Westenberg County Jail, Oma visited him. She read from the Bible words that, much to his regret now, Silas ignored.

Had Oma's prayers truly done any good? What if Silas wasn't really the Lord's? What if it was all a façade? What if all the time he sought to do good was just a guise?

"Lord, am I Yours? And if I am, how will I know for sure?" he asked in the silence of the night. No response, only the sound of a calf calling to its mother, coyotes in the distance, and crickets outside his window.

Silas blinked as he stared at the ceiling. Hurst, Kylian, and Engstrom proved their false allegiance to him more than once. It had taken Silas years to trust someone enough to call them "friend" again. John Mark Eliason was the first one he'd given that title to. Nowell and Pritchard soon followed.

And so far, none of them had betrayed him the way the gang had.

The next morning, Silas wrestled with whether or not to ride over to John Mark's before chores took up the entirety of his day. Leaving his ranch in the capable hands of Barney, his ranch foreman, Silas finally decided to seek the guidance he needed from his closest friend.

Would John Mark mock him for his question? Deride him for not having the faith to believe he was truly a Christian?

No, not John Mark. Surely not the man he attended church with and was invited as a guest into the Eliason home. Not the man Silas rode alongside numerous times to apprehend outlaws. Still, Silas's ability to trust in the loyalty of others was shaken anew.

The Eliason house came into view minutes later. From this distance, Silas saw Ambrose and Little Russell in the garden with Hannah and an older man who appeared to be Reverend Solomon. Should Silas turn around given that the Eliasons had company?

But something urged him on.

The boys dashed toward him as Silas dismounted.

"Uncle Silas!"

"Uncle Siwus!"

Hannah and Reverend Solomon followed the youngsters, and something deep inside Silas brought about an overwhelming feeling of emotion at the warm greeting.

Little Russell raised his arms toward Silas, and Silas scooped him up. "I an outwah," the boy said in his animated vernacular.

"How did you manage to be the outlaw, Little Russell?"

Little Russell shrugged, but a glance toward Ambrose told Silas all he needed to know. "Are you the sheriff, Ambrose?"

"I'm always the sheriff."

Hannah tossed Ambrose a stern look before turning her attention to Silas. "What brings you here today?"

"Just wondering if I might have a word with John Mark."

"I'm sorry, Silas. He's at work. Normally he doesn't work on Tuesdays, but Winslow needed his help today, given the two other deputies are doing rounds in the rest of the county."

Reverend Solomon offered a firm handshake. "Good to see you, son."

Not many people had ever called Silas son. His own pa certainly hadn't.

"Well, I reckon I'll take my leave then. Would you tell him I stopped by?" Silas set Little Russell back on the ground and the boys ran again toward the garden, followed by Grumbles, their pet pig.

"Is there anything I can help you with?" Hannah asked.

"Nah, and I'm sorry to bother you when you have company."

"Not a problem at all. You know you're welcome here any time."

The mention, as it always did, comforted him. "Thank you. I just have a few questions for John Mark is all. I can talk to him later."

"Something weighing heavily on your mind, son?"

How had the reverend known? Was it that obvious from Silas's countenance?

Would the reverend betray Silas's trust? Taunt him for his questions? Think less of him if he asked his questions? "I..."

"I'll leave you two be," said Hannah. "Good to see you, Silas."

"Walk with me to the corral," suggested Reverend Solomon. He led the way toward the far end, and against what might be his better judgment, Silas followed.

They faced the mountains, the view always reminding Silas of the fact that such a magnificent creation couldn't have just occurred without the hand of an artistic Creator.

"I have some questions about the Lord, but I don't want to burden you." There he'd said what was on his mind. Perhaps Reverend Solomon would agree that such a topic was a burden and send Silas on his way.

"I've never known a time when I was burdened by questions about the Lord. I may not know the answers, but I do know Who to pray to for guidance."

Before Silas could stop the flow of words, he blurted the inquiry weighing on his mind. "I'm not sure I really belong to the Lord. That I'm a Christian. I think I am, but how does a man truly know?"

They stood there in silence for a few awkward moments. Should Silas even talk to the reverend about it? While he also considered Reverend Fleming a friend, he'd never before discussed the deep sorrows of his heart with the man. Men just didn't do that, and Reverend Fleming lived in the same town. He'd likely think differently of Silas if he knew the truth.

But Reverend Solomon lived in Willow Falls. Silas likely wouldn't see him for months, maybe years, after today. But what if the reverend did hold his sins against him? Suggest perhaps Silas not visit the Eliasons after hearing all that Silas had done? "Reckon I'll take my leave. Thank you, Reverend."

Reverend Solomon clapped him on the back. "No need to take your leave, Silas. I remember wondering that myself a time or two."

"You have?"

Reverend Solomon closed his eyes and folded his hands. Was he praying?

Finally, the older, shorter version of John Mark opened his eyes and stared out across the pasture. "It's one of the enemy's biggest lies. To make us think we aren't the Lord's. It's not a new tactic, but it's a successful one."

"My past has caught up with me, sir, and I found myself tempted to be prone to anger yesterday. I thought that was in the past."

Seconds ticked by before Reverend Solomon answered. "Recently, I was a bit abrupt with a friend of mine. I had a lot to do in the day, and this friend likes to talk as much as a chattering hen. Nice fellow, but talkative. I was impatient as he spoke to me about what ailed him. Then yesterday before I traveled here on the new spur from Nelsonville to Poplar Springs, I complained about the meal my wife made for me. A meal that she took time to lovingly prepare and to serve to me. Truth was, I hoped she would have made something else, rather than the same meal we'd had so recently. I hurt her feelings, the feelings of the person I love most in this world. Such impatience with my friend and rudeness with my wife is unbecoming of a Christian, and for sure a man of the cloth."

While Silas didn't know much about Reverend Solomon, he had figured him to be as near perfect as a man this side of Heaven could be. "Did you ask your wife for her forgiveness?"

"I did. And of course my Lydie is the most gracious woman I've ever met. She's had to bear with me all these years, after all." He chuckled. "Yes, she forgave me, for which I am grateful. I also apologized to my friend for my impatience. He truly needed to bend my ear, and I'm glad I realized he was more important than the list of things I'd created for myself to do that day."

Reverend Solmon paused, closed his eyes briefly again, then continued. "Silas, we will never get everything right until we are someday in Heaven with our Savior. We will be tempted—and sometimes give in to that temptation—many, many times in our lives. Temptation to lie, be rude to those we love, create an idol in our lives that comes before the Lord, gossip, and the like. Such things don't mean we aren't His."

"I just wasn't sure how I'd know for sure if I am a Christian."

"The Lord tells us the road is narrow, and many who claim to be His aren't. You're right to ponder the possibility you may not have surrendered fully to Him. We know from what the Lord tells us in His Word that we are all sinners. A condition that warrants spending an eternity apart from Him. But we also know from the Bible that there is a cure. His name is Jesus."

"Yes, sir, and I believe that."

Reverend Solomon nodded. "One of my favorite verses is found in Romans ten. *'That if thou shalt confess with thy mouth the Lord Jesus, and shalt believe in thine heart that God hath raised him from the dead, thou shalt be saved.'* When we repent of our sins—God knows about them all anyhow—and declare our faith in Jesus, that He died for us, and was raised from the dead, this verse tells us we will be saved. When we fully surrender to Him, our lives begin to change. Not all at once, although that would be nice. I'd like nothing more than to always be kind and loving to my wife and patient with my friend, but it can be a slow process."

"But I knew right away I didn't want to do the things I had done before I surrendered my life to Him."

"And sometimes those convictions arrive right away. But there will always be some things we struggle with. Over time, those things may lessen, only to re-emerge again when we least expect it. Tell me, Silas, have you done as Romans ten indicates?"

"I have. And I have asked God to change me."

"And has He answered your prayer?"

"In many ways, yes. Like those things I no longer want to do." Silas shifted. Should he elaborate about his time in jail? The pain he caused Oma? His selfish motives when stealing and lying?

"You don't have to share with me where you were before you decided to follow Jesus unless you want to," said Reverend Solomon as if to read Silas's mind.

Silas debated whether to share the things he'd only shared a portion of with John Mark and Nowell. He stared at the man beside him. Would he be a different man if he'd had Reverend Solomon for a pa? A better man?

"Sir, I just want to do what's right."

"With what motive?"

"In gratitude for the Lord giving me a second chance."

Reverend Solomon lifted his eyes heavenward. "He is a giver of second chances for certain. He's also permanent. When we are truly His, nothing and no one can snatch us from His hand. When you make mistakes, and you will, you will remain His. Held forever in His grasp from now through eternity. Someday He'll call you home, and you will no longer face the temptations you face here. Until then, steady reliance on Him, keeping our gaze upon Jesus at all times, constant prayer, worship, and time in the Word and in fellowship with others will assist in living the life that would glorify Him."

"I've professed that faith in Him. I do believe all those things about Jesus dying and raising again. I have repented and have done my utmost best to turn from my sin."

"Then I would say that while a man's salvation is between him and the Lord, from my best knowledge of what you are telling me, you are His."

The tears formed in Silas's eyes, tears he'd not allow anyone—not even the reverend—to see. He swallowed hard and took a deep breath as the emotion washed over him. "Thank you, sir. For everything."

Silas rode into town after meeting with Reverend Solomon to warn John Mark the Farris Hill Gang had arrived in Poplar Springs. While that thought greatly concerned him, his heart was lighter than it had been in a long time thanks to Reverend Solomon.

CHAPTER TWENTY-TWO

UNFORTUNATELY, THE EXTENSIVE HOURS riding the ranch gave him too much time to think. Ponder Amaya's rejection. Contemplate the visit from the gang. Remind himself of the hurt he'd caused Oma and his struggle to forgive himself. Reflect on Reverend Solomon's wise words.

Silas checked on the fence on the far side of his ranch. The area, surrounded by a grove of aspen trees, wasn't far from town. If his house hadn't already been built when he purchased the land, he would have built it on this small spread. The view of the mountains was breathtaking from any place on his acreage, but this area had a perfect view of the tallest peak with its snow-covered height adding to its majesty.

An old sheepherder's wagon sagged by the creek on the left-hand side. Silas had meant to inspect it and see if there was anything worthy of saving, but hadn't yet found the time. At some point, the bottom portion of it had been painted green and the spoked wheels red, but now much of the paint had chipped. The door, also once green, boasted weathered and splintered wood and a missing hinge. The stovepipe leaned to the right, and one of the four wheels was missing most of its spokes.

He passed by it on occasion when he needed to mend a fence or herd his growing number of cattle toward this end of his property. Someone, probably the herder himself, had built a wide four-step ladder to access the wagon, but it too was in severe disrepair with one rung missing. Two old barrels lay tipped over on the ground outside the wagon, and a rusted tin can thrown haphazardly nearby indicated the numerous years that had passed since someone resided in the rickety abode.

The mode of transportation likely had a story to tell. Maybe a Basque family resided there while herding their sheep. Or maybe a reclusive, elderly man once called it home.

Silas was about to continue riding until he noticed something different about the sheepherder's wagon. A meager stack of canned goods located at the rear of it caught his attention. He rode closer, noting they'd been stacked. But it wasn't the arrangement of the cans that drew his eye.

It was the fact the cans were not rusted.

He rested his hand on his revolver. Had a squatter taken up residence?

In the wilds of Wyoming, it could be anyone. An innocent vagabond or a criminal hiding from the law. Wisdom dictated he ride into town and fetch John Mark or the sheriff.

Curiosity dictated otherwise.

Besides, Silas had never feared the unknown, and he for certain didn't fear criminals.

The wagon creaked. Not once, but twice.

Was someone inside?

Could be something. Could be nothing.

Silas scanned the area, dismounted, and strode to the door of the wagon and knocked. He pressed his ear to the door and heard coughing, muffled voices, and more creaks and groans from within the wagon. He knocked again, then stepped back.

The door opened slightly. "Owen?" a young voice asked.

"It's Silas."

"Silas?" The door shut again and he heard whimpering followed by a "shh."

Something hard hit his leg then, followed by several more items rapidly pummeling him. He winced when something pelted him in the lower back.

Silas spun around, hand on his revolver.

A young boy stood throwing rocks at him with the aim and speed that rivaled even the best baseball player at the last Poplar Springs town celebration.

"Stop!" he bellowed, his voice echoing throughout the area. Silas regretted the harshness in his voice when he saw the boy drop to the ground and cover his head with his hands.

The door to the wagon opened again, and a young girl peeked her head out. "Owen?"

The young boy, presumably Owen, lifted his head slightly enough so one eyeball peered at Silas and the girl. "It's okay, Effie. Go back inside."

"Is he a bad man?" Effie asked.

"No, I won't hurt you," Silas answered before Owen could.

A hoarse cough sounded again, and Effie closed the door.

"Son, I'm not going to hurt you. I just needed you to stop throwing rocks. You could cause some serious harm."

"We're not going back," Owen murmured.

Back where?

Silas crouched to Owen's level. A blue eye peered at him, but the boy said nothing.

"Was that your sister in the wagon?"

A slight nod.

"Can I talk to you a minute? Man to man?"

Owen unfolded his arms and slowly placed them at his sides, a wary expression on his face. Stringy, matted blond hair and an unbathed body smell greeted Silas.

Where were the child's parents? And why had they neglected him?

"Owen...can I call you Owen?"

"Yes, sir."

"I'm Silas. Silas McFadden." He offered a hand and Owen shook it. "Are you and your sister living in the wagon?"

The boy blinked and shrugged his thin shoulders. "Yes, and Dudley."

Silas blew out the breath he'd been holding. Good. It sounded like an adult at least resided with them, although whoever the adult was needed to mend Owen's shirt. Silas counted three holes just in the front of it. He perused the area again noting a pile of three unopened food cans. Obviously from the boy's appearance, food was scarce. Was there more in the wagon?

"Owen?"

"It's all right, Effie."

"Can we come out?"

"Yes."

When the wagon door swung wide open, Silas caught a glimpse of the wagon's dilapidated interior. While a rusted stove stood in the corner, there was nothing else but a quilt, a dirty rug, and a few more food cans.

Silas stood to assist the girl, who wore a stained dress and two shoes, one which was so worn he could see her toes. Her tangled blonde hair hung in greasy clumps, and she swiped it from her eyes with her hands. "I gotta get Dudley." She turned, then stood at the top of the stairs, attempting to lift a much younger boy, her emaciated arms straining at the weight.

"Here, let me help."

The youngest boy, his size indicating he wasn't much older than a baby, coughed violently, causing green mucus to flow freely from his nose. Large brown eyes stared at Silas and nearly-black uncombed hair hung past his ears. Silas lifted the boy and set him carefully on the ground.

The boy didn't resist. Silas could feel the heat of fever radiating from him. "This little one is sick," he said, more to himself than to the other children.

"His name is Dudley," said Effie. She rushed to his side, patted his head, and placed a dingy quilt over him. "He shakes a lot. I think he's cold."

"That's Dudley?" So much for thinking the children had an adult caregiver.

Silas knelt beside him, concerned for the young boy who shook with fever. The sooner he fetched Doc, the better.

"He's our brother." Effie placed a hand on his arm. "It's all right, Dudley."

"We need to fetch Doc." Silas removed his canteen from his saddle gab and lifted it to Dudley's lips. The boy guzzled the water.

"No. We can take care of ourselves. Don't need no doctor," declared Owen. He stood, hands on his hips. "Please, sir. Just leave us be. We aren't hurting no one."

Effie's gaze traveled toward the pile of cans.

"How did you get the food?" Silas asked.

Owen shifted. "Don't rightly know."

Effie's blue eyes widened, and she again swiped a greasy hair from her cheek. "Owen," she said.

"Did you take it?" Silas attempted to make his tone as neutral as possible.

"Maybe."

"The Bible tells us stealing is wrong." Even as Silas said the words, glimpses of his own past haunted him. He hadn't cared in the slightest what God's Word said.

"Ain't wrong if you're starving," said Effie.

"It's never right to take things that don't belong to you."

Owen cowered, his shoulders slumping. "You gonna punish us for it?"

"No, son, I'm not. But you should know it's never right."

Effie wrapped her arms around herself. "I told him that."

210

"We'll pay for it one way or another."

Silas sighed. "Are you the one who broke into the mercantile the other night?"

Owen said nothing, and Effie gasped. "How'd you know?"

"The food pile over yonder looks just like the food missing from the mercantile."

Tears slid down Effie's face. "Are you gonna tell the sheriff?"

"If you do," said Owen, "I'll go to jail, but I won't let you take Effie and Dudley."

Spoken like the protective older brother Owen likely was. "You won't have to go to jail, Owen, but the right thing to do is pay the people you stole it from. Make amends."

Dudley coughed again, and Effie rushed to his side.

Silas untethered his horse. "Right now we need to get Dudley some medical care. Are there any adults here?"

"No," Owen and Effie chorused.

"All right. I live not far from here. We'll go to my place and I'll have someone fetch the doc."

Effie stood beside him. "We're gonna go with you, mister?"

"Yes, and we'll see to it that Dudley gets some medicine and you two get something to eat.

Owen rubbed his stomach. A fleeting look of indecision crossed his face. "All right, we'll come with you. But if you hurt my sister or brother..." he balled his fists.

"No one is going to hurt any of you," Silas said, placing a gentle hand on the boy's shoulder. He half expected

Owen to shrug off his hand, but the young boy instead peered up at him, his brow furrowing.

"No one? Not even him?"

Silas wasn't sure whom Owen referenced, but his heart broke for what these children had likely endured. "Not even him," he promised, hoping he could keep his word.

They mounted the horse, and Silas took advantage of the silence to lift his petitions to the Lord for wisdom and guidance.

Several minutes later, they arrived at the house. Thankfully, Barney was near the barn when they arrived. "Can you fetch Doc, Amaya, John Mark, and Reverend Fleming?" he asked his hired hand.

Barney scrutinized the children, then turned his focus to Silas. "What do you want me to tell them?"

"Just that I need their assistance at the ranch." Protectiveness toward the children settled over him. He'd do what he could to keep them safe until John Mark or Winslow found their parents. "We don't need rumors starting," he added as Barney mounted his own horse. "Keep it under your hat about the children."

"Sure thing, boss."

Dudley coughed again, the hoarse bark unrelenting as the little boy's body shook. "We need to get you inside." Silas carried him to the extra bedroom and covered him with the thin blanket.

"Wow, I like this house." Effie ran her hand along the side of the stove, then sat in the rocking chair by the unlit fireplace. "Is this your place, mister?"

"It is, and you can call me Silas."

But Effie wasn't listening. Instead she rocked forward and back in the chair, wearing the first smile Silas had seen since meeting her.

"How old are you, Effie?"

"Six, and Owen is seven, and Dudley is three."

Owen scowled. "Don't tell him so much about us."

"Why not?" asked Effie, her short legs coming off the ground as she nearly rocked the chair too far back.

"Owen, did you see the barn when we arrived?"

"Yes."

"Beyond it just a few paces is the chicken coop. Would you take this," Silas handed him the metal bowl from the table, "and collect some eggs? I'll make us some grub."

Effie stilled even as the rocking chair continued its motion. Seconds ticked by. "Can they be scrambled eggs?" she finally asked.

"Sure."

Owen clutched the bowl. "Do you think there'll be enough eggs for a big meal?"

"I think so. I haven't yet had the opportunity to collect the eggs, so there should be a fair amount."

"I really like scrambled eggs," said Effie.

Owen licked his lips. "We all do."

Effie squinted at Silas. "Wait. Are you gonna make the eggs?"

"I am. As a matter of fact, I know how to make about four food items." Silas ticked off the meals on his fingers as he spoke the words. "Eggs, steak, buttered bread, and carrot cake."

"Carrot cake?" Effie flew out of the rocking chair and rushed to his side. "You know how to make cake?"

"I do."

"We like carrot cake. Even more than eggs."

Silas laughed. "Well, we won't have cake today as I'm out of flour, but another time." He thought of Oma's carrot cake recipe and his own stomach growled.

"No matter," said Owen. "We can wait on the cake. I'll go get us them eggs." He scurried out the door and towards the coop.

Effie put her hands on her hips and narrowed her eyes. "If you know how to only make four things, how'd you get so big?"

Silas chuckled. "People feed me. For instance, Mrs. Alvarado. She's always making a lot of food." He thought of the homemade bread she'd sent with him the other day.

"Who's Mrs. Alvarado?"

"She owns the mercantile."

Effie's countenance fell. "Oh. She won't be taking too kindly to us and making us any food since we stoled from her."

Silas knelt to the petite girl's height. "We'll take back the food you and your brothers haven't eaten along with the quilt and offer to work off the food you did eat. We'll also ask for her forgiveness."

A tear trailed Effie's cheek. "Do you think she'll forgive us?"

"Yes, I think she will. Let's go check on Dudley while we wait for Owen to bring the eggs."

Effie followed him to the room where Dudley rested. Loud nasally snores filled the air. Dudley's wide-open mouth and the drool trickling down his chin indicated he was getting some well-needed shut-eye.

Effie covered her mouth with her hand. "Aren't Dudley's snores funny?"

"Yes, they are."

"He's always snored. Even when he was just a young'un."

The way both Effie and Owen proclaimed to be miniature adults tore at Silas's heart. Who had placed such heavy burdens on such young children?

Effie took a step toward Dudley and patted his long dark brown hair. "Once upon a time, me and Owen decided Dudley would be our brother. And we all lived happily ever after."

Except that Silas knew the trio wasn't living happily ever after. But with God's help and the assistance of a few friends, he aimed to change that.

Grandmama hadn't accepted Amaya's nonchalant answer of nothing being out of the ordinary when she asked what was wrong.

After all, Amaya could only hide the pain in her heart from her grandmother's perceptive observations for so long.

"Did I ever tell you about Ganiz?"

Amaya dabbed at her eyes and shook her head. "Ganiz?"

"He was my first husband."

Grandmama had been married before?

"Allow me to explain." Grandmama poured them each a cup of coffee,.

Amaya inhaled, the smoky aroma temporarily calming her.

"Once upon a time, I was in love with a young and dashing man named Ganiz. He was a sheepherder in Nevada. We lived there a brief time before moving to Wyoming." Grandmama paused to take a sip of her coffee. "Ganiz and I were in love. We were both orphans and both enjoyed the solitary lifestyle of living in a sheepherder's wagon. Don't get me wrong, while it was a good life, it was a hard life." She closed her eyes fleetingly before reopening them. "I remember when Ganiz carved important things on the walls of the wagon."

"Important things?"

"Yes. Things like the year his parents moved to America from Spain. Ganiz was born here, and he also carved the date of his birth, the date we met, my birthdate, and the day we married. There was another date carved in the wood, and one day I asked Ganiz what that date meant. He said it was the exact day he knew he loved me." Grandmama stared into the distance as if her memories placed her in that exact moment with Ganiz.

Amaya ruminated on all that Grandmama had told her. Her dear and sweet grandmother had been married before? Did Ma and Pa know? Did she miss the life she once had with Ganiz? What happened to him?

Grandmama's expression dulled, and tears glistened in her eyes. "One day— it was our first day back in the mountains among the timber after residing in town for the winter. There were still patches of snow here and there and especially on the hills and mountains. The temperatures were still a mite bit chilly. But, oh, we could already see that summer would be beautiful as it always was. I longed to see the wildflowers sprout their faces in a few weeks. The mud, well, I never have cottoned to mud, and there was plenty of it. I feared we would get stuck at times, but Ganiz, he never worried about a thing. So composed and unconcerned."

Amaya rested a hand on Grandmama's arm.

"Ganiz loved to hunt, and he was a sure shot, always bringing home deer, rabbit, or pheasant. He said he was going to go towards the slope of the mountains. I said to him, 'Ganiz, please don't go that close to the mountains. There's still plentiful snow and what if you lose your way?' My Ganiz relished adventure and never was one to sit still for long. He gave me a kiss and told me not to agonize, that he would return post haste. It was our last kiss and the last time I saw him alive."

"Grandmama, if this is too painful..."

"It is painful, dear child, but it is a story that must be told, especially to you." Grandmama dabbed at her eyes. "I was pregnant with your father at the time and didn't do well with the pregnancy. The doctor told me this should be our only child." Grandmama's lower lip trembled. "I hadn't seen Ganiz for hours, and my spirit was troubled. I prayed and prayed for the Lord to bring back my Ganiz, but it was not His will."

Amaya's own eyes welled with tears. "What happened to him?"

"An avalanche. It buried him and no one found him until all the snow melted. I kept praying."

"I'm so, so sorry."

"I was angry at God for some time. Later, I would realize that the Lord had seen fit to save me and your pa when some fellow sheepherders happened upon us two days later. By that time, I knew for certain something had happened to Ganiz. My fears were confirmed when they found his body."

Grandmama choked a sob. "I couldn't see anything good coming from my predicament. An orphan and now I had no husband. A baby who would grow up without his pa." She shook her head. "I saw nothing good at all. But then one day, I realized my baby and I could have perished on the mountain as well. When they found Ganiz, and we buried him in late July, I couldn't believe he would leave me. Leave *us*. I knew there would never be another love for me. Ever."

"But Grandfather..."

Grandmama's eyes crinkled at the corners. "Ah, yes. I was so sure I would never love again until one day I met a young man at the mercantile in town. He'd moved there recently and was oh so very different from Ganiz. He introduced himself as Iker Alvarado, and I wanted nothing to do with him. But two years later, my heart began to soften, and I realized Iker was a good and kind man. I'd taken in sewing and washing to support your father and me, and of course, the church assisted when they could. Iker had a heart of generosity. There were times I couldn't pay for the necessary provisions, but Iker would not hear of it. He would sneak the items into the crate and send me on my way, with him carrying the crate, of course. He was slim and wiry, just barely taller than me, and oh so handsome with thick, black hair and those dark brown eyes you inherited. So opposite from Ganiz, who was tall, stocky, and thickset."

Amaya realized her coffee had grown cold from her rapt attention to Grandmama's story, and she poured more for both her and her grandmother. "And you married and lived happily ever after."

"Yes. Iker loved your father as if he were his own, and your father adored Iker from the beginning. Those two are more alike than if your pa had been born to Iker. He gave us his last name, loved us, cherished us, and never let a day pass that he didn't tell me he loved me. And, oh, how I love my Iker. An ornerier man there never was, but such a benevolent and considerate man. We moved here in 1884 when the town was first incorporated."

Amaya set her coffee cup on the nearby table and hugged Grandmama. "Thank you for sharing that with me."

"You are most welcome, but I must admit have an ulterior reason for doing so."

"Oh?"

"You lost your Russell to a horrific circumstance, and you loved him with all your heart. Now along comes Silas."

"Grandmama, we are only friends."

"Oh, but that sweet boy would like to be more."

How did Grandmama figure Silas cared for her in a way that exceeded friendship?

"Just remember, Amaya, a woman can have a heart big enough for two men and can have love enough for both. Ask me. I know."

CHAPTER TWENTY-THREE

AMAYA RODE BESIDE JOHN Mark, Doc, and Reverend Fleming to Silas's ranch. Barney had been vague when summoning her. Was Silas ill? Why else would Barney fetch Silas's best friend, Doc, and the reverend?

Sorrow clutched her heart. What if something happened to Silas, and she'd never had the chance to tell him she loved him?

The ride took much longer than it usually did or maybe it just seemed that way due to Amaya's uneasiness. She thought again of the conversation she'd had with Grandmama just days ago. The Lord had blessed her with the opportunity to find love again. To open her heart. To possibly share her life with a good and godly man. Why had she not seen before what a blessing that was?

For a moment, she wished she could ride as quickly as she had in the horse race. Silas's face when they'd won flashed through her mind. They'd made an outstanding team that day, taking home the prize purse.

Amaya thought of the way she'd felt in Silas's arms when he'd comforted her after she'd visited Russell's grave. Memories of their time spent together and the friendship they'd developed over the past couple of months endeared him all the more to her.

But it was the realization after speaking with Grandmama that made her recognize she loved him.

Loved him for his strong faith, tender heart, kind and thoughtful gestures, his willingness to help her and Grandmama care for Grandfather, and the way he always offered to eat the overabundance of food Grandmama always prepared.

Then there was his appearance. Secondary, of course, but Silas was a handsome man. Strong and muscular with blue eyes that drew her in. Large in size and in character with a gentle side she'd been privy to on many occasions.

Yes, she loved Silas McFadden.

Now she just needed to be able to tell him.

Not fretting was a struggle, as it oftentimes was, but Amaya did her best to shove the worry aside. *"If you keep your eyes on Jesus, you'll have no room for fretting."* Ma always said. Easier to say than to achieve.

She prayed again, lifting her eyes toward the One who could give her peace.

They rounded the corner to Silas's ranch, proceeded through the gate, and came upon the cabin. Amaya scarcely halted her horse before dismounting and hastening up the two stairs onto the rectangular-shaped porch.

Before she could lift a hand to knock, Silas opened the door.

"Silas!" she breathed, taking a step toward him and nearly colliding with his broad chest.

"Amaya? Is everything all right?"

She searched his face, allowing her gaze to travel over him. He appeared well. "I was worried when you had Barney summon John Mark, Doc, and the reverend."

A smile lit his face. The dapper smile she had grown to love. "Sorry I worried you. It wasn't about me."

"Who are all these people?" An unkempt little girl sidled up next to him.

Amaya released a sigh of relief. "I'm so thankful. I thought..." she paused and peered at the girl. "I'm Amaya."

"I'm Effie. Are you Mr. Silas's wife?"

Heat infused Amaya's face. "I—no—I'm a good friend of his."

Effie tilted her head to one side. "You can come in. My brothers, Owen and Dudley, are here too. But Dudley is sick."

Amaya heard John Mark's chuckle behind her as he and the other men crowded into Silas's house. It was then that she noticed a boy who strongly resembled the girl, but a bit older, sitting at the table consuming food faster than she'd ever seen anyone eat.

"I will need to speak with you all about the children, but we do have a mighty sick young'un in the extra room. Doc, we can wait until you check him before I share with you the details."

Doc nodded and carried his bag toward the room.

Several minutes later, Amaya met the others on the porch.

"Effie, would you check on Dudley for me, please?" The girl hesitantly left Silas's side and wandered inside, turning around to face Amaya and the others several times as she did so.

"I recognize these children," said Reverend Fleming. "When I went to pay a visit to the Wimmer household to invite them to church, they were there. It was from afar, but I reckon it was them. I believe they're the ones he and the missus adopted from the orphanage in Laramie."

"Do you know anything more about them?" John Mark asked.

Reverend Fleming raised a brow. "I am not one to say unkind things about anyone, but neither Mr. Wimmer nor his wife left me with a favorable impression. As I mentioned, I only saw the children from afar, so I couldn't ascertain their condition. If I had..." Reverend Fleming blew out a deep breath. "There was nothing on that day that gave me cause for concern for the children's wellbeing, although seeing them now causes me serious unease."

Doc nodded. "Dudley is quite ill with the croup. Not only that, but I did find a few bruises on his legs. Now, he is a young boy, so this could be perfectly normal, but I'd like to examine the other two before making a judgment."

"You think they may have been abused?" The thought shook Amaya. No child deserved such an atrocity.

Silas explained how he had come upon them after finding them. "They'd been there for a few days, and I believe they were the ones who stole from the mercantile."

"That would make sense," said John Mark. "If they were starving, as they appear to be, they would be desperate. What are your thoughts on the next step to take, Reverend?"

"Obviously we will need to notify the Wimmers. But honestly, based on Doc's findings, I'm of the mind they don't deserve those children. I'll attempt to push my own biases aside, but I say we notify them and then take whatever action necessary to remove them from the home. The Keisels have been hoping to adopt. Perhaps they might be an option."

Everyone agreed with the reverend's suggestion, and his concerns were confirmed after Doc examined Effie and Owen. "Effie does have a few bruises on her upper arms. All of the children are severely malnourished, and Effie has nits in her hair." Doc paused. "The most appalling of all is Owen."

Owen?" Silas asked.

"Yes. The boy has welts in several stages of healing on his upper back consistent with continual beatings with a switch."

Amaya gasped and tears clouded her vision.

Silas clenched his fists at his sides. "Is this Wimmer's doing?"

John Mark placed a hand on Silas's shoulder. "We have no way of knowing that for sure."

"But if the children resided with him..."

Reverend Fleming took a deep breath. "I'll be the first to admit that I'd think the worst of Wimmer. He's an abrasive and contemptible man. But the children did reside at the orphanage before moving to Poplar Springs. Is it possible, Doc, that Owen's wounds could be from that time?"

"It is indeed possible," said Doc. He stroked his gray beard. "But I'm not inclined to think so due to the approximate age of the wounds. They are relatively recent. We don't know the length of time they've lived on their own in the sheep wagon, but it can't be long. In my estimation, those marks are a week or two old at best."

John Mark narrowed his eyes. "Any man who hurts a child should be hanged, or at the very least, locked up for life."

"Agreed," said Silas. "That is *if* we don't get our hands on him first."

"And then the congregation remembered revenge is not ours," Reverend Fleming quipped. "Of course, prayer is our best action. Secondly, I suggest we find a way to nurse the children back to health in safe surroundings. In the meantime, John Mark, you and Winslow should speak with Wimmer. There could be an explanation, or this could have occurred at the orphanage or even at a home between the children residing at the orphanage and with the Wimmers.

"Regardless of the physical wounds, these children are severely malnourished, especially Effie, and that didn't happen just in the couple of days they were on their own." Reverend Fleming took a breath before continuing. "It's likely we will need to see what can be done about rescinding the Wimmers's adoption. If it looks as though we will be successful in that endeavor, I will speak with the Keisels about potentially adopting the children. But only after the Wimmers are no longer their legal guardians."

Everyone agreed to the reverend's proposal. "I like your idea of us nursing the children back to health. Is there someone who could take them temporarily until the matter with the Wimmers is settled?"

"I would be the first to volunteer, but with recently adopting the Chvatal children, the parsonage is crowded, but the missus and I would be happy to take them for a few days."

"Us as well," said John Mark.

Doc nodded. "I like the idea of each of us taking the children for a few days."

"While it will be difficult for them to go from home to home, at least we'll know they're being appropriately cared for." Amaya thought of the mercantile. While the space was limited, she would find a way to fit the children. "Silas, since the children are here now, would you be amenable with keeping them here first?"

"Yes, I was going to suggest that. Why not leave them here for two or three days? Things are temporarily slower on the ranch right now and my men can handle what needs to be done."

Reverend Fleming nodded. "Good. Amaya, why don't you take them next, followed by John Mark, then Doc, and finally, we'll take them. Hopefully justice will move swiftly in this matter if our theory proves accurate."

Silas milked the cow early the next morning and returned to the house. The first night with the children had gone relatively well. Dudley, while coughing throughout the night, was sleeping soundly when Silas checked on him at dawn.

He opened the door and inhaled the aroma of eggs. Owen was sweeping and Effie was at the stove. She stood on a chair stirring something, presumably eggs, in the frypan.

"Effie?"

"Good morning, Mr. Silas. Breakfast will be ready soon."

He set the milk bucket on the table. "Owen, I sure appreciate you sweeping the house this morning. It looks nice."

Owen stood straighter. "Thought you might 'ppreciate it and all."

"I do, very much." Silas strode toward Effie. "I appreciate you making breakfast, Effie, and it smells mighty fine in here, but you're far too young for such a chore."

Effie shook her head. "No, I'm not. I do it all the time at the mean people's house."

"That's 'cause if you don't..." Owen's voice trailed, and he cowered toward the corner.

Silas lifted Effie from the chair. "Here little girls don't have to *make* breakfast. They can help, but it's not their job to make breakfast all by themselves."

Effie's head dropped. "I'm sorry, Mr. Silas." She peered at the stove. "I did get some shells in the frypan, but I'm awfully sorry for it."

Silas saw several shells among the yolks. "It's all right. Those can be removed."

The girl's mouth gaped open. "You're not gonna punish me?"

He crouched to her level. "No, I'm not going to punish you for a mistake. But will you promise me you won't try to make breakfast all by yourself again?"

Effie shrugged. "I do like to cook."

"Yes, and when you're older, you'll be doing a fair amount of cooking." He hoped Mrs. Keisel would be a patient teacher to her new daughter.

"Can I help you when you bake the cake?"

"I will need help with that for certain, especially the icing part."

"Ooh! We like icing, don't we, Owen?"

"Sure thing." He grinned. "Can we stay with you for a few days, Silas?" He and Effie crowded around him.

"Yes, you can." Silas returned to the stove and plucked the shells from the eggs. "Do you remember my friends that were here yesterday for a visit?"

"I remember them," said Effie. "Amaya and the doctor and the reverend and the lawman."

Silas flipped the fried eggs, checking for any more shells. "We all decided you could stay with each of us for a while."

Owen scowled. "But that doesn't sound fun. We'd like to just stay here. I promise I'll sweep, muck out the stalls, and mend the fences."

"And I'll cook..." Effie paused, her eyes wide. "Help you cook, that is. And I'll scrub the laundry, and take care of Dudley, and..."

"You two are hard workers, and I appreciate that. I think you'll enjoy visiting my friends. Amaya's grandma makes the best food, and a whole lot of it. The lawman's name is John Mark, and he has two little boys, one about your age named Ambrose. The reverend also has several children, and Doc's horse had a new foal you'll want to see." Silas removed the pan from the heat. "Reckon you won't want to miss any of those opportunities."

Owen's eyes darted from side to side and he shifted. "What about the mean people?"

"Would that be the Wimmers?"

"Yes. Do we gotta go back to them?"

Silas didn't want to make any promises, but surely after what he and the others suspected, no judge would return the children to those who abused them. "We are going to do our best so you don't."

Chapter Twenty-Four

OWEN, EFFIE, AND DUDLEY apologized for their thievery. Grandmama assured them they were forgiven, but would have to work to pay for the stolen items. Owen and Effie both unloaded the crates and organized the items on the shelves. Dudley sorted the thread by color. After the noonday meal, Amaya accompanied the children to the area in an open field just past the church for hopscotch.

"We played this at the orphanage," said Owen. "'Member that, Effie?"

Effie nodded.

"Can I pway too?" Dudley asked.

"Of course you can," Effie answered before Amaya could reply.

Effie found a stick and drew lines in the shape of a square in the soft dirt. She then wrote the numbers one through seven in the boxes. "You go first, Owen."

Owen didn't need further convincing. He hopped forward on one leg in the first square, then both legs in the next two horizontal squares, then repeated it again. Effie went second, followed by Dudley who did a combination of a teetering hop and an exuberant skipping-motion far beyond the confines of the squares.

Effie giggled and covered her mouth with her hand. "You are silly, Dudley. Come on, I'll show you how to do it.

"Miss Amaya, are you going to take a turn?" Owen asked.

"I believe I will." Bounding through the hopscotch squares brought back fond memories of hours spent playing the game with Zurina.

Amaya's heart broke for the three orphans. She prayed diligently that the Keisels would love them and provide a good home for them.

The following day, Grandmama cinched one of her red aprons around Effie's waist, then handed her the bronze measuring cup. "And then you add the sugar."

Effie obliged, her skinny legs teetering on the chair as she reached over the table and added the next ingredient. "I really love cooking, Grandmama," she said.

Grandmama squeezed her into a hug.

And Amaya realized for the second time that day that she, Grandmama, and Grandfather had almost immediately fallen in love with the orphans.

"I do love gâteau Basque," declared Effie. She took a swipe at the pastry cream batter with her finger.

Dudley giggled. "Can I have some?"

Effie scooped some batter onto a spoon and fed it to Dudley. His eyes rounded. "More, please?"

Grandmama shook her head. "If you two eat all of the batter, there will be none left for making the gâteau Basque."

Amaya planted a kiss on Grandmama's cheek. "I'll open the mercantile this morning."

"Thank you, dear. Effie and I will be down shortly after we finish baking."

"Which might take all day, right, Grandmama?" Effie's beaming countenance lit the entirety of the somewhat drab upper living quarters.

Grandmama laughed. "It just might. Of course, Grandfather knows we're baking today, so he'll be expecting us to bring him some dessert after the noonday meal."

Amaya noticed Owen sitting in one of the chairs observing the ongoings. He was, without question, the most reserved of the three. "Owen and Dudley, would you care to help me in the mercantile today?"

Dudley reached for her hand and glimpsed up at her, curiosity in his expression. Owen pushed in his chair. "Yes, ma'am."

Fifteen minutes later, Amaya waited on several customers as Owen and Dudley played quietly in the corner with some wooden blocks. When the last customer left, she noticed Owen reaching for a book from the sparse offerings for sale on the shelf above a few random toys, including a bag of marbles and a top. Amaya was about to offer to obtain it for him when the thick book toppled into Owen's hands.

She knew the book well.

Owen perched on the floor and opened it to the first page. He bent forward, engrossed in the illustrations.

Amaya had leafed through the pages of *God's Amazing Birds* so often that she'd memorized most of it.

Owen's eyes widened, and he pointed with his finger at the script, his lips moving as he attempted to pronounce the words as he read them. A smile lit his face, and he pulled the book closer before turning the page. "The raw-b-ih-n eats worms. They also eat bugs, nuts, and b-eh-rr..." He paused and attempted to decipher the word again. Finally, he tore his gaze from the book. "Miss Amaya? What is this word?"

She leaned beside him, and he pointed at a word with his dirt-crusted fingernail.

"That word is 'berries.'"

Owen beamed. "The robin eats worms. They also eat bugs, nuts, and berries."

"Good job, Owen. Do you like birds?"

He bobbed his head. "I wish I could hold one. Do people have birds for pets?"

"Some do. I once read a book about a woman with a pet cardinal who lived in an ornate cage in her parlor. Chickens are also birds, so they can sometimes be pets."

Owen wrinkled his nose. "There was a mean chicken at the orphanage. I think I'd rather have a cardinal. What do they look like?"

Amaya flipped through the pages to find an illustration to show Owen.

"I like that bird."

"Do you have a favorite type of bird?"

Owen pinched his chin in between his thumb and finger and peered at the ceiling. "I like all the birds, but woodpeckers are my favorite."

Amaya turned to page eighty-seven where an artist had drawn a woodpecker with its long beak, tapping at a tree. "We definitely have many of those in Wyoming."

Her heart soared that Owen should appreciate birds as much as she did.

"Will you read me this book?"

Amaya began reading. A few moments later, she noticed Dudley was missing. "Where's Dudley?"

"He was sitting here playing with the blocks before I started looking at the book."

Panic rippled through. "Dudley?"

No answer.

Amaya checked behind the counter, at the far end of the store, and in the new living quarters.

Nary a sign of a little boy.

"Owen, can you please go upstairs and see if Dudley is with Grandmama and Effie?"

He reluctantly set the book down and hastened to the stairs.

Amaya's heart pounded, and dread twisted in her gut. Wagons at times traversed the street far too fast, as did horses. Especially in a town like Poplar Springs. If Dudley wasn't paying much mind and ventured into the street...

"Dudley!"

Owen returned from upstairs, stopped halfway down the steps, and shrugged. "No, Dudley didn't go see Grandmama and Effie."

Lord, please help me find him.

And she desired to be a mother someday? Yet she failed to oversee a three-year-old boy placed in her care?

Her throat tightened, and she bit her lip. Where else could he be? She again checked the downstairs living quarters, behind the counter, to the back of the shelves, and in the scanty area where they now kept supplies. No sign of Dudley.

Amaya again lifted her petition to the Lord before grasping the door knob. She needed to check outside. What if he was halfway down the boardwalk by now? What if a nefarious individual had found him? While Poplar Springs was far safer than it had once been according to those who permanently resided here, outlaws still lived and traveled here.

Preparing herself for what she might see, Amaya flung open the door and peered first to the right. Several passersby lined the boardwalk all the while conversing. She glimpsed to the left.

And that's when she saw him.

Grandfather sat in his wheelchair with Dudley on his lap with his wooden blocks. Dudley snuggled against Grandfather as content as a puppy on a rug near the fireplace.

Amaya released the panicked breath she'd been holding. "Dudley, I was so worried about you."

Dudley swung a thin arm around Grandfather's neck. "I wike Grandfather."

Tears burned Amaya's eyes—tears of both gratitude and of joy.

Silas leaned an elbow on the counter in the mercantile. "How did it go with the children?"

"It went well. I almost wanted..."

She stopped mid-sentence, and organized some tins full of buttons. Tins that didn't need organizing.

"And?" he prompted her.

"I just—" she released a sigh, "I just hope the Keisels appreciate what wonderful children they are about to adopt. Owen loves birds, and he and I nearly read the entire *God's Amazing Birds* book after supper. Effie adores cooking with Grandmama, and Dudley, whom I thought I had lost, was actually sitting outside on Grandfather's lap watching the passersby."

Silas wanted to reach across the counter and take her hand in his. He knew somewhat of how she felt, as he too had been drawn to the orphans. "I haven't ever met the Keisels, but I reckon it will be good for the children to have a permanent home, rather than being passed around to several of the townsfolk, no matter how fond of them we've become."

"Yes, you are right. They deserve to have parents." She paused. "On our way to deliver the children to Reverend and Mrs. Fleming's house, Owen spied a nest. I wish I could have taken a photograph with one of those fancy cameras a traveling photographer in Bowman owned. I'd capture the three red-winged blackbird babies in their nest in a photograph and have it to view forever." Her face lit up as she spoke, and her cheeks flushed at the joy that bubbled within her.

Silas's breath caught, as it always did when he found himself thinking of her. Oma told him to find a woman who possessed inner beauty because that was what counted. *"Outer beauty is lovely, but the only thing that lasts forever is a person's character."*

He doubted Amaya would ever be anything but pretty, but she was one of those somewhat rare women he'd encountered who possessed both inner and outer beauty.

"They had this little tuft of grayish hair on their heads, skinny necks, and their chirping and twittering as they awaited their mother's return—" Amaya held a hand to her heart. "But goodness! Listen to me going on and on about birds."

Amaya could talk about nothing but spools of thread and he would still be mesmerized by her. "I'd like to see the baby birds," he said.

"It's just down the road a bit behind the church. If you're not busy this evening perhaps we could..." Amaya paused as she often did when she suggested something with him. Was her mind on Russell? Did she worry she would betray him by spending time with Silas? "I'm sure you're busy with the ranch and helping at the sheriff's office."

"I'm not busy this evening. What time should I stop by?" Even if he was busy, he'd make time for her.

A deeper hue of red covered her face and she cast a glance to the boardwalk. "Six o'clock, perhaps? By then we will have closed the mercantile and I could arrive back in time to assist Grandmama with supper."

"Six o'clock it is."

Silas enjoyed these talks with Amaya when he visited the mercantile, which if he was honest, were much more often than necessary in recent days. He doubted she would ever feel for him what he felt for her given the fact that she'd insinuated there would only be one man in her life, and that man was Russell.

Still, Silas figured he could always use another friend, even if he wanted more than friendship with Amaya. Oma would giggle at his romantic notions, although she was the only other person who had known of Silas's dream of being a husband and father. The dream to have a family. Not that Oma wasn't family enough, for she was. But Silas entertained on numerous occasions the thought of marrying a godly woman, settling down on the ranch, and raising several children.

There was much he knew about Amaya. Like the fact she loved to sing and had a melodious voice. That she had an amazing memory and could quote scripture verses. Or that she had a heart for children and loved birds. That she came to his shoulder in height and was slender and graceful in her movements. Or that her soft brown eyes were perfectly-spaced and were expressive when she was excited about something. Or that she had a habit of pressing on the folds of her skirt although he'd never noticed it wrinkled.

Oh, yes, Silas had noticed much about Amaya Alvarado. He'd lost his heart to her some time ago. But while he cared for her and yearned to someday court her, he knew it was futile to entertain such thoughts. She'd never be interested in anyone other than Russell. She'd made that clear the day he'd walked with her through Bird Haven.

She'd especially never be interested in a man with a past.

"I best go sweep in front while there are no customers." Amaya grabbed the broom. He opened the door for her and followed her out into the sunny afternoon.

"I'll be by at six o'clock."

She smiled at him again, and a peculiar feeling settled in his stomach. "I'll see you at six o'clock, then."

"Yes."

Silas stood there like an awkward school boy. It was then that three men caught Silas's eye.

And something inside him thudded.

They were back.

CHAPTER TWENTY-FIVE

"WELL, WELL, LOOK WHO we found on the dusty streets of Wyoming." Engstrom spit a wad of phlegm onto the boardwalk.

Kylian glared at Silas, his gaze unwavering. "Have you missed us, McFadden? We enjoyed ourselves at your place a few weeks back. Matter of fact, Poplar Springs ain't such a bad place. Maybe we oughta move here."

"Who's your pretty lady?" Hurst leered at Amaya.

Silas's pulse sped and his shoulders tensed. He levied a glare at Hurst and opened his mouth to reprimand Hurst for his uncouth actions. Then thought better of defending Amaya. For if they knew she meant something to him, there could be trouble, especially if they sought revenge.

"She's not *my* pretty lady."

"Didn't look like that to me," scoffed Kylian. "Looked to me like you two was enjoying some pleasant conversation when we rode up."

Silas shrugged. "No way she'd be my pretty lady. Just some woman who works at the mercantile."

"Maybe she oughta be *my* pretty lady." Hurst leered again at Amaya, and Silas barely resisted the urge to set him straight on how he should treat a lady.

These men could *not* know they agitated him. That was the difficult part. In the two years they rode together, they'd all become adept at each other's habits. "She's someone else's pretty lady, that I do know." *Russell's.*

Amaya needed to disappear into the mercantile where she'd be safe.

"Now, what can I do for you fellas?"

"Silas?" Amaya asked, a tremor in her voice.

He touched the brim of his hat. "Thank you, ma'am. I believe we're finished with our discussion. I would be much obliged if you could send someone to fetch me when my order arrives. That will be all."

Amaya's hurt and confusion from his blatant dismissal bothered him. She blinked rapidly and chewed on her lower lip. What must she think of him? She opened her mouth, presumably to speak, but before she could do so, Silas dismissed her with a wave of his hand. "Best you go back to the mercantile."

This time, she pressed her lips in a firm line and crossed her arms across her chest. "I don't know what has..."

"Ma'am, you are no longer needed out here. I've already discussed the order with you. Go back inside where you belong. Now go." His tone was harsh, as he intended, but having to speak to Amaya sharply was arduous.

Amaya narrowed her eyes at him, the hurt deep within their depths. She spun on her heel and nearly stomped in the mercantile, turning to glance at him twice as she did so.

"You sure she ain't your woman?" Hurst asked. "Seems to me she wanted to spend more time with you."

Silas shrugged. "She's not my woman. Like I said, she's someone else's by the name of Russell." He hoped his indifference proved effective.

Engstrom ripped a nail from his thumb and tossed it on the ground. "We been talkin' some more, and we want you to come back and ride with us again."

"You mentioned that the other night at my place, and my answer remains the same. Not going to happen. Sorry, men."

Engstrom, the tallest and most robust of the three, took three strides forward and butted his chest against Silas's. "What? Are you too good for us now, is that it?"

"Just have a different life is all. We've already discussed this. No need to do so again."

"Does the pretty lady know your past?"

"Look, Engstrom, I'm content where I am. You three can ride along."

This time Kylian took a few steps toward him, his thin, wiry frame no threat to anyone, much less Silas. "Seems to me you don't have any rights in telling us what we will and won't do."

Pritchard strode by, hands in his trouser pockets. "Is everything all right here, Silas?"

"It is. Thank you."

From the doubtful expression on Pritchard's face, he didn't believe a word Silas said. That was the nice thing about Pritchard. When he knew there was trouble, he was suave and calm, but should someone need help and the mayor noticed it, he would be the first to volunteer, even if he did so covertly.

"As if someone like you could do anything if there was trouble. What are you, a wannabe lawman?" Hurst's comment toward Pritchard caused all three men to chortle.

Pritchard said nothing, but tipped his hat and went on his way. Silas inwardly chuckled. If they knew what a sure shot Pritchard was, he'd be the last man they would mock.

"We have some news we think you'll want to hear," said Kylian, obviously trying a different tactic. "Maybe you could join us for some whiskey at the..." he stepped back and focused down the street. "The Sticker Weed. Yeah. You could join us there."

"I'm sorry, but no." Silas rarely stepped foot in a saloon since that fateful day years ago unless it was to assist John Mark or Sheriff Winslow.

"You're sorry?" Engstrom asked, uttering a stream of curses that caused a few passersby to take notice. "We been making good money in our venture. A lot more than you'll ever see ranching."

"Money doesn't matter to me."

Kylian narrowed his eyes. "Not anymore?"

Silas regretted that money ever *had* mattered to him. Yes, he needed it to survive and to grow his herd, but his focus on it—and obtaining it under false pretenses in the past—still bothered him. "No, not anymore."

Hurst strutted toward him again. "Let me guess. It's because you claim to have found Jesus?"

"That's exactly what I did."

"Although he didn't find enough of Him because Mc-Fadden here is still temper prone." Engstrom quirked an eyebrow as if to dare Silas to contradict him.

Reverend Solomon's words rang through Silas's mind. *"When we are truly His, nothing and no one can snatch us from His hand. When you make mistakes, and you will, you will remain His. Held forever in His grasp from now through eternity."*

Still, while Silas was now more confident in his salvation, he needed God's help to remain calm and to handle this in a way so as not to provoke the men and, more importantly, not to ruin his Christian witness.

But such a feat would be impossible without the Lord's guidance. He offered a prayer for wisdom, guidance, and a way out of the situation.

"You still worried you'll disappoint ol' Oma? No worries about that now since she's in the ground."

The fury rose within Silas. His breathing came in spurts and he clenched his jaw. These men knew how to aggravate him. "Leave Oma out of this."

"Or what?" Hurst cocked his head to one side. "Three against one. Hmm. Wonder who will win that one?" He rested his hand on his revolver, curling his lip, as a vein throbbed in his prominent forehead. "Don't matter how quick a draw you are, McFadden. If you want to a duel, you'll lose."

"Not interested in a duel."

Hurst's eye twitched. "Lucky for you." He strutted towards Silas. "Now here is how it is. You're a traitor. Because of you, the three of us did unnecessary jail time in Farris Hill. It wasn't no lowly jail like in Westenberg. Let's just say it wasn't pleasant."

"Wasn't pleasant at all," said Kylian, also taking several steps toward Silas.

"Because of that, we aim to exact revenge on you."

Silas's heart pounded. He wasn't concerned about himself, but he *was* concerned about the passersby in the nearby proximity. Amaya and Grandmama inside the mercantile behind them. Gertrude and Mrs. Fleming discussing something outside the church. The mother pushing her baby in the carriage by the millinery. The children playing in the schoolyard. The elderly white-haired man sitting on the bench near the barbershop.

Lord, please keep the innocent bystanders safe. Guide my tongue and my actions.

"Revenge is unnecessary," he found himself saying.

Engstrom shoved Silas in the chest with the heel of his hand. "Oh, but it is necessary."

Silas fought the urge to close his eyes and turn his head at Engstrom's foul breath. A three-day-old dead skunk couldn't smell worse.

Engstrom hissed some curse words under his breath before backing up a few steps.

Hurst placed a hand on Engstrom's shoulder. "We have a deal for you."

He must be firm but cautious. "I'm of no mind to make a deal." Silas's gaze flickered toward the mother with her child. She was only a few paces away now. "Ma'am, please turn around. There's nothing you ought to be seeing here."

The woman dipped her head and veered toward the opposite direction. Silas watched as she ducked inside the millinery.

"All troubled an innocent might get hurt, are you?" Engstrom chortled.

"Oh, he's more than a little troubled an innocent might get hurt. He's as yellow-bellied as they come. I ain't never known a bigger coward than McFadden here." Hurst gritted his teeth, his words seething. "Any man who would leave his friends to get caught and thrown in jail is a rapscallion of the worst kind. You're a leaky mouth who ratted us out to that lawman in Farris Hill."

Silas held up his hands. "I did not rat you out. That lawman discovered your wrongdoings on his own. I just left because I wanted no part of it."

Kylian hit him hard in the shoulder. "We don't know that for sure."

"No," said Hurst. "We don't. But here's what we're gonna do. We're gonna give you another chance. You're gonna join us when we head to Thornsby to rob that train."

"I'm not interested."

It was Hurst's turn to bridge the distance between him and Silas. He shoved Engstrom out of the way and put his face just inches from Silas's. Yes, the man was shorter. Yes, he was less muscled. But he was a callous and despicable outlaw who'd likely taken more than one life during his heinous crimes. "You listen here, McFadden, and you listen good. You will go with us or we will exact revenge. It might be on you when you're not looking and you take a bullet to the back. Or it may be on that pretty lady you claim ain't yours. Or it may be some innocent just walkin' along enjoying the day." Hurst shrugged. "Who knows? Only we do. Now tell me, is that what you want? If someone died at your hands because of your cowardice, would that have pleased Oma?" Hurst released a stream of oaths that burned Silas's ears.

"Hurst..."

"No, you listen to me." Hurst seized a fistful of Silas's shirt in his right hand. "You will listen, and you will do what we say or lives will be lost. And don't be letting your mouth run about our plans." Hurst's eyes bugged, the depravity in their depths clearer than Silas had ever before seen.

Silas's heart pounded in his chest. Could he pretend to proceed with the gang's plans, but in reality alert John Mark and Winslow? Or should he reiterate his refusal to participate in their nefarious scheme in the hopes there would be no repercussions for doing so?

The hammering of his heartbeat in his ears almost caused Silas not to hear Grandmama's gentle words as she exited the mercantile with a plate of gâteau Basque in her hands.

Hurst took a step back, and Silas jerked his head in the direction of the store in an attempt to nonverbally suggest to Grandmama to retreat back inside. If nothing else, Grandmama's ears would burn at the words these three used. But Grandmama only grinned at him, her short stubby legs carrying her towards him at a quicker-than-usual pace.

"Thought you would enjoy some of this today, Silas," she said, arms outstretched and her eyes crinkling at the corners with her broad smile.

"No thank you, ma'am."

As quickly as Grandmama's face shown happiness, disappointment lined her features. "No thank you? Silas what has gotten into you?"

"Yeah, *Silas*, what has gotten into you?" Engstrom mocked Grandmama's words, his harsh tone causing Grandmama to flinch.

"I'm not interested. Maybe another time. Now, please, go back inside the mercantile." Silas hated the harsh tone and the words that must be said to protect those he cared about, especially since Grandmama clearly had no idea why he uttered them.

"Silas..."

Silas released a deep breath. "Look, ma'am, just please leave."

He couldn't look at the elderly woman who had become a surrogate grandmother to him. Couldn't bear to see the pain in her eyes. She hastily retreated back to the mercantile, her shoulders slumped.

"Weren't you just speaking about innocents being in danger?" Engstrom asked.

"I was." Hurst smoothed a hand over his holster.

"That old woman who just offered McFadden something to eat might be another one who loses her life when we exact revenge."

The thought of Grandmama losing her life for any reason, but especially due to his choices, distressed him.

He couldn't let it happen. "When are you planning on carrying out the heist?"

"Now that's more like it," said Kylian. He patted Silas on the back twice. "Right answer, my friend."

"Be ready to ride out in two days. And if you say any word of this to anyone, best you be prepared when we exact our revenge tenfold. There won't be a time when one of us isn't keeping a watch on you." Hurst lowered his voice. "And don't believe something won't happen if you tell the sheriff, 'cause it will." To Kylian and Engstrom he added, "Let's go see what the Sticker Weed has to offer. After that, let's pay ourselves a visit to the brothel."

Silas cringed. That could have been him—visiting the saloon and then the brothel, were it not for the Lord's mercy. And a woman's continual prayers.

Amaya had taken one last look at Silas and fled into the mercantile. Tears fogged her vision and she nearly tripped over the men's boots for sale lined against the far wall. Emotion welled in her throat, and she hastened past Grandmama and up the stairs to her living quarters.

"Amaya?"

She pivoted at the top of the stairs. Grandmama stood below, concern etched in her features.

Amaya choked back the sob surging to the forefront and cleared her throat. "I'll be back in a moment." Her voice wavered, and although she would prefer to keep her distress from her grandmother, such a feat would be nearly impossible.

Besides, Grandmama likely felt the same after she herself was spurned by Silas's words and actions. Amaya clutched the handrail with one hand, lifted her skirts with the other, and trudged back down the steps.

"I don't know what has gotten into that sweet boy, but he must have a good reason."

But even Grandmama's voice didn't sound reassuring.

"Or maybe he's not who we thought he was." The possibility caused a chill in her heart.

As Amaya drew nearer, she witnessed the tears brimming at the corners of Grandmama's eyes. Thankfully no customers were in the mercantile, but if she tilted her head just slightly, Amaya could still see Silas standing outside with the other men.

"I'm not sure his reasons..."

Grandmama's sentence remained unspoken.

"If he arrives this evening to accompany me to see the bird nest behind the church, please tell him I will have to decline his offer as I'm otherwise occupied."

"Otherwise occupied? I won't lie for you, Amaya."

"I'm not asking you to lie. I will be otherwise occupied upstairs penning a letter to Zurina, and as such, will be declining his offer."

Grandmama's expression softened. "All right."

"Thank you. I need but a moment, and then I will return to assist you with the customers." She folded her grandmother into a hug.

The questions clouded her mind. Why had Silas been so quick to dismiss her? Who were the men? And why had he been discourteous to Grandmama as well?

CHAPTER TWENTY-SIX

HEAVINESS WEIGHED ON SILAS'S heart. If only Amaya and Grandmama realized his actions were to protect them. But while he wasn't sure he *could* explain to them without causing more trouble, he would have been much obliged if they would have allowed him to clarify what happened.

Of course, it could be for the best that he hadn't loitered near the mercantile. Especially since he spied Kylian across the street watching him. Knowing Hurst, one of the men would be posted near his place after their visit to the brothel. Silas knew how they operated. He'd once been one of them.

Silas would report the men in a minute if he could be reassured Amaya, Grandmama, and other innocents wouldn't incur the gang's revenge if he did so. He scowled at Kylian and continued on his way, pondering how he could protect those he cared about and prevent a train robbery at the same time.

Lord, reckon I could use some wisdom right about now.

He perched for a moment on the bench outside the post office still noting Kylian following his every move. Wasn't he supposed to be at the brothel?

A used newspaper, likely left by accident on the bench, flapped in the breeze. Were it not for the rock that weighted it, the paper would have long blown away in the warm summer breeze. Silas lifted it and skimmed the headlines of all four pages of the *Poplar Springs Weekly*, a venture created by a Mr. Mayes last year. Several advertisements, including one for a local attorney from Thornsby, who promised to reach Poplar Springs within two days for "critical" cases, one for a pair of men's fine satin calf shoes on sale for a dollar and thirty-five cents at the mercantile instead of their usual two dollar and twenty-five cent price, and Gertrude's Matrimonial Agency offering a five-percent discount until month's end.

On the next page were the weekly happenings, including church services and a listing of the city officers, including Pritchard, five trustees, the city clerk, and city treasurer. More news followed on the nearby Bighorn National Forest having been established several months back in February.

Lastly, a court case was dismissed in Prune Creek, a town over the mountain from Poplar Springs, due to what the judge termed a "complaining witness".

A peek above the paper indicated Kylian continued to watch him. Did the men think they were going to follow Silas's every move? If their intent was to intimidate him, they were sorely mistaken. Silas did need some way to alert John Mark, Winslow, or one of the other deputies about the gang and their intent in Thornsby in two days. But he could wait until the opportune time.

Silas rolled up the paper and replaced it on the seat beside him, covering it with the rock. He had much work ahead of him at the ranch. Work he'd fallen behind on. Cattle to be moved, fences to be mended, and mundane tasks like milking the cow and collecting the eggs from the chicken coop. The garden could use some attention if he expected to have more than a potato or two come harvest time.

Nowell, who should also be working his ranch today, strolled by, Gertrude on his arm. She smiled up at him and fluttered her eyes. Nowell, not even realizing Silas was sitting on the bench in front of him, lifted Gertrude's hand and kissed it. Gertrude giggled and rested her head on Nowell's shoulder.

A lovelorn and giddy buffoon was all Nowell was. Would his cattle even be ready for market if he stayed in town spending all of his spare time with Gertrude?

Pritchard stood near City Hall speaking with one of the men from the bank. While Silas would incur the gang's suspicion if he visited the sheriff's office, no one would suspect a thing if spoke with Pritchard. Especially if...

Silas grabbed the paper and entered the post office, away from Kylian's watchful eye. Once inside, he asked the clerk for a pencil.

Mr. Lodderman, likely Wyoming's very first settler, happily obliged, then went back to his work sorting mail.

Silas tore off a sizable piece of the *Poplar Springs Weekly* and wrote the words on the narrow white margins:

Men going to rob the train in Thornsby in two days. Am and Gr will be in danger if I tell JM, Win, or No. Alert JM but tell him to keep it under his hat until I know more details.

He paused, turning the paper over as he sought more blank space in which to write.

The men are the ones you saw me speaking with earlier today. Destroy this paper after reading. Si.

Intelligent and vigilant, Pritchard would do what needed to be done. Silas removed his bandana, wrapped the note inside, and exited the post office.

Kylian must have wandered off somewhere, or maybe finally to the brothel, because he'd disappeared from his location across the street. Pritchard remained prattling on like a hen with the banker. They finally finished their conversation, and before Pritchard could find someone else to converse with, Silas purposely strode toward him. "Pritchard."

"Si. What takes you away from your ranch today?"

Silas scanned the area. Kylian inched his way toward them, lurking as he did so.

"Errands and such. Say, Pritchard, would you ask Ina to mend this handkerchief for me? I'd be much obliged seeing how it's my most important one." He handed Pritchard the red kerchief, ensuring the piece of newspaper inside remained intact.

Pritchard arced a fuzzy blond eyebrow, but otherwise remained nonchalant. "Be happy to."

"Isn't this the puny fella you were talking to earlier?" Kylian asked, interrupting the conversation.

Pritchard rocked back on his heels and snapped a suspender with his free hand. "Puny in size maybe, but not in wit."

Silas chuckled at his friend's comment. "That's the truth."

Kylian sneered. "Don't care about your stupid wit."

"Don't worry, I'm not offended. Well, Si, I promised the missus I'd stop by and retrieve some flour on the way home." To Kylian, he added, "I'd say nice to meet you, but frankly it really wasn't that memorable of an experience."

Without another word, Pritchard ambled off, the handkerchief folded in his hand.

"We're watching you, McFadden. Don't do anything dumb. That pretty lady you were talking to? Hurst will be paying her a little visit if you don't behave."

Grandmama pushed Grandfather's wheelchair into the mercantile. "Will you be all right if I take Grandfather for a short stroll?"

"I'll be fine. Enjoy your time."

Attempting to distract herself from the disappointment of Silas's earlier rebuff, Amaya commenced to accomplishing the lengthy list of chores around the mercantile.

The door rattled, and Amaya looked up from unpacking the latest shipment to see one of the men who'd been on the boardwalk speaking with Silas earlier. "May I help you?"

"I'm needing some tobacco and bullets."

Amaya pointed to the far wall which housed the requested merchandise. "You'll find the tobacco on the second shelf and the bullets slightly to the right on the top shelf."

"Much obliged."

His perusal of her lasted longer than necessary, his eyes boring into her and settling on places other than her face. Knots coiled in her belly and fear washed over her. She glanced about, noting the man was the only other person in the mercantile besides herself. A glimpse out the window indicated few people on the boardwalk directly outside of her grandparents' store.

She prayed for Grandmama and Grandfather to return soon from their stroll. or at the very least, another customer to enter the store. With difficulty, Amaya attempted to return her attention to unpacking the crates of goods. The man stared a few more seconds before retreating to the far corner for the items he sought.

Amaya lifted a box of sewing notions from the crate of wares that had been delivered this morning and set it on the shelf near the money box. Bemoaning the visible tremor in her hands, she offered a prayer seeking God's protection. Why she was so nervous around this fellow, she couldn't be sure, other than knowing that if he had ill intent, she would be an easy victim.

Her fingers fumbled the box, and it slipped and crashed to the floor. Amaya stooped to retrieve the items.

"Allow me to help."

She looked up, her face nearly colliding with the man's. His hard, icy blue eyes bored into her, temporarily paralyzing her for a moment. "I—thank you," she stuttered.

He handed her two thimbles and some thread, and she unintentionally flinched.

"Name's Hurst. And you are?"

She hesitated before answering, "Miss Alvarado."

"Pleasure to meet you, Miss Alvarado." Hurst placed the tobacco tin and box of bullets on the counter, then inclined himself toward her, his close proximity unnerving. He averted his gaze to the plate of gâteau Basque Grandmama had made earlier for Silas. The plate he insolently refused. "Mind if I have one?"

"Please do."

The man removed a slice from the plate and shoved an oversized bite into his mouth. He smacked his lips as he chewed the dessert noisily and in a most unrefined manner. "Mighty good stuff. McFadden was a fool to decline it when the old woman offered it to him earlier."

Amaya said nothing, but turned her focus to the window, hoping to alleviate the nausea that broiled in her stomach from watching the man eat.

Hurst downed three more slices, released a revolting belch that echoed inside the mercantile, then wiped his hands on his trousers. "Tell me, how well do you know Silas McFadden?"

An unexpected question.

"Poplar Springs is a small town, so everyone pretty much knows everyone else."

Hurst's peculiar blond mustache—in the shape of two long, slightly inwardly curved strings of disheveled hair on either side of his downturned mouth—twitched. A fuzzy tuft of hair beneath his lower lip and a coarse, unkempt beard crawling up the sides of his chin and toward his ears gave him an ominous appearance. She angled herself away from him.

Hurst stood up straight and removed his hat. Oily dark blond hair clung to his head and dirt marred his high forehead. "I'm sorry, ma'am. I didn't mean to be off-putting. I'm just concerned."

"Concerned?"

He smiled, revealing yellowed misshapen teeth. Ragged chewed nails crusted with dirt and filth tapped in a rhythmic pattern on the counter. "Yes, because of Mr. McFadden."

"Is he in some sort of trouble?"

"Could be." Hurst scanned the room, then inclined himself toward her once again.

Amaya inhaled at the wrong time, nearly gagging on Hurst's musty-smelling breath. She took a step back and waited for him to continue.

"Are you aware Silas was part of an outlaw gang in Texas?"

She gasped. Not the answer she'd been expecting.

A tightness formed in her chest. Silas an outlaw? "Surely you're incorrect."

"Wish I was, ma'am. You see, he was found guilty and sent to do time in the Westenberg County Jail. Ask him next time you see him. 'Course he probably ain't gonna tell the truth, especially if he wants you to think well of him." Hurst shook his head. "Sad shame he committed those crimes. One was a felony."

A numbing chill rippled through her, and her chest tightened. Not Silas. Not the man who had so gently carried Grandfather up and down the stairs. Not the man who took care of three orphan children with such kindness. Not the man who had done all he could to assist her and Grandmama in their time of need. No. She wouldn't believe it. "I highly doubt that."

"Much to my dismay, it is true."

"He's friends with the sheriff. I doubt he would be an outlaw."

A flash of something briefly crossed Hurst's face. Annoyance? Vexation?

He scrutinized her and tweezed the strands of his mustache between his fingers. "Not sure I should share this, but..." Hurst lowered his drawl. "I was hired to locate him and haul him back to Texas for a court hearing on another matter. Apparently, he's a suspect. That discussion you heard earlier? Mr. McFadden won't surrender. It's going to be an unpleasant situation."

While Silas's abrupt and discourteous behavior earlier had both annoyed and saddened her, Amaya struggled to believe he could be—or ever had been—an outlaw.

She computed the total of the purchase and relayed the amount to Hurst.

Hurst removed some coins from his pocket and plunked them on the counter, causing a quarter to roll near the edge before retrieving it. "As a lawman myself, I just want to warn pretty, law-abiding citizens such as yourself to be aware of Mr. McFadden." He shrugged. "He's done time in Westenberg County for theft, and it is a curious state of affairs that he should have such an impressive herd of cattle." He perused the mercantile before his gaze again settled on Amaya. "Be a sad shame if he duped the fine folks of Poplar Springs out of their money as well."

Amaya sucked in a deep breath. She'd ponder all the man said later. But for now, she wished nothing more than to see him leave. "Here's your change." She held out the nickel.

When she dropped it into his hand, he closed his fingers over hers, and his eyes again roamed over her.

Amaya had an immense inclination to flee from this man who caused her apprehension. She jerked her hand away, causing him to offer her a frigid smile that caused the hairs on the back of her neck to stand.

"My dear lady, keep the change." Hurst rolled his hand over hers to return the nickel. "But do be cautious around Silas McFadden. He's not as he seems."

At promptly six o'clock, Silas strode to the mercantile. He needed to explain to Amaya and Grandmama the reason for his abrupt actions earlier. He only hoped they would understand.

The door was locked when he arrived. He knocked, and Grandmama unlocked it, although she didn't invite him in.

"Hello, Grandmama. Is Amaya here? We were going to see the bird nest."

"She must decline your offer as she's otherwise occupied."

A sharp jab of pain squeezed his heart. "Otherwise occupied?"

261

"Yes, and I must see to Grandfather." She dismissed him.

"I can explain about earlier."

"Perhaps later."

Anguish lodged in his throat from the rejection from the two people he'd recently come to care greatly for.

Chapter Twenty-Seven

THE FOLLOWING DAY, AMAYA methodically pushed Grandfather in his wheelchair out the door, and onto the boardwalk. "It's the perfect day for some fresh air," she said, easing the chair around a bowed board. She did her best to push the chair, gripping each side as the rickety chair jostled along the narrow walkway and Grandfather's head lolled. And while Amaya couldn't see his expression, she imagined his smile. His improvement in recent weeks was profound. She and Grandmama thanked the Lord each day for Grandfather's steady recuperation.

The walk to the bank took a mere five minutes, and Amaya's arms strained to swerve the wheelchair into the doorway, the tight fit nearly impossible.

Mr. Oberholtz, the banker, sat at the corner desk. Mr. Gorski, a customer, reclined in a chair while the two talked about cattle prices and Mr. Gorski's need for a loan, while several other customers waited for Mr. Simpson, the lone bank teller, to conduct their business. Amaya recognized all but one, a stooped elderly man with an abundance of wayward gray-white hair who was first in line. He inclined his head toward Mr. Simpson, paired with a numerous-times repeated, "What's that you say?"

Behind the elderly gent was Jolene, who was rumored as having been one of the women Gertrude attempted to arrange a courtship with Silas. She smiled and waved as she, Gertrude, and Doc's wife, Florence, all chatted.

Gertrude took a step toward her and Grandfather. "Oh, hello, Amaya and Mr. Alvarado."

"It seems the bank is a busy establishment today." Florence, an affable woman, about Amaya's mother's age, said.

"Indeed," added Jolene who wore a slim yellow skirt of the latest fashion that hung straight in the front with a fuller back. She clutched a leather handbag with a gold-colored clasp.

A peculiar thought entered Amaya's mind. Had Silas contemplated courting Jolene? Especially now since Amaya had rejected his offer of courtship? With effort, Amaya pushed the thought aside. It shouldn't matter to her, especially since Silas's brash and peculiar behavior yesterday.

Florence discussed something with Grandfather, and he nodded and answered, the clear pronunciation of his words still a struggle. To Amaya, Florence added, "We're to have the children again beginning tomorrow. They are such delights. I hear Mr. and Mrs. Keisel have consulted an attorney for the adoption."

"I'm thrilled to hear that. I know they've wanted to adopt for some time."

"Yes, although Owen, Effie, and Dudley are older than the ages they previously mentioned they'd prefer to adopt."

Gertrude peered out the window. "I heard they only wanted one and a baby at that."

Florence shook her head. "I heard that as well, but be that as it may, perhaps God's will is that they provide a home for these young ones."

The elderly gentleman left the counter and Jolene replaced him. Amaya reached for the money box she'd tucked behind Grandfather. The mercantile had done well in recent days with several folks paying their bills. For the first time in a long time, Grandmama was encouraged they'd make a profit after paying their own debts.

"I do hope the Keisels adopt them," said Amaya. "Those children have been through a lot, likely more than they've let on. It would be a blessing for them to have a permanent home."

Gertrude pressed her skirt. "Nowell said something about them having to be sent back to the orphanage if the Keisels decide to forego the adoption."

"That would be a sad shame." Florence pursed her lips. "If Doc and I were younger, we'd adopt them as our own."

"Reverend and Mrs. Fleming mentioned that if the parsonage had more room, they'd seek to keep them." Amaya thought of the children and how they'd been shuffled between her, Silas, Hannah and John Mark, Doc and Florence, and the Flemings. While such arrangements proved beneficial in light of the children's homelessness, there was no doubt Owen, Effie, and Dudley wondered whether anyone would keep them forever rather than only a few days at a time.

Florence placed a hand on her hip. "Did you hear that the Wimmers are still attempting to have the children returned to them? I say that no judge in his right mind would allow such an atrocity."

"Nowell says they'll likely be rounded up and thrown into jail for their treatment of those children," added Gertrude, who obviously listened intently to every word her betrothed said.

Grandfather watched it all and uttered a word or two, his voice low and the words somewhat garbled. "They can't go back."

Amaya placed a hand on Grandfather's shoulder. "I find it highly doubtful they'll be returned."

"We as a town will fight for them," said Florence.

Gertrude stepped up to the counter next to conduct her business. Amaya turned to briefly peer out the windows with bars on them. Passersby walked down the boardwalk, and wagons rumbled down the main street. She was growing quite fond of this town and was eager for Ma, Pa, and Zurina to move here. While there was considerably more crime here than in Bowman, there were a lot of good people here as well. People like Florence, Gertrude, Hannah and John Mark, the Flemings, Ina and Pritchard, the Pearsons, Sheriff and Mrs. Winslow, and others who truly cared about those who resided in Poplar Springs.

Jolene finished her business as well, and Florence chatted with Mr. Simpson before asking him to deposit the funds she'd brought.

"Are you doing all right, Grandfather?"

Grandfather nodded. While his appearance had much improved in the past weeks, he remained pale, his cheekbones more pronounced, and dark circles underlined his once-vibrant eyes.

Florence just finished with Mr. Simpson, and Amaya was about to push Grandfather's wheelchair closer to the counter when another customer entered through the rear entrance.

An entrance no one used, with the exception of the bank employees.

Two other men followed the latest customer, and Amaya gasped.

"Well, well, Miss Alvarado, is it?" The man known as Hurst strutted up alongside her, revolver pointed in her direction, while one of the other men flipped the wooden *open* sign to *closed* and the third one held a gun on Mr. Oberholtz and Mr. Gorski.

"Please allow us to leave," Florence pleaded.

"Sorry, lady. Well, not really sorry, but no, you can't leave." Hurst chortled before his expression immediately changed to a glower.

He grabbed Amaya's arm and squeezed it, causing her to wince in pain. "All of you, get against that wall."

Amaya pushed Grandfather's wheelchair in the direction Hurst pointed. What did these men want? Why was Silas consorting with them yesterday? Was he one of them? Did they plan to shoot her and the others? Rob the bank?

Two of her questions were answered immediately when one of the others, a tall, thickset man, ordered Mr.

Simpson to put all the money from the drawer and the safe into a burlap sack. "And the gold too. And don't no one move at all or y'all be shot." He spun the revolver, caught it in his grip, and aimed it first at Mr. Oberholtz and Mr. Gorski, then at Amaya, Grandfather, and Florence.

Amaya needed to secure help. And what of Grandfather? Would this cause his health to suffer? *Lord, please protect us, and please give me wisdom. An idea. Anything.*

Seconds, maybe even minutes, passed, before a plan came to her.

"Sir?" she asked Hurst.

"What is it, pretty lady?"

"Can we please let this old man leave?"

"Ain't no one leaving," Hurst growled through his bandana.

"Please. He doesn't understand English as he's Basque and only speaks Spanish. He'll be of no harm."

Hurst's right eye twitched and a muscle in his jaw bunched. "He don't speak English?"

"No, sir. Only Spanish. He's from the Old Country." Did the robbers speak Spanish? What then of her plan?

"And you know this how?"

"Don't believe her none," sneered the third man who kept his attention focused on the ongoings outside the window.

Amaya disregarded his words. There had to be a way to release Grandfather. "I know him because I work at the mercantile, and he shops there with his wife on occasion."

"What's his name?"

"Obtener Ayuda."

Hurst narrowed his eyes and looked up at the ceiling as if attempting to comprehend the name Amaya had given Grandfather— "get help".

"I know some Spanish, and that don't sound like no name," the thickset man said.

Amaya patted Grandfather on the arm. "Señor Ayuda?"

"Sí?"

Grandfather's voice was barely audible, but it had been heard.

The man peering out the window continued to do so. "Don't care what his name is or what language he speaks. Git this done and let's git outa here."

"His wife will be waiting for him at the livery. When she notices he's not there, she may come to the bank." Amaya's heart pounded. Would they believe her story?

Hurst shifted from one foot to another. "All right, we'll let him go, but the rest of you are stayin' here."

"Thank you."

Amaya stood and pushed Grandfather to the front door of the bank. Would he understand that she needed him to get help? Was he cognizant of the hidden words she'd used when she referred to him by a different name?

Hurst gripped her wrist, his strength causing her arm to go numb. "You're stayin' here. Push the old man out the door and get back against the wall or we'll shoot her." He pointed at Florence, and the thickset man held his revolver near her ear.

Amaya trembled beneath his hold on her. "Yes," she said. Hurst released her, and she said to Grandfather, one more time as she pushed his wheelchair out the door, "Adiós, obtener ayuda."

The watchman at the window shut the door, locked it, and shoved Amaya back toward the wall. She stumbled forward and landed hard on her knee before scooting herself once again beside Florence.

Tears burned the back of her throat. God would protect them.

Wouldn't He?

CHAPTER TWENTY-EIGHT

AFTER RECEIVING THE NEWS from Grandfather, it took Silas, John Mark, Winslow, Nowell, Pritchard, and the other two deputies exactly four minutes to plan their strategy and an additional minute for John Mark to lead the prayer for wisdom and that they'd all return home safely to their respective supper tables.

Someone would get hurt or worse if there was a stand-off in the bank. Silas would lure the outlaws away to avoid casualties. He planted his least favorite revolver in the holster at his hip and tucked his Colt in the back waistband of his trousers. Then he strutted toward the rear of the bank with more confidence than he felt. No doubt Kylian or Engstrom would be guarding the front and wouldn't allow entry. But there was a back door, and from what Silas knew of the gang, that was likely how they gained entrance to avoid being noticed.

Thinking like an outlaw was imperative.

At one time, a whoosh of exhilaration flooded Silas when he committed crimes. Now that same whoosh surged through him when he joined the posse to apprehend criminals.

Just another example of how the Lord could take a man and change him for the good.

Silas kicked at a brown-green sagebrush bush behind the buildings. A piece of yellowed paper was trapped in the prickly branches of the bush, and he retrieved it and stuffed it into his trouser pocket to discard later.

Because at this moment, he was on a mission to save the woman he loved and several other innocents trapped in the bank at the hands of his former comrades.

The breeze blew a foul odor through the air, and he gagged at the smell of a dead animal, likely a prairie dog, somewhere in the vicinity. Several old barrels in various states of disrepair were discarded near the back of one of the businesses, along with a crude, haphazardly-built table leaning on three legs near a splintered trough. Pritchard aimed to clean up the filthy area behind all the businesses on the main street. For too long, it had been neglected.

Silas knew the back of the businesses as well as he knew his own ranch. He'd been back here several times for various reasons. Namely to locate an outlaw or a drunkard who figured concealing himself amongst the refuse was a surefire way to avoid the law.

Nowell had tethered Silas's horse to the rail, where three other horses waited, presumably those of the gang. He'd then sauntered off and waited for their carefully-orchestrated plan.

Silas sidled up to the back of the bank, its weathered door in dismal condition compared to the well-maintained front door. Through the thin walls, he could hear activity inside, especially Hurst's harsh tone.

The man had never been known for being inconspicuous, although he'd been successful in many of his endeavors, namely because of his cunning deviousness, accurate aim with his revolver, and horsemanship skills.

Silas drew a deep breath, prayed for the Lord to guide his words and protect the hostages, then slowly opened the door.

In a matter of seconds, the outlaws had their revolvers trained on him.

Silas held up his hands. "Is that any way to treat an old friend?" he asked, hoping his voice sounded somewhat confident.

"What are you doing here, McFadden?" Kylian sneered.

"Saw your horses outside and thought I'd take a gander at what you all are up to." Silas scanned the room and barely contained the emotions that rose to the forefront when he saw Amaya crammed into a corner on the floor with several others.

"Toss your revolver toward me."

Averting his attention back to Hurst, Silas did as requested and unholstered his gun, and with his left hand still in the air, slid it across the wood floor.

Kylian scrambled for it. He held up the weapon and scrutinized it. "This ain't your Colt. Where's your Colt?"

"Don't use it anymore. Found me this one in Colorado. I like it better." Silas would never surrender his Colt unless lives depended on it. He resisted the urge to reassure himself it remained safely tucked in the back of his trouser waistband.

Kylian guffawed. "You always were an idiot, McFadden. Who trades in their Colt for this? Least we ain't gonna fight over who gets it after you meet your demise."

Despite his words to the contrary, Kylian was quick to slip the gun into his own waistband.

A gun was a gun, and even if the smaller and less accurate revolver wasn't Silas's top choice, it *was* a necessary possession for any man who made his home in lawless areas like parts of Wyoming.

Hurst nodded toward Kylian and Engstrom. "Lower your weapons, men. Kylian, keep watch out front. Engstrom, check out back and make sure no one followed our *friend*."

"No one followed me." Silas leaned an elbow on the counter.

Hurst, like the others, wore a bandana over his face. He stalked toward the hostages and motioned for Amaya to stand before yanking her roughly by the arm with his free hand. She cried out softly, Hurst's aggressive grip obviously causing her pain.

With extreme effort, Silas tempered the fury that rose within him. Every muscle in his body tensed, and his heartbeat pounded in his ears, temporarily deafening him.

Hurst's eyes flashed with hostility, and he put his face dangerously close to Amaya's as he barked his intentions. "Here's how it's gonna be. We're gonna ride out of here with the money and with her. If you want these other people to live, you'll allow us passage. And you better make sure no one follows us."

What about Amaya's life? Once Hurst and his gang had no use for her, they'd likely discard her somewhere along their route where she'd succumb to the harsh and desolate Wyoming terrain.

Silas had to agree to allow them to take Amaya if he wanted the other hostages to live? Silas flicked a glance toward Florence, Oberholtz, Gorski, and Simpson. Each and every life was valuable, but Silas wouldn't allow them to sacrifice Amaya for the others.

He quivered with indignation. None of the hostages would lose their lives if he had anything to say about it.

Yet, he couldn't allow Hurst to suspect that Amaya meant something more to him than just another acquaintance. He would endeavor to do whatever it took to discount his feelings for her in Hurst's presence, even if he'd never possessed the skill of pretense. Only with the Lord's help could he be effective with the guise he prayed he could achieve. Silas shrugged. "Why take her?"

Amaya gasped as her terrified expression met his. She blinked rapidly and her shoulders shook. Her pallor matched freshly-fallen snow. How could he communicate to her that his nonchalant attitude was only a façade? Words uttered to save her life? He couldn't let them take her. *Wouldn't* allow them to leave with her, even if it meant sacrificing his own life.

If only Hurst and the gang had never found him. If only they'd been arrested and sent to prison for their various crimes.

"Why take the pretty lady? I'll tell you why. To exact revenge. Or did you forget what you done?"

"Taking her won't exact revenge. She means nothing to me."

Hurst chortled, and Amaya flinched as his obnoxious laugh emanated throughout the room. Then he sobered just as quickly. "You tellin' me that is like me saying I'm a reverend."

Kylian, always somewhat slow in comprehension, added, "You ain't no reverend, and you know it."

"And you're a simple-minded, empty-headed half-wit."

Kylian glowered at Hurst, but said nothing.

Hurst forcefully pulled Amaya closer to him and held his gun on her. Amaya's eyes widened and her eyebrows raised to create horizontal worry lines in her forehead. A lone tear slid down her cheek.

Silas resisted the urge to rush forward and attempt to save Amaya, which he knew would be futile when he met the barrel of Hurst's gun if Kylian and Engstrom didn't shoot him in the back first. Instead, he offered another prayer, unknotted his fists, and did his utmost best to remain calm all the while doubt threatened to seep into his mind.

The pleading look in Amaya's eyes tore at Silas. How could he reassure her in some way that he was an ally rather than an enemy?

Hurst's demands interrupted Silas's thoughts. "Let's get the loot and get out of here."

"Let her go."

Hurst tightened his stronghold, and Amaya released a whimper. The terror flashing in her eyes was nearly Silas's undoing.

"Like I said. She means nothing to me. She works at the mercantile, I see her from time to time when I retrieve provisions. I got my eye on someone else here in town."

Hurst rested his head against Amaya's cheek. She closed her eyes and winced. "She is a comely woman."

"Not as pretty as some. Release her, Hurst. She'll only slow you down. If you aim to make a swift getaway, taking a hostage with you isn't the answer."

"You know how I know you're lying about her not meaning something to you? Because you've always been a fool when it came to life. Always babbling on about human life meanin' something, no matter whose it was. You don't want nothing to happen to any of these people." Hurst waved his gun toward Florence, Oberholtz, Simpson, and Gorski, all of whom remained sitting on the floor. Florence crouched lower and covered her mouth with her hand.

"Can't see why you're wasting precious time arguing with me," said Silas. "Here's how I see it. You want to exact revenge on me? I have a proposition for you."

Engstrom stomped towards him. "You are in no position to give propositions, McFadden."

Hurst chortled again and retained his tight grip on Amaya. "McFadden, McFadden, McFadden. Always thinking you're the leader when you ain't nothin' but a peon. No one really cares what you have to say, especially seeing as how you're nothing but a traitor."

"You want revenge on me? That's easy. But you best hurry yourselves up if you want this heist to be successful. You've drawn the curtains on the windows, and it'll be a matter of time before someone figures something isn't right. For someone so experienced at robbery, you're severely lacking in common sense when it comes to this one."

"Did you just say I was lacking in common sense?" Hurst shouted, his booming voice causing Amaya to recoil.

Silas needed to be careful as to not stir up more ire than necessary. Hurst had always been a tinderbox with a violent temper. Perhaps he should have taken a different approach with him.

Hurst started to get jittery, unable to stand still as he often did when anxious or provoked. As if someone drugged him with strong coffee and kept him up all night for three nights in a row.

Lord, help me not to infuriate him further. Please help me with this volatile situation.

"If you're gonna say something, get on with it!" Hurst shouted, his venomous tone causing Amaya to recoil.

"You keep it noisy like that and folks will hear you." Silas straightened his posture to increase his height, which was significantly taller than any of the three men. "Let the woman go and take me instead. I'll help with the train robbery in Thornsby. You know I'm the best shot you've seen this side of the Mississippi."

Kylian mumbled, "A sure shot *and* big. Always was a dangerous combination."

"Yep, and one that will help make the robbery a success."

"Why would you want to go with us?" Engstrom asked. "You didn't want to when we asked you before. And how is that exacting revenge?"

"I'll ride with you and make amends. It'll be the four of us once again."

"That ain't no revenge." Engstrom waved the gun at the hostages. "We'd be better off to take the woman."

Someone knocked on the door, and the room went silent. Silas knew for this plan to succeed, he needed to hurry. After a few seconds, he continued. "My horse is tethered next to yours at the rail outside. I know the quickest route away from here and a good place to hide where no one will find us. That's a lot more help than what you'll get from the woman." He nodded toward Amaya. "Leave her here. Let's grab the gold and ride off. If you don't like that idea, I could instead delay the law so you can get a head start. When they discover I'm part of the gang and have aided you in your plans, they'll arrest me."

Indecision flickered in Hurst's hardened eyes. He glowered. "Naw, that won't do. That's not enough of a punishment for the likes of your sorry self." Hurst's shoulders heaved and he muttered a string of oaths.

All in the presence of two ladies.

If the Holy Spirit didn't dwell in him, Silas would take revenge on Hurst right now.

Kylian lifted the curtain away from the window and, from the side to avoid being seen by passersby, peered outside. "We best hurry, boss. Some ne'er-do-well is loitering around outside."

Silas inwardly smiled. One could always count on Pritchard.

Hurst released Amaya and shoved her hard towards the wall, she stumbled and struggled to maintain her balance before collapsing to the floor. She rubbed her neck where Hurst had pressed his arm into it. And Silas inwardly grimaced. What he wouldn't give right now to hold her and reassure her. To comfort her and ensure she was all right.

But he unfortunately had other matters to tend to.

Hurst stormed towards Silas, his footsteps thundering across the wood floor. "Kylian, keep your gun on the hostages. Engstrom, keep watch outside." He paused and pulled his bandana down to his chin so only Silas could see his mouth. "As for you, you idiot, I don't trust you for a minute. You prattle on like some ninnyhammer, expecting me and the others to believe you will do the right thing when you ride with us out of here." He expectorated, and a wad of phlegm landed on Silas's right shoulder. "I don't trust you at all, McFadden. You had your chance to be a part of the Farris Hill Gang. To be somebody, instead of a worthless nobody that even his parents didn't want."

A fresh swell of rage rose in Silas. No, his parents hadn't wanted him. Not his pa who left when his ma was pregnant, and not his ma, who saw him as a burden and decided he wasn't worthy of her time or love. Silas took a step closer to Hurst, their faces mere inches from each other. "No, you listen, Hurst." Were it not for the Lord's aid, he would have squandered the opportunity to see these men caught and justice served.

"Want me to start shooting hostages?" Kylian asked, as if such a question were akin to asking if he should hitch horses to a wagon.

"I say we just take the woman and get out of here," seethed Engstrom. "We ain't never took this long during a robbery. Get the woman, get the loot, and let's go!"

Silas didn't dare remove his attention from Hurst, but he could imagine that the prominent vein in Kylian's forehead pulsed with the man's rage.

Hurst held the gun at Silas's forehead. A quick wrangling of a few moves, and Silas could extract it from Hurst rather easily. However, with Kylian and Engstrom, such a feat would be foolish on Silas's part. Besides, he wouldn't risk the hostages. Hurst shoved Silas hard on the shoulder, but it failed to move him.

In the most convincing authoritative tone he could muster, Silas bellowed, "Engstrom, get the money from the safe. Kylian, keep watch on the hostages until we are out of the building. Hurst, grab two of the bags of gold and cash. I'll grab the other two. If we ride toward the east behind the buildings for as long as we can, we'll have some cover. Folks see a bunch of masked men, they'll likely cause a fuss and fetch the sheriff."

Hurst's draw dropped before he quickly collected himself. "You ain't in no position to order us around, McFadden."

"Want the silver too?" asked Silas, ignoring him.

"Naw. It's too heavy. It'll slow us down."

"Listen here, Hurst, do you want my help or not? Let's leave and I'll show you a hideout I discovered while riding on the ranch one day. I'll ride with you to Thornsby and aid you in the train robbery. If you decide to kill me after that, so be it. I will prove to you that I'm serious about making amends and earning your trust."

CHAPTER TWENTY-NINE

WITHOUT AWAITING HURST'S ANSWER, Silas slithered out the back door. He searched up one side of the street and then the other. All quiet, save for Nowell.

He hurried back inside the bank. "Only one man out there. He's a drunkard known for dawdling."

Keeping his gun on those in the room, Hurst backed up and peered outside. "Who is he?"

"Just another drunk. He'll topple over soon."

Nowell teetered on long, lanky legs as he muttered something unintelligible before nearly losing his balance.

Hurst edged back inside and grabbed one of the bags. "You two, grab the other ones. No one else move until we're out of here. Any quick movements and you'll regret it."

Once outside, Hurst hissed, "You best just ride with us. I don't trust you one bit that you won't side with the law." He muttered a stream of oaths describing, in his opinion, what kind of man Silas was.

Silas shrugged. "There are some rock formations that offer plenty of hiding places. Follow me there."

Kylian shook his head. "I don't believe you," he sneered, his face inches from Silas's. "You better not be a

282

traitor again." He pressed his revolver into Silas's chest. "You might be able to fool Hurst, but you can't fool me."

"I appreciate your concern, Kylian. But you men were like brothers to me." Silas paused for effect. "The brothers I never had. The biggest mistake I ever made was turning my back on you. I know you want revenge. And I hope to atone for my actions." Kylian lowered his gun, and Silas poked him in the chest with his finger. "That's what loyalty is, and that's what I plan to do."

"Quit with the sentimentality, McFadden," growled Hurst. "If we don't hurry it ain't gonna matter what revenge we exact."

He hoped—no, prayed—that Amaya would understand this was only an act. That he would never be on the wrong side of the law again. That he cared for her and the others and was only trying to protect them.

Rule number one when riding with the Farris Hill Gang. Ride alongside them and not in front of them. It lessened the chances of being shot in the back.

Silas did his best to veer the men toward the south once they'd traveled east for a good two miles. John Mark, Nowell, Winslow, Pritchard, and the other two deputies would find them within an hour or two.

But Hurst was a stubborn one. He'd unknowingly deviated from the planned route twice. Was he wise to the law's plan? Maybe if Silas suggested they stop and water the horses at the creek, he'd succeed in redirecting their path. "Let's stop and water the horses," he yelled over the thunder of the hooves.

Hurst had lowered his bandana some time back and muttered something Silas couldn't hear. He beckoned his horse even faster, and Silas figured that meant they'd wait to take a break. They passed old man Bezemek's place when Kylian led them to the left.

Finally, after some time, Kylian led along the ridge of reddish-brown cliffs, the area Silas had discussed with John Mark and Winslow. They rode to the top of the canyon where Silas took a gander at the incredible view. Were it not for the circumstance in which he found himself, he might pause and marvel all the more at the fascinating view. Sporadic pine covered rocky terrain, and a glimpse in three of the four directions yielded mostly flat land with gentle hills swelling above the earth. Parts of the craggy interior wall were plush green, while others boasted brown and cream-colored rock layers. "We'll stop here for the night," said Hurst.

"It's only mid-day," argued Engstrom. "I say we ride on."

Hurst shook his head. "No. We'll stop here and look for the perfect hideout."

They tethered their horses and drank from a nearby stream. Engstrom counted the loot. "We done good, men. Some two thousand in gold coins."

"Put that away, you half-wit," growled Kylian.

"It's time to exact some revenge." Hurst held his revolver on Silas. "As we was ridin' out here, I thought to myself that we didn't need you anymore. 'Course, we never did. But you were right. This is as good a place to hide as any, 'cept from what I'm seeing, up ahead appears to be some caves and such."

Silas knew the caves of which Hurst spoke. A short distance away, the holes in the rock formations provided a habitat for animals—and an effective place to hide from the law. Much better than where they now stood.

"I told you I wanted to join you at Thornsby."

"Naw, we don't need you at Thornsby after all."

Kylian and Engstrom drew their guns, the sound causing Hurst to momentarily glance sideways.

Silas took cover behind the rock formations and simultaneously grappled for his revolver. He didn't want to shoot anyone. Didn't want to take a life. But knew he would do what he'd have to in order to defend himself.

Gunshots echoed in the formerly quiet surroundings. A bullet whizzed past his head before a second one hit him in the shoulder.

The pain took him off guard and he willed himself to remain alert. Silas rolled to one side and peered around the rock formations. Hurst, Engstrom, and Kylian drew closer, their goal obvious.

Yes, he was at a disadvantage with having been shot, and never before had Silas's hands shook as he reloaded his Colt. He aimed and returned fire, striking Engstrom.

Another bullet buzzed near Silas's ear, barely missing him. He again returned fire, hitting Hurst.

The pain seared in Silas's shoulder, and he rolled back behind the rocks, his breath coming in gasps. Rock crunched before Kylian rounded the boulder, shoving him before he could react.

Hurst's raucous voice was the last thing Silas heard before everything went black.

⁕

The sun beat down on him, the heat of its relentless rays searing into Silas's exposed skin. Birds circled above him, likely looking for an evening meal. He moistened his parched lips and knew he'd never take water for granted again.

It still surprised him that Hurst and his men hadn't shot him again. They could have solved their need for revenge much quicker with another bullet. Hurst's voice rang in Silas's ears: *"He rolled down the cliffside. Leave him for dead. Won't take long in this heat, especially with him hidden from the road. No one will find him."*

The roll down the cliffside could have killed him as Hurst surmised. But it hadn't. God had protected Silas. He did, however, need to seek shelter from the sun and find water if he was to survive.

Later.

He'd do all of that later. For now, all he wanted was to catch some shuteye. With a prayer on his lips, Silas allowed his eyes to close, and for a brief moment, the pain in nearly every part of his body was an afterthought. Images passed through his mind.

Oma kneeling beside her bed praying for him. Taking his hands in hers and begging him to surrender his life to Jesus.

Amaya and how she felt in his arms. Her lovely face when she smiled at him. Her enthusiasm when they'd walked through Bird Haven at his ranch.

Supper with John Mark, Hannah, Ambrose, and Little Russell. Ambrose pretending to be a sheriff and leaving Little Russell with no choice but to be the outlaw.

Rescuing Owen, Hattie, and Dudley. Hattie at the oven attempting to cook, Owen asking a million curious questions, and Dudley smiling up at Silas. A fleeting thought of what it would be like to be their pa.

Grandmama and Grandfather accepting him like he was their own grandson. Grandmama's fine cooking and how she generously shared it with him.

Nowell and Gertrude and their courtship and how Silas and Amaya had arranged it.

Amaya again and what it would be like to court her. To love and care for her. To start a life with her as his wife. If only she'd have him.

The images continued, rapidly flashing through his mind as if he were watching his entire life including the sad parts. His barely-recognizable ma as she left him behind and never looked back. The children at school taunting him. The gang inviting Silas to be one of them. The inside of a jail cell.

Amaya found it difficult to sleep that night. Thoughts of the robbery and the pain Hurst inflicted replayed through her mind over and over again. She tossed to one side, the tears from both gratitude and thoughts of what might have happened sliding down her cheeks and onto her pillow.

Tears also from the confusion that lingered about Silas being a part of an outlaw gang.

How had she not known who he really was? How had she fallen for the façade he so carefully exhibited?

She, Florence, Mr. Oberholtz, Mr. Gorski, and Mr. Simpson remained in the bank petrified with fear as they waited until believing it was safe enough to emerge from the building. Amaya half expected it to be sunset as the time held captive in the bank seemed much longer than mere minutes.

Grandmama had held her in her arms when Amaya arrived at the mercantile. She'd patted Amaya's hair and prayed in both English and Spanish, thanking the Lord for His protection and mercies over her granddaughter.

Mrs. Fleming had seen Grandfather sitting outside of the bank and pushed his wheelchair to the sheriff's office, where he'd told John Mark about what was happening. She knew no more details, but she prayed for God's protection over the posse who rode out of town to capture the criminals.

Silas among them.

Her heart broke again at the thought of the man she was growing fond of being on the wrong side of the law.

Amaya heard a noise outside her window, which wasn't uncommon, especially given that she lived on Main Street with saloons and a brothel in close proximity. Since she wasn't sleeping at all that night anyway, she might as well see what all the commotion was.

She padded across the floor and, avoiding the left-most square of glass as it remained shattered from a wayward bullet years ago, peered through the window. Expecting to see a drunkard stumbling in the middle of the street, two men from The Sticker Weed in an altercation, or a rambling wagon on its way to its destination, the sight she did see stunned her.

In the moonlight, Amaya observed six men on horseback, two of them each dragging a stretcher with what appeared to be men atop them covered in blankets. She squinted and pressed her nose against the window. Something on one of the men's shirts glinted in the dim light.

A sheriff's badge.

Indeed. She could see now that it was Winslow, John Mark, Nowell, and a short, skinnier figure—Pritchard—and two other men, presumably the other deputies. A horse, being led by Nowell, carried a man slung over the back of it.

Amaya's heartbeat raced. Had they apprehended the outlaws? If so, where was Silas?

The group had passed her line of vision by now, with two of the deputies and the man slung over the horse veering toward the sheriff's office, and the others going straight, presumably to Doc's.

Silas.

Had he survived?

Was he the one on the horse or in one of the stretchers?

Panic seared through her, and she hurriedly replaced her nightgown with a dress, retrieved her wrap, and started downstairs.

Grandmama appeared in the doorway of the downstairs living quarters. "Amaya? What's all the din outside?"

Amaya planted a kiss on Grandmama's cheek. "It was the sheriff and the posse. They've captured the men who robbed the bank. I'll be back in a moment."

"Amaya Erdutza Alvarado, you will not go out at this time of the night by your lonesome."

For this one time, and this one time only, she would disobey Grandmama. "It'll be but a moment." She flung open the door, and bolted through it, her steps quick and light across the boardwalk as she made her way toward Doc's.

Foolish? Perhaps. But she must find out if Silas was all right. Had to ascertain whether he was the man slung over the horse or if he was on one of the stretchers. *Lord, please...*she breathed, her fifth petition to God since first witnessing the group of the men.

The moonlight cast an eerie glow on windows of the businesses, and Amaya shivered. Rowdy yelling and cursing from the saloon across the street nearly caused her to retreat back to the safety of the mercantile, but she forged ahead.

Doc's office was on the same side as the mercantile, and when Amaya arrived, John Mark and Nowell were lifting one of the men from the stretcher. Doc and Florence appeared from the opposite direction. The physician darted toward the door and unlocked it.

Amaya rounded the other side of one of the horses to the other stretcher.

A heavy feeling settled into her stomach, and time slowed to nearly a stop. Silas rested upon the stretcher, head lolled to one side, blood spattered on the blanket that covered him, his breathing shallow. "No!" she gasped, kneeling next to him. She found his hand and held it in hers. No response from him and no indication he was conscious. Dirt smudged his face. A bloody wound on his head and a cut just below his left eye drew her attention.

"Amaya?" A gentle hand grasped her shoulder, and she turned to see John Mark standing above her." We need to get him inside."

She couldn't move, and dizziness swirled through her mind. "No...I can't..."

Arms lifted her to her feet and steadied her. "We have to get him inside so Doc can tend to him."

"But—" Her chest tightened.

John Mark worked around her and, together with Nowell and Pritchard, carried Silas into the infirmary. Amaya remained in the street watching. Praying. Pleading with the Lord.

Nowell returned a moment later and guided her into Doc's office. "Not likely you'll be able to go in there for a bit, but maybe Doc can give you an update as soon as he knows Silas's condition."

Amaya covered her mouth and attempted to restrain the sobs.

John Mark put an arm around her. "Amaya, Doc says he'll likely make it."

"But—how—why?" Had Silas been shot by one of the lawmen? She needed to know what had transpired, but her words wouldn't come. Only grief.

"We need to get you back to the mercantile. This is no time to be out by your lonesome."

"I have to make sure he's all right."

Doc closed the door to where they'd taken Silas, and Amaya attempted to trudge toward it on lethargic feet.

"Come on. Let's get you home."

She paused, looked into the eyes of the man who ought to be home with his family, and begrudgingly acquiesced. John Mark led her out of the building, past the other men, and down the boardwalk.

"I can make it alone," she said, not really knowing why she mentioned such an imprudent suggestion.

John Mark ignored her and continued to walk with her toward the mercantile.

"You need to get home. Hannah will be beside herself with worry."

"As soon as we get you back to the mercantile, I'll be on my way."

John Mark's words left no option for her to disagree. Two men emerged from the saloon, guns aimed toward the sky, their crass words echoing through the night.

A few moments later, Amaya and John Mark reached the mercantile. "Get some rest. You can visit him tomorrow."

The words she wanted—needed—to ask lodged in her throat. She stuttered before finally uttering them. "I don't understand why he was riding with the outlaws."

Grandmama opened the door, and John Mark delivered her safely inside. "Amaya, you need to trust that he's the man you know him to be."

John Mark tipped his hat. "Mrs. Alvarado." He then turned on his heel and disappeared into the night.

Leaving Amaya with no further answers to her lingering questions.

Where was he? Silas attempted to shift, but pain radiated through his shoulder. He groaned, willing the throbbing to subside. Was he still near the cliffs? Silas blinked, then forced his eyes open. Closed them again, then one last time reopened them. He inhaled an unfamiliar odor. Medicine, perhaps?

"Where am I?" he croaked, wishing for a drink of water.

"You're at Doc's office."

An older woman patted his arm, her face blurry.

"Doc's office?"

"Yes. Would you care for some water?"

How had she known?

The woman placed a hand beneath his head and assisted him so he could drink from the cup she offered. He sputtered and choked, causing water to spew from his mouth and dribble down his chin. She rested him back on the pillow and set the pitcher beside him on a table.

She looked familiar. But if so, why couldn't he remember who she was? A haze, much like a fog filled his mind and again clouded his vision when he peered up at her.

The plump woman with gray-brown hair in a bun and a white apron pressed a hand against his forehead. "Good, no fever," she said.

"You...you, who are you?"

"Florence. Doc's wife."

Ah, yes. Florence. She'd been at the bank earlier—or was that yesterday—or several days ago?

"How long have I been here?"

"Two days."

"How—who brought me here?

Florence sat in a chair beside his bed. "John Mark, Winslow, Nowell, and Pritchard hauled your sorry self here." She pursed her lips. "You had me and the others at the bank concerned that you were one of them."

"One of them?"

The woman tilted her head. "The outlaws." There was no malice in her voice, just a matter-of-fact statement.

"An outlaw?"

"Yes. Do you remember the bank robbery?"

The bank robbery. Yes, recollection began to set in. Hurst and his men threatening the customers. He jerked his head toward Florence. "Amaya! Where is she?"

Florence placed a warm hand on his arm. "She's fine, as are the others. Doc will return soon to check on you and the other gentleman. He had to deliver a baby."

He blew out a deep breath. Amaya was fine. *Thank You, Lord.* He needed to explain to her that he wasn't one of Hurst's men. That it was a ploy to capture them. "Where's Amaya?"

"She's been by three times just today, not to mention yesterday."

"She's been by?" The thought gave him hope.

"I'm going to check on the other man. You just rest here, and in a while, we'll see if you can manage to eat something."

"The other man?"

Florence stood, and Silas followed her with his gaze as she walked to a bed beside him.

If Silas remembered correctly, Doc's office was far too small for two beds crammed inside.

He tried to turn onto his left side to get a better view of the other patient, but his shoulder reminded him of the impossibility of such a feat. He bit his lip, hoping to alleviate the pain.

"You've still got that raging fever," Florence was saying to the other patient. The distance between the two beds was so narrow Silas was surprised she could fit between them. "I'll give you some more medicine to reduce the fever, and we'll see what Doc says when he returns." Silas watched from his side-eye as Florence poured some of Dr. Wilhoft's fever reducer from a glass bottle onto a spoon.

He couldn't see the other person, but could hear his shallow breathing.

"Florence?"

The woman turned around and pulled the blankets up to his chin. "Yes, Silas?"

"Who is the other man?"

"One of the outlaws. I believe Doc said his name was Hurst."

Silas jerked upright as the pain ripped through him. He emitted a loud cry and flopped back on the bed.

"Hurst?" His voice sounded like a disgruntled growl in his ears.

"Yes."

"McFadden?" Hurst's raspy voice was barely recognizable.

"I don't want to be in the same room as him." Silas closed his eyes, bit his lip and clutched the side of the uncomfortable mattress in an effort to ease the twinge that radiated down his entire left arm.

"He's not long for this world, so you needn't worry." Florence assisted him with another sip of water. "I have some matters to tend to in the front office. I'll be back momentarily."

"No, don't..." *leave me here with him.*

Bits and pieces of memories clouded his mind. Hurst, Kylian, and Engstrom shooting at him.

Three against one.

Silas returning the gunfire and striking Engstrom. The man falling to the ground, and Silas realizing he'd taken a fatal bullet.

More gunshots. Silas taking cover behind the rocks. A bullet whizzing past his head, then another hitting him in the shoulder. Hurst and Kylian coming closer, firing rapidly as they neared him. Silas crouching behind the rocks and reloading his Colt. Rising and firing with perfect aim and hitting Hurst, not once, but twice.

Rolling down the cliffside.

Hurst and Kylian mounting their horses, leaving him for dead.

No. Silas didn't want to share any space with Hurst.

How and who had found Hurst? How had he survived? Where was Kylian?

Hadn't Winslow once told him that mean people were more robust than the nice ones? If that was true, Florence could be wrong about Hurst. And if she was wrong...

"Florence?"

Silas wanted to be relocated to somewhere far away from Hurst. No telling what the man might do, and Silas didn't have the wherewithal nor the ability to keep guard over himself. Where was John Mark? Nowell? Winslow? Pritchard? Why were they not here watching Hurst? The man could escape again and on his way out the door exact that revenge he was so bent on accomplishing.

Florence either hadn't heard him or chose to ignore him. Likely the former.

"McFadden?"

He could barely hear Hurst's weak and muffled voice above some noise outside on the boardwalk.

"What do you want?" he groaned.

Hurst said nothing, but within minutes, Silas heard the familiar snores of a man who'd once upon a time been his friend.

Daylight streamed through the window. How long had he been asleep?

Doc stood near Silas's bed. "Glad to see you awake, son. Florence went to Pearson's Restaurant to fetch some oatmeal for both you and Hurst."

It hadn't been a nightmare? Hurst *was* in the room?

And Silas had allowed himself to fall asleep?

Doc listened to Silas's heartbeat, checked for a fever, gave him a sip of water, inspected his wound, and gave him some Mexican Mustang Liniment for the pain. "You are doing well. I suspect you'll be up and about in no time."

Silas didn't *feel* well. For one, he was starving.

For two, he wasn't thrilled about his roommate and the harm Hurst could inflict on him if given the chance.

"I remember being shot."

"Yes, twice."

"Twice?"

Doc nodded. "One is more of a graze, but still enough to do some damage."

"Can I move somewhere else?"

The doctor chuckled, his rotund stomach shaking as he did so. "This is as good a place as any for you."

"With Hurst?"

"Don't worry yourself, son. He's not long for this world."

The same thing Florence had said.

"You're sure?"

"Believe me when I tell you that your friends would have my hide and then some if I put you in any danger."

Silas released the breath he'd been holding.

"Florence will be here soon with your breakfast. I have to ride out and tend to Hank's broken leg. Seems he thought he was just a kid again and decided he needed to climb a ladder. Fell plumb off. It's only by God's grace he didn't break more of himself."

"Has Amaya been by?"

"She has. Came in early before the mercantile opened. I suspect she'll be by again later. Perhaps one of these times, she'll actually find you awake. You've had many visitors, but you've always been asleep."

Doc grabbed his bag and left the room before Silas could ask any further questions.

"McFadden?"

Silas turned his head and, for the first time, saw Hurst's still form in the bed next to his. Matted hair clung to Hurst's forehead, and perspiration dotted his entire face.

When Silas didn't answer, Hurst continued. "Kinda ironic you and me in the same infirmary." He drew a breath and winced as he did so. "Did you hear Doc say I'm not long for this world?"

"I did."

If Hurst was expecting sympathy, Silas would be hard-pressed to provide it. Amaya's face flashed before his mind. Hurst roughly imprisoning her in a stronghold, his gun held on her. The thought angered Silas, and he clenched his right fist. If Hurst died today, so be it.

"I ain't sure I wanna die."

"No one wants to die, Hurst, but you didn't give any thought to that when you were shooting at me, or killing those men in Farris Hill, or holding Amaya hostage at the bank." The words came out harsh. Just as Silas intended.

There was only the sound of Hurst's breathing, and for a moment, Silas figured he fell asleep.

"Engstrom is gone. So is Kylian. Both dead." He paused. "I done a lot of bad stuff."

"Yep." There would be no sympathy from Silas if that was what Hurst was seeking.

Hurst released an agonizing cry before calming himself.

Silas's stomach growled. He hoped Florence would be here soon with the oatmeal.

"I know I'm gonna die soon."

"Likely so." But even as Silas attempted callousness, a stirring within his conscience prompted him to react otherwise.

"Do you think Jesus will forgive me?"

Hurst worried about the Lord's forgiveness? Silas turned again to look at Hurst. It wasn't perspiration that streamed down the side of his face, but tears.

Silas's stomach clenched, and he fiddled with the knob on the drawer on the table beside him.

"Do you think he will, Silas? I mean, I done a lot of stuff wrong. I killed...I killed people." Hurst sniffled. "Sure wish I had me a handkerchief right about now."

A squeezing in Silas's chest temporarily made it more difficult to breathe.

"I killed people, I robbed people, I took advantage of women. I hurt them too. I..."

Thankfully when Silas rode with Hurst and his men, they hadn't yet committed the atrocious crimes they one day would.

Hurst's body shook, and Silas suspected it wasn't from the cold or the fever. Would Florence return soon?

"Do you think—do you think Oma prayed for me too?"

A brief, selfish thought entered Silas's mind. Oma would *only* pray for those she loved, and she would *never* love someone like Hurst. But then Silas recalled the day he'd come home from causing mischief and found Oma in front of the fireplace praying. Her wrinkled hands folded and her Bible in her lap.

Oma hadn't realized Silas was there. Just like she rarely knew when she prayed beside her bed. Her hearing had begun to fail in those days. However, Silas heard the words loud and clear as if they'd been spoken yesterday.

"My precious Lord. You desire for no one to perish. You want all to come to repentance. Even those we might not care for or like."

Silas had stood as still as he could, his ear inclined toward her voice, attempting to hear it over the rocking of the chair.

"You tell us to pray for our enemies. Well, Father, that is hard for me at times, and I need to be reminded that You exhort us to do that. If only it was as easy as praying for my precious Silas. Bring him to You, Lord."

Her voice quivered, and Oma had paused, gathering her emotions before continuing. *"My sweet boy is so far from You. Lord, I also pray for those friends of his. Hurst, Kylian, and Engstrom. Where they went wrong, I don't know. It's not too late for them, and I pray that You, in Your grace, would also bring them to You."*

"Naw, Oma wouldn't pray for someone like me. I wasn't never kind to her."

Hurst's voice interrupted Silas's memory.

"She did pray for you. Kylian and Engstrom too."

"She did?"

As much as Silas didn't want to admit to it, Oma had cared about his friends. Had cared for someone like Hurst enough to pray for him.

"Do you think Jesus heard her?"

Silas learned long ago that even when he wanted nothing to do with the ways of the Lord, He heard all prayers. "Yes, I'm sure He did."

Hurst was silent for a moment, and Silas chastised himself for being thankful for some peace and quiet. But that niggling feeling in his stomach started up again, and it wasn't hunger.

"Doc says I ain't gonna make it."

"Yes, you mentioned that."

"If I ain't gonna make it, then that means I'm going to have to see Jesus."

Hurst was staring at him now, one eye partially obscured by the pillow.

"McFadden?"

"Yes?"

"I'm so sorry for all that I done. I wish I could go back and make amends."

Silas had his own regrets, but thankfully he hadn't ever killed anyone or harmed a woman.

"Will Jesus forgive me?"

Verses from God's Word lingered on the edge of Silas's mind. "Hurst..."

"Look, McFadden, I know I haven't treated you well. When you turned your back on us in Farris Hill, well..." he paused, his speaking becoming more labored. "You were supposed to be one of us. But then you went off and found Jesus."

Oma's prayer had been answered. Had it not been for the Lord's mercy, where would Silas be? He deserved to have been left to his own inclination. If he had been, would he have become a hardened criminal like Hurst, Kylian, and Engstrom?

The Lord's mercy.

The Lord's grace.

The Lord's forgiveness.

The realization hit Silas in the gut. What if Hurst needed that same mercy? That same grace? That same forgiveness?

From the Lord?

From him?

It wasn't easy to see things the Lord's way. Silas didn't want to care if Hurst perished for eternity. But the truth was, he *did* care.

Although such an awareness was a difficult bite to swallow.

"McFadden?"

"I'm here, Hurst."

Hurst released a breath and sniffled again.

"God wants no one to perish. That's what it says in His Word."

"Perish?"

"He wants everyone to spend eternity with Him."

Silas thought of Reverend Solomon. Wouldn't that have been something if the man paid a visit to Poplar Springs just now. Silas wasn't equipped to be a preacher.

"I don't want to perish. I don't even want to die."

In the hours after chores, Silas spent a fair amount of time reading the Bible. He had a hunger for the Word of

God, and if he was honest with himself, wanted to recoup that lost time he'd so willingly thrown away during his rebellious years.

"Have you asked God to forgive you?"

"Never figured you to be a preacher, McFadden." His voice wavered. "No, reckon I ain't never asked Him to forgive me. Thought He'd never be interested in the likes of me."

"He cares about you, more than you know."

"But what if He don't forgive me?"

Silas searched into the far recesses of his foggy mind. He was tired. Exhausted. In pain. Did he really have to answer Hurst's multitude of questions? "If you are sincere in your request, He will forgive you."

Hurst cleared his throat. "I used to want to be you. To have someone care about me the way Oma cared about you. Ain't no one ever really cared about me. I used to wish I had someone who loved me the way she loved you. Someone to pray for me."

Throughout the time Silas had known Hurst, he'd found him to be manipulative and insincere. Was that the case this time? The man just wanted reassurance he wasn't going to spend eternity apart from Jesus? Would Hurst still be this worried if he wasn't going to die soon?

That niggling in his stomach returned. The verse from Romans that Reverend Solomon shared, entered his mind. "Hurst, if you are sincere in your words, the Lord will forgive you. If you confess with your mouth and believe that Jesus is Lord, you will be saved."

"Reckon I'm gonna do that." Hurst's voice wavered. "I believe in Jesus, and I'm gonna ask Him to forgive me for all I done. All the bad stuff. Will you help me talk to Him, McFadden?" His voice broke, and his body shook. "Please?"

"I'll help you."

It was the first time Silas had ever helped lead anyone to Christ. As were all things, this too was in the Lord's timing as Hurst passed that evening.

Doc had just finished checking Silas's wounds when Grandmama arrived. The aroma of sausage, cabbage, and vegetables filled the air, and Silas inhaled a deep breath. Surely if Grandmama was willing to bring Basque vegetable soup, she had forgiven him.

At least he hoped.

Doc took the bowl from her, and placed it on the table beside Silas's bed. "It's good to see you today, Mrs. Alvarado. How is Iker?

"He's doing well today, although I would appreciate it if you could stop by and check on him. If nothing else, he'd enjoy the company."

"I'd be happy to do that right now, if that would be amenable to you."

"Thank you, Doc. He just woke from his nap, so this time is as good as any."

Doc retrieved his leather bag, stuffed the stethoscope and a few other items inside, and nodded at both Grandmama and Silas. "I'll be back soon, Silas. Mrs. Alvarado, please fetch me immediately if our patient here decides to escape." A glint shone in the doctor's eyes.

"You'll be the first to know if he attempts such a feat."
Grandmama pressed her lips into a firm line. "Although
he'd better not."

The fact that Grandmama was her jovial self gave Silas
hope. Had she stopped by while he slept as so many others had? She hadn't the liberty to visit freely with caring
for Grandfather and the mercantile, but the yearning
that she might do so constantly lingered in his mind.

There was only one other person he hoped would forgive him more.

Grandmama took a seat in the chair next to his bed and
removed the brightly-colored red, blue, and green scarf
from her head, exposing her thinning, curly gray hair.

The scent of the robust soup alone caused the ache
in his shoulder to feel better. It overpowered the usual
medicinal scent of the infirmary, and Silas breathed in
the aroma and closed his eyes. When he opened them
again, Grandmama was stirring the soup with a spoon.
"I thought you might need some nourishment."

"Oh, yes!" Silas plumped up the flattened pillow and
held out his hands for the bowl. "The food from Pearson's Restaurant is tasty, but there's nothing like your
Basque vegetable soup." He paused. "Except for your
gâteau Basque."

Grandmama arched a gray brow. "I'll allow you to eat,
but then I'd appreciate some answers."

Silas would provide answers without eating, but it
would make life a whole lot easier if he could do so with
a full belly. "Yes, ma'am."

She handed him the bowl, and the heat seeped through
to his hands. While the hot summer day didn't necessi-

tate warm foods, he'd not complain. He bowed his head and thanked the Lord for Grandmama's visit, for the food she brought, and for keeping Amaya safe. Then he appealed to God for Grandmama's mercy.

Even as a young'un, Silas had always been bigger and stronger than other boys his age. Oma mentioned on several occasions that he reminded her of his grandpa. Tall, muscular, brawny, hale, and hearty. There were numerous times when he and Oma were so poor there was but a loaf of bread, watery broth, and a few carrots from the garden to sustain them. Unbeknownst to her, Silas witnessed Oma deferring her portion to him one time. A generosity he could not accept. She'd finally acquiesced and ate her meager share, even as Silas attempted not to devour his all in two bites.

After that day, Silas determined they'd never starve again. Oma taught him how to hunt at a young age, and he regularly brought home white-tailed deer and squirrels. Unfortunately, there were times when he came home empty-handed. On those days, rather than witness the disappointment in Oma's eyes—disappointment she tried so hard to hide—he'd "borrowed" some vegetables from a neighbor's garden. It amazed him how easy it was to steal and not get caught.

An ability that served a purpose well in his dark days of fraternizing with the gang.

He took a bite, then another, then a third. The meal soothed him in ways he couldn't articulate. Silas relished the taste of the onions, potatoes, and sausage. When he finished, he stretched toward the table to set the bowl on it. "Thank you, Grandmama."

"I'm honored you found it to be a delectable meal." A spark lit her brown eyes, and Silas breathed a sigh of relief. Perhaps she would forgive him, for the thought of losing two grandmas was too painful to contemplate.

Her forehead creased. "Now tell me, dear boy, why did you do what you did?"

"It was the only way I could think of to protect you and Amaya. Vile and calloused, these men planned to stop at nothing to administer revenge."

"Revenge?"

Silas had hoped he wouldn't have to share the sordid details of a past long left behind. He knew he was not the man he was. More importantly, the Lord knew he was not the man he used to be, but would Grandmama and Amaya believe it? Could he convince them he'd changed? Would they accept it?

"Grandmama, I know I hurt you and Amaya, and I will regret that to my dying day. But there was no other way I could think of that would make the gang believe you meant nothing to me. If they knew how much I cared about you both, they would do something to harm you—to spite me."

"The men...they were friends of yours?"

It pained him to admit they'd once been friends, but if he wanted Grandmama's forgiveness, and more importantly, if he desired to honor the Lord with the second chance he'd been given, honesty was crucial. "Yes. I..." It was as if a heavy stone had settled in his belly. A mixture of emotions swarmed through him: guilt, regret, anger at himself for being so foolish those years ago, gratitude that Hurst surrendered his life to Christ, craving to be accepted by Grandmama, the woman who'd become a surrogate grandmother to him, and pleading with the Lord that he and Amaya's friendship would be restored.

Grandmama's eyes misted from unshed tears.

"I was once a man who didn't care what anyone thought. I stole things that didn't belong to me. I lived for myself. In doing so, I hurt and disappointed Oma and the Lord. Eventually, I decided that life wasn't for me anymore and turned my back on the gang. Their outrage lasted the several years it took them to find me. They vowed revenge, and they knew that one of the easiest ways to achieve that was to harm someone I loved. I'm sorry, Grandmama. It was the only way I saw fit to do what I did. Will you please forgive me?" His throat tightened. Had there been another way?

Grandmama scooted her chair toward him, scraping it across the floor. She reached a wrinkled hand toward his arm. "My dear boy. You are forgiven."

He expelled the breath he'd been holding and fought to choke back the emotion that rose within him. "You forgive me?"

"I do. And so will Amaya. But you must explain this to her as well. I'll not do it for you."

"I wouldn't expect you to."

Grandmama's hand remained on his arm, comforting him like Oma's had all those times in his youth when he only wanted other kids at school to accept him. Not call him names because his parents weren't married when they decided to bring him into this world.

"She considers you a friend, and Amaya is a tender soul."

Silas knew that well. It was one of the things he loved about her.

"Thank you, Grandmama. I'll be forever in your debt."

That familiar twinkle shone in her eyes once again. "In that case, I do have a few chores I'd like to ask of you once you've recovered."

Amaya finished with a customer when Grandmama returned to the mercantile, empty bowl in hand. She wanted to ask how it went with Silas. But then, did she really want to know? Thoughts warred within her about his actions and his supposed connection to a nefarious outlaw gang, who, according to John Mark, had been wanted in several states.

Silas wasn't the man she thought he was.

"Hello, Grandmama. Doc visited and said Grandfather has improved much. He's taking a nap now, but I suspect he'll want to go for a ride in his wheelchair later."

"Have you spoken any more to Mayor Pritchard about the hero celebration planned in honor of him and the others?"

Amaya shook her head. "No, but I know Grandfather will be so honored."

Grandmama hung up her scarf on the nail hook and put the apron around her waist. "I visited with Silas."

Amaya knew she had, but she didn't say as much. "Oh?"

"I think you ought to go see him."

"I've tried several times, but each time he's been asleep."

"Doc says he'll be leaving for home in two days. Best catch him before that boy decides he has to herd cattle and fix the fence the day he returns to the ranch."

If the pain in her heart at Silas's betrayal hadn't taken up such a significant residency, she might have laughed and nodded at Grandmama's response. After all, Silas took his ranching seriously and undoubtedly was antsy and eager to return to his land.

But what if he had truly decided to ride with the outlaws and partake in the train robbery? What if he had decided to leave you, his ranch, and Poplar Springs behind? What then? Amaya fixed a crooked tin on the shelf. No sense in wondering about what was thankfully not to be. She returned her attention to Grandmama. "Did he have a reasonable explanation?"

Grandmama reached up and patted her gray bun, assuring the wispy hairs were still in place. "There's a verse in the chapter of Luke that says *'Be ye therefore merciful, as your Father also is merciful.'*"

Amaya knew the verse of which Grandmama spoke.

Her grandmother continued. "When you visit Silas, and I suggest that it be soon, remember to imitate the Lord in His merciful ways."

CHAPTER THIRTY

SILAS SAT UP IN the bed, feeling better than he had in days. Doc had to perform surgery to remove some remaining pieces of one of the bullets. He'd be sore for a while, but the doctor expected him to make a full recovery.

Which was good news because he had a ranch to manage.

John Mark had rallied folks to assist with some of the duties until Silas could return. He was grateful they still considered him an upright member of their town.

But did Amaya?

He nodded off after the stream of visitors, which included John Mark, Hannah, and the boys, Pritchard and Ina, Winslow, Nowell, and Reverend Fleming. Florence brought him a meal from Pearson's Restaurant, which he ate so fast it gave him indigestion. But nothing had been better than Grandmama's visit and her Basque vegetable soup, both of which were the best remedies so far for his injuries.

Silas thanked the Lord again for Grandmama's forgiveness.

"Silas?"

He stirred and opened his eyes to see a blurred vision of Amaya. He thought of her often, so it was no surprise he'd dream about her too.

"Silas?"

A tap on his arm caused him to reopen his eyes. The same hazy view of Amaya greeted him, and he allowed himself to again drift to sleep.

"I was hoping I would arrive when you were awake."

Wait. Maybe this wasn't just a dream. He blinked and forced his eyes to focus.

She sat beside his bed, her lovely face just as he remembered it. A tinge of pink touched her cheeks, and her gaze rested on her hands, which were folded in her lap.

Amaya had come to see him. The realization sent warmth through him. While she may never feel for him the way he felt about her, if they could remain friends after all that happened, Silas would consider it a victory.

He cleared his throat, suddenly needing a glass of water. Silas reached for the half-filled cup beyond comfortable reach as pain seared through him. He settled back against the stack of pillows, determined to try again in a few seconds.

"Do you need help?" Amaya asked, bending toward the worn square table next to his bed. She retrieved the cup, stood, and offered it to him.

Silas breathed in her flowery scent, one he'd become accustomed to in the time knowing her. Some perfume from the mercantile, he supposed. He forgot his thirst for a brief moment. "Thank you," he said, after drinking the remaining water.

Amaya returned the cup to the table and again took a seat in the chair.

He needed to explain to her why he'd done what he did. Would she understand? Would she forgive him? The muscles in his neck tightened as Silas again revisited the words he sought to say.

"Amaya, there are some things I need to explain."

She regarded him with wary eyes and offered a hesitant nod.

Silas had been in many awkward and uncomfortable situations in his life, but this one was one of the worst.

Finally, she spoke. "Please help me to understand."

He wanted to reach for her hand. To explain to her the reasons for his actions in the bank. To reassure her he was the same man she'd considered as a friend. Would he be able to fully express his rationale for the decisions he made? Would it sound anything like what he'd spent hours last night pondering when he should have been sleeping?

"If I would have let him—" Silas turned and briefly peered at the other bed in the room where Doc previously tended to Hurst. A range of emotions engulfed him, from sadness to relief. Hurst's actions had been odious and contemptible. But then, mere hours before his death, he'd sought forgiveness from his Creator. Such a feat was nothing short of a miracle.

Silas cleared his throat and again focused on Amaya. "If I would have let them know you meant something to me, they would have harmed you as an act of revenge."

Her brown eyes rounded. "An act of revenge?"

Would she think less of him when she heard about the man he used to be? Should he be forthright about his past?

Grandmama had understood, and so with much the same words he used to describe it to her, he again explained some of his past to Amaya.

"I couldn't let them hurt you," he said when he finished.

"I was sure I didn't mean anything to you in those moments." Tears skipped down her cheeks.

Her statement grieved him, and a throbbing pain in his chest that had nothing to do with his wounds reminded him of the turmoil he'd caused. "Amaya," he whispered, wishing again that he could take her hand in his. "You mean everything to me."

Last night, Amaya wondered how she could forgive Silas. But in this moment, she wondered how she could *not* forgive him.

"Thank you for explaining that to me. I was so worried—" she rubbed her forearms, remembering the horrific time she'd spent in the bank during the robbery. "I was so worried you were one of them. That I didn't really know the *real* you."

"I'm not proud of what I did. The people I disappointed. The ones I stole from. The times I carelessly ruined another's property. But I know without a doubt that the Lord is the giver of second chances, and He gave me a second chance. My Oma never once stopped praying for me. And while I'd do anything for another day with her, or even another few minutes, I *will* see her again someday. Her prayers are the reason I am a changed man."

Gratitude was written in his gaze. He reached toward her, hand open.

Without a second thought, she placed her hand in his, and his long fingers closed over her hand. Her heart galloped in her chest at his touch. Likely from the reconciliation they now experienced. "Thank you for sharing that with me. I forgive you."

Silas closed his eyes and nodded. His Adam's apple bobbed. "Thank you, Amaya."

They visited for the next several minutes before she prepared to return to the mercantile. "I have a surprise for you that I'll bring later this afternoon."

If Florence hadn't threatened him that she'd round up the entire town to track him down and return him to Doc's office, Silas would have headed home. Staying in the small infirmary for several days while he healed was not his idea of time well spent. His ranch needed him, and while his hired hand was competent, Silas couldn't wait to return to the saddle and devote his time to the job he loved.

He thought of Florence again and their lengthy conversation a day after he'd arrived at Doc's office. She'd graciously accepted his explanation for the ongoings at the bank. Her words still rang in his ears. *"Do not fret another moment about it, Silas. For as long as I've known you, and it's been a few years now, you've always been an upright man with exemplary character."*

Florence's words meant a lot to him. Grandmama's forgiveness was also an encouragement. But no one's acceptance of his past meant as much as Amaya's did. As it had been for some time now, he couldn't get her out of his mind.

And now, he impatiently waited for her return this afternoon. He thought of how they'd talked, how her hand felt in his, how pretty she looked when she sat in the chair next to his bed.

How much he loved her.

Amaya mentioned she'd be bringing him a surprise, and he hoped it was some of Grandmama's gâteau Basque.

Silas strained to see the clock on Doc's desk. Two o'clock. Doc hummed as he unpacked a box of medical supplies, a wagon roared past on the street outside, and two men had stopped to chat on the boardwalk.

He shifted and swung his legs over the side of the bed. Doc wanted him to move about, and truth was, he was antsy and restless. Tomorrow couldn't come soon enough for him to return to the ranch.

Less than ten minutes later, children's voices sounded outside. Silas sat up straighter in his bed and craned his neck to see who caused the commotion. Amaya entered the infirmary, followed by Owen, Effie, and Dudley.

"Mr. Silas! I have a loose tooth!" Effie dashed toward Silas's bed, opened her mouth, and reached her finger in to wiggle the tooth. "It's almost ready to fall out. Grandmama says it's barely hanging by a thread."

"Then why don't you pull it out?" asked Owen, always the voice of reason.

Dudley said nothing, only climbed onto the bed and rested his head against Silas.

"We're staying with Miss Amaya, Grandmama, and Grandfather the rest of today and tomorrow and the tomorrow after that," said Effie, her words tumbling from her mouth with barely a pause in between.

Silas allowed his gaze to meet Amaya's. She smiled, and for a minute, he forgot to breathe. "Your surprise was to see the children, but we also managed to bring along a piece of the gâteau Basque Grandmama made yesterday."

"Much obliged for that."

She placed it on the table beside the bed for him to eat later.

Effie leaned across the bed and gave Dudley a hug. "It's going to be Dudley's other birthday in a few months."

"Dudley's other birthday?" Amaya asked.

"Yes. He has his birthday when he gets older and his other birthday. Isn't that right, Owen?"

Owen nodded, but didn't interrupt his sister's enthusiastic chatter.

"His other birthday is when Owen and I decided Dudley would be our brother because we had room in our family for him." Effie gave her younger brother a second hug. "Isn't that right, Dudley?"

"Yes," Dudley answered, hugging her back, but not relinquishing his place on Silas's lap.

Silas saw the emotion in Amaya's eyes. Owen and Effie had adopted Dudley into their family of two.

Now if only the Lord saw fit to give the children a home with a mother and father where they would be loved and cherished.

Chapter Thirty-One

ON THE DAY OF the celebration honoring those who'd assisted in the Farris Hill Gang's capture, Owen and Effie could barely contain their excitement. They hopped up and down and clapped their hands, barely able to stand still. This was the first time Amaya had witnessed such behavior in the contemplative and stoic Owen. "Can we have some ice cream?" Effie asked, her blue eyes rounded. Their ebullient behavior made Amaya smile. "Yes, after the presentation, we'll have ourselves some ice cream."

Owen licked his lips. "I like ice cream."

Dudley peered up at her with a creased brow and clutched her hand more tightly. "Have I had ice cweam, Miss 'Maya?" His navy knickerbockers that came to his knee, combined with black cowboy boots and a tweed button up collarless jacket made him appear much older than his three years. So many in town had donated clothing for the children, including the Ottoways, a generous couple with a son a year older than Dudley, who'd donated the knickerbockers and jacket. Grandmama had slicked Dudley's now-short dark brown hair, courtesy of a visit to the barber a few weeks ago.

"I'm not sure, Dudley. But I do know that if you haven't, you will indeed enjoy it."

"I know I'll indeed enjoy it," declared Effie. "I'm not sure I can even wait." She and Owen jabbered on about the time they had ice cream at the orphanage.

And the realization hit Amaya that she loved these children.

She scanned the crowd for Silas. Would he be here? No one had told him he'd also be honored, and to Amaya's knowledge, he believed the celebration to be for Grandfather only. Anticipation at possibly seeing him caused her heart to pitter-patter against her ribcage.

"Oh, look!" said Owen, standing on tiptoe. "It's Mr. Silas. Can we go greet him? Can we?"

Amaya's eyes connected with Silas's as he weaved his way through the massive amount of people—perhaps the entire population of Poplar Springs. "Yes, you may, but do be courteous to others and use your manners."

Owen and Effie squealed in delight, and Amaya was unsure they'd heard her instruction. They bounded toward Silas, and if his shoulder was not still healing, Amaya had no doubt he'd lift them and twirl them around. She watched as the children fought over his one available hand, Effie eventually winning.

"Hello, Amaya."

"Hello, Silas."

His handsome smile caused a peculiar sensation in her belly. Why was she suddenly nervous around him? They'd gone from friendship to her questioning his loyalties, and now to something more. Could Grandmama be correct? That true love *could* happen twice in one lifetime?

Mayor Pritchard took to the stairs of city hall. The crowd hushed, and he folded his hands on the lapels of his coat. "Hello, ladies and gents! I'm Mayor Pritchard, and this is my beautiful wife, our first lady, Ina."

The crowd cheered, and Pritchard took a bow before claiming his wife's hand. Ina tittered, her smile broad as she gazed at him adoringly, her pink cheeks contrasting her normally pale pallor.

"Thank you for joining us for this exceptional moment in Poplar Springs history. As you well know, several days ago, three members of the Farris Hill Gang descended upon our town in an attempt to commit a crime. They entered our bank, took hostages, and demanded all of the gold and cash in the safe."

The crowd booed.

"My sentiments, exactly. But we here in Poplar Springs do not cotton to ruthless outlaws bent on taking what doesn't belong to them."

This time, the onlookers cheered, some whistled, and others raised their hands and let out roars of agreement.

"Yes, my friends and fellow residents, such foolhardy and imprudent behavior on the part of any gang will only be met with resistance as we continue to make our town the best in Wyoming."

The supportive shouts grew louder, and Dudley covered his ears with his hands.

Pritchard waited until the noise waned before continuing. "Today, we call a meeting of sorts to commend those who aided in the capture of the sinister and nefarious Farris Hill Gang. Each of those we honor today are true heroes. They are the ones who ensured that our women and children were safe. That no lives were lost. And that the bank received back the stolen money."

Those in attendance grew silent as Pritchard released Ina's hand and unfolded a sheet of paper. Through the multitude of people, Amaya saw Grandmama and Grandfather just in front of the stairs. Grandmama stood with her hand on the back of Grandfather's wheelchair. She'd told him they should attend the celebration, most importantly in support of the lawmen, but also because there would be ice cream at Pearson's Restaurant afterwards.

Grandfather loved ice cream, and this would be the first time ever it would be available in Poplar Springs.

"We'll begin with the man who alerted the lawmen that something was amiss at the bank." Pritchard and Ina stepped down to Grandfather. "Please give your applause to Mr. Alvarado!"

Grandmama turned Grandfather around to face the crowd, and even from where she stood, Amaya could see the tinge of red that lit her grandpa's pale face. His eyes crinkled at the corners as he grinned. He mouthed the words, "thank you", although it was doubtful anyone but Grandmama, Pritchard, and Ina could hear him.

"Mr. Alvarado, on behalf of the town of Poplar Springs, I present you with a portion of the reward money." Pritchard handed Grandfather an envelope.

Although Grandfather's articulation had improved significantly in recent weeks, this unexpected circumstance rendered him speechless. His mouth moved, but no words emerged. Grandmama planted a kiss on his bald head and stepped aside, tears in her eyes. Grandfather looked up toward Heaven, then said, "Thank you. Thank you to everyone." Loud clapping responded to his muted and slightly garbled tone.

"We also have another man to thank. Silas McFadden, having hailed from Texas, had some knowledge about this gang. His quick thinking likely saved the lives of those held hostage in the bank. Not only that, but he risked his life to ride with them, find their hideout, and suffered two gunshot wounds while doing so. He's our second hero."

Silas peered at Amaya, then at Pritchard, then at those around him who were slapping him on the back and voicing their appreciation. Owen and Effie, who both beamed at him with adoring glances, joined him as he strode through the throngs of people toward the stairs of city hall.

Pritchard continued with recognizing John Mark, Winslow, Nowell, and the other two deputies, who all received accolades and a portion of the reward money.

"Thank you again for joining the first lady and me to celebrate our Poplar Springs heroes. Because of them, our town is safer. As many of you know, Poplar Springs will now offer ice cream. This savory dessert is available only at Pearson's Restaurant. You'll not find it anywhere else in our fine town. Also, as a show of appreciation, our heroes will receive free ice cream this afternoon."

Owen ran his tongue across his lips. "Miss Amaya says we can have ice cream too, Mr. Silas."

"You most certainly can."

From Owen's sparkling eyes, one might have thought Silas offered him much more than a dish of ice cream. Amaya marveled at how the children revered and admired Silas.

He was a good man.

How could she have ever doubted such a truth?

"One other thing I might add..." said Pritchard, his arm now around Ina while she clearly basked in his love for her. "Pearson's Restaurant is the best restaurant, not only in Wyoming, but also west of the Mississippi. Be sure to have your noonday meal there today and for as many days of the week as is possible. Enjoy the rest of your day!"

Several minutes later, Amaya and Silas led the children to Pearson's Restaurant to stand in line for ice cream. Dudley's eyes doubled in size when one of Ina's sisters handed him a dish of the frozen dessert. He smelled it, stuck his finger through the white delicacy, then plopped the dripping liquid into his mouth. "I like ice cream, Miss 'Maya. I like it a lot!"

Silas accompanied Amaya and the children to the mercantile one early September evening after a full day of picking the remaining huckleberries on the mountain slopes at the far end of his ranch and eating supper at Pearson's Restaurant. In the days since the bank robbery, he'd basked in the company of the woman he'd grown to love and the children that had secured a place in his heart.

In recent days, much had changed. His shoulder continued to heal, and he saw Amaya most days of the week. She'd cared for the children the past few days and would do so until tomorrow when they again went to stay with Doc and Florence before visiting John Mark and Hannah again. They would stay with Silas again after another visit with the Flemings. And hopefully, at some point, the Keisels would proceed with their adoption. The children deserved a loving and permanent home.

Silas's feelings for Amaya had only grown. He thought maybe she might feel the same about him. While herding cattle yesterday, he'd pondered things long and hard. Things like asking her to court him again. Things like a life together with her. Waking up next to her and falling asleep beside her each night. Praying together, rejoicing in the good times, and being there for each other during the difficult times.

Would she be amenable to it? Or should he forego asking her in light of her devotion to Russell?

Silence greeted them when they entered the mercantile. Grandfather was likely already asleep, and Grandmama waved at them and resumed her knitting in the other room near the potbelly stove. Silas promised that when Amaya's family arrived from Bowman next month, he'd do whatever was necessary to revamp the upstairs to accommodate them.

Silas assisted Amaya with tucking the children into bed before preparing to leave. She joined him as he started down the stairs. "I'll see you at church on Sunday," he told her when they reached the lower level of the mercantile.

"Thank you for the delightful day," she said. "The children ought to sleep well."

"Dudley won't be waking up in the night asking for a drink of water?"

Amaya laughed. "He does that at your house as well?"

"He does. Owen and Effie are sound sleepers, but I think Dudley is afraid he'll miss something and fights going to sleep."

"Indeed. Of course, he's come so far since that day you found him. All of them have."

Silas nodded. "Reverend Fleming mentioned that the Keisels have a court hearing for the adoption next week. Hopefully the children will adjust to living with them permanently."

They paused by the counter, and Silas could see Grandmama's feet through the doorway of the room he'd built for her and Grandfather.

Amaya lowered her voice to a whisper. "The children have grown accustomed to moving around every couple of days or weeks. And the Keisels have only visited with them once. I'm rather concerned."

He loved that about her. Loved that she cared for others and had such a compassionate nature. Silas caressed her cheek with his thumb. "Something to continue to lift up to the Lord."

She closed her eyes, and his gaze traveled to her full lips. How many times in days past had he wanted to ask her if he might kiss her? Silas leaned toward her and breathed in the scent of huckleberries from their excursion today. "Amaya," he whispered.

Either she had fallen asleep or was unable to hear them. Shouldn't he ask her to court him first? Shouldn't he ask if he might kiss her and then share his feelings for her? Stop being a hopeless ninnyhammer?

Staring at her and taking in her beauty and being this close to her had rendered him a simpleton.

"Will you court me?"

In the light of the lantern flickering on the counter, he thought he saw pink color her cheeks. She dipped her head and stared at the floor for a second.

He never should have asked.

Never should have assumed she felt the same for him as he did for her. That her stance had changed.

"Silas..."

He took a step back, feeling as though someone had punched him in the stomach. He had no right to ask her to court him again when she'd lost Russell. Hadn't he attempted to share his feelings before to his detriment?

"I should go."

Amaya lifted her head again. He couldn't read her expression.

A snore from the other room indicated Grandmama had fallen asleep. Best she not witness his heart again breaking in two million pieces.

"I'll see you tomorrow at church."

"No, wait." She reached for his arm, and he felt the warmth through her grasp. Her slender hands, with fingers dyed purple from the huckleberries, drew his attention away from her face.

"I'm sorry, Amaya."

Grandmama's chair creaked, and Silas shifted his attention towards her. Just a slight movement of Grandmama's legs was all he could see.

Should he pull away? Act like he'd never asked such a foolish question? Ask Amaya to forgive him for asking again?

"I would very much like that."

In his mind, he imagined she'd say yes. He'd prayed at least two hundred times yesterday and today that if it was the Lord's will, she'd agree to court him and someday become his wife.

"I best be on my way."

Confusion lit her eyes and her brow furrowed. She released her hand from his arm.

"Amaya, I'm sorry I asked," he continued. "It's just that I love you. I have for the longest time. I think about you all the time and wonder what it would be like to court you. I know I have no right when you still love Russell. But truth is, I'll never be Russell."

"Silas..."

He needed to leave. Needed to hop on his horse and ride to the ranch nice and slow to gather his thoughts. She would be the only one he'd ever love, but he'd prayed about it, and if it was God's will for him to remain unmarried, so be it. Only, that wasn't all right with him.

"Well, goodness, Silas McFadden!" Grandmama's normally soft-spoken voice was boisterous in the otherwise quiet room.

"Grandmama?"

He and Amaya both turned to see Grandmama gaping at them, her mouth pinched. She was nearly folded in half from her position on the rocking chair, her knitting in her lap. "Amaya said she'd very much like to court you, and you are going on and on like a senseless cad. If you would listen for a moment and not be so daft, you would have heard her say yes to you."

Silas's jaw dropped. He never before heard such a lecture from Grandmama. "She said yes?"

"Well, I said I'd very much like that. To court you, I mean." A sparkle lit Amaya's eyes.

"I—you—you said you would like to court me?"

Grandmama shook her head. "Young folks these days. When Iker proposed to me, and I said yes, he heard me straightaway."

"Reckon I—you said yes?"

"Yes, Silas McFadden, I'll court you."

"She'll probably marry you too," insisted Grandmama. She leaned back in her chair, and Silas saw her hands again working the knitting needles.

"I thought...nevermind. May I kiss you?"

Amaya nodded and her lips parted. He drew closer to her, pulled her gently into his arms, and kissed her.

CHAPTER THIRTY-TWO

AMAYA REQUESTED THAT THE children stay with her, Grandmama, and Grandfather the day before the court hearing for their adoption by Mr. and Mrs. Keisel. It had been rescheduled twice before this day arrived.

She braided Effie's hair and attempted to assuage her fears.

"But what if they take us back to the orphanage?" Effie asked.

"We will run away," vowed Owen, in a candid voice as if such a feat were an everyday occurrence for those not wanting to reside with their new parents.

Amaya started to correct him, then thought better of it. The Keisels were kindly folks from what she knew of them, and it was likely that they would come to love and cherish the children.

At least, she prayed so.

On numerous occasions.

She knew Silas was praying as well. So were Hannah and John Mark, Pritchard and Ina, the Flemings, and Doc and Florence. So many people had come to adore the children.

"Can we have ice cream?" Dudley asked, rubbing his stomach. The little boy didn't mind that it was already

October, and the fall chill in the air wasn't conducive to eating cold desserts. But she wouldn't say as much. Not today.

"Perhaps." Would the Keisels take the children for the refreshing dessert? Would they tuck them into bed at night, pray with them, and kiss their little foreheads? Would they know about Dudley's fear of the dark, Owen's protective nature, and Effie's penchant for being a chatterbox? Would they know how much Owen enjoyed checking on the cattle with Silas and Effie's hope to someday be a baker? Would they give extra attention to Dudley since he'd likely been without anyone truly caring about him often in his young life?

Tears flooded her eyes. Grandmama's words played through her mind: *God will take care of them, Amaya. He loves them even more than you do.*

And what of Silas? He'd grown fond of the children too. Not that the other families hadn't, but she and Silas had become attached to them.

Grandmama knocked on the door. "We should go to the courthouse," she said.

"Are you all right, Grandmama?" Dudley asked, gazing up at her.

"Yes, my sweet Dudley. I'm fine." Grandmama dabbed at her nose with her handkerchief, and her puffy eyes belied her words of assurance.

Fifteen minutes later, Amaya, Grandmama, and the children met Silas and Reverend Fleming at the courthouse. The impressive red brick-and-stone square structure, with its Italianate architecture, loomed on a hill on the outskirts of Poplar Springs. Erected in 1884 and surrounded by mature pine trees and cottonwoods, it boasted about twenty steps up an incline to the front doors.

Effie clutched Amaya's hand, and Owen stalled near the railing on the fourth step. Silas pivoted back towards him and knelt to his height. "Is everything all right, Owen?"

A young boy of few words, Owen shook his head, folded his arms across his chest, and peered down at his brown leather boots someone had donated to the church along with the brown trousers and button-up gray shirt. His lips twitched downward, and his shoulders sagged, as if he carried the problems of the world upon them. While Effie would voice her fears, Owen held them all inside.

"We will all be here with you." Silas set a hand on the boy's shoulder.

"Don't wanna go with the Keisels."

Had Amaya not been listening intently, she would have missed Owen's whispered words.

Silas lifted Owen. "I know that, son."

Owen wrapped his skinny arms around Silas's neck and buried his face in his shoulder. He sniffled, and Amaya hazarded a guess that he was doing all he could to hide the tears that likely fell down his face.

Silas held him closer, and whispered something in his ear. Owen shook his head and a sob racked his body. At that moment, Dudley released Amaya's hand and bolted toward Silas. He held his arms upward. "Mr. Silas?" he whimpered.

Obviously paying no mind to his formerly-injured shoulder, Silas hoisted Dudley up in his other arm and held both boys. Dark circles beneath his eyes told of his lack of sleep and concern.

Effie clutched Amaya's hand tighter, then buried her face in Amaya's skirts.

Grandmama gasped and covered her mouth, and Reverend Fleming bowed his head, likely lifting a petition to the Lord.

Amaya's eyes welled with tears. *Lord, if there is some way...some way that these precious little ones might be protected, please, I pray for You to be their safeguard. Go before them in this new life.*

Silas walked toward her, his somber face drawn and pinched. Amaya's own sorrow closed up her throat, and she choked on the emotion.

Grandmama patted each child on the back, tears streaming down her cheeks. "We will pay you many visits," she said.

But Amaya wasn't so sure if the Keisels, in their desire to start a family, would be amenable to the constant flow of guests—folks who'd grown to love Owen, Effie, and Dudley—converging on their home on a routine basis.

"We best be on our way," Reverend Fleming said.

A musty odor greeted them as they entered through the doors of the courthouse. A man passed them and nodded, and Reverend Fleming led everyone up a set of stairs to the second floor.

Mr. Keisel appeared from around the corner, leaving his attorney and wife behind. "Reverend Fleming, might we speak with you for a moment?"

The reverend nodded and followed Mr. Keisel to his wife and their attorney.

"Miss Amaya?" Effie asked, a tremble in her voice.

"Yes?"

"Do we have to go with those people?"

How could Amaya tell her that yes, if the court deemed it necessary, they would have to reside with the Keisels? "They're nice people, Effie, and they'll take good care of you, Owen, and Dudley."

Effie's lip quivered, and she buried her face in Amaya's skirts.

Silas carried Dudley to the entrance of the courtroom. "It's empty," he said. Silas then placed a hand on Amaya's arm. He needn't say a thing for Amaya to know exactly what he was thinking.

She attempted to allow her mind to drift to other things. Good things like Silas's marriage proposal and how she'd agreed to be his wife just last week. Would a winter wedding be in their future? Grandmama told of how she and Grandfather married on December 1.

Reverend Fleming strode toward them a few minutes later, his shoulders slumping and weariness in his countenance. "Amaya and Silas, could I speak with you? Children, would you please stay with Grandmama?"

Amaya noticed that the Keisels' attorney had ushered them in the opposite direction, and Mrs. Keisel hadn't so much as given any notice to the children.

A sense of foreboding settled deep in her stomach. It mingled with a sense of protection over the children she'd come to love as her own.

Silas offered his arm, and together they met with Reverend Fleming inside the courtroom.

Reverend Fleming released a deep breath. "I have some unpleasant news."

A shadow crossed Silas's face. "Oh?"

"Mr. and Mrs. Keisel wanted only to adopt one of the children."

"Let me guess," said Silas. "Dudley."

"No, actually, they wanted to adopt Effie."

Amaya shook her head. "Effie?"

Reverend Fleming stroked his beard, opened his mouth as if to say something, then shut it again before finally speaking. "Yes, Effie. They traveled to Thornsby last week to the small orphanage there."

"I wasn't aware Thornsby had an orphanage." Silas's eyebrows drew together.

"Nor was I. But apparently there is one, and they found a baby to adopt. Mrs. Keisel has always wanted a baby rather than an older child."

Irritation surged through Amaya. "The children can't help it that they are no longer babies, and that doesn't explain why they still wanted to adopt Effie."

"Exactly," said Reverend Fleming. "The children cannot help their ages." He paused, his gaze dropping to the floor. "They want Effie to help care for the baby and assist with household chores."

Every muscle in Amaya tensed, and her indignation flared. "So they wanted to adopt her to be a nanny and a maid, instead of their child?"

Silas clenched his fists at his sides. "If that's what they will consider Effie to be, they don't deserve to adopt her. She's a little girl. Not a servant."

Reverend Fleming strode toward the open door, presumably to check on the children. "I know we are all furious about this, but we musn't allow the children to hear us."

"I'm sorry," said Silas. "I just can't believe it.

"Nor can I. What did you tell them?"

"I told them the details of the adoption weren't up to me, but up to the judge." Reverend Fleming thick brows knit together. "I will be honest and tell you if it wasn't for the Lord reining in my tongue, I may have said all sorts of things to them regarding my opinion. However, I did say in no uncertain terms that we cannot split the children up since they are siblings."

"Was the attorney agreeable with that?" Silas asked.

"He was. When I explained the detrimental effect it would have on each of them, he understood. Mr. and Mrs. Keisel didn't argue."

Amaya wrapped her arms around herself. "I'm thankful for that. The children shouldn't be separated, and to do that to Effie would be unthinkable. But what happens to them now?"

"I refuse to allow them to have to go back to the orphanage," Silas said, straightening his posture. "We'll do whatever it takes."

"No one will allow them to go back to the orphanage. We will pray that God will lead us to another family."

Amaya caught Silas's eye. Was he thinking what she was thinking? "We'll..." she began.

"Adopt them," finished Silas.

"The two of you?"

"We are already planning to marry," said Amaya. "And we love them."

Silas took her hand in his. "What do you say, Reverend? Would Amaya and I be fitting to be their parents?"

For the first time since they'd entered the courthouse, a broad smile covered Reverend Fleming's face. "Oh, yes, I think you two would be just the parents God has planned for these children."

Chapter Thirty-Three

THE WEEKS PASSED QUICKLY, and at the end of October, Nowell and Gertrude married. Soon after, Ma, Pa, and Zurina relocated to Poplar Springs.

It was good to have Ma and Pa residing in the same town. Both Pa and Grandfather were doing much better. Until spring when work could begin on their cabin just outside of town, Amaya's family would reside with Grandmama and Grandfather.

On Wednesday, December 1, swirling flakes of peaceful snow drifted to the ground outside, while inside the church, Amaya begged her knees not to wobble as Pa walked her down the aisle to marry Silas.

Mrs. Fleming played the organ in the corner, and Ma, Grandmama, Grandfather, Zurina, and the children sat in the front pews.

The children. As if a wedding wasn't thrilling enough, the news she and Silas would be sharing with Owen, Effie, and Dudley would add to the day's excitement.

John Mark and Hannah, Ambrose, and Little Russell; Pritchard and Ina and their brood; Nowell and Gertrude; Sheriff and Mrs. Winslow; Doc and Florence; and a host of other friends from town packed the remaining pews.

Amaya tucked her hand in Pa's arm. Silas awaited her at the altar, looking especially dapper in his Sunday best. A familiar little boy's voice said, "Hi, Miss Amaya!" as she passed by him.

"You look so pretty," declared Effie.

When they reached the front of the church, Pa patted her hand, nodded at Silas, then took his seat next to Ma.

Silas caught her gaze, and for a moment, she nearly forgot to breathe. His white shirt stretched across his muscular shoulders. He'd shaved and combed his blond hair, and she caught a faint hint of pine soap. Amaya's stomach turned jittery and the heat suffused her face.

Reverend Fleming prayed, welcomed those in attendance, and recited the vows to which both Amaya and Silas agreed.

"You may kiss the bride."

Silas wrapped her in his arms and kissed her thoroughly before releasing her to the sound of clapping from those in attendance.

Well-wishers greeted and hugged Amaya and Silas, and Grandmama ushered everyone toward a table in the back of the church where she served gâteau Basque as the wedding cake.

An hour later when it was time to leave, Silas beckoned the children to meet them outside with their coats.

Ma kissed Amaya's cheek. "We'll bring them tomorrow morning," she said, her hushed voice drowned out by the commotion of those in attendance.

"Thank you, Ma."

They bid everyone farewell, then Silas assisted her with her wrap, took her hand, and together they meandered outside into the cold day.

"Why did you want us to come outside?" asked Effie, towing Dudley behind her.

Dudley held a sizable piece of gâteau Basque in his free hand. Most of what he'd already tried to devour covered his face. He attempted to reach it with his tongue.

Owen's shoulders slumped. "When will we see you again, Mr. Silas and Miss Amaya?"

"Yes, we will miss you." Effie released Dudley's hand and wrapped her arms around Amaya's waist. "We'll make cookies again, right?"

Dudley bent over and swiped a handful of snow. "Brr," he said, his hand becoming red from the half-melted moisture, although he didn't allow it to deter him.

Silas put an arm around Amaya's shoulders. "Children, Amaya and I would like to discuss something with you."

"Out here in the cold?" Effie released her hold on Amaya and took a step back. She peered into the distance where billowing snow settled into a glistening velvety pile.

"Mr. Silas and I have something to ask you."

Owen squinted against the winter sun, his expression wary. He shuffled his feet in the snow, causing it to collect on the top of his boots.

Effie rubbed her hands together in anticipation.

Dudley plopped himself down in the snow and began to giggle, oblivious to anything transpiring around him.

Silas squeezed her hand. "Miss Amaya and I would like to know if you would like to be our children."

"Your children?" Effie's blue eyes rounded. "You would be our ma and pa?" She enunciated her words slowly and clearly.

"I think I would like that," said Owen.

Dudley stretched out on his back and waved his arms side to side and his legs in and out. "I like snow."

"I would *love* it!" Effie jumped up and down.

A smile transformed Owen's normally fretful countenance. "I would answer yes."

Dudley sat up and nibbled a handful of snow, which replaced the piece of gâteau Basque half buried in the snow beside him. "Can I eat snow for the noonday meal?"

"We love you all very much and would like for you to be in our family," said Amaya, the tears freezing as they slid down her face.

Silas captured Amaya, Owen, and Effie in a hug. Effie started to cry, and Owen clung to Silas.

Dudley stood and zigzagged through the snow before joining the embrace.

"Tomorrow morning, Abuela and Abuelo will bring you to the ranch."

Effie took a step back. "Tomorrow? How come not today?"

Silas patted her on the head. "We have some things to do first."

"Like get our rooms ready?" Owen asked.

"Yes, we need to get your rooms ready."

"I can't wait for my new room!" Effie danced around in the snow.

Awe transformed Owen's face. "Can me and Dudley have the loft for our room?"

"You sure can," said Silas, affection for the children glowing in his eyes.

Dudley tilted his head back and caught a snowflake on his tongue. He giggled before asking, "Is there snow at the ranch?"

"Plenty of it."

"I don't care about snow at the ranch, Mr. Silas. I care about baking cookies with my new ma."

"You would care about that, Effie," said Owen. "As for me..." he thumbed his chest. "I can't wait to ride the horses again and help Mr. Silas..."

Effie shook her head. "You mean, Pa. His name is gonna be Pa now. And Miss Amaya is gonna be our ma forever and ever and ever." She grasped Amaya's hand. "I suppose I can wait until tomorrow. I do like Abuela and Abuelo."

"And they adore you." Amaya's parents and Zurina had taken to the kids upon meeting them. But how could anyone not love the three precious children with their distinct personalities?

Grandmama opened the church door a few seconds later and retrieved Owen, Effie, and Dudley.

"I borrowed the sleigh from the livery," Silas told Amaya as they navigated their way through the snow. When she nearly slipped, he swept her up into his strong arms.

Amaya rested her head against his muscular chest. Joy bubbled through her, and she reveled in the wonder of the day and in a new life with the man she loved.

A new life that was just beginning.

EPILOGUE
THREE WEEKS LATER

SILAS AND AMAYA FINISHED tucking in the children and praying for them before placing the presents beneath the tree, a spindly pine with strings of popcorn and trinkets. Silas wasn't sure who was more excited—the children or he and Amaya.

When they finished, he wrapped his arms around his wife. "Just think, Mrs. McFadden, tomorrow will be our first Christmas."

"I'm very much anticipating it, Mr. McFadden. Won't the children be delighted when they see their presents?"

"That they will."

It had been a blessing that this year's cattle prices were better than expected. While Silas prided himself on being cautious with his money and saving what he could for lean times, he also wanted to make this Christmas an especially memorable one. He eyed the five parcels wrapped in brown paper beneath the tree. The Barney & Berry's ice skates cost fifty cents a pair, but it would be worth it to see the children's faces. "Reckon I hope we can make a tradition out of going ice skating."

"Provided I can learn how without falling."

He pulled her closer. "Well, that will make two of us," he said, "but don't worry, I'll catch you as I'm falling down."

Amaya laughed, the tinkling sound tickling his ears. He loved her laugh. Loved her heart for others. Loved her strong faith. Loved her beauty. Loved how she fit perfectly in his arms. He breathed in her flowery scent and closed his eyes as he circled her waist. Would he wake up and realize the wife and family the Lord had blessed him with was all a dream? He released a sigh of gratitude and contentment.

"I do have a special present for you," he said.

"Before tomorrow?"

"Yes." Silas placed the wrapped gift in her hand.

Amaya removed the paper and gasped. "This is lovely."

"It was Oma's."

She fingered the brooch then held it to her heart. "Thank you."

"Oma would have wanted you to have it."

The fire crackled in the fireplace, the only other sound besides Amaya's soft breathing and the sound of his own heartbeat in his ears.

Silas hoped Amaya would be delighted when she opened her other gift from him—the bowl and pitcher with a painting of her favorite bird, a black-capped chickadee, painted on it with brightly-colored yellow and purple flowers and green leaves. He'd specially ordered it from the catalog at a sales price of eighty-seven cents, and with Grandmama's assistance, hid it from Amaya until Christmas arrived.

He took a step back from her and cupped her chin in his hand. "I love you, Amaya."

She closed her eyes and leaned her head toward him. "I love you too, Silas."

His mouth captured hers for a series of kisses that ended all too soon when a little voice interrupted them. "Ma? Pa?" The hesitancy in the words could only come from Owen who, of the three, most cautiously guarded his heart.

Silas reluctantly released Amaya, and they both turned toward Owen, who stood near the table, his shoulders lowered and his arms at his sides.

"Owen? Are you all right?" Amaya rushed towards him.

"It's Dudley. He's having a bad dream."

"Don't worry. I'll check on him." Amaya rushed from the room and up the ladder to the loft where Silas had built a bedroom for the boys.

He watched her go, grateful that the Lord had made her such a loving and caring mother to their children. But he'd always known she would be from her tender care of her grandparents.

Owen remained in the room, his head lowered and a dejected expression on his round face. "Owen? What's wrong? Is it Dudley?"

The boy shook his head and stared down at his hands.

Silas didn't know much about children, and even less about being a pa. What did one do when his son experienced melancholy? He prayed for guidance, pulled out a chair from the table, and took a seat.

Owen didn't need any further encouragement. He hastened towards Silas and climbed into his lap. The little boy laid his head against Silas's chest, and Silas could hear the hushed whimpers. He said nothing, only put his arms around Owen and prayed God would give him the words to say.

Amaya's inaudible voice in the loft as she comforted Dudley and the sound of an owl's continuous and persistent hooting mixed with Owen's quiet sobs.

Silas would sit with his son and wait for as long as it took.

Finally, Owen peered up at him with dampened cheeks. "Mr...I mean, Pa?"

"Yes, Son?" Of all the children, Owen struggled the most with not calling his new parents Mr. Silas and Miss Amaya.

"Will you always be our parents?"

Silas choked on the emotion that filled him. He knew what it was like to wonder about the future and if there would be anyone to love you. "Yes, we will always be your parents."

Owen's eyes searched Silas's face. "But what if we do something bad?"

"We'll always love you, Owen, even when you make mistakes." The desire in his heart to be a father like his Heavenly Father gripped him with an unrelenting hold. "It's just like how God loves us even when we make mistakes."

"But what if someone else wants to adopt us? What if Mr. and Mrs. Keisel decide they do want us?"

The fear in Owen's words caused Silas's own throat to tighten. He put a finger on Owen's chin and raised his head. "Owen."

Owen looked him in the eye as another tear slid down his cheek. God had created him with such a tender heart.

"Your ma and I love you. We chose you to be our son. No one can take you away from us. Not Mr. and Mrs. Keisel or anyone else. We signed special papers that say you are ours forever. You, Effie, and Dudley are McFaddens now and always will be."

Owen's brow furrowed. "Forever?"

"Forever."

"And can we always live here?"

A low rumble vibrated in Silas's chest. "Yes, for as long as you'd like. Although I think someday you might want to get married. But, yes, you can live here as long as you want."

"I don't think I'll get married because girls are featherheaded and talk too much."

Silas laughed. "You might change your mind someday."

"No, I won't. But I do want to be a rancher. Just like you."

"I'd be honored to have you be a rancher. You are already a big help when we mend fences and herd the cattle. I'll for sure need some help during calving season in the spring."

Owen nodded, the first glint of a smile on his face. "All right." He paused. "Pa?"

"Yes?"

"Will you and Ma have other children?"

"We hope to have other children, yes." Silas and Amaya had spoken of having a large family if God willed it.

Owen blinked. "But when you have other children, will you love them more?"

Silas put his arm around Silas's shoulders. "No, we won't love them more. We will love you all the same. Just like God loves all of His children the same."

"But Effie always says she's yours and Ma's favorite daughter."

"Well, right now she is because she's our only daughter, but someday if we have other daughters, we will love them all the same amount. Did you know that I was adopted by Oma?"

"Oma?"

"My grandmother."

"You mean like Grandmama? Or our new grandma, Abuela?"

Amaya's parents had taken to the children just as her grandparents had. "Yes, like Grandmama and Abuela. I loved Oma very much, and she took me in and cared for me when I was just a young'un."

"Where were your parents?"

How could Silas explain it to Owen without giving too much detail? "Well, they weren't able to care for me, so Oma did."

"That's how Dudley's parents were. When he came to the orphanage, me and Effie had room in our family, so we adopted him as our brother."

"Thank you for adopting him as your brother. He's a blessed boy to have both of you."

Owen nodded. "We think so too. He was just a baby when we decided to make him our brother. Well, I best get to bed so tomorrow can be here soon. I can't wait to open them presents under the tree!"

Amaya assisted Dudley with his new skates before clutching Silas's hand as they walked carefully in their own skates toward the pond at the farthest edge of the property. "I've never attempted this before."

"That makes two of us."

His handsome grin caused her heart to skitter. He leaned over and planted a gentle kiss on her waiting lips.

"You sure must like Ma a lot," declared Effie as she and Owen clomped along in their own skates behind Amaya and Silas.

"I do like her a lot," said Silas.

Amaya's stomach did a somersault when his eyes met hers. God had blessed her richly with a husband like Silas. Why had she waited so long to realize he was the one God planned for her?

"I know you like her a lot," continued Effie in her high-pitched voice, "because you give her lots of kisses."

"Eww," said Owen. "That's why I'm never getting married. I don't want to ever have to kiss a girl."

Amaya giggled and whispered to Silas, "Poor Owen. He might think that now, but I suspect there will be no shortage of young ladies in Poplar Springs who will be fond of him when he's older."

"I think you're right." Silas squeezed her hand. "I'm quite fond of a certain young lady."

"Oh, really? Pray tell who might that be?"

"I know who he's fond of," interjected Effie as she and Owen caught up and walked alongside Amaya and Silas. "He's fond of you, Ma."

Owen ribbed Effie in the side. "You're such a prattling hen."

"I am not. It's true. He is fond of Ma."

"Husbands are supposed to like their wives." Owen cautiously took a step onto the ice with one foot, then the other while Effie sauntered onto the frozen pond with quick steps, nearly losing her balance.

"I love how they're so different," said Amaya. "Effie never met a stranger and is daring and loves to talk." She thought of how she and her new daughter had grown close. Owen had grown even closer to Silas since the adoption, and everyone loved Dudley.

"And Owen is the more cautious and reserved type."

"Look at Dudley," Amaya said, pointing at their youngest perched on a rock not far from the pond eating snow. "I don't think he'll be joining us skating anytime soon."

Silas laughed. "No, probably not."

They ventured further from the side, taking slow and methodical steps, with Amaya clutching Silas's arm. "Thank you for suggesting this tradition." The crisp, sunny day caused the snow to sparkle, and on the gentle breeze, the smell of a wood burning fire from a nearby house tickled Amaya's nose.

"Reckon we're not doing too bad," Silas said just before his foot slipped out from underneath him. He toppled onto the pond, Amaya falling right beside him.

"You were saying?"

He chuckled and brushed a kiss on her forehead before allowing his lips to travel towards hers and seal the hope of love's promise.

WHERE ARE THEY NOW?

One of the fun things about ending a series is imagining where the characters are now. Read on...

Reverend Solomon and Lydie Eliason continue to encourage and serve the residents of Willow Falls. Reverend Solomon continued in his capacity as a reverend part-time when his granddaughter, Esther's, husband became the new full-time pastor. Before Esther married, she followed in the footsteps of her mother and grandmother and taught school in Willow Falls.

Caleb and Annie Eliason continue to ranch in Willow Falls and recently welcomed their first grandson, born to their daughter, Lola, and her husband.

John Mark and Hannah Eliason welcomed a daughter, whom they named after both of their mothers. John Mark continues to apprehend dangerous criminals in his role as deputy.

Tobias and Charlotte Hallman added twins—a daughter and a son—to their family. They continue to live in the former Peabody home. While blacksmithing has changed with the times, Tobias continues to operate a well-respected business in Prune Creek.

Silas and Amaya McFadden added four more children to their brood, including one they adopted from the Thornsby orphanage.

Lanie Hallman opened Aunt Myrtle's Bakery in Prune Creek and married one of her father's apprentices. She and Effie McFadden became fast friends and share recipe ideas on a regular basis. Lanie's "new twist" on Aunt Myrtle's famous huckleberry pie recipe has been well-received.

Rebecca Hallman married a carpenter and moved into a small house on the edge of Prune Creek.

Aunt Myrtle continues to bake her huckleberry pies and enter them in the county fair. Quimby and Lanie remain the biggest (and only) fans of her cooking.

Aunt Fern and Stanley were instrumental in planting flower gardens throughout Prune Creek. Stanley remains a popular barber.

Lena Eliason married Freddy Morton. They assist Freddy's parents, Millicent and Frederick, with the daily operations at the Willow Falls mercantile.

Frederick Morton also works part-time as an official candy-tester for a Wyoming-based candy company.

Evangeline Eliason married a business owner and moved to Nelsonville.

Ambrose Miller Eliason served as the Poplar Springs County Sheriff for several years and earned the award of Wyoming Lawman of the Year. He married and is the father of three children.

Little Russell Eliason grew to a hefty 6'5 and became a rancher in Poplar Springs. He married one of Reverend Fleming and Mrs. Fleming's daughters.

Owen McFadden became a rancher and works alongside his pa on the McFadden Ranch. He married one of Doc and Florence's granddaughters, a vivacious, petite, and talkative redhead who was visiting Poplar Springs from Montana.

Effie McFadden started a bakery adjacent to Grandmama and Grandfather's mercantile. She later married a young, handsome, quiet, and studious lawyer.

Dudley McFadden became a barber in Poplar Springs and married one of Pritchard and Ina's two daughters.

After a successful stint as the mayor of Poplar Springs, Pritchard served as a Wyoming State Senator for two terms.

Nowell and Gertrude welcomed four sons. Nowell joins the posse when needed, but mainly runs their ranch with the assistance of their sons. Gertrude continues to assist with matchmaking whenever the opportunity arises.

Poppy Morton became a writer and married an artist from Nelsonville. Together, they write and illustrate children's books.

And they all lived happily ever after!

READ A SNEAK PEEK FROM

OVER THE HORIZON

HORIZON SERIES
BOOK ONE

A MOST UNUSUAL PROPOSAL...

Over the Horizon
Sneak Peek

PAISLEY HURRIED THROUGH THE town of Cornwall, lost in an area she'd never before been. Passersby paid her no mind. But why would they when they didn't know her? Didn't know why she stumbled along the boardwalk in search of somewhere to hide?

Lord, please help me.

Behind her, Ivan called her name. He'd arranged for them to exchange wedding vows at one o'clock, and she feared his demands of her becoming his wife might come to fruition.

She scanned the businesses located along the board-walk. Where was the sheriff's office? The church? She'd only been to Cornwall a handful of times since her family moved to the Idaho Territory. It was at least five times larger than the town of Pringle where she lived.

Perhaps she could confide in the reverend, a man whom she'd never met, and express to him her reasons for refusing to marry Ivan. Would he help her? Or would Ivan convince the reverend otherwise?

There was no time to ponder what may or may not happen.

Paisley ducked into an alley and pressed herself against a building's wall. Her chest heaved and her breath emerged in gasps.

"There you are."

She startled and spun around to see cold, harsh eyes boring into her. She attempted to run, but Ivan yanked her by the arm and clamped his fingers over her wrists. Pain seared through her as he dug his fingernails into her flesh. "And don't you dare scream. They'll only believe you are of unsound mind just like your father."

"Someone would believe me." But even in her own ears, her voice sounded doubtful.

Ivan chortled, his evil laugh sending shivers down Paisley's spine. "No, my dear, no one will believe you." In an instant he sobered again, a scowl covering his face. A vein throbbed in his jaw, and his warm breath, smelling of stale tobacco, lingered in the air. He bridged the distance between them, his face mere inches from hers. "You will marry me, Paisley. Your pa agreed to it." A spit particle spewed from his mouth.

She recalled that moment when Papa, his voice muffled and incoherent, gave Ivan Marchesi the blessing to marry his only child.

Papa, why did you promise Ivan my hand in marriage? What have you done?

This was a nightmare. It had to be. For in real life, her father never would have promised her hand to a cruel man.

She wouldn't marry Ivan Marchesi. Couldn't marry him. Among other reasons, she knew what he'd done to poor Mr. Leander when he refused to sell Ivan his farm.

Heavenly Father, please help me.

Ivan's gaze traveled the length of Paisley's appearance, lust filling his sinister brown eyes. Bile rose in her throat, and despite the heat, she shivered.

"And don't you cause a fracas when we arrive at the church," he warned.

Even if she did cause a disturbance at the church, would anyone help her?

Tears threatened at the hopelessness of the situation, but she refused to allow them to fall lest Ivan see her weakness. "I won't marry you." The words escaped her mouth before she could give a thought to the consequences.

He released one of her wrists and raised his hand to slap her. She held her breath, preparing for the impact.

A woman and her young child crossed the street at the edge of the alley. The woman looked toward them, then prompted the child to move quickly as they proceeded on their way. Would anyone hear Paisley if she screamed?

Ivan lowered his hand. "You *will* marry me and you *will* give me the deed to the land. Not owning the Abbott farm is one of the only things preventing me from owning most of Pringle." Ivan clenched his teeth, and his already-large nostrils flared. "You *will* do it, Paisley."

The deed. She'd folded and tucked it into her coin purse, then slipped the purse into the pocket in her skirt.

Ivan mustn't find it.

"Why would you want the farm? Most of it was destroyed by the flood."

"Makes no difference to me. The waters will recede, and when they do, I'll have added more fertile farmland to my holdings. You know I aim to own the entire town of Pringle."

Yes, she did know Ivan's goals of obtaining acreage, and she also knew his manipulative and oftentimes dangerous methods of attaining it. Greed was a prevalent part of his nature. While marrying her would make his scheme appear legal to onlookers, Paisley doubted he would hesitate to use whatever means necessary to seize the deed—and then convince the law he'd obtained it legitimately.

Ivan again grabbed her other wrist and shook her hard, giving in to the volatile temper that ruled him. Why he would want to marry her was a question that plagued her ever since Ivan visited Papa and asked for his blessing. While she would never willingly give him the deed or sell the farm to him, he didn't *need* her to procure the land he thought he was entitled to. The vile man had other methods of obtaining what he wanted.

"Now. Are you ready to go to the church?" he hissed, his hands again at his sides.

A man strode by them. "Everything all right here?" he asked.

"All is well, my friend." Ivan pasted on a grin.

"Sir, if you could please..."

But the man had already gone about his way.

Ivan shoved her against the wall. She struggled to maintain her footing as she stumbled backward, her heel catching the hem of her dress.

It was then Paisley noticed the pile of discarded items on the ground beside her. A rusty kettle rested among the heap. She'd needed strength so often in the past few days, and this moment was no exception.

A noisy wagon clamored past, drawing Ivan's attention. She snatched the kettle and swung it toward his head, catching him hard on the shoulder. Stunned and caught unaware, Ivan staggered and gripped the injured area while emitting a stream of profanities.

Paisley dashed from the alley and searched for the main thoroughfare, her sense of direction altered in the unfamiliar area of town. How many precious minutes did she have before Ivan came after her?

Lord, I beseech Thee to help me with this plight.

She passed several buildings before pausing in front of the livery. Standing on tiptoe, she peered about. After a few seconds of obscured vision, she noticed Ivan stumbling down the boardwalk in her direction.

Paisley's heart pounded in her ears, and she staggered forward on weak legs. Should she hide inside one of the businesses?

A horse neighed and she flinched. Paisley hurried down another nearby alley, halting when she noticed an abandoned wagon full of lumber.

The perfect place to hide.

Not caring how unladylike she appeared, Paisley gathered her skirts and climbed into the back of the deserted wagon, sliding into a narrow spot between the lumber and some tools. Then, spying a bedroll, she quickly unrolled the dingy brown sleep sack. Grasping the ends of it with trembling hands, she pulled it over her body and most of her head, leaving just enough space to breathe.

Paisley shifted beneath the bedroll, wishing for a handkerchief to dab at the perspiration collecting at the back of her neck from both the heat and her jumbled nerves. Periodically, she heard the clip-clop of horses' hooves, the sound of wagon wheels, or voices in conversation.

Then came the dreaded sound of Ivan's sharp, raucous voice. "Where is that impertinent woman?"

She fought the rising panic. Would Ivan see the tip of her head in the wagon? Or realize someone hid beneath the bedroll with a few pieces of lumber strewn on top? No. He mustn't find her. His disheartening obsession with her left an uneasy feeling in her stomach.

She moved slightly, but enough to bump her left elbow on something hard in the wagon. Tears filled her eyes, and she barely contained the gasp that threatened to escape from her lips. Ivan would find her for sure if she uttered even the most reticent of sounds.

"Excuse me, sir," Ivan said.

"Yes?" another man answered.

"Have you seen a woman about twenty-two or twenty-three years of age? She's slender with brown hair and hazel eyes and is wearing a blue dress."

"Not that I recollect. What is your reason for wanting to locate her?"

"She's my wife."

Paisley's eyes widened and she gritted her teeth. Ivan was so adept at lying that he likely believed himself.

"I'm sorry, I haven't seen her. Best of luck finding her."

She heard footsteps, followed by what sounded like the tipping over of barrels. After what seemed like an interminable amount of time, all was quiet.

Paisley released the breath she'd been holding. She was safe. For now.

If you want to be among the first to hear about the next Horizon installment, sign up for Penny's newsletter at www.pennyzeller.com. You will receive book and writing updates, encouragement, notification of current give-aways, occasional freebies, and special offers.

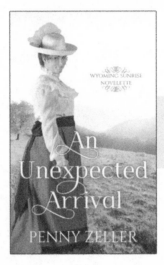

A
WYOMING
SUNRISE
NOVELETTE

AUTHOR'S NOTE

Dear Reader,

It was a bittersweet moment when I typed THE END on the manuscript for *Love's Promise* because it was not only the end of this story, but also the end of the Wyoming Sunrise Series. I hope you enjoyed the tidbit about where all of the characters are now.

I always knew Caleb, John Mark, and Charlotte would have their own stories, but Lydie and Amaya were surprises. Silas came out of left field when I was writing John Mark's story. I knew he needed a story, and who better to pair him with than Russell's fiancée? As often happens, the ideas came faster than my fingers could type them.

You may have noticed that adoption is a reoccurring theme in this series (as well as in most of my other books). Owen, Effie, and Dudley begged to be written into the story and be given a forever home. Most writers will tell you they are people watchers who get their ideas and inspiration based on numerous real-life characters from which tiny bits and pieces of appearance and personality are taken. Such was the case for Dudley, whose brown eyes and nearly-black hair were inspired by a baby boy at church. Of course, I then fictionalized Dudley by giving him his own personality and an older age than his inspiration.

I loosely based the area where Silas and the Farris Hill Gang rode to after the robbery on the Hole in the Wall Hideout near Kaycee, Wyoming. The courthouse where the adoption was to have taken place was inspired by photos of the historical Johnson County Courthouse in Buffalo, Wyoming. It was built in 1884 and is still used today. I spent numerous hours researching costs, mercantile wares, and other items to make this story as historically accurate as possible. As one who grew up in a community with a vibrant Basque population, I was thrilled to include Amaya's heritage in *Love's Promise*. Dr. Price's Special Flavoring Extracts were real items sold in stores. Mexican Mustang Linament was also a popular medicine. The Barney & Berry's ice skates were real as well. In chapter twenty-six, it was mentioned that a court case was dismissed in Prune Creek due to what the judge termed a "complaining witness". This occurred at an actual court case I stumbled upon in my research.

For purposes of the story, I didn't have the stagecoach stop at a station on the way from Bowman to Poplar Springs as most stagecoaches did every 10-20 miles according to my research. I also did take some fictional liberties with the stagecoach accident, although during my interview with a stagecoach restoration specialist, much of what happened could have definitely happened the way it was written.

For those of you who have been with me throughout this Wyoming journey, thank you. While there is always a possibility of adding a novella for a minor character to this series, it is, for the most part complete. The journey has been an enjoyable one with some tears along the way—yes, we writers are known for shedding a few tears during the especially poignant scenes. Books two and three in my Horizon Series are next on the agenda, followed by a brand-new four-book series taking place in late 1800s Montana. It's been a while since we ventured back to that beautiful state. And as you have probably guessed, my states of preference for my books are Wyoming, Idaho, and Montana.

As always, thank you for taking a visit to the past with me. Until we meet again, happy reading!

Blessings,

Penny

ACKNOWLEDGMENTS

To my family for their love and encouragement. It's not easy living with an author, especially one who spends a large majority of her hours in another century. I am so, so grateful God has blessed me with the best family ever.

To my Penny's Peeps Street Team. Thank you for spreading the word about my books. I appreciate your continued encouragement and support.

To my beta team. Thank you for reading my manuscript when it was in its early phase and offering awesome suggestions.

To Marie Concannon, Head, Government Information & Data Archives, University of Missouri Library, whose help is always so appreciated and whose research gave me the idea for the quilt contest Silas entered.

To Catherine Richmond, occupational therapist and author of inspirational romances and Anna Zogg, author of *Frontier Secrets*, who both helped me immensely with information regarding Grandfather's stroke.

To Dawn LeGros for her assistance in naming the outlaw gang in the book.

To my readers. May God bless and guide you as you grow in your walk with Him.

And, most importantly, thank you to my Lord and Savior, Jesus Christ. It is my deepest desire to glorify You with my writing and help bring others to a knowledge of Your saving grace.

Let the words of my mouth and the meditation of my heart be acceptable in your sight, O Lord, my rock and my redeemer.
- Psalm 19:14

About the Author

Penny Zeller is known for her heartfelt stories of faith and her passion to impact lives for Christ through fiction. While she has had a love for writing since childhood, she began her adult writing career penning articles for national and regional publications on a wide variety of topics. Today, Penny is the author of nearly two dozen books. She is also a homeschool mom and a certified fitness instructor.

When Penny is not dreaming up new characters, she enjoys spending time with her husband and two daughters, camping, hiking, canoeing, reading, running, cycling, gardening, and playing volleyball.

She is represented by Tamela Hancock Murray of the Steve Laube Agency and loves to hear from her readers at her website www.pennyzeller.com and her blog, *random thoughts from a day in the life of a wife, mom, and author*, at www.pennyzeller.wordpress.com.

WYOMING SUNRISE SERIES

— HORIZON SERIES —

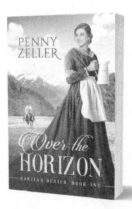

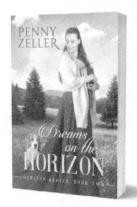

HOLLOW CREEK

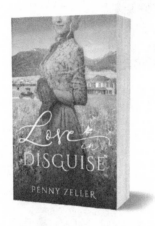

LOVE LETTERS FROM ELLIS CREEK

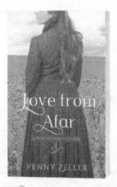

Love from Afar

PENNY ZELLER

Love Unforeseen

PENNY ZELLER

Love Most Certain

PENNY ZELLER

Freedom's Flight

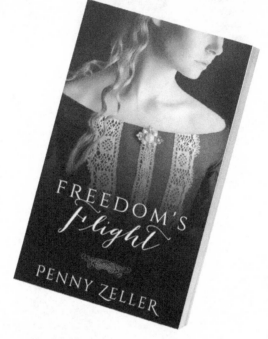

LIVES IN JEOPARDY.

A RACE AGAINST TIME.

WILL MISTRUST PROVE FATAL FOR ALL INVOLVED?

CHRISTIAN
CONTEMPORARY ROMANCE

Love in the Headlines

Chokecherry Heights

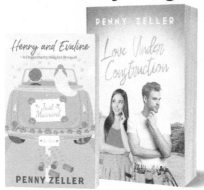

Made in United States
Orlando, FL
10 March 2024

44610655R00232